The presentation of the Nebula Awards took place at the Science Fiction Writers of America's first annual banquets in New York and Los Angeles on March 11, 1966. This was the first time that the science fiction writers themselves chose the best science fiction stories of the year. The awards consist of a spiral nebula made of metallic glitter and a specimen of rock crystal, both embedded in a block of lucite. Combining elements of chemical synthesis, geology, and astronomy, they appropriately symbolize the far-ranging concerns of science fiction.

Nebula Award Stories Four
was originally published by
Doubleday & Company, Inc.

NEBULA
AWARD
STORIES
FOUR

Edited by POUL ANDERSON

PUBLISHED BY POCKET 🖋 BOOKS NEW YORK

NEBULA AWARD STORIES FOUR

Doubleday edition published December, 1969

Pocket Book edition published January, 1971

This *Pocket Book* edition includes every word
contained in the original, higher-priced edition. It is printed
from brand-new plates made from completely reset, clear, easy-to-read
type. *Pocket Book* editions are published by Pocket Books, a division
of Simon & Schuster, Inc., 630 Fifth Avenue, New York, N.Y. 10020.
Trademarks registered in the United States and other countries.

L

Standard Book Number: 671-75646-X.
Library of Congress Catalog Card Number: 66-20974.
Copyright, ©, 1969, by Science Fiction Writers of America. All rights
reserved. This *Pocket Book* edition is published by arrangement
with Doubleday & Company, Inc.

Printed in the U.S.A.

CONTENTS

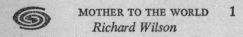
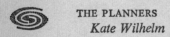
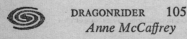

For service to SFWA over and above the duty
he helped create, this book thanks

Lloyd Biggle, Jr.

INTRODUCTION

This book is more than a collection of science fiction stories. Of course, it is mainly that, and rightly so. After all, we have here the fourth annual set of Nebula Award winners and as many runners-up on the final ballot as could be fitted in. But in view of the growing acceptance of science fiction as a valid literary form, it seems time to offer some history and commentary besides.

So widely are the assumptions and conventions of that form disseminated these days, that nobody feels surprised or puzzled when they are used by someone as respectable as, say, John Hersey. At the same time, their regular users are more and more adopting techniques which, if not yet absolutely contemporary (being associated with such names as Joyce, Kafka, Čapek, Dos Passos), are light-years in advance of cut-and-dried pulp narration.

Most science fiction has also preserved its own traditional virtues. It still tells stories, wherein things happen. It remains more interested in the glamour and mystery of existence, the survival and triumph and tragedy of heroes and thinkers, than in the neuroses of some sniveling fagot. And *pace* Will McNelly, I don't believe "hard" science is on the way out of it. The impressive terminology always did include plenty of gobbledygook. If anything, we get more genuine science and technology now, from writers like Hal Clement, Joseph Martino, and Larry Niven, than ever before.

This combination of new skills and old values has completely revitalized a field which, a decade or so back, had decayed to a frighteningly low proportion of stories *not* flat, imitative, or idiotic. I don't know what brought on the change. It wasn't just the many talented new writers, though obviously they're responsible for a lot. Quite a few old-timers suddenly caught fire again. Whatever the cause, heightened quality is earning us a wider, more discriminating audience. The rewards go well beyond such benefits for the writer as decent income and expenses-paid trips to symposia in Brazil. Mainly, he's getting across.

We still have a long way to fare, but it looks like an exciting journey ahead.

Among reasons for optimism is our organization, Science Fiction Writers of America. Let's be blunt, the typical writers' group—and I include some of the most prominent—is a farce. The vitality of science fiction is reflected in the virility of SFWA. It has won, or created, genuine benefits for its membership, such as improvements in the contracts of several publishers and the increasingly prestigious Nebula awards.

The year 1968 was almost as stressful for SFWA as it was for mankind in general. Not only did we suffer a Year of the Jackpot—see the obituary section—but for a while, political disagreements threatened to tear us apart. Two opposing groups were collecting signatures and contributions for two opposing statements on the Vietnam War, to be published as advertisements in some of the magazines.

I happened to spearhead one of these, which involved me in a blizzard of correspondence with SFWA members as well as officers. Practically without exception, every letter I got from any side—more than two sides exist, you know—was both patriotic in tone and humane in spirit. The statements appeared simultaneously, and I haven't heard of any friendships that they broke. The experience gives me a bit of hope for our poor flayed world. Science fiction people obviously can't save it by themselves. But are they perhaps representative of a larger community of people who'd rather think than scream?

Let's turn from the writers to what they write, a subject doubtless more interesting to readers. I don't agree with everything that Will McNelly has to say about the year in novels; neither, probably, will you; and it is obvious that a substantial plurality of SFWA's professional writers won't, since their votes bestowed the Nebula on a book that leaves him cool but that they (and I) think is a credit to the award. And so what's wrong with a little controversy? Professor McNelly's remarks are well worth your attention, both for their own sake and as a strong assault on those Berlin Walls of categorization which have for too long kept the various literary forms artificially isolated from each other. The year in magazines can be summarized quite briefly, since this whole book is itself a commentary upon that.

Analog offered the mixture as before: stories running heavily to ideation, interesting fact articles, and provocative —sometimes deliberately infuriating—editorials. Or was it really quite the old blend? John Campbell has never stopped pioneering. He has, however, recognized that even a science fiction audience is basically conservative and newness must be sneaked in. For example, you don't see much about "psi" any more; it's simply there, as Anne McCaffrey's yarn bears witness. *Analog* also enjoyed a gratifying rise in circulation.

The Magazine of Fantasy and Science Fiction continued in its own tradition, quite a different one except for Isaac Asimov's column. It was especially noteworthy how many stories here bore immediate relevance to our real, mid-twentieth-century world. Editor Edward Ferman also encouraged the continued development of such comparatively new writers as Bruce McAllister, K. M. O'Donnell, and Josephine Saxton, who rewarded him with fine contributions.

Amazing and *Fantastic* had their problems, including a midstream change of editors, but nonetheless published a good deal of fresh and worthwhile material. Under Harry Harrison, book reviews came to be handled by such as Fritz Leiber and James Blish; the anthropologist Leon Stover began a series of regular reports from the frontiers of his science; and besides old hands, we got extremely promising recruits like Robert Taylor and James Tiptree, Jr. When Barry Malzberg took command, he proved especially sympathetic to experimental writing: which is not the same thing as amateurish writing.

But Frederik Pohl was unquestionably the innovator of the year. He was not content with good solid periodicals like *Galaxy*—which regularly includes articles by Willy Ley—and *If*—which has thrice in a row taken the annual Hugo Award for best magazine, bestowed through vote of fans rather than writers. He also launched two new, at present irregular, publications. One is called *Worlds of Fantasy* and is devoted to precisely what the title implies. If you don't like spaceships but do like Tolkien or Lovecraft, this is probably for you. The other is *International Science Fiction*, featuring stories from places as remote as Japan and the Soviet Union. I hope both of these will become firmly established. Everyone would benefit.

When he ran the two head-on Vietnam declarations, Fred Pohl and his publisher did not go out and spend the five hundred dollars they had collected. Instead, they announced that it would be paid out in prizes for the best ideas they received on what the United States might actually do about the situation. Response was large and imaginative. After winnowing, it was turned over to a professional study group which in turn may well call some of the suggestions to the attention of the government. Again, this does not mean that science fictioneers can bail out the human race. But it does mean that, far from being escapists, they are uncommonly aware of and concerned about reality.

In addition, Galaxy Publishing Corporation instituted its own awards, cash, for the best stories it has printed within a year. These are determined by a poll of subscribers, employing standard statistical methods of sampling and validation. It is interesting that none of the winners (first was Clifford Simak's novel *Goblin Reservation*) made the final Nebula ballot. I suspect this indicates not so much a failure of either system as it does the diversity of science fiction.

In fact, the range is so very healthily wide that what's going on in Britain today is often too much for me, even though I consider myself to have catholic tastes. Rather than scold what I seldom understand, I asked one of that country's most distinguished writers in our field to comment on it. Ladies and gentlemen, Brian Aldiss:

"New Worlds totters from strength to strength. The appearance of every issue is a triumph of hope over economics; the persistence of the editor, Michael Moorcock, who is now also publisher, is perhaps a triumph over himself.

"New Worlds is no longer a magazine but a cause: thrown away the magazine, kept the courage. The November 1968 issue contained only stories by new authors—they were being given a chance to speak before the magazine sank forever. In December, the magazine bobbed up again, with stories by such Nebula winners as Delany, Moorcock, and Aldiss. Disch and Bill Butler were also present, and there was an article on Andy Warhol. So the vessel still floats, despite severe trouble with distributors during the year, when Spinrad's *Bug Jack Barron* was running. Of course, a hefty Arts Council grant (now extended into 1969) helps buoyancy.

"Subject matter in the stories is sometimes thin, inexpertise sometimes shows below the wish to set convention at nought;

but what matters most is the attitude of questioning: the good hard look at what is going on, the wish to interpret without falsifying.

"English science fiction has never been too greatly subjected to the enervating pressures of pulp markets. Moorcock's *New Worlds* merely uses its liberty to the full; it's for writers and not for publishers (under either system, readers, as readers must, fend for themselves). Writers respond to this policy by writing freely—and sometimes for free, if necessary. This dedication finds an echo in the staff, and more than an echo in the editor himself. Moorcock, as he ascends into legend, begins to look like a Gerald Scarfe portrait of the French philosopher René Descartes.

"Many of Moorcock's contributors are American—Zelazny, Disch, Sladek, Spinrad, Leiber, Zoline, Jacobs, et al. The typical *New Worlds* story is pretty cool, has connections with the attitudes of the 'underground,' and shares little in common with the American New Wave, which is characterized by heavier breathing. It is against nothing but mediocrity: which is why it has aroused so much anger here and there."

I take special pleasure in having Brian's remarks because one of my great regrets in editing this book was that there turned out to be no way of including his novelette *Total Environment.* Look for it elsewhere, together with the other fine runners-up. If 1968 had more than its share of catastrophes, it also had some very special glories—among them the return of the *Pueblo* crew, Apollo 8's Christmas journey around the moon . . . and, not altogether bathos in the present context, a great deal of first-class science fiction.

Poul Anderson

FOREWORD

The Science Fiction Novel in 1968
by Willis E. McNelly
Professor of English, California State College, Fullerton

The Wandering Jew is alive and an activist in Berkeley. Seven billion human beings are trying to stand on Zanzibar; there is conflict in Utopia; puberty rites in space end with the death of a planet; the Apocalypse will come either with Black Magic or with the approaching Millennium. Electric sheep graze, unmolested by fallout, and all is not well on Paradise.

These visions of the future—some might term them nightmares—with their extensions, extrapolations, and involvements are the subject matter of the best science fiction novels published during 1968. Seven of them were the Nebula finalists[1]; the eighth was a superior work overlooked in the voting.[2] Together they continue a trend begun some years ago, demonstrating again the growth of the novel as the most representative, if not the most distinctive, form for the presentation of science fiction.

Thirty-five novels were listed on the preliminary ballot used by the members of the Science Fiction Writers of America to nominate candidates for 1968 Nebula Award. They were a diverse lot, including a few fantasies, dozens of spanner and grommet stories, some high jinks in time, and several serious explorations of certain new views of the hell man continually shapes for himself. It was, in general, a good year for the

---

[1] James Blish, *Black Easter,* Doubleday; John Brunner, *Stand on Zanzibar,* Doubleday; Philip K. Dick, *Do Androids Dream of Electric Sheep,* Doubleday; R. A. Lafferty, *Past Master,* Ace; Alexei Panshin, *Rite of Passage,* Ace; Joanna Russ, *Picnic on Paradise,* Ace; Robert Silverberg, *The Masks of Time,* Ballantine.

[2] John Boyd, *The Last Starship from Earth,* Weybright & Talley.

science fiction novel, although space operas, by and large, are not really worth considering seriously. They are mostly good adventure stories, told, as usual, with a maximum of action and dialogue, a minimum of characterization, and a general banality of style: "Starwolf, whispered the void . . ." They end up as half of an Ace double, thud and blunder among the stars.

The serious works, like the Nebula finalists, sometimes show great originality. Indeed, if the editors of the *Saturday Review* or *The New York Review of Books* had read some of the Nebula nominee novels published during 1968, they might have discovered that the gap between so-called mainstream fiction and first-rate science fiction is narrowing. In fact, there are times when the difference disappears completely, so completely that even the case-hardened iconoclasts who occupy the pages of *The New Yorker* might be unable to detect the gap at all. For example, John Barth's *Giles Goat Boy* is science fiction, but no reviewer bothered to mention the fact. Barth's McLuhanesque *Lost in the Fun House* was also science fiction—a non-novel, perhaps, or even an anti-novel, or a non-book, a piece of mclunacy, but science fiction nonetheless—a fact ignored by every reviewer who tried to make conventional, representational mainstream sense out of Barth's fragmented vision.

Good as the Nebula nominees were, they did not produce a science fiction novel in a class with Frank Herbert's *Dune*, Alfred Bester's *The Demolished Man*, Robert A. Heinlein's *Stranger in a Strange Land*, or Walter Miller's *A Canticle for Leibowitz*. Yet the general quality of the better novels is certainly above that of any year within recent memory. To be sure, even among the finalists there were certain failures, but the failures were often failures of excess and were not due to lack of imagination, paucity of conception, or lapses of style.

The outstanding feature of the finalists was how much involvement or response they demand of the readers. The best novels, such as James Blish's *Black Easter*, Robert Silverberg's *The Masks of Time*, John Brunner's *Stand on Zanzibar*, or John Boyd's *The Last Starship from Earth*, were written for what might be called a "maximum" audience. The authors all seem to have realized that creative writing requires creative reading. Thus they are no longer content to spoonfeed space pablum to adolescents. Instead, the authors have written up to their readers, not down to them. Consequently, the passive reader is forced, by every device in the writer's arsenal, to become involved, to read between the lines, behind the lines, and under the lines. The stories are often told by indirection, suggestion, allusion. The characters begin to assume a life as independent human beings, rather than cardboard stereotypes. Readers unwilling or unable to provide what the artists demand remain blissfully unaware of some genuinely superior work. And that is their loss, not that of the writers. What is most important, any reader who approaches the principal novels of the year with a quickened ear, a sensitive eye, and an awakened imagination will realize that in a few instances at least, the writer deserves the appellation "artist."

The 1968 Nebula nominees demonstrated a wide variety of styles, types, techniques, and modes. They ranged from the wildly experimental *Stand on Zanzibar* to the controlled discipline and form of Panshin's *Rite of Passage,* the Nebula winner. Certainly Panshin's first novel had been widely anticipated; he had, after all, demonstrated both his commitment to science fiction and his undeniable talent in numerous short stories and his full-length critical analysis, *Heinlein in Dimension.* What kind of novel could be expected from this man, reputed to be a member of the New Wave, who was at the same time a merciless dissector of Heinlein? The result: a smooth, competent, professional reworking of tired, worn-out science fiction characters and devices. One is tempted to say that *Rite of Passage* is a mini-splendored thing.

Yet withal, it *was* the Nebula winner, voted the best science fiction novel of the year by the members of SFWA. Their choice was both difficult and easy to understand. *Rite of Passage* is, on one hand, banal, at least to this reader. On the other hand, it is well constructed, smooth, slick, thoroughly professional. Unquestionably the writers who named *Rite of Passage* were responding to the professionalism everywhere evident in the novel, the tight plotting, the crisp transitions, the clear statement of a problem that, if minor, was nonetheless intriguing. In the last analysis, the votes for *Rite of Passage* were a tribute to the writer from whom Panshin had learned so much and to whom he owed so much, Robert A. Heinlein.

Brunner's *Stand on Zanzibar,* the Nebula third-place winner, is another matter indeed. It may be a non-novel or an antinovel, it may be the ultimate "New Worlds" novel, the *Ulysses* or *Finnegans Wake* of the New Wave, but one can hardly be indifferent to it. Indeed, *Stand on Zanzibar* may be the most important science fiction novel of the last decade. Unfortunately, it may also be the most difficult. *Stand on Zanzibar* requires a patience of eye and ear that many fans will be unwilling or unable to give. After all, fans don't have to read McLuhan's *The Gutenberg Galaxy* or Joyce's *Ulysses* to appreciate any of the other Nebula nominees, and none of the others are even half the length of *Zanzibar's* 507 pages. However, those who pay it the attention it deserves, who are willing to follow Brunner through his maze of characters, situations, typographical eccentricities, and triple or quadruple levels of writing will find here both a richness of conception and depth of execution rarely matched in contemporary fiction. *Stand on Zanzibar* is no sterile, naturalistic-representational novel about people whose miseries are merely aching groins and whose griefs, to quote William Faulkner, grieve on no universal bones, who write not of the heart but of the glands.

For all of his dazzling pyrotechniques, Brunner is neither deliberately obscure nor obtusely difficult. To create his twenty-first-century world where seven billion humans consume mass-marketed psychedelics and otherwise sweat, struggle, and die, Brunner writes a careful multidimensional prose. The major clue to understanding the book is, curiously enough, the seven-page table of contents. Here Brunner leaves his clues: utilizing styles he calls "context," "the happening world," "track with closeups," and "continuity," he builds a multilayered contrapuntal novel. These four fugal styles interweave continually while each still maintains its complete artistic integrity. The McLuhanesque quality of the novel is everywhere evident. The four parts cannot simply be considered as linear, independent developments, each telling a simple beginning, middle, and end story. Instead, the artistic construct becomes a single entity, an art object-as-form, a medium whose message is its totality. Brunner demands sensory involvement on all levels, from the thematic to the stylistic, as he searches for "retribalization" in the midst of sterile linearity. All in all, *Stand on Zanzibar* is a dexterous performance, at once as facile as a Bach motet and as gripping as one of the German master's chorales.

One of the most conspicuous, as well as one of the most

interesting, trends in many of the science fiction novels written during the last dozen years is the emergence of the so-called "soft" sciences as thematic material. Among these are anthropology, sociology, psychology, semantics, and recently, religion or theology. Once the enemy of knowledge in such works as Raymond F. Jones's *Renaissance,* religion has recently become primary source material, used sympathetically and provocatively by many different sf authors. Recall, for a moment, *A Canticle for Leibowitz,* considered by many critics to be one of the two or three best science fiction novels ever written. Miller's novel untilizes the structure, mystique, language, and theology of Roman Catholicism. Remove the Roman Catholic Church from its pages, and *Canticle* is nothing, mere vapidity unredeemable even by Miller's flashing word magic. Also religiously oriented are James Blish's *A Case of Conscience,* Roger Zelazny's *Lord of Light,* Herbert's *Dune,* and Heinlein's *Stranger in a Strange Land,* to cite only a few. It matters little whether the religious constructs and background be Catholicism, Hinduism, Islam, or pantheism. What is important is that these writers, all skilled craftsmen, felt impelled to utilize religious themes as artistic material and to utilize them so profoundly that their novels would not otherwise be complete. Moreover, each of these writers has handled the religious symbols as if they were standard science fiction devices.

Yet the nature of the material has seemingly forced the writers to consider some genuine problems, problems as real as violence in Chicago or dangling bodies in Iraq. Suppose, asks Herbert, we have a genuine avatar, a messiah, a true manifestation of the Deity who is forced by the incredible horror of living conditions to choose violence, not love or charity, as his method of redeeming Arrakis and the Fremen. So Paul Atreides' internal sufferings, the clash of love with violence, become a crucial ethical problem that would be essentially trivial without the religious background against which the ethics can be weighed.

No author has explored these theological implications as consistently, or as profoundly, as James Blish. Beginning with the Hugo-winning *A Case of Conscience* and continuing with *Doctor Mirabilis,* the second book in the trilogy, which has been published only in England, Blish has pursued the ramifications of evil as has no writer since the late Charles Williams. The final volume of Blish's sequence, *Black Easter,* another Nebula finalist, is perhaps the most frightening novel of the year in its implications. Theron Ware—the name is derived from a greatly underestimated novel by Harold Frederic, *The Damnation of Theron Ware,* written fifty years ago—is a master of the arcane, a materialistic magician who has turned the black art of necromancy into an instrument of personal profit. Simply to see what might happen, this modern Faust undertakes to let all of the major demons out of hell for one night, turning them loose on the world with no orders and no restrictions except that they must return to hell at dawn. His undertaking is successful beyond belief because his actions bring Armageddon and the resultant destruction of the world. What all of the diabolists had not realized, they are told by the ravening Sabbath Goat, is that God is dead. When the bounds are loosed, the powers of evil must finally conquer. End of novel.

Here Blish again asks ancient questions: What is the role of evil in the world, and by implication or extension, what is the position of suffering? In addition Blish raises the great Manichaean problem once more: Is evil creative? If so, what are its implications for our contemporary society, because the society of *Black Easter* is uneasily like that of 1969. And if evil is creative, perhaps diabolists such as Huysmans' des Essientes or the Marquis de Sade were right after all to worship Lucifer. Perhaps Rosemary's baby is real, alive and well in Manhattan, awaiting His Infernal Kingdom and His *Black Easter.*

Some readers may cavil with Blish, maintaining that his artistic viewpoint is essentially one of fantasy rather than science fiction. That may very well be, but at best it is a quibble over form or shadow which ignores the substance of Blish's arguments. Like Ivan, in *The Brothers Karamazov,* Blish seems to imply that if God did not exist, everything is permitted and the doing of evil becomes virtually a mandated "good."

This kind of probing into the depths of man's consciousness is impossible within the traditional science fiction novel. Involvement with scientific gimmickry has too often robbed science fiction of its humanity. It may be that the inclusion of theology—and the other "soft" sciences—as viable subject matter is one step toward the restoration of its human element. Where fiction loses its ability to concentrate on the human being, where it no longer informs, entertains, or enhances life, it becomes simply a mechanical recitation of fantasized fact, a trap that too much science fiction has fallen into. Theology may help restore the balance.

First novels have many characteristics. Sometimes they are so bad that about all that can be said for them is that the punctuation and spelling display a startling originality. Too often mainstream writers who attempt a science fiction novel know almost nothing about the form. George Orwell's *1984* or Aldous Huxley's *Brave New World* seem to them the apotheosis of the genre, and their own reading of real science fiction ended with Carl Claudy's pastiches of H. G. Wells in the old *American Boy* magazine. They had fading memories of the Buck Rogers radio program or the superior draftsmanship but inferior plotting of Prince Valiant. The results would be laughable if they weren't so pitiable. Don't fail to miss them all.

Often enough a first science fiction novel is written by someone like Panshin who has obviously learned his trade well in the rigorous workshops of John W. Campbell, Fred Pohl, or Ed Ferman. Of course, writing a short story with its limited vision, singleness of effect, controlled plotting, minimal characterization, and qualified range is not the same as writing a novel. Essentially, the problem of the novelist is to create an entire world, populate it with believable people, and construct a problem that requires careful, detailed elaboration. Further, he must accomplish this in prose that moves the story toward its denouement while remaining unobtrusive. There are those writers, like Ray Bradbury, whose talents seem to lead them to the short story as a natural medium. It is not that Bradbury lacks the artistic vision for the novel; it is rather that his concepts seize him, shake him, and emerge explosively after two or three hours of writing into a short story. Other writers think galactically or epically; no microcosm for them. Their dreams encompass entire worlds, their characters emerge from ink into reality, and their prose can be lean, supple, poetic, highly charged with cosmic tensions.

Critics often maintain, with some justification, that it is more difficult to write a good short story than an average novel. Perhaps. But when any author masters his trade so well that his novel is a richly panoplied accomplishment, he deserves recognition and praise from those who should appreciate the extent of his achievement.

Nineteen sixty-eight produced at least one such novel, John

Boyd's *The Last Starship from Earth*. It is so good that it caused Heinlein to break his strongest resolution: never to comment in public on anything a colleague has written. He said, "It is terrific . . . the best anti-utopia, the strongest satire on trends in our present culture that I have seen since *1984* appeared . . . it belongs up at the top, along with *Brave New World*."

Yet despite Heinlein's praise, Boyd's novel had a very mixed reception. It received a few votes for the Nebula Award and almost no reviews, even delayed ones, in any of the science fiction magazines. Why was it ignored? No one knows for sure, but the sometimes justified xenophobia of both science fiction writers and fans might have accounted for part of it. Fans and writers are clannish—indeed, have had clannishness forced upon them by those who think that science fiction is easy to write or simply Buck Rogers updated. Thus, uncertainty about Boyd's identity or background might have caused a certain reluctance to vote for his book. All anyone knew was that *The Last Starship from Earth* was a first novel, that it had been picked up by the Doubleday Science Fiction Book Club as the June-July selection.

All of these suppositions did not alter the fact that *The Last Spaceship* was a superior first achievement, better than most authors' tenth. It is, on the surface, a parallel universe story—the Pope is a computer, the City of God is on Mt. Whitney, Lincoln has given "The Johannesburg Address," Byron is an eighteenth-century poet, laser science has produced theological cybernetics, and Hell is a pariah planet. Beyond the surface, the novel is a virtuoso performance combining word magic of all kinds, half-buried topical allusions, thinly veiled references to "reality," and unobtrusive, penetrating comments on our society. Its ending is at once so subtle in execution and yet so bold in concept as to defy description. Only the theologically ingenious innovation at the conclusion of *A Canticle for Leibowitz* has equaled Boyd's accomplishment at the end of his novel, but the quality of *Canticle* must be the standard for comparison. *The Last Starship from Earth* did not win any awards, but it will be winning readers when most of the finalists will be forgotten. His new novel, *The Pollinators of Eden*, due from Weybright & Talley in mid-1969, is sure to get a much wider readership. If it is anywhere nearly as good as *The Last Starship from Earth*, it will be a strong Nebula contender a year from now.

If 1968 was the year science fiction explored certain devices and techiques derived from McLuhan, psychology, and the impact of the mass media, it was also a year in which very little old-fashioned humor was published. Science fiction has often been too intensely serious for its own good, too self-conscious, and too sycophantic. It has usually lacked the blessed ability to stand outside of itself, take a good look at the warts and the freckles, and then break into raucous laughter at the sight. Perhaps the somberness of reality was reflected in the somberness of the writing, but science fiction could have used some outrageous spoofs, more rollicking comedy, or even some gentle self-satire.

Arthur C. Clarke's novel *2001: A Space Odyssey*, based on Stanley Kubrick's epic motion picture of the same name, solved some of the many questions raised by the film itself. Not eligible for a Nebula nomination, *2001* was in many ways a better book than the picture really deserved. Flashy, expensive, and magnificently photographed, Kubrick's movie had everything—except characters who lived, a plot which made sense, dialogue which sounded human, and action of any kind. It did have, of course, the mysterious Formica tabletop upon which everyone grooved, a drag computer for a hero, the loudest and most distracting sound track of any film ever made, and unrelieved boredom. After the press preview before Kubrick eliminated an hour of non-action, several perceptive critics booed.

There was no booing of Clarke's novel, however. Not only was it assured of vast sales because of its connection with the movie, *2001* was snatched up by eager film viewers who looked for answers to questions raised by the motion picture. Clarke provided those answers literately, intelligently, and provocatively. Readers familiar with his earlier *Childhood's End* might have expected as much. Fortunately for science fiction, the tens of thousands of readers attracted to the novel by the film were treated to serious probing of some profound questions: What is the nature of man in space? What are some of the implications of genuine interstellar contact? What is the mutation beyond man?

These questions are part of the common coinage of science fiction, to be sure, but Clarke's handling of them insured many sympathetic readers for science fiction, particularly among people who would not otherwise know an Apollo capsule from a Heuristically programmed ALgorithmic computer, otherwise known as HAL. If only for performing this service, Clarke's *2001: A Space Odyssey* is probably the most valuable novel of the year.

Persistent rumors during the last year or two have told of a coming sequel to Frank Herbert's Nebula-winning novel, *Dune.* Herbert finally confirmed the rumors when he finished the actual writing in mid-1968. While the continuation of the story of Paul Muad'Dib as emperor must await 1969 publication and evaluation, Herbert's 1968 novel, *The Santaroga Barrier,* was not one of the Nebula finalists. The critics may have subconsciously compared the limited scope of *The Santaroga Barrier* with the epic vision of *Dune,* but *The Santaroga Barrier* perhaps deserves more consideration than it was given. One more variation on Herbert's basic theme, the necessity for communication, *The Santaroga Barrier* has been praised by many college students who are overly aware of the invidious consequences of the lack of understanding: alienation, anomy, despair.

One of the principal charges laid against many science fiction novels is that they are exasperating. Too often they combine startling ingenuity with shabby characterization, or complexities of plotting with inanities of style. Some 1968 novels are no exception. What makes them so exasperating is the realization that they are, on the whole, so good that there is no reason for their not being superior. What is even more disappointing, the novels sometimes demonstrate an unrealized potential. Editors groan when they get a manuscript embodying an original concept, very badly handled. The editors, to their credit, usually insist that a writer learn his trade and that his execution be at least half as good as his imagination, before they will print a single mediocre word. For that matter, even the very best novels of the past dozen years too often betray symptoms of this same unrealized potential, or are marred in one way or another. *Stranger in a Strange Land* breaks apart in the middle, *Dune* has stylistic lapses, and even *A Canticle for Leibowitz* lacks centricity, to cite only three examples. Mainstream novels, of course, do not lack flaws, as they too often concentrate on representational confessionalism, replete with sexual aberrations or psychological hang-ups.

However, the fact that a science fiction novel—or any other for that matter—is flawed should not detract from the immediacy of its appeal. Students or fans do not really care whether *Stranger in a Strange Land* sometimes reads like two different novels or that Joyce's *Ulysses* is overly complex. One writer's forte may be dialogue, another's style, a third's character or action, and we should appreciate their techniques. Someday a writer may combine all these elements and the result may be a great novel, by whatever standards one uses to define "great." Many writers now active have the ability. Aldiss, Boyd, Brunner, Delany, Dick, Disch, Ellison, Herbert, Lafferty, Moorcock, Sturgeon, Zelazny . . . the list could include a dozen more . . . all are capable of writing a distinguished work. To that list perhaps should be added Joanna Russ, whose *Picnic on Paradise* is an agonizingly good but flawed novel. Miss Russ's major accomplishment here is that she may have created one of the first memorable women in a very masculine field. Save for Lady Jessica of *Dune*, there are few other women of the stature of Alyx, the tough heroine of *Picnic*, in the annals of science fiction. Alyx can charm, antagonize, hate, love, please, anger, and most of all, survive. A typical woman perhaps? Yes, but Alyx breathes the way that too many "real" painted dolls do not.

Miss Russ may learn more as her talent matures—learn how to remove the flaws that make *Picnic on Paradise* so enchantingly exasperating. For example, she may learn more about techniques of plotting, or learn not to depend on too much willing suspension of disbelief by her readers—but as she learns she will still have her talent, a vibrant verbal dexterity. Her words chime with a ring of genuine silver, not the clunk of the ersatz sandwich coinage spewed out by so many writers. Miss Russ's promise is measured by the fact that, for all its flaws, *Picnic on Paradise,* her first novel, was a Nebula nominee. How good her second or sixth will be boggles the imagination.

Robert Silverberg's *The Masks of Time* was the Nebula runner-up. It looks to the past and projects that vision to the future. How will people in the mass behave as they approach the end of the millennium thirty years from now? he asks. Much the same as they behaved a thousand years ago, with fears of the coming of the Antichrist or hopes for the Second Coming; with riots, depredations, religious intolerance, vast excesses of lust, rage, and power. Silverberg might have prefaced his novel, which is both realistic and terrifying, with Yeats's words, "And what rough beast, its hour come round at last, Slouches toward Bethlehem to be born?" The twenty-first century thus may be the age of the rough beast, the era of enlightenment, the beginning of the new dark ages. The conditions are here now, Silverberg posits: the superstition, the ignorance, the susceptibility to vast stimulation through the Cyclopean eye of the TV monster, the potential for mass hysteria. Combine these elements and transform "the rough beast" into a charismatic figure, and you have the makings of a very provocative novel indeed. The entire book is seen through the eyes of a dispassionate University of California at Irvine physics professor, and told in his words. He becomes involved with the antihero, Vornan-19, as a jealous sexual rival, and through the professor's narrow vision, life at the end of our century lurches to its whimpering conclusion. Wisely, Silverberg never reveals whether his visitor out of time is a demonic demiurge, a *homo superior* from the future with incredible charm, or simply the personalized extension of the bastard in all of us. Even though the novel may appear to be limited by the narrowness of the first-person point of view which Silverberg adopts, close examination reveals that he has created a universal micro-world. And as Scott Fitzgerald once put it, "Life is much more successfully looked at from a single window, after all." So with *The Masks of Time*.

The role of sex in contemporary science fiction has been a limited one, at best. Formerly magazine editors would not even suggest that a spaceman ever had to urinate, to say nothing of wanting to fornicate now and then. Today when D. H. Lawrence has emancipated all novelists, few science fiction writers treat sex as anything except a biological curiosity. Silverberg is a notable exception, and *The Masks of Time* is his best example. To be sure, any treatment of sex runs the risk of becoming mere titillation, not integral to plot, character, or action. But by personalizing Vornan-19 as an object of sexual idealization by both men and women, Silverberg makes the sexual conflict an important part of the book. Thus sex becomes relevant, not prurient or extraneous to the action or characters. In the end, Silverberg's utilization of hitherto proscribed materials may be as important to the future of science fiction as the introduction of the soft sciences as subject matter.

The last two finalists, Lafferty's *Past Master* and Dick's *Do Androids Dream of Electric Sheep* are two more examples of books being written for a maximum audience. Both require the reader to extend himself, to stretch his imagination almost to the breaking point past a willing suspension of disbelief. The authors lead the reader through worlds of time into nightmares of anti-utopian vision. To be sure, in Lafferty's book Sir Thomas More is alive in his Utopia, but faced with what enemies and what alternatives that extend from More's original vision? And Dick asks the reader some elemental questions: When is a human being? Are machines more real than man if they are worshiped by man, if they are immune to fallout, and if humans can program their daily moods with a few simple flicks of a dial?

All of these extrapolations derive from conditions actually existing in our present society. This ability to indicate the logical conclusions of what we now do when projected into a future scene is, of course, at the very heart of science fiction. Throughout the past thirty years the imagination of science fiction writers has often surpassed their ability to incarnate that imagination into form. Now talent is beginning to catch up with imagination, and the combination will ultimately produce novels of distinction, particularly when writers continue to insist on maximum readers. Refusal to demand more of the readers means that writers will produce competent, slick, professional novels that may win a prize or two but will do nothing to make science fiction into literature. When writers utilize their imaginations and talents in concert with the awakened sensitivities of their audience, science fiction may well become the genuine literature of the future.

MOTHER TO THE WORLD

Richard Wilson

His name was Martin Rolfe. She called him Mr. Ralph.

She was Cecelia Beamer, called Siss.

He was a vigorous, intelligent, lean and wiry forty-two, a shade under six feet tall. His hair, black, was thinning but still covered all of his head; and all his teeth were his own. His health was excellent. He'd never had a cavity or an operation and he fervently hoped he never would.

She was a slender, strong young woman of twenty-eight, five feet four. Her eyes, nose and mouth were regular and well-spaced but the combination fell short of beauty. She wore her hair, which was dark blonde, not quite brown, straight back and long in two pigtails which she braided daily, after a ritualistic hundred brushings. Her figure was better than average for her age and therefore good, but she did nothing to emphasize it. Her disposition was cheerful when she was with someone; when alone her tendency was to work hard at the job at hand, giving it her serious attention. Whatever she was doing was the most important thing in the world to her just then and she had a compulsion to do it absolutely right. She was indefatigable but she liked, almost demanded, to be praised for what she did well.

Her amusements were simple ones. She liked to talk to people but most people quickly became bored with what she had to say—she was inclined to be repetitive. Fortunately for her, she also liked to talk to animals, birds included.

She was a retarded person with the mentality of an eight-year-old.

Eight can be a delightful age. Rolfe remembered his son at eight—bright, inquiring, beginning to emerge from childhood

 Nebula Award, Best Novelette 1968

1

but not so fast as to lose any of his innocent charm; a refreshing, uninhibited conversationalist with an original viewpoint on life. The boy had been a challenge to him and a constant delight. He held on to that memory, drawing sustenance from it, for her.

Young Rolfe was dead now, along with his mother and three billion other people.

Rolfe and Siss were the only ones left in all the world.

It was M.R. that had done it, he told her. Massive Retaliation; from the Other Side.

When American bombs rained down from long-range jets and rocket carriers, nobody'd known the Chinese had what they had. Nobody'd suspected it of that relatively backward country which the United States had believed it was softening up, in a brushfire war, for enforced diplomacy.

Rolfe hadn't been aware of any speculation that Peking's scientists were concentrating their research not on weapons but on biochemistry. Germ warfare, sure. There'd been propaganda from both sides about that, but nothing had been hinted about a biological agent, as it must have been, that could break down human cells and release the water.

"M.R.," he told her. "Better than nerve gas or the neutron bomb." Like those, it left the buildings and equipment intact. Unlike them, it didn't leave any messy corpses—only the bones, which crumbled and blew away. Except the bone dust trapped inside the pathetic mounds of clothing that lay everywhere in the city.

"Are they coming over now that they beat us?"

"I'm sure they intended to. But there can't be any of them left. They outsmarted themselves, I guess. The wind must have blown it right back at them. I don't really know what happened, Siss. All I know is that everybody's gone now, except you and me."

"But the animals—"

Rolfe had found it best in trying to explain something to Siss to keep it simple, especially when he didn't understand it himself. Just as he had learned long ago that if he didn't know how to pronounce a word he should say it loud and confidently.

So all he told Siss was that the bad people had got hold of a terrible weapon called M.R.—she'd heard of that—and used it on the good people and that nearly everybody had died. Not the animals, though, and damned if he knew why.

"Animals don't sin," Siss told him.

"That's as good an explanation as any I can think of," he said. She was silent for a while. Then she said: "Your name —initials—are M.R., aren't they?"

He'd never considered it before, but she was right. Martin Rolfe—Massive Retaliation. I hope she doesn't blame everything on me, he thought. But then she spoke again. "M.R. That's short for Mister. What I call you. Your name that I have for you. Mister Ralph."

"Tell me again how we were saved, Mr. Ralph."

She used the expression in an almost evangelical sense, making him uncomfortable. Rolfe was a practical man, a realist and freethinker.

"You know as well as I do, Siss," he said. "It's because Professor Cantwell was doing government research and because he was having a party. You certainly remember; Cantwell was your boss."

"I know that. But you tell it so good and I like to hear it."

"All right. Bill Cantwell was an old friend of mine from the army and when I came to New York I gave him a call at the University. It was the first time I'd talked to him in years; I had no idea he'd married again and had set up housekeeping in Manhattan."

"And had a working girl named Siss," she put in.

"The very same," he agreed. Siss never referred to herself as a maid, which was what she had been. "And so when I asked Bill if he could put me up, I thought it would be in his old bachelor apartment. He said sure, just like that, and I didn't find out till I got there, late in the evening, that he had a new wife and was having a houseparty and had invited two couples from out of town to stay over."

"I gave my room to Mr. and Mrs. Glenn, from Columbus," Siss said.

"And the Torquemadas, of Seville, had the regular guest room." Whoever they were; he didn't remember names the way she did. "So that left two displaced persons, you and me."

"Except for the Nassers."

The Nassers, as she pronounced it, were the two self-contained rooms in the Cantwell basement. The NASAs, or the

3

Nasas, was what Cantwell called them because the National Aeronautics and Space Administration had given him a contract to study the behavior of human beings in a closed system.

Actually the money had gone to Columbia University, where Cantwell was a professor of mechanical and aerospace engineering.

"A sealed-off environment," Rolfe said. "But because Columbia didn't have the space just at that time, and because the work was vital, NASA gave Cantwell permission to build the rooms in his own home. They were—still are—in his basement, and that's where you and I slept that fateful night when the world ended."

"I still don't understand."

"We were completely sealed off in there," Rolfe said. "We weren't breathing Earth air and we weren't connected in any way to the rest of the world. We might as well have been out in space or on the moon. So when it happened to everybody else—to Professor and Mrs. Cantwell, and to the Glenns and the Torquemadas and to the Nassers in Egypt and the Joneses in Jones Beach and all the people at Columbia, and in Washington and Moscow and Pretoria and London and Peoria and Medicine Hat and La Jolla and all those places all over—it didn't happen to us. That's because Professor Cantwell was a smart man and his closed systems worked."

"And we were saved."

"That's one way of looking at it."

"What's the other way?"

"We were doomed."

From his notebooks:

Siss asked why I'm so sure there's nobody but us left in the whole world. A fair question. Of course I'm not absolutely positively cross-my-heart-and-hope-to-die, swear-on-a Bible convinced that there isn't a poor live slob hidden away in some remote corner. Other people besides Bill must have been working with closed systems; certainly any country with a space program would be, and maybe some of *their* nassers were inhabited, too. I hadn't heard that any astronauts or cosmonauts were in orbit that day but if they were, and got down safely, I guess they could be alive somewhere.

But I've listened to the rest of the world on some of the finest radio equipment ever put together and there hasn't been a peep out of it. I've listened and signaled and listened and signaled and listened. Nothing. Nil. Short wave, long wave, AM, FM, UHF, marine band, everywhere. Naught. Not a thing. Lots of automatic signals from unmanned satellites, of course, and the quasars are still being heard from, but nothing human.

I've sent out messages on every piece of equipment connected to Con Ed's EE net. RCA, American Cable & Radio, the Bell System, Western Union, The Associated Press, UPI, Reuters' world news network, *The New York Times*' multifarious teletypes, even the Hilton Hotels' international reservations system. Nothing. By this time I'd become fairly expert at communications and I'd found the Pentagon network at AT&T. Silent. Ditto the hot line to the Kremlin. I read the monitor teletype and saw the final message from Washington to Moscow. Strictly routine. No hint that anything was amiss anywhere. Just as it must have been at the Army message center at Pearl Harbor on another Sunday morning a generation ago.

This is for posterity, these facts. My evidence is circumstantial. But to Siss I say: "There's nobody left but us. I know. You'll have to take my word for it that the rest of the world is as empty as New York."

Nobody here but us chickens, boss. Us poor flightless birds. One middle-aged rooster and one sad little hen, somewhat deficient in the upper story. What do you want us to do, boss? What's the next step in the great cosmic scheme? Tell us: where do we go from here?

But don't tell me; tell Siss. I don't expect an answer; she does. She's the one who went into the first church she found open that Sunday morning (some of them were locked, you know) and said all the prayers she knew, and asked for mercy for her relatives, and her friends, and her employers, and for me, and for all the dead people who had been alive only yesterday, and finally for herself; and then she asked why. She was in there for an hour and when she came out I don't think she'd had an answer.

Nobody here but us chickens, boss. What do you want us to do now, fricassee ourselves?

Late on the morning of doomsday they had taken a walk down Broadway, starting from Cantwell's house near the Columbia campus.

There were a number of laughs to be had from cars in comical positions, if anybody was in a laughing mood. Some were standing obediently behind white lines at intersections, and obviously their drivers had been overtaken during a red light. With its driver gone, each such car had simply stood there, its engine dutifully using up all the gas in its tank and then coughing to a stop. Others had nosed gently into shop windows, or less gently into other cars or trucks. One truck, loaded with New Jersey eggs, had overturned and its cargo was dripping in a yellowy-white puddle. Rolfe, his nose twitching as if in anticipation of a warm day next week, made a mental note never to return to that particular spot.

Several times he found a car which had been run up upon from behind by another. It was as if, knowing they would never again be manufactured, they were trying copulation.

While Siss was in church Rolfe found a car that had not idled away all its gas and he made a dry run through the streets. He discovered that he could navigate pretty well around the stalled or wrecked cars, though occasionally he had to drive up on the sidewalk or make a three-block detour to get back to Broadway.

Then he and Siss, subdued after church, went downtown.

"Whose car is this, Mr. Ralph?" she asked him.

"My car, Siss. Would you like one, too?"

"I can't drive."

"I'll teach you. It may come in handy."

"I was the only one in church," she said. It hadn't got through to her yet, he thought; not completely.

"Who were you expecting?" he asked kindly.

"God, maybe."

She was gazing straight ahead, clutching her purse in her lap. She had the expression of a person who had been let down.

At 72nd Street a beer truck had demolished the box office of the Trans-Lux movie house and foamy liquid was still trickling out of it, across the sidewalk and along the gutter and into a sewer. Rolfe stopped the car and got out. An aluminum barrel had been punctured. The beer leaking from it was cool. He leaned over and let it run into his mouth for a while.

The Trans-Lux had been having a Fellini festival; the picture was $8\frac{1}{2}$. On impulse he went inside and came back to the car with the reels of film in a black tin box. He remembered the way the movie had opened, with all the cars stalled in traffic. Like Broadway, except that the Italian cars had people in them. He put the box in the rear of the car and said: "We'll go to the movies sometime." Siss looked at him blankly.

At Columbus Circle a Broadway bus had locked horns with a big van carrying furniture from North Carolina. At 50th Street a Mustang had nosed gently into the front of a steak house, as if someone had led it to a hitching post.

He made an illegal left turn at 42nd Street, noting what was playing at the Rialto: two naughty, daring, sexy, nudie pix, including a re-run of "My Bare Lady." He didn't stop for that one.

At the old Newsweek Building east of Broadway, an Impala had butted into the ground-floor liquor store. The plate glass lay smashed but the bottles in the window were intact. He made a mental note. Across the street, one flight up, was the Keppel Folding Boat Company, which had long intrigued him. Soon it might be useful to unfold one and sail off to a better place. He marked it in his mind.

Bookstores, 42nd Street style. Dirty books and magazines. Girly books. Deviant, flagellant, homosexual, Lesbian, sadistic books. Pornographic classics restored to the common man— *Memoirs of a Woman of Pleasure. The Kama Sutra,* quaint but lasciviously advertised. Books of nudes for the serious artist (no retoucher's airbrush here, men!).

Nudie pix in packets, wrapped in pliofilm, at a buck and a half the set. Large girls in successive states of undress. How big can a breast be before it disgusts? What is the optimum bosom size? A cup? D cup? It would depend on the number to be fed, wouldn't it? And how hungry they were? Or was that criterion passé?

He looked over at Siss, who wasn't looking at him or the bookstores or the dirty-movie houses but straight ahead. She had a nice figure. About a C.

But it was never the body alone; it was the mind that went with it and the voice with which it spoke.

"What are you thinking, Siss?" he asked.

"Nothing," she said. It was probably true. "What are *you* thinking?"

Riposte. How could he tell her?

He improvised. They were passing Bryant Park. "Pigeons in the park," he said. "I'm thinking of the pigeons. Hungrier

7

than yesterday because nobody's buying peanuts for them, bringing slices of bread from home; there's no bread lady buying bagfuls for them at Horn & Hardart's day-old bakery shop."

"It's a sad time, isn't it, Mr. Ralph?"

"Yes, Siss; a sad time."

They got to First Avenue and the U.N. There wasn't anybody there, either.

Notes for a History of the World was what he wrote on page one of his notebook.

On page two he had alternate titles, some facetious:

The True History of the Martin Rolfe Family on the Planet Earth; or, *Two for Tomorrow*.

Recollections of a World Well Lost.

How the Population Crisis Was Solved.

What Next? or, if *You* Don't Do It, Marty, Who the Hell Will?

From his notebooks:

Thank God for movies. We'd be outen our minds by now if I hadn't taught myself to be a projectionist.

Radio City Music Hall apparently's only movie on Con Ed's EE list. Bit roomy for Siss and me but getting used to it. Sometimes she sits way down front, I in mezzanine, and we shout to each other when Gregory Peck does heroic things.

Collected first runs to add to 8½ from all major Manhattan houses—Capitol, Criterion, Cinema I & II, State, etc.—so we have good backlog. Also, if Siss likes, we run it again right away or next night. I don't mind. Then there are the 42nd St. houses and the art houses and the nabes & Mod. Museum film library. Shouldn't run out for a long time.

Days are for exploring and shopping. I go armed because of the animals. Siss stays home at hotel.

(*Why* are there animals? Find out. *Where* find out; how?)

The dogs in packs are worst. So far they haven't attacked and a shot fired in the air scares them off. So far.

Later they left the city. It had been too great a strain to live a life half primitive, half luxurious. The contrast was too much. And the rats were getting bolder. The rats and the dogs.

They had lived there at first for the convenience. He picked

8

a hotel on Park Avenue. He put Siss in a single room and took a suite down the hall for himself.

He guessed correctly that there'd be huge refrigerators and freezers stocked with food enough for years.

The hotel, with its world-famous name, was one of the places the Consolidated Edison Company had boasted was on its Emergency Electricity net, along with City Hall, the Empire State Building, the tunnels and bridges, Governors Island and other key installations. The EE net, worked out for Civil Defense (what had ever become of Civil Defense?), guaranteed uninterrupted electricity to selected customers through the use of deep underground grids and conduits, despite flood, fire, pestilence or war. A promotional piece claimed that only total annihilation could knock out the system.

There was a hint of the way it worked in a slogan that Con Ed considered using before the government censors decided it would have given too much away: ". . . as long as the Hudson flows."

Whatever the secret, he and Siss had electricity, from which so many blessings flowed, for as long as they stayed in the city.

From his notebooks:

I've renamed our hotel the Living End. Siss calls it our house, or maybe Our House.

I won't let her go out by herself but she has the run of the hotel. She won't use the self-service elevators. Doesn't trust them. Don't blame her. She cooks in the hotel kitchen and carries our meals up two flights on a tray.

Garbage disposal no problem. There's an incinerator that must work by electricity. So far it's taken everything I've dumped down it. I can't feel any heat but it doesn't stink.

We're getting some outdoor stinks, though. Animal excrement that nobody cleans up (I'd be doing nothing else if I started). Uncollected garbage. Rotting food in supermarkets and other places without EE.

There are certain streets I avoid now. Whole sections, when the wind is wrong.

Bad night at the Living End. Had a nightmare.

I dreamed that Siss and I, home from the Music Hall

9

(Cary Grant and Audrey Hepburn in something from the sixties), were having a fight. I don't know about what but we were shouting and I was calling her unforgivable names and she was saying she was going to climb up to the 20th floor and jump, when the phone rang . . .

I woke up, seeming to hear the echo of the last ring. The phone was there on the floor, under the night table.

I didn't dare pick it up.

It must have happened just before dawn, when Manhattan was as deserted as it ever got.

I took a chance on the EE and went up in the elevators to the top of the Empire State Bldg. First time I'd ever been up—also the last, probably. What a sight. Plenty of cars, cabs, trucks, buses rammed into each other & sides of bldgs but lots more just came to natural(!) stop in midstreet or near curb. Very feasible to drive around and out of town, tho probably not thru tunnels. GW Bridge shd be okay, with its 8 lanes. Have to get out of town one day anyhow, so best explore in advance.

Planes. No sign that any crashed but bet lots did somewhere. Everything looks orderly at NY airports.

Fires. Few black spots—signs of recent fires. Nothing major.

Harbor & rivers. Some ships, lots of boats drifting around loose. No sign of collisions; nothing big capsized.

Animals. Dog packs here and there. Sound of their barking rises high. *Nasty* sound. Birds, all kinds.

Air very dry.

Down in the street again, Rolfe began to think about the animals other than the dogs that ran in packs. How long would it be until the bigger ones—the wolves and bears and mountain lions—found their way into the city? He decided to visit Abercrombie & Fitch and arm himself with something heavier than the pistol he carried. Big-bore stuff, whatever they called it.

Rolfe was admiring an elephant gun in the fantastic store (Hemingway had shopped here, and probably Martin and Osa Johnson and Frank Buck and others from the lost past) when he remembered another sound he'd heard from the top of the Empire State Building. It had puzzled him, but now he could identify it. It had been the trumpeting of an elephant.

An elephant in Manhattan? The circus wasn't in town— He knew then, but for the moment he pushed aside the thought and its implications.

After he had picked out the guns, and a wicked gas-operated underwater javelin for good measure, he outfitted himself in safari clothes. Khaki shorts and high socks, a big-pocketed bush jacket, a sun helmet. Hurrah for Captain Spalding! He looked a true Marxman, he thought, humming the song Groucho had sung and admiring himself in a full-length mirror.

He took a cartridge belt and boxes of shells and first-aid and water-purification kits and a trapper's knife and a light-weight trail ax and a compass and binoculars and snowshoes and deerskin gloves and a tough pair of boots. He staggered out into Madison Avenue and dumped everything into the back of the cream-colored Lincoln convertible he was driving that day.

The trumpeting of the elephant had come from the Central Park Zoo, of course. He drove in from Fifth Avenue and parked near the restaurant opposite the sea lions' pool. He could see three of them lying quietly on a stone ledge, just above the water, watching him. He wondered when they'd last been fed.

First, though, he went to the administration building and let himself in with lock-picking tools. He had become adept at the burglary trade. He found a set of what seemed to be master keys and tried them first at the aviary. They worked.

The names of the birds, on the faded wooden plaques, were as colorful as their plumage. There were a Papuan lory, a sulphur-crested cockatoo, the chiffchaff and kookaburra bird, laughing jackass and motmot, chachalaca, drongo and poor old puffin. He opened their cages and watched their tentative, gaudy passage to freedom.

A pelican waddled out comically, suspicion in its round eyes. He ducked a hawk and cowered from a swift, fierce eagle. An owl lingered, blinking, until he shooed it toward the doors. He left to the last two brooding vultures, hesitating to free creatures so vile. But there was a role for scavengers, too. He opened their cage and ran, to get outdoors before they did.

After the cacophony of the aviary, he was surprised at the silence as he neared the monkey house. He'd have to be damned careful about the gorilla, which obviously had to be shot. The big chimps were nothing to fool around with, either. But the monkey house was empty. The signs were there and the smell remained but the apes, big and little, were not. Could they have freed themselves? But all the cages were locked.

Puzzled, he went on to the smaller mammals, freeing the harmless ones, the raccoons, the mongooses, the deflowered skunks, the weasels and prairie dogs—even the spiny porcupine, which looked over its shoulder at him as it shuffled toward the doors.

He freed the foxes, too, and they bounded off as if to complete an interrupted mission. "Go get the rats," Rolfe yelled after them.

He marked the location of the wolves and the big cats. He'd come back to them with his guns.

Last of all he freed the lone elephant, scarcely grown, whose trumpet call had summoned him. The elephant—an unofficial sign said it was a female, Geraldine—followed him at a distance almost to the car, then broke into a clumsy trot and drank from the sea lions' pool.

As Rolfe was returning to the cages with the guns he knew why there weren't any monkeys. The big and little apes were hominids, like man. Their evolutionary climb had doomed them, too.

He killed the beasts of prey. It was an awful business. He was not a good shot even at close range and the executions took many bullets. A sinuous, snarling black panther took six before he was sure. The caged beasts, refusing to stand still for the mercy killings, made it hot, bloody, stinking work. He guessed it was necessary.

Finally he was done. Quivering and sweating, he returned to the car. The sea lions honked and swam across to his side of the pool. He could see now that there were three babies and two adults.

What was he to do with them? He couldn't bring himself to a final butchery. And what was he to do about all the other captive animals—in the Bronx Zoo uptown, in zoos all over the world? He couldn't be a one-man Animal Rescue League.

Rolfe had a momentary fantasy in which he enticed the sea lions into the car (four in the back, one in the front) and drove them to the East River, where they flopped into the water and swam toward the sea, honking with gratitude.

But he knew that in his present state of exhaustion he

couldn't lift even the babies, and there was no way for them to get out of their enclosure unaided. Maybe he could come back with a truck and plank and fish to tempt them with. He left the problem, and that of the Bronx and Prospect Park Zoos and the Aquarium (not to get too far afield) and started the car.

Geraldine looked after him. He would have liked a little trumpet of farewell but she had found some long grass and was eating.

As he drove back to the Living End through the wider streets, weaving carefully around the stalled cars, his mind was full of other trapped beasts, great and small, starving and soon to go mad from thirst, as if in punishment for having outlived man.

Only then did the other thought crash into his consciousness—what of the millions of pets, trapped in the houses of their vanished owners? Dogs and cats, unable to open the refrigerators or the cans in the pantries. Some would have the craft to tear open packages of dried food and would learn to drink from leaking faucets or from toilet bowls. But at best they could prolong their miserable existence for only a few more days.

What was he to do about the pets? What could he do? Run around the city freeing them? Where would he start? Should he free all those on the north sides of odd-numbered streets? Or those on the ground floors of houses in named streets beginning with consonants? What were the rules? How did you play God?

He resolved not to talk to Siss about it. He wouldn't have her breaking her heart over a billion doomed animals; she had enough to mourn.

From his notebooks:

What should I call today? Rolfeday? Sissuary the 13th? Year Zero?

Shd hav kept track but don't really know how many days it's been since I walked out of Bill's storage vault and found myself ½ the human pop. of the whole furshlugginer world.

Asked Siss. *She* remembers. It has been exactly 11 days since the holocaust. She accounted for every one of them. Moren I cld do: they started to run together for me after the first three.

13

OK, so it's Sissuary the 11th, Year One, Anno Rolfe. Some-body's got to keep a record.

How many days in Sissuary? We'll see. Got to name the second month before closing out the first.

It was difficult for him to look back and remember exactly when he had first realized with certainty that this was the woman with whom he was fated to spend the rest of his life, when it had dawned on him that this moron was to be his bosom companion, that he had to take care of her, provide for her, *talk* with her (and *listen* to her), answer her stupid questions, *sleep* with her!

The realization must have come about the time he began to experience his stomach-aches. They weren't pains; they were more like a gnawing at the vitals of his well-being, a pincers movement by the enemy that was trapping him where he didn't want to be, with someone he didn't want to be with, a leaden weight that was smothering his freedom.

Some of her traits nearly drove him out of his mind. He was oversensitive, he supposed, but he had to wince and tried to close his ears every time she converted a sneeze into a clearly-enunciated "Ah *choo!*" and waited for him to bless her.

Worse because more frequent was her way of grunting audibly when she was picking up something, or pushing some-thing or moving something around. This was to let him know that she was hard at work, for him. After a while he forced himself to praise her while she was at it—her diligence; her strength, her unselfishness—and she stopped making so much noise. He hated himself for being a hypocrite and felt sure she would see through him, but she never did and in the end his exaggerated praise became a way of life. It stood him in good stead later, when he had to tell her white lies about the degree of his affection for her and the great esteem in which he held her.

From his notebooks:

Asked Siss if she'd ever read a book and she said oh yes the Good Book. Parts of it. It used to comfort her a lot more in the old days, apparently. She'd read two books all the way thru—Uncle Wiggily and Japanese Fairy Tales, and parts of a Tarzan book. She sometimes used to look at the paper—read the comics, the horoscope, picture captions, the TV listings. Lord save us from ever having to hold a literary conversation.

To be fair I've tried to remember the last 10 books I read before doom. Probably be a pretty stupid list if I was following my usual random reading pattern—off on an Erle Stanley Gardner or James Bond kick and reading everything available all at once.

Aside from his obligation to humanity to sire a new race, what was there for him to do? Rolfe considered the possibilities, dividing them into two groups: necessities (duties or obligations) and pastimes (including frivolities).

Under necessities he put:

Keep a journal for posterity, if any. He was already doing that.

Give Siss the equivalent of a grammar school education; more if she could take it.

Try to elevate her taste for the sake of the unborn children she would one day influence.

Keep his family fed and sheltered. Would it be necessary to clothe them, except for warmth in the winter? Nudity might be more practical, as well as healthier.

Then he jotted down on a separate piece of paper "Obligation to self paramount" and looked at it. He felt that he had to come first, with his duty to Siss a little lower (on the paper and in his estimation) because he was smarter than she was and therefore more worth saving.

Then he had another look and amended it. Siss was more worth saving because she was a woman and able to reproduce her kind.

But not without his help, of course.

Finally he put himself and Siss at the top of the list. No good saving one without the other.

Pastimes. Take up a sport to keep fit. What one-man sports were there? Woodchopping? Fat chance. Too blister-prone, he. Hiking? Maybe he and Siss should hike around the world to make positively sure there was nobody else. Or around the eastern United States, anyhow. Or just up and down the Hudson River Valley? Somehow walking didn't seem to be his sport, either.

He might take up cooking. Men had always been the best chefs and now ingenuity would be needed to make nourishing and palatable meals from what was available to them. They couldn't depend on canned and preserved food forever. Okay, he'd be a cook. Of course that was a sport that tended to put pounds on, not take them off. He'd better find an antidote, like swimming or handball.

How about collecting? What—money? Diamonds? Great art? Neither money nor diamonds, obviously; neither had any intrinsic value in a World of Two—and then art was best left where it was, as well-protected as anything in the poor old world. If he wanted Siss to see a Rembrandt or an Andrew Wyeth, he'd take her to it.

From his notebooks:

Collecting old-fashioned windup phonographs against the day when no elec. Also old-fashioned 78 records. Got to keep so many things I can't reproduce.

Music. Good; Siss likes. She enjoys Tchaikowsky, Wagner and Beethoven (what wildness must stir within her poor head sometimes!) She'll sit still for Bach. I can't complain.

We're both crazy about Cole Porter, she for the music, I for the words, those great words, so much more ironic now than he had ever meant them to be.

"It's All Right With Me," for instance.

We've found a place. We—Is that the first time I've used the word?

It's far enough away from the city to be really country; beyond the stink and the reminders of dead glory; yet close enough so I can get in for supplies if I need them. I've stored up enough good gassed-up cars so that travel is no problem, but I think I'll try to stay here as much as I can. I used to be a fair woodsman. Let's see how much I remember.

It's peaceful here. My stomach-ache is better, all of a sudden.

He insisted on thinking of her as a person who had come into his custody and for whom he was responsible. For a long time all he felt toward her was pity; no desire. And for that reason he also pitied himself.

Because she was what she was, it would be unthinkable for her to touch him in any but the most innocent of ways, as she would one of her animal friends.

And when she called him anything but Mr. Ralph, using a word like honey, he was not flattered because he had heard her apply it also to a squirrel, a bluejay and a field mouse.

"Mr. Ralph, can I ask you a favor? Would you mind if you took me for a ride?"

It wasn't that she particularly wanted to go anywhere; apparently her enjoyment lay in sharing the front seat with him; he noticed that she sat very close to him, in almost the exact center of the seat and did not, as he had speculated she might, sit at the far right, next to the window.

For her ride she chose an ornate costume which included a hat, a silk scarf, dark glasses, jacket, blouse and skirt, stockings and half-heel shoes.

She picked the costume at what she called the Monkey Ward store while he shopped down the block for a fairly clean convertible with sound tires and a fair amount of gas in the tank.

They rode out past the quarry. Long ago he had stored away the fact that Quarry Road was the highway probably least littered with debris.

There was one bad place where he had to get off into a field to skirt what looked as if it had been a 50-car chain-reaction smashup. Otherwise, it was good driving all the way to the lake.

He parked near the old boat-launching site and automatically scanned the watery horizon for any sign of sail or smoke. He had never entirely abandoned hopes of finding other people.

He had brought from the liquor store (catty-corner from Monkey Ward's) a fifth of a high-priced Scotch and as they sat looking out over the lake he carefully opened it, preserving the tinfoil for her.

Then he ceremoniously offered her a drink. She declined, as he knew she would, saying:

"Not now, thanks. Maybe some other time." Apparently a piece of etiquette she'd learned was that it was bad manners to refuse anything outright—especially something to eat or drink.

Rolfe said: "I'll have one, though, if you don't mind." And she replied, in what must have been a half-remembered witticism, "Take two, they're small."

He took two in succession, neither small.

The lake was serene, the sun was warm but not hot, a breeze blew from the east and the bugs were infrequent.

"Doesn't it bother you that there's nobody else?" he asked her. "Don't you get *lonesome?*"

17

But she said: "I'm always lonesome. I was. Now I'm less lonesome than I was. Thanks to you, Mr. Ralph."

Now what could he say to that? So he sat there, touched but scowling out at the horizon, and then he reached for the very old Scotch (the world had still lived when it was bottled) and took a very big swallow. Only later did he think to offer her one.

"Some other time, maybe," she said. "Not right now."

There came a day when her last brassiere lost its hooks and she obtained his dispensation to stop wearing it. And another when her blouses lost their buttons and refused to stay closed by the mere tucking of their tails into her skirts, and he told her it didn't matter in the least; until finally her last rags fell from her.

She said to him: "You're my Mr. Ralph, honey, and it's not wrong to be this way with you, is it, Mr. Ralph?"

This touched him so that he took her naked innocent body in his arms and kissed the top of her clean, sweet head and he said:

"You're my big little girl and you couldn't do anything wrong if you tried."

And only then, for the first time, he felt a desire for this waif—this innocent in whom the seeds of the whole human race were locked.

She gave him a quick daring kiss on the cheek and ran off, saying: "It's time I started supper now. My gosh, we have to get you fed."

He remembered with shame a pathetic scene early in their life together. They had gone to Monkey Ward's and dressed from the skin out in brand-new evening clothes. He'd had to help her cancel some tasteless combinations but at last she stood before him like an angel. Or, as he'd said: "Damned if you don't look like a Madison Avenue model."

"You shouldn't swear, Mr. Ralph," she'd said. "But thanks anyhow."

"And you shouldn't talk. You're welcome. Look, we're going to play a game. We're going to a fancy night club. We're going to make believe you're a mute—that you can't talk. No matter what, you must not say a word. Not a word."

"All right, Mr. Ralph."

"Starting right now, damn it! I'm sorry. I mean starting right now. All you can do is nod or smile. You can touch me

18

if you want to. But you can't talk at all. That's part of the game. Do you understand?"

She started to say yes, then caught herself and nodded.

The silent nod from this beautifully gowned woman immediately made her ten times more attractive. Pleased with himself and with her, he gave her his arm and bowed her into the front seat of the Bentley he had searched out for this evening.

The night club had once been a major one, with a resident big-name band. Changing fashion had turned it into a discothèque, so that it had a juke box. He fed it a handful of coins to pay his way into a night of illusion. But the tables were bare and therefore wrong. He found a linen closet and set them with tableclothes and silverware, glasses, candlesticks.

The illusion grew. He found a switch that set in motion a set of colored lights which played on multi-faceted colored globes which hung from the ceiling. Another switch set them spinning slowly.

"What do you do in your spare time?" he asked her, knowing she wouldn't reply but wanting to see how she would react.

She shrugged, smiled a little and shook her head in what he tried to imagine was an attitude that she had so little spare time that it was negligible.

She was carrying out her part of the bargain. She did it extremely well. She listened without a word to his conversation, looking into his eyes as he pretended they were two among hundreds of elegant diners. He reconstructed talk from pre-holocaust nights out. He pretended she was a girl he had once been engaged to and told her extravagant things. She looked back at him and smiled, as if mockingly, as the old girl would have done. He pretended it was a later time, with the engagement in ruins and him solacing himself with the wife of his best friend, with the best friend's knowledge and consent, and the girl across from him gave him silent looks of profound sympathy. He pretended he had hired a call girl and spoke foully to her. She smiled bravely, her lips quivering, saying nothing.

Angered by the illusion which he had created and which mocked him, he drank too much and continued to abuse her —for herself, now; for doing as he had asked, for remaining silent.

The juke box was playing "Begin the Beguine" and ghostly

19

dancers danced inside the circle of tables, under the soft colored lights. He saw them and cursed them for their non-existence. He got up, knocking his chair over backwards, and shouted at her.

"Speak!" he said. "I release you from your muteness."

She shook her head, no longer smiling.

"Speak! You misbegotten halfwit! You monstrous bird-brained imposter! You scullery maid in a Schiaparelli gown! Speak, you—mental case."

But still she said nothing; merely looked at him with those deep eyes that seemed to understand and forgive.

Only at the very end of their evening out, when he had drunk himself into a stupor and stared across the room over her right shoulder, as if transfixed by his misery, did she speak. And then she said only:

"We better go home, Mr. Ralph, honey."

Then with a strength greater than his she half carried him there to the car and drove him home and put him to bed. It was a good thing he'd taught her to drive.

He woke up contrite, half remembering that he'd behaved unforgivably.

But she forgave him, as perhaps no one else ever would have, using these words:

"I forgive you, Mr. Ralph. You knewd not what you dood."

He was delighted. "Do not what I would," he said. "Had I but dood what I could, who knew what would have been dood?"

"I don't think that's very nice, Mr. Ralph. I said I forgive you. You're supposed to say thank you and say you're sorry, even if you're not sorry."

He was still laughing at her, even after the realization that he had a hangover.

"Okay, I'm sorry even if I'm not sorry and it's very good of you to forgive me for my insufferable behavior, even if nobody asked you to."

"Thank you for saying that, Mr. Ralph. Now I'll fix you a hangover remedy."

"Where did you learn to concoct a hangover remedy, for God's sake?"

"I was a working girl once for a poor man who got intoxicated and his wife. I learned it there."

She gave him no magic potion but an ordinary tomatoey

thing laced with pepper and Worcestershire sauce. He drank it down but stubbornly declined to feel better for a full hour. By then he had persuaded Siss he needed a cold beer and she'd brought him one—disapproving but proud of her ingenuity in having produced it, since they kept no store of alcoholic beverages. She must have made an ingenious search to find a cold beer; he was suddenly proud of her.

But, remembering his performance of the night before, he hated himself.

From the holding of hands to the kiss is not so far a thing as from the not holding of hands to the holding.

One thinks of the innocence of holding hands (children do it; men shake hands) but it is a vast journey from a platonic handclasp, over which there is no lingering, to the clasp which is so intense and telegraphic (accompanied, as it may be, by ardent gazing) that it would be a great surprise if the kiss to which it soon led were rebuffed.

And a kiss may lead anywhere. This he knew. He wondered how much she knew, or felt or surmised.

Dared he take her hand to help her across a stream or a rocky place? So far he had taken her arm, holding her firmly just above the elbow as if she were an elderly woman and he a large Boy Scout. He had no wish yet for anything more intimate.

It was a hesitant, tentative beginning to their romance.

"Do you mind my touching you?" he asked. Lately he had found that it gave him pleasure to touch her hair or trace the outline of her ear, or run his finger along her breastbone. Nothing carnal.

"No; I enjoy it."

And so they married. He arranged a ceremony, not only for her sense of propriety but to satisfy his demand for a kind of stability amid chaos.

He made it as elaborate as possible. He found a big flat rock to be the altar. He picked flowers and garlanded them into a headpiece for her. Let her head be covered, though her body was not.

She surprised him with a piece of writing. Crudely written in pencil on a sheet from a lined pad, it said:

"To my Mr. Ralph—

"This is our day to mary to-gether. My day and your day.

21

I feel real good about it even if nobody else cant come. I'll try and make you a good wife with all my heart.

"I know you do the same thing for me because you are kind and good dear Mr. Ralph.

"Your freind and wife
"Cecelia Beamer"

It was the first time he knew what Siss was the nickname for.

Never before a sentimental man, Martin took his wife, Cecelia Beamer Rolfe, in his arms and kissed her with tenderness and affection.

He put her wedding-letter, as he thought of it, away in his desk, where it would be safe.

He wanted to consummate the marriage outdoors. It was a perfect June day, the sun warm, the grass soft, a breeze gentle. Lord knew they could not have asked for greater privacy than that of their own planet. But he felt Siss would have been, if not shocked, embarrassed unless four walls surrounded them.

Therefore he took her indoors, where she removed her flowery hat and put it in water, in a bowl.

Then she returned to him and said: "Tell me what to do, Mr. Ralph. I don't know what to do for you."

"For us, child," he said. "What we do—whatever we do from now on, is for us. Together."

"I like you saying that. Tell me what I should do."

"You don't have to do anything except be loved and love back in whatever way you feel. Anything you feel and do is right because you're my wife and I'm your husband."

"Would it be wrong for me to want you to hold me—here?" she asked. Eyes cast down, she touched her breasts. "I feel as if I'm bursting, I'm so full of love for my Mr. Ralph. I never thought—back then, that—"

He had to stop her talking and kissed her.

For a ring he had made a circlet of grass. When it broke apart or fell to pieces he made her another. In a way, he thought sometimes, it was like renewing the vows.

Once, years later, when he was looking for a pencil he found in the back of her drawer a collection of hundreds of wisps of strands of dried grass. She had saved each of the worn-out rings, obviously. She had kept them in a cheaply-manufactured container of plastic masquerading as leather which said in gaudy lettering "My Jewel Box." These were her gems, her only treasure.

He sometimes asked Siss, suddenly, intently: "Are you my friend?" And she would reply: "Yes, I am. Didn't you think so?" And he would be ashamed, but also gratified, and his heart would swell because she had said more than just Yes.

A woman is a race apart, a friend had told him once. "But," Rolfe added to himself, "this is ridiculous." He and Siss could not have been more unlike mentally.

Well, of course. That could have been true even if he'd had the whole world to choose from. Suppose she had been a selfish, empty-headed teenager; how long could he have stood someone like that? Or she could have been a crone, a hag; work-worn, fat, diseased, crippled. You're a pretty lucky guy, Martin Rolfe; Mr. Ralph, sir!

Sexually they were complementary, for instance. But was that enough? Except for little bits of time, no. But those are very important little bits of time, aren't they, Marty? Precious, even. Each a potential conception, a possible person.

But aside from that, no; it was not enough.

But because her entire existence was one of trying to please him, she learned eventually to make acceptable verbal responses and their mating became more satisfactory to him. His stomach ached less frequently.

By trial and error and by diligence, as she learned any task, she learned to speak to him in bed with an approximation of high intelligence, murmuring words of sympathy, approval, surprise, delight, playfulness, even shock at appropriate times. She learned that a few words, sincerely but carefully expressed, did more for their mutual happiness than a babble, or an ungrammatical gush.

Her physical responses, as of a slave to a beloved master, had always been gratifying to him, except for her one unbreakable habit—her tendency to say "Oh, praise God!" whenever she achieved orgasm, or whenever she thought he had.

Once she had asked him to tell her about his life.

"What about it?" he had asked.

"All about it," she'd said.

"That would be a lot to tell."

23

"As much as you want to, then, Mr. Ralph."

Without a word of introduction he would start: "I was sixteen when I first kissed a girl. Awfully old . . ."

He'd always thought it shameful that he'd been unkissed so long and had never confessed it before. It was years later before Siss got up the courage to say: "Mr. Ralph, you told me once you didn't get a kiss till you were sixteen and that's too bad, but do you know how old I was?"

And he had said No, he didn't and she'd said:

"Twenty-eight, Mr. Ralph: that's how old. So don't you feel so bad."

And he'd asked her, though he was practically certain: "You mean I was the first one ever to kiss you?"

"The first man, except my father, yes, sir, Mr. Ralph. And do you know what? I'm awfully glad it was you that was the first, and that now nobody else ever will. I'm glad of that."

And so he had to postpone his confession. He had been on the point of telling Siss about his previous marriage—how he had chosen his wife from those available for matrimony among the fairly large number of women he had known.

What a fantastically wide choice he had had! The irony of now, with no choice at all, made him marvel to think that he could have picked from among millions, had he known doom was to come and that he and his mate, if she too were saved, would be parents to the entire human race. With what care he would have searched, what exacting tests he would have applied, to screen the mass of womanhood for a fitting mate for the last man!

But because he had expected all life to continue he had chosen from an extremely small sample. Nevertheless he had chosen well.

Later he would tell Siss; not now. He would not hurt her at this time with talk about what, by hindsight, had been a perfect marriage; nor did he feel like hurting himself by contrasting a happy past marriage to an intelligent woman with what he had now.

Now he would tell Siss about another time in his adult past, a sad interlude during which he and his perfect wife had separated and he was living alone.

How foolish to have had that quarrel with his dead perfect wife, he thought. How senseless to have lost all the time that they might have had together.

Yet he had achieved a certain peace in his solitude. And their marriage had been stronger when he returned to her.

"I'm going to tell you about a time I was living all alone in a little trailer in the woods," he told Siss.

He had been a free-lance editor in those days, doctoring doddering magazines, doing articles for his editor friends, and reading for a publishing house, and so was able to avoid the frenzied daily commute. He used the mails and phone and got into the city a couple of times a month.

He enjoyed an occasional dinner or cocktail party in his exurb; but he valued his privacy enough to decline many invitations and to withdraw to his trailer.

Rolfe himself never entertained. His truck-back trailer home was unsuited for anything but the shortest of visits. He'd have the mailman in for a drink of bourbon on Christmas Eve, or chat with the man who came around to collect for the volunteer ambulance corps, or play ten-second-move chess with the route man who delivered the only food Rolfe ate at home—eggs, and the butter he fried them in.

The truck-back home normally sat in the middle of Rolfe's eighteen acres—far enough out of town so that there were woods to surround him and a damned-up stream in which to swim, but close enough for an electric power line to be run in.

If Rolfe's choice of this way to live during his separation was an eccentricity, then he was eccentric. One other thing about him was a little odd. He had nailed a sign to a tree at the beginning of the track which led off the county road to his place. It said:

PRIVATE ROAD
MINED

The police came around after he put up the sign, which he'd burned into the end of an egg crate with an electric pen. The policemen, a lieutenant and a sergeant, left their car at the county road and walked carefully along the edge of Rolfe's track to the pickup truck in the clearing near the dammed-up stream. A pheasant moved without haste into some undergrowth as they came up to the door over the tailgate.

Rolfe invited them in, making room for them to sit down by lifting a manuscript off the one easy chair and motioning the sergeant to the camp chair in front of the typewriter on the bracket that folded down from the wall. Rolfe sat on the single bunk along the driver's side, having first got cokes out of the tiny refrigerator. He knew better than to offer liquor to policemen on duty. They chatted for a while before the lieutenant said: "About your sign, Mr. Rolfe; we've had some complaints."

"Call me Martin. Complaints? I like my privacy, that's all."

"My name's Sol," the lieutenant said, "and this is Eric." They shook hands all round again, now that the first-name basis had been established, and Sol said: "About the road being mined. Sure it's private property and nobody respects the principle of that more than I do, but somebody might get hurt. Somebody who couldn't read, maybe, or who wandered in after dark—not really meaning to trespass, you know."

"Sure," Rolfe said. "I can understand that."

"Besides," the sergeant—Eric—said, "anybody with war surplus ammunition was supposed to have turned it in years ago. It's the law."

"I don't know what you mean," Rolfe said. "I haven't booby-trapped the road. I wouldn't hurt a rabbit, much less a human being. Why, I'm so soft-hearted I don't even fish the stream."

Sol said: "I get it. You just put up the sign to keep people away—like 'Beware of the Dog,' even if you don't have a dog."

"And there really aren't any bouncing Bettys out there then?" Eric said. "I'm relieved. Believe me, we walked mighty easy along the edge."

Martin Rolfe grinned. "Gentlemen, I think I begin to understand. And it's all my fault because I'm such a poor speller. What I was trying to do was to call attention to the fact that it isn't a public road or a hiking trail or a place for young vandals to go if they have a hankering to break windows or set fires in out-of-the-way places. I believe there've been a few such incidents around town."

"Too many," Sol said. "But I still don't know what you mean about being a poor speller."

"What I intended to say on the sign, I guess, was 'Mind you, this is a private road.' It's a kind of New England expression."

"I've heard it," Eric said. "They have signs like that in London, where my wife's from—she was a war bride, you know, Lieutenant—that say 'Mind the step.' "

"That's m-i-n-d, not m-i-n-e-d," Sol said.

"Is that right?" Rolfe asked with a grin. "I told you I wasn't much of a speller. I'd better change the sign, then, hadn't I?"

Instead of replying directly, Sol asked: "Ever have trouble with kids back in here?"

"Kids and grown-ups both," Rolfe said. "Different kinds of trouble. Kids broke a window one night. I was asleep and got a shower of broken glass all over my face. Another time a big brave man with a gun shot the hell out of a mother partridge and her brood and left them flopping around. He wasn't even planning to eat them. Did you ever put a living thing out of its misery with your bare hands, Sol? That same day I put up the sign. The partridges and I haven't been bothered since."

Sol got up and let himself out into the clearing. "I had to kill a doe once that some mighty hunter put a hole into but didn't think worth following into the brush." Eric went out with Martin Rolfe behind him and all three walked along the middle of the track to the county road. Birds chirped at them and a leisurely rabbit hopped away.

At the blacktopped road Martin Rolfe went to his sign. He took a pencil out of his shirt pocket and scratched a vertical line through the *E* in *mined*. Then he joined the *N* and *D* with a copyreader's mark.

The sergeant said, "I don't know that that's too highly visible. Besides, a couple of rains'll wash it off."

"Oh, come on, Eric," the lieutenant said, getting into the car. "It's as plain as day."

"Thanks, Lieutenant," Martin said, going over to the police car to say goodbye. "I never could spell worth a damn."

"Oh, yeah?" Eric said. "I'll bet you can outspell both of us any day." He was looking back at the sign as he got into the car and he tripped, so that he had to grab for the door to steady himself.

"Mind the step," Martin said.

It was achingly poignant for him to leaf through the pages of a copy he'd saved of *The New York Times Magazine*.

How lovable and childlike seemed the people doing the weird things fashion advertising demanded of them! How earnest were the statements made in the articles and the letter pages. For example, there was the ironic, the heart-breakingly laughable article about the population explosion—about the

27

insupportable hundreds of millions there soon would be in India, or the six billion there'd be on Earth in just a few more years.

Would that there were only as many people as had read that particular Sunday issue of the *Times*. A million and a half? World enough. Or even if there existed on Earth only the few hundred people it had taken to write, edit and print that particular issue of *The New York Times Magazine*. Even if there were only *one* other than Siss and himself. One man to play chess with, or to philosophize with.

He thrust away from him the thought that the third person on Earth might be another woman. It was too dangerous, too explosive a thought. Would he betray Siss for a normal woman? Certainly he would never abandon her, but betrayal was certain—she would be so easy to fool. What form, other than an intellectual one, would it take? Would he take the new woman blatantly as his mate, with a facile explanation to Siss? Would the new one try to banish Siss (he'd never stand for that—would he?), or decree a demeaning role for her in a reorganized household—something he might rationalize himself into accepting? (He could hear the new one saying: "You want our children—Earth's only children—to be intelligent, don't you? You don't want the new world peopled by feeble-minded brats, do you?")

His thoughts went back to the possible consequences if a third person were male. Suppose the man were not a chess player? Suppose he were a mere brute, with brutish instincts? Would Martin have to share Siss with him, Eskimo style? Even if he could bring himself (or Siss) to accept such an arrangement, how long could it continue without an explosion?

No—as long as he was fantasizing it would be simpler to dream up two other people, a man and a woman who had already arranged their own lives, who had made the adjustment.

Still—how long could two couples—and only two—live side by side without something boiling over? Wife-swapping was too prevalent an institution in the bad old days, when there was all kinds of other entertainment, not to be a daily temptation in an all-but-depopulated world.

No—it would be best to have no third or fourth person— not unless there could be an infinity of others besides . . .

Ah, but he was so *lonely!*

"I'm going to the city," he told Siss.

They had done without the city for a long time. They had made do with the things they had, or could make; they'd let their clothing drop away and hadn't replaced it; they'd grown their own food; made their country house the center of their universe. But now he wanted to go back.

She must have seen something in his eyes. "Let me go for you," she said. "Just tell me what you want."

Sometimes she chose such an ironic way of saying things that he fleetingly suspected her of having not only intelligence but wit.

"Just tell you what I want! As if—" He stopped. As if he could tell her. As if he knew.

He knew only that he had to get away for a little while. He wanted to be alone, with his own memories of a populated Earth.

He also wanted a drink.

Long ago he had made it a rule never to have liquor in the house. It would be too great a temptation to have it handy. He could see himself degenerating into a drunken bum. With an unlimited supply close at hand and a devoted woman to do all the work that needed to be done, he could easily slip into an animalistic role—become a creature with a whiskey-sodden, atrophied brain.

A fitting father and mother to the world such a pair would be!

And so he had made his rule: drink all you want when you have to—in the city—but never bring it home.

And so he had told Siss: "I don't know what I want, exactly. I just want to go to the city."

And she had said: "All right, Mr. Ralph, if you have to."

There was her perception again, if that's what it was. "If you have to," she'd said, though he'd talked of want, not need.

"I do," he said. "But I'll come back. Is there anything I can bring you?" She looked around the kitchen and began to say something, then stopped and said instead: "Nothing we really need. You just go, Mr. Ralph, and take as long as you have to. It'll give me a chance to go do that berry-picking I been wanting to."

She was so sweet that he almost decided not to go. But then he kissed her—very thankful, just then, that she was his Siss and not some too-bright shrew of a problem wife—and went. He drove in, naked in a Cadillac.

He had rolled the swivel chair out of the store onto the sidewalk and was sitting in it in the afternoon sunshine. Beside him on the pavement were half a dozen bottles, each uncapped. He was talking to himself.

"As the afternoon sun, blood-red through the haze of the remnants of a once overpopulated world, imperceptibly glides to its bed, one of the two known survivors becomes quietly plastered." He had a drink on that, then went on:

"What thoughts pass through the mind of this pitiful creature, this naked relic of a man left to eke out the rest of his days on a ruined planet?

"Does he ever recall the glory that once was his and that of his fellows? Or is he so sunk in misery—in the mere scratching of a bare existence from an arid soil—that he has forgotten the heights to which his kind once had risen? Subject pauses in thought and reaches for bottle. Drinks deeply from bottle, but not so deeply as to induce drunken sickenness. Aim of subject is quiet plasterization, happy drunkdom, a nonceness of Nirvana, with harm to none and bitterness never. Sicken drunkenness?

"A respite of reverie, perhaps, as subject casts mind back to happy past. Mr. Martin Rolfe in Happier Days."

He picked up his *New York Times Magazine* and leafed through it. It was almost as good as having another drink. There they were—they couldn't have been more than 17—leaping in their panty girdles to show the freedom of action and the elasticity of the crotch. He remembered once having heard a newsman, waiting in the rain for the arrival of a President, say: "Being a reporter is essentially an undignified occupation." So had been being a model, obviously.

Things of the past . . . He thought: "A title for my memoirs—*Things of the Past*." He took up the *Times* again and turned to an ad of a debonair young man in a revolving door holding a copy of the *Wall Street Journal*. "I dreamt I was trapped in a revolving door in my Arcticweave tropical worsted," Rolfe said, summing up the situation. He looked like the 28-year-old Larchmont type; five years out of college, with a Master's, two kids, wife beginning to drink a little bit too much. "If he's trapped there long enough he may read the paper right through to the shipping pages and ship out to the islands."

Rolfe looked pityingly at the trapped Larchmont type, armed against his predicament only with his Arcticweave suit, his *Wall Street Journal* and, presumably, a wallet full of wife-and-baby pictures, credit cards and a commutation ticket issued by a railroad company petitioning to suspend passenger service.

"You poor bastard," Rolfe said.

Of course he was saying it to himself, too. He said it all the way home: "You poor bastard. You poor bastard."

Siss was waiting for him in the cool garden. Gently she led him indoors. She said, with only the slightest hint of reproach (he could stand that much—he deserved more): "You been drinking too much again, Mr. Ralph. You know it's bad for you."

"You're right, Siss. Absolutely right."

"You got to take care of yourself. I try to, but you got to try, too."

Tenderly she put him to bed. He knew then, among other times, how much he needed her, and he struggled to say something nice to her before he dropped off to sleep. Finally he said: "You know, Siss, you're nicer than all those crazy leaping girls in the York Times." That's what she called it, the York Times. "You got a lot more sense, too, than they look as if they had."

From his notebooks:

Got drunk saft. Downtown. Dangerous. Not fair to Siss. Liable get et up by dogs while stinko. Bad show.

Can't bring bottle home, tho. Too great a temptation to get sozzled daily and twice on Sunday.

Why is Sunday worse than other days? I tried to rename it but Siss insisted we keep it. She also demanded it come every seven days, just like in good old days. Had to give in. So much for calendar reform.

He sought other ways of escaping. He hiked and climbed and explored.

Once he found a spot on the brow of a hill from which one (that is, he) could see for miles but from which no work of man was visible except the top of a silo at the top of a similar hill across a wide valley.

Having found the spot, he cleared wild strawberry plants from beneath a young maple tree, leaving the ferns and the cushiony moss, and lay down to rest. It had been a strenuous climb, and hot, and now the insects were upon him. But though the flies buzzed they did not often land and the

31

mosquitoes were torpid and easily slapped. After a while—it was almost noon (as if the hour mattered)—he had a couple of swallows from the flask in his rucksack and ate some cheese. He thought of the flask as his iron rations.

As he rummaged in the rucksack he found a roll of plastic tape he'd brought along to help him blaze a trail. He hadn't needed it; instead he'd marked his way by cutting branches with a long-handled pruning tool.

But as he lay in the solitude he had sought out and found (how odd to seek solitude in an empty world), under one of a myriad of trees, where the only sounds were of buzzing insects, chirping birds, the soughing of trees in a soft wind— he knew what to do with the plastic tape. He printed something on a little square of paper, small but legible, and, with the tape, attached it to the lowest bough of his young maple. Now he lay under it, savoring what he had done.

The little sign said: THIS TREE RESERVED.

One June night it rained in great, warm, wind-driven sheets. He had not experienced such a storm since a visit a decade earlier to the tropics.

The pleasure he took in the soaking, bath-temperature rain was enhanced by the danger from the lightning. It stabbed down from the sky as if seeking him out, destroying and burning only yards away, as if it would be a great cosmic joke to strike that one spot on the surface of the Earth and kill the last man.

He defied it, prancing wildly, then halting deliberately as if transfixed when it flashed, posing with outthrust or upthrust arms, yelling, defying the thing or Being that had sent the storm, loosing his pent-up frustrations, his disappointments and hates in the elemental power of the storm.

He had trapped the beast in a pit, unfairly. It had nearly exhausted itself in attempts to leap the sheer walls. At least he hadn't lined the bottom with spikes.

Rolfe could have killed it from above, poisoned it, let it starve. Instead he jumped into the pit, armed with two knives, to risk mauling and death.

He realized his folly instantly. The creature was far from helpless. Its claws were sharp, though its movements were clumsy in the cramped pit-bottom, and its fetid breath was as much a weapon as its fangs.

Only by the sheerest of luck, he felt, did he avoid the claws and fangs long enough to plunge first one knife then the other into the beast's heart.

As its death struggles subsided he lay there, his face buried in the back of its neck, hugging the thing he'd killed, a sadness coming over him as he felt the fading heartbeat.

Later he skinned the beast. He and Siss ate the meat and slept under the pelt. But first he had buried the head, in tribute to a worthy antagonist, a kind of salute to another male.

And unto them was born a son.

Siss seemed to know just what to do, by instinct. Clumsily he helped. He cut the umbilical with a boiled pair of scissors. Made a knot. Washed the red little thing.

Eventually Siss lay quiet, dry, serene, holding her swaddled child. He sat on the floor next to the bed and looked and looked at the mother and child. A holy picture, he thought. He sat for hours, staring, wondering. She looked at him, silent, wondering.

The new human being slept, serene.

It could not have been more perfect.

His son. His boy. His and hers but, he felt it fair enough to say, mostly his.

His son Adam. What else had there been to name him? Adam. Trite but noble. He had considered calling him Ralph, but only briefly. It would be too comical to have his mother go around introducing him to their near circle of friends—relatives all, come to think of it—as Ralph Ralph.

There'd be no need for introductions for many years, of course, in a closed society such as theirs. The years did pass.

There was his son, tall for his age, straight, brown, good with his hands . . .

But bright? Intelligent? How was a father to know? A prejudiced parent sees only the good, ignores what he doesn't want to accept, can be oblivious to faults obvious to anyone else.

He talked to him and got gratifying responses. But wouldn't almost any response be gratifying to a parent? Parents are easily satisfied. Especially fathers of sons.

Had he conditioned himself to the point where he would be satisfied if his son showed more than animal intelligence? The conditioning encompassed an agony of watching as his son grew—watching for signs of mental retardation, of idiocy, of dullness, of bigheadedness, of torpor.

And then they had a daughter.

From his notebook:

My son. Brown as a penny. Naked as a jaybird. Slender, muscled, handsome, active, good with his hands.

Bright? Seems so. Obviously too soon to really tell.

Five years old and just made his first kill. Wild dog, attacking our goat. Got him in the right eye with a .30-30 at_____ yards (measure and fill in).

Strong and brave and skilled and good looking.

Let's hope intelligent, too.

Please, God.

My daughter. My precious, my beauty. What a delight you are, with your serene smile and your loving way of wrapping your arms around my leg and looking up at Old Daddy. You're your mother's child, aren't you? So good, so quiet. But you're quick on your feet and your reflexes (I've tested them) are sound. I think we're all right.

The Diary of Siss

(Siss was not very faithful about her diary. The printed word was not her medium. Although her intentions were obviously good, there are fewer than a dozen entries in all, and they are reproduced below. She did not date them. The handwriting in the last entry is slightly better than that of the first, but maybe only because she was using a sharper pencil. A more revealing diary probably would be found in her heart, if that could be read, or in her children.)

Mr. Ralph told me write things down when they big & inportant I will start now. Today Mr. Ralph married me.

Very happy today. Learning to please my husband.

Very very happy. Today moved to our country house. I like it better than the big city.

Today I had a baby, a boy.

My word for today is contentment. I have to spell it and

tell what it means. Mr. Ralph says I need an eddukaton, he will eddukate me.

My word for today is education. Mr. Ralph seen what I wrote in my dairy yestdy.

I have 2 words for today diary & yesterday. Also saw not seen.

Today I had a baby, a girl. Ralph said now everything is going to be alright.

And presumably it was. Having doubled the population, the human race seemed to be on a firm footing. There was love in the world; a growing, proud family, and a new self-assurance in Siss—note that he was Ralph now, not Mr. Ralph. We may be sure, though, that the strict if loving father gave her two words for tomorrow: all right. A father, a mother, a son, a daughter. A little learning, a lot of love.

In the summer of his eighth year Adam and his father were in the woods back of the pasture, in the little clearing at the side of the stream that ran pure and sparkling before it broadened into the shallow muddy pond the livestock used. Martin and the boy were eating lunch after a morning of woodcutting and conversation.

Adam, naked like his father, had asked: "Am I going to grow some more hair, like you?"

And Martin said: "Sure, when you get bigger. When you begin to be a man."

And Adam had compared his smooth skin with his father's hard, muscled, hairy body and said: "Mom's got hair in that place, too, but she's different."

So Martin explained, sweating even though he was sitting still now, and his son took it all in, nodding, just as if it were no more important than knowing why the cow had her calf. It was obvious that until now Adam had not connected the function of the bull with the dropping of the calf. Martin explained, in human terms.

"That's pretty neat," Adam said. "When do I get to do it?"

Martin tried to keep his voice matter-of-fact. How do you instruct your son in incest?

The explanation was completed, finally, and it was Martin's turn to ask a question. "Think carefully about this, son. If you could save the life of one person—your mother or me but not the other—which would you save?"

Adam answered without hesitation. "I'd save Mother, of course."

Martin looked hard at his strong, handsome son and asked the second part of the question. "Why?"

Adam said: "I didn't mean to hurt your feelings, Dad. I'd save both of you if I could—"

"I know you would. You've been a crack shot since you were five. But there might be only one chance. Your answer is the only possible one, but I have to know why you gave it."

The boy frowned as he struggled to reason out the reply he had made instinctively. "Because—if necessary—she and I could—" Then it came out in a rush: "Because she could be the mother to the world and I could be the father."

Martin shuddered as if a long chill had just passed. It was all right. He embraced his fine, strong, *intelligent* son and wept.

After a little while Siss appeared, walking the path beside the stream, naked as the two of them but different, as Adam had said, and riding the naked baby on her hip.

"Thought we'd join the menfolks for lunch," she said. "I picked some berries for dessert." She carried the blackberries in a mesh bag and some had been bruised, staining the tanned skin a delicate blue just below her slim waist.

Martin said: "You sure make a good-looking picture, you two. Come here and give me a kiss."

The baby kissed him first, then toddled off to smooth up for Adam, who gave her a dutiful peck.

Their father held open his arms and Siss sat beside him, putting her berries aside. She rested her head on his shoulder, serene. Martin folded her to him and kissed her eyes and cheeks and hair and neck and finally her lips, there in the sunshine, by the side of the pure stream, in the presence of all the world.

"Do you think—" she started to say, but Martin said, "Hush, now. It's all right. Everything's all right, Siss darling." She sighed and relaxed against him. He had never called her darling before. He kissed her again for a long time and she gradually lay back on the soft ground and raised one knee and bent the other to accommodate her husband.

The baby lost interest and went to wade in the stream but Adam watched, his elbow on his knee, and once he said,

"Don't crush the blackberries," and reached out to get them. He ate a handful, slowly.

Then he heard his mother gasp, "Oh, praise God!" and after a moment both his parents became still. And after a little while longer he looked to see that the baby was okay and then went to the intertwined, gently-breathing bodies, which were more beautiful than anything he had ever seen.

Adam knelt beside them and kissed his father's neck and his mother's lips. Siss opened her arms and enfolded her son, too.

And Adam asked, with his face against his mother's cheek, which was wet and warm, "Is this what love is?"

And his mother answered, "Yes, honey," and his father said, in a muffled kind of way, "It's everything there is, son."

Adam reached out for the berries and put one in his mother's mouth and one in his father's and one in his. Then he got up to give one to the baby.

THE DANCE OF THE CHANGER AND THE THREE

Terry Carr

This all happened ages ago, out in the depths of space beyond Darkedge, where galaxies lumber ponderously through the black like so many silent bright rhinoceroses. It was so long ago that when the light from Loarr's galaxy finally reached Earth, after millions of light-years, there was no one here to see it except a few things in the oceans that were too mindlessly busy with their monotonous single-celled reactions to notice.

Yet, as long ago as it was, the present-day Loarra still remember this story and retell it in complex, shifting wave-dances every time one of the newly-changed asks for it. The wave-dances wouldn't mean much to you if you saw them, nor I suppose would the story itself if I were to tell it just as it happened. So consider this a translation, and don't bother yourself that when I say "water" I don't mean our hydrogen-oxygen compound, or that there's no "sky" as such on Loarr, or for that matter that the Loarra weren't—aren't—creatures that "think" or "feel" in quite the way we understand. In fact, you could take this as a piece of pure fiction, because there are damned few real facts in it—but I know better (or worse), because I know how true it is. And that has a lot to do with why I'm back here on Earth, with forty-two friends and co-workers left dead on Loarr. They never had a chance.

There was a Changer who had spent three life cycles planning a particular cycle climax and who had come to the moment of action. He wasn't really named Minnearo, but I'll call him that because it's the closest thing I can write to approximate the tone, emotional matrix, and associations that were all wrapped up in his designation.

When he came to his decision, he turned away from the crag on which he'd been standing overlooking the Loarran ocean, and went quickly to the personality-homes of three of his best friends. To the first friend, Asterrea, he said, "I am going to commit suicide," wave-dancing this message in his best festive tone.

His friend laughed, as Minnearo had hoped, but only for a short time. Then he turned away and left Minnearo alone, because there had already been several suicides lately and it was wearing a little thin.

To his second friend, Minnearo gave a pledge-salute, going through all sixty sequences with exaggerated care, and wave-danced, "Tomorrow I shall immerse my body in the ocean, if anyone will watch."

His second friend, Fless, smiled tolerantly and told him he would come and see the performance.

To his third friend, with many excited leapings and boundings, Minnearo described what he imagined would happen to him after he had gone under the lapping waters of the ocean. The dance he went through to give this description was intricate and even imaginative, because Minnearo had spent most of that third life cycle working it out in his mind. It used motion and color and sound and another sense something like smell, all to communicate descriptions of falling, impact with the water, and then the quick dissolution and blending in the currents of the ocean, the dimming and loss of awareness, and finally the awakening, the completion of the change. Minnearo had a rather romantic turn of mind, so he imagined himself recoalescing around the life-mote of one of Loarr's greatest heroes, Krollim, and forming on Krollim's old pattern. And he even ended the dance with suggestions of glory and imitations by others, which was definitely presumptuous. But the friend for whom the dance was given did nod approvingly at several points.

"If it turns out to be half what you anticipate," said this friend, Pur, "then I envy you. But you never know."

"I guess not," Minnearo said, rather morosely. And he hesitated before leaving, for Pur was what I suppose I'd better call female, and Minnearo had rather hoped that she would join him in the ocean jump. But if she thought of it she gave no sign, merely gazing at Minnearo calmly, waiting for him to go; so finally he did.

And at the appropriate time, with his friend Fless watching him from the edge of the cliff, Minnearo did his final wave-dance as Minnearo—rather excited and ill-coordinated, but that was understandable in the circumstances—and then performed his approach to the edge, leaped and tumbled downward through the air, making fully two dozen turns this way and that before he hit the water.

Fless hurried back and described the suicide to Asterra and Pur, who laughed and applauded in most of the right places, so on the whole it was a success. Then the three of them sat down and began plotting Minnearo's revenge.

—All right, I *know* a lot of this doesn't make sense. Maybe that's because I'm trying to tell you about the Loarra in human terms, which is a mistake with creatures as alien as they are. Actually, the Loarra are almost wholly an energy life-form, their consciousness coalescing in each life cycle around a spatial center which they call a "life-mote," so that, if you could see the patterns of energy they form (as I have, using a sense filter our expedition developed for that purpose), they'd look rather like a spiral nebula sometimes, or other times like iron filings gathering around a magnet, or maybe like a half-melted snowflake. (That's probably what Minnearo looked like on that day, because it's the suicides and the aged who look like that.) Their forms keep shifting, of course, but each individual usually keeps close to one pattern.

Loarr itself is a gigantic gaseous planet with an orbit so close to its primary that its year has to be only about thirty-seven Earthstandard Days long. (In Earthsystem, the orbit would be considerably inside that of Venus.) There's a solid core to the planet, and a lot of hard outcroppings like islands, but most of the surface is in a molten or gaseous state, swirling and bubbling and howling with winds and storms. It's not a very inviting planet if you're anything like a human being, but it does have one thing that brought it to Unicentral's attention: mining.

Do you have any idea what mining is like on a planet where most metals are fluid from the heat and/or pressure? Most people haven't heard much about this, because it isn't a situation we encounter often, but it was there on Loarr, and it was very, very interesting. Because our analyses showed some elements that had been until then only computer-theory —elements that were supposed to exist only in the hearts of suns, for one thing. And if we could get hold of some of them . . . Well, you see what I mean. The mining possibilities were very interesting indeed.

Of course, it would take half the wealth of Earthsystem to outfit a full-scale expedition there. But Unicentral hummed for two-point-eight seconds and then issued detailed instructions on just how it was all to be arranged. So there we went.

And there I was, a Standard Year later (five Standard Years ago), sitting inside a mountain of artificial Earth welded onto one of Loarr's "islands" and wondering what the hell I was doing there. Because I'm not a mining engineer, not a physicist or comp-technician or, in fact, much of anything that requires technical training. I'm a public-relations man; and there was just no reason for me to have been assigned to such a hellish, impossible, godforsaken, inconceivable, and plain damned *unlivable* planet as Loarr.

But there was a reason, and it was the Loarra, of course. They lived ("lived") there, and they were intelligent, so we had to negotiate with them. Ergo: me.

So in the next several years, while I negotiated and we set up operations and I acted as a go-between, I learned a lot about them. Just enough to translate, however clumsily, the wave-dance of the Changer and the Three, which is their equivalent of a classic folk-hero myth (or would be if they had anything honestly equivalent to anything of ours).

To continue:

Fless was in favor of building a pact among the Three by which they would, each in turn and each with deliberate lack of the appropriate salutes, commit suicide in exactly the same way Minnearo had. "Thus we can kill this suicide," Fless explained in excited waves through the air.

But Pur was more practical. "Thus," she corrected him, "we would kill *only* this suicide. It is unimaginative, a thing to be done by rote, and Minnearo deserves more."

Asterrea seemed undecided; he hopped about, sparking and disappearing and reappearing inches away in another color. They waited for him to comment, and finally he stabilized, stood still in the air, settled to the ground, and held himself firmly there. Then he said, in slow, careful movements, "I'm not sure he deserves an original revenge. It wasn't a new suicide, after all. And who is to avenge us?" A single spark

41

leaped from him. "Who is to avenge us?" he repeated, this time with more pronounced motions.

"Perhaps," said Pur slowly, "we will need no revenge—if our act is great enough."

The other two paused in their random wave-motions, considering this. Fless shifted from blue to green to a bright red which dimmed to yellow; Asterrea pulsed a deep ultraviolet.

"Everyone has always been avenged," Fless said at last. "What you suggest is meaningless."

"But if we do something great enough," Pur said; and now she began to radiate heat which drew the other two reluctantly toward her. "Something which has never been done before, in *any* form. Something for which there can *be* no revenge, for it will be a *positive* thing—not a death-change, not a destruction or a disappearance or a forgetting, even a great one. A *positive* thing."

Asterrea's ultraviolet grew darker, darker, until he seemed to be nothing more than a hole in the air. "Dangerous, dangerous, dangerous," he droned, moving torpidly back and forth. "You know it's impossible to ask—we'd have to give up all our life cycles to come. Because a positive in the world . . ." He blinked into darkness, and did not reappear for long seconds. When he did he was perfectly still, pulsing weakly but gradually regaining strength.

Pur waited till his color and tone showed that consciousness had returned, then moved in a light wave-motion calculated to draw the other two back into calm, reasonable discourse. "I've thought about this for six life cycles already," she danced. "I must be right—*no* one has worked on a problem for so long. A positive would *not* be dangerous, no matter what the three- and four-cycle theories say. It would be beneficial." She paused, hanging orange in midair. "And it would be *new*," she said with a quick spiral. "Oh, how *new!*"

And so, at length, they agreed to follow her plan. And it was briefly this: On a far island outcropping set in the deepest part of the Loarran ocean, where crashing, tearing storms whipped molten metal-compounds into blinding spray, there was a vortex of forces that was avoided by every Loarra on pain of inescapable and final death-change. The most ancient wave-dances of that ancient time said that the vortex had always been there, that the Loarra themselves had been born there or had escaped from there or had in some way cheated the laws that ruled there. Whatever the truth about that was, the vortex was an eater of energy, calling and catching from afar any Loarra or other beings who strayed within its influence. (For all the life on Loarr is energy-based, even the mindless, drifting foodbeasts—creatures of uniform dull color, no internal motion, no scent or tone, and absolutely no self-volition. Their place in the Loarran scheme of things is and was literally nothing more than that of food; even though there were countless foodbeasts drifting in the air in most areas of the planet, the Loarra hardly ever noticed them. They ate them when they were hungry, and looked around them at any other time.)

"Then you want us to destroy the *vortex?*" cried Fless, dancing and dodging to right and left in agitation.

"Not *destroy,*" Pur said calmly. "It will be a *life*-change, not a destruction."

"Life-change?" said Asterrea faintly, wavering in the air.

And she said it again: "*Life*-change." For the vortex had once created, or somehow allowed to be created, the Oldest of the Loarra, those many-cycles-ago beings who had combined and split, reacted and changed countless times to become the Loarra of this day. And if creation could happen at the vortex once, then it could happen again.

"But how?" asked Fless, trying now to be reasonable, dancing the question with precision and holding a steady green color as he did so.

"We will need help," Pur said, and went on to explain that she had heard—from a windbird, a creature with little intelligence but perfect memory—that there was one of the Oldest still living his first life cycle in a personality-home somewhere near the vortex. In that most ancient time of the race, when suicide had been considered extreme as a means of cycle-change, this Oldest had made his change by a sort of negative suicide—he had frozen his cycle, so that his consciousness and form continued in a never-ending repetition of themselves, on and on while his friends changed and grew and learned as they ran through life cycle after life cycle, becoming different people with common memories, moving forward into the future by this method while he, the last Oldest, remained fixed at the beginning. He saw only the beginning, remembered only the beginning, understood only the beginning.

And for that reason his had been the most tragic of all Loarran changes (and the windbird had heard it rumored, in

43

eight different ways, each of which it repeated word-for-word to Pur, that in the ages since that change more than a hundred hundred Loarra had attempted revenge for the Oldest, but always without success) and it had never been repeated, so that this Oldest was the only Oldest. And for that reason he was important to their quest, Pur explained.

With a perplexed growing and shrinking, brightening and dimming, Asterrea asked, "But how can he live anywhere near the vortex and not be consumed by it?"

"That is a crucial part of what we must find out," Pur said. And after the proper salutes and rituals, the Three set out to find the Oldest.

The wave-dance of the Changer and the Three traditionally at this point spends a great deal of time, in great splashes of color and bursts of light and subtly contrived clouds of darkness all interplaying with hops and swoops and blinking and dodging back and forth, to describe the scene as Pur, Fless and Asterrea set off across that ancient molten sea. I've seen the dance countless times, and each viewing has seemed to bring me maddeningly closer to understanding the meaning that this has for the Loarra themselves. Lowering clouds flashing bursts of aimless, lifeless energy, a rumbling sea below, whose swirling depths pulled and tugged at the Three as they swept overhead, darting around each other in complex patterns like electrons playing cat's-cradle around an invisible nucleus. A droning of lamentation from the changers left behind on their rugged home island, and giggles from those who had recently changed. And the colors of the Three themselves: burning red Asterrea and glowing green Fless and steady, steady golden Pur. I see and hear them all, but I feel only a weird kind of alien beauty, not the grandeur, excitement and awesomeness they have for the Loarra.

When the Three felt the vibrations and swirlings in the air that told them they were coming near to the vortex, they paused in their flight and hung in an interpatterned motion-sequence above the dark, rolling sea, conversing only in short flickerings of color because they had to hold the pattern tightly in order to withstand the already-strong attraction of the vortex.

"Somewhere near?" asked Asterrea, pulsing a quick green.

"Closer to the vortex, I think," Pur said, chancing a sequence of reds and violets.

44

"Can we be sure?" asked Fless; but there was no answer from Pur and he had expected none from Asterrea.

The ocean crashed and leaped; the air howled around them. And the vortex pulled at them.

Suddenly they felt their motion-sequence changing, against their wills, and for long moments all three were afraid that it was the vortex's attraction that was doing it. They moved in closer to each other, and whirled more quickly in a still more intricate pattern, but it did no good. Irresistibly they were drawn apart again, and at the same time the three of them were moved toward the vortex.

And then they felt the Oldest among them.

He had joined the motion-sequence; this must have been why they had felt the sequence changed and loosened—to make room for him. Whirling and blinking, the Oldest led them inward over the frightening sea, radiating warmth through the storm and, as they followed, or were pulled along, they studied him in wonder.

He was hardly recognizable as one of them, this ancient Oldest. He was . . . not quite energy any longer. He was half matter, carrying the strange mass with awkward, aged grace, his outer edges almost rigid as they held the burden of his congealed center and carried it through the air. (Looking rather like a half-dissolved snowflake, yes, only dark and dismal, a snowflake weighed with coal-dust.) And, for now at least, he was completely silent.

Only when he had brought the Three safely into the calm of his barren personality-home on a tiny rock jutting at an angle from the wash of the sea did he speak. There, inside a cone of quiet against which the ocean raged and fell back, the sands faltered and even the vortex's power was nullified, the Oldest said wearily, "So you have come." He spoke with a slow waving back and forth, augmented by only a dull red color.

To this the Three did not know what to say; but Pur finally hazarded, "Have you been waiting for us?"

The Oldest pulsed a somewhat brighter red, once, twice. He paused. Then he said, "I do not *wait*—there is nothing to wait *for*." Again the pulse of a brighter red. "One waits for the future. But there is no future, you know."

"Not for him," Pur said softly to her companions, and Fless and Asterrea sank wavering to the stone floor of the Oldest's home, where they rocked back and forth.

45

The Oldest sank with them, and when he touched down he remained motionless. Pur drifted over the others, maintaining movement but unable to raise her color above a steady blue-green. She said to the Oldest, "But you knew we would come."

"Would come? *Would* come? Yes, and *did* come, and *have* come, and *are* come. It is today only, you know, for me. I will be the Oldest, when the others pass me by. I will never change, nor will my world."

"But the others have already passed you by," Fless said. "We are many life cycles after you, Oldest—so many it is beyond the count of windbirds."

The Oldest seemed to draw his material self into a more upright posture, forming his energy-flow carefully around it. To the red of his color he added a low hum with only the slightest quaver as he said, *"Nothing* is after me, here on Rock. When you come here, you come out of time, just as I have. So now you have always been here and will always be here, for as long as you are here."

Asterrea sparked yellow suddenly, and danced upward into the becalmed air. As Fless stared and Pur moved quickly to calm him, he drove himself again and again at the edge of the cone of quiet that was the Oldest's refuge. Each time he was thrown back and each time he returned to dash himself once more against the edge of the storm, trying to penetrate back into it. He flashed and burned countless colors, and strange sound-frequencies filled the quiet, until at last, with Pur's stern direction and Fless's blank gaze upon him, he sank back wearily to the stone floor. "A trap, a trap," he pulsed. "This is it, this is the vortex itself, we should have known, and we'll never get away."

The Oldest had paid no attention to Asterrea's display. He said slowly, "And it is because I am not in time that the vortex cannot touch me. And it is because I am out of time that I know what the vortex is, for I can remember myself born in it."

Pur left Asterrea then, and came close to the Oldest. She hung above him, thinking with blue vibrations, then asked, "Can you tell us how you were born?—what is creation?—how new things are made?" She paused a moment, and added, "And what *is* the vortex?"

The Oldest seemed to lean forward, seemed tired. His color had deepened again to the darkest red, and the Three could

46

clearly see every atom of matter within his energy-field, stark and hard. He said, "So many questions to ask one question." And he told them the answer to that question.

—And I can't tell you that answer, because I don't know it. No one knows it now, not even the present-day Loarra who are the Three after a thousand million billion life cycles. Because the Loarra really do become different . . . different "persons," when they pass from one cycle to another, and after that many changes, memory becomes meaningless. ("Try it sometime," one of the Loarra once wave-danced to me, and there was no indication that he thought this was a joke.)

Today, for instance, the Three themselves, a thousand million billion times removed from themselves but still, they maintain, *themselves,* often come to watch the Dance of the Changer and the Three, and even though it is about them they are still excited and moved by it as though it were a tale never even heard before, let alone lived through. Yet let a dancer miss a movement or color or sound by even the slightest nuance, and the Three will correct him. (And yes, many times the legended Changer himself, Minnearo, he who started the story, has attended these dances—though often he leaves after the re-creation of his suicide dance.)

It's sometimes difficult to tell one given Loarra from all the others, by the way, despite the complex and subtle technologies of Unicentral, which have provided me with sense filters of all sorts, plus frequency simulators, pattern scopes, special gravity inducers, and a minicomp that takes up more than half of my very tight little island of Earth pasted onto the surface of Loarr and which can do more thinking and analyzing in two seconds than I can do in fifty years. During my four years on Loarr, I got to "know" several of the Loarra, yet even at the end of my stay I was still never sure just who I was "talking" with at any time. I could run through about seventeen or eighteen tests, linking the sense-filters with the minicomp, and get a definite answer that way. But the Loarra are a bit short on patience and by the time I'd get done with all that whoever it was would usually be off bouncing and sparking into the hellish vapors they call air. So usually I just conducted my researches or negotiations or idle queries, whichever they were that day, with whoever would pay attention to my antigrav "eyes," and I discovered that it didn't

47

matter much just who I was talking with: none of them made any more sense than the others. They were all, as far as I was concerned, totally crazy, incomprehensible, stupid, silly, and plain damn no good.

If that sounds like I'm bitter, it's because I am. I've got forty-two murdered men to be bitter about. But back to the unfolding of the greatest legend of an ancient and venerable alien race:

When the Oldest had told them what they wanted to know, the Three came alive with popping and flashing and dancing in the air, Pur just as much as the others. It was all that they had hoped for and more; it was the entire answer to their quest and their problem. It would enable them to create, to transcend any negative cycle-climax they could have devised.

After a time the Three came to themselves and remembered the rituals.

"We offer thanks in the name of Minnearo, whose suicide we are avenging," Fless said gravely, waving his message in respectful deep-blue spirals.

"We thank you in our own names as well," said Asterrea.

"And we thank you in the name of no one and nothing," said Pur, "for that is the greatest thanks conceivable."

But the Oldest merely sat there, pulsing his dull red, and the Three wondered among themselves. At last the Oldest said, "To accept thanks is to accept responsibility, and in only-today, as I am, there can be none of that because there can be no new act. I am outside time, you know, which is almost outside life. All this I have told you is something told to you before, many times, and it will be again."

Nonetheless, the Three went through all the rituals of thanksgiving, performing them with flawless grace and care—color-and-sound demonstrations, dances, offerings of their own energy, and all the rest. And Pur said, "It is possible to give thanks for a long-past act or even a mindless reflex, and we do so in the highest."

The Oldest pulsed dull red and did not answer, and after a time the Three took leave of him.

Armed with the knowledge he had given them, they had no trouble penetrating the barrier protecting Rock, the Oldest's personality-home, and in moments were once again alone with themselves in the raging storm that encircled the vortex. For long minutes they hung in midair, whirling and darting in

48

their most tightly linked patterns while the storm whipped them and the vortex pulled them. Then abruptly they broke their patterns and hurled themselves deliberately into the heart of the vortex itself. In a moment they had disappeared.

They seemed to feel neither motion nor lapse of time as they fell into the vortex. It was a change that came without perception or thought—a change from self to unself, from existence to void. They knew only that they had given themselves up to the vortex, that they were suddenly lost in darkness and a sense of surrounding emptiness which had no dimension. They knew without thinking that if they could have sent forth sound there would have been no echo, that a spark or even a bright flame would have brought no reflection from anywhere. For this was the place of the origin of life, and it was empty. It was up to them to fill it, if it was to be filled.

So they used the secret the Oldest had given them, the secret those at the Beginning had discovered by accident and which only one of the Oldest could have remembered. Having set themselves for this before entering the vortex, they played their individual parts automatically—selfless, unconscious, almost random acts such as even non-living energy can perform. And when all parts had been completed precisely, correctly, and at just the right time and in just the right sequence, the creating took place.

It was a foodbeast. It formed and took shape before them in the void, and grew and glowed its dull, drab glow until it was whole. For a moment it drifted there, then suddenly it was expelled from the vortex, thrown out violently as though from an explosion—away from the nothingness within, away from darkness and silence into the crashing, whipping violence of the storm outside. And with it went the Three, vomited forth with the primitive bit of life they had made.

Outside, in the storm, the Three went automatically into their tightest motion sequence, whirling and blinking around each other in desperate striving to maintain themselves amid the savagery that roiled around them. And once again they felt the powerful pull of the vortex behind them, gripping them anew now that they were outside, and they knew that the vortex would draw them in again, this time forever, unless they were able to resist it. But they found that they were nearly spent; they had lost more of themselves in the vortex than they had ever imagined possible. They hardly felt alive now, and somehow they had to withstand the crushing powers of both the storm and the vortex, and had to forge such a strongly interlinked motion-pattern that they would be able to make their way out of this place, back to calm and safety.

And there was only one way they could restore themselves enough for that.

Moving almost as one, they converged upon the mindless foodbeast they had just created, and they ate it.

That's not precisely the end of the Dance of the Changer and the Three—it does go on for a while, telling of the honors given the Three when they returned, and of Minnearo's reaction when he completed his change by reappearing around the life-mote left by a dying windbird, and of how all of the Three turned away from their honors and made their next changes almost immediately—but my own attention never quite follows the rest of it. I always get stuck at that one point in the story, that supremely contradictory moment when the Three destroyed what they had made, when they came away with no more than they had brought with them. It doesn't even achieve irony, and yet it is the emotional high-point of the Dance as far as the Loarra are concerned. In fact, it's the *whole* point of the Dance, as they've told me with brighter sparkings and flashes than they ever use when talking about anything else, and if the Three had been able to come away from there *without* eating their foodbeast, then their achievement would have been duly noted, applauded, giggled at by the newly-changed, and forgotten within two life cycles.

And these are the creatures with whom I had to deal and whose rights I was charged to protect. I was ambassador to a planetful of things that would tell me with a straight face that two and two are orange. And yes, that's why I'm back on Earth now—and why the rest of the expedition, those who are left alive from it, are back here too.

If you could read the fifteen-microtape report I filed with Unicentral (which you can't, by the way: Unicentral always Classifies its failures), it wouldn't tell you anything more about the Loarra than I've just told you in the story of the Dance. In fact, it might tell you less, because although the report contained masses of hard data on the Loarra, plus every theory I could come up with or coax out of the mini-comp, it didn't have much about the Dance. And it's only in things like that, attitude-data rather than I.Q. indices, psych reports and so on, that you can really get the full impact of what we were dealing with on Loarr.

After we'd been on the planet for four Standard Years, after we'd established contact and exchanged gifts and favors and information with the Loarra, after we'd set up our entire mining operation and had had it running without hindrance for over three years—after all that, the raid came. One day a sheet of dull purple light swept in from the horizon, and as it got closer I could see that it was a whole colony of the Loarra, their individual colors and fluctuations blending into that single purple mass. I was in the mountain, not outside with the mining extensors, so I saw all of it, and I lived through it.

They flashed in over us like locusts descending, and they hit the crawlers and dredges first. The metal glowed red, then white, then it melted. Then it was just gas that formed billowing clouds rising to the sky. Somewhere inside those clouds was what was left of the elements which had comprised seventeen human beings, who were also vapor now.

I hit the alarm and called everyone in, but only a few made it. The rest were caught in the tunnels when the Loarra swarmed over them, and they went up in smoke too. Then the automatic locks shut, and the mountain was sealed off. And six of us sat there, watching on the screen as the Loarra swept back and forth outside, cleaning up the bits and pieces they'd missed.

I sent out three of my "eyes," but they too were promptly vaporized.

Then we waited for them to hit the mountain itself . . . half a dozen frightened men huddled in the comp-room, none of us saying anything. Just sweating.

But they didn't come. They swarmed together in a tight spiral, went three times around the mountain, made one final salute-dip and then whirled straight up and out of sight. Only a handful of them were left behind out there.

After a while I sent out a fourth "eye." One of the Loarra came over, flitted around it like a firefly, blinked through the spectrum, and settled down to hover in front for talking. It was Pur—a Pur who was a thousand million billion life cycles removed from the Pur we know and love, of course, but nonetheless still pretty much Pur.

I sent out a sequence of lights and movements that translated, roughly, as, "What the hell did you do that for?"

And Pur glowed pale yellow for several seconds, then gave me an answer that doesn't translate. Or, if it does, the translation is just "Because."

Then I asked the question again, in different terms, and she gave me the same answer in different terms. I asked a third time, and a fourth, and she came back with the same thing. She seemed to be enjoying the variations on the Dance; maybe she thought we were playing.

Well . . . We'd already sent out our distress call by then, so all we could do was wait for a relief ship and hope they wouldn't attack again before the ship came, because we didn't have a chance of fighting them—we were miners, not a military expedition. God knows what any military expedition could have done against energy things, anyway. While we were waiting, I kept sending out the "eyes," and I kept talking to one Loarra after another. It took three weeks for the ship to get there, and I must have talked to over a hundred of them in that time, and the sum total of what I was told was this:

Their reason for wiping out the mining operation was untranslatable. No, they weren't mad. No, they didn't want us to go away. Yes, we were welcome to the stuff we were taking out of the depths of the Loarran ocean.

And, most importantly: No, they couldn't tell me whether or not they were likely ever to repeat their attack.

So we went away, limped back to Earth, and we all made our reports to Unicentral. We included, as I said, every bit of data we could think of, including an estimate of the value of the new elements on Loarr—which was something on the order of six times the wealth of Earthsystem. And we put it up to Unicentral as to whether or not we should go back.

Unicentral has been humming and clicking for ten months now, but it hasn't made a decision.

THE PLANNERS

Kate Wilhelm

Rae stopped before the one-way glass, stooped and peered at the gibbon infant in the cage. Darin watched her bitterly. She straightened after a moment, hands in smock pockets, face innocent of any expression what-so-goddam-ever, and continued to saunter toward him through the aisle between the cages.

"You still think it is cruel, and worthless?"

"Do you, Dr. Darin?"

"Why do you always do that? Answer my question with one of your own?"

"Does it infuriate you?"

He shrugged and turned away. His lab coat was on the chair where he had tossed it. He pulled it on over his sky-blue sport shirt.

"How is the Driscoll boy?" Rae asked.

He stiffened, then relaxed again. Still not facing her, he said, "Same as last week, last year. Same as he'll be until he dies."

The hall door opened and a very large, very homely face appeared. Stu Evers looked past Darin, down the aisle. "You alone? I thought I heard voices."

"Talking to myself," Darin said. "The committee ready yet?"

"Just about. Dr. Jacobsen is stalling with his nose-throat spray routine, as usual." He hesitated a moment, glancing again down the row of cages, then at Darin. "Wouldn't you think a guy allergic to monkeys would find some other line of research?"

Darin looked, but Rae was gone. What had it been this time: the Driscoll boy, the trend of the project itself? He

 Nebula Award, Best Short Story 1968

wondered if she had a life of her own when she was away. "I'll be out at the compound," he said. He passed Stu in the doorway and headed toward the livid greenery of Florida forests.

The cacophony hit him at the door. There were four hundred sixty-nine monkeys on the thirty-six acres of wooded ground the research department was using. Each monkey was screeching, howling, singing, cursing, or otherwise making its presence known. Darin grunted and headed toward the compound. The Happiest Monkeys in the World, a newspaper article had called them. Singing Monkeys, a subhead announced. MONKEYS GIVEN SMARTNESS PILLS, the most enterprising paper had proclaimed. *Cruelty Charged,* added another in subdued, sorrowful tones.

The compound was three acres of carefully planned and maintained wilderness, completely enclosed with thirty-foot-high, smooth plastic walls. A transparent dome covered the area. There were one-way windows at intervals along the wall. A small group stood before one of the windows: the committee.

Darin stopped and gazed over the interior of the compound through one of the windows. He saw Heloise and Skitter contentedly picking nonexistent fleas from one another. Adam was munching on a banana; Homer was lying on his back idly touching his feet to his nose. A couple of the chimps were at the water fountain, not drinking, merely pressing the pedal and watching the fountain, now and then immersing a head or hand in the bowl of cold water. Dr. Jacobsen appeared and Darin joined the group.

"Good morning, Mrs. Bellbottom," Darin said politely. "Did you know your skirt has fallen off?" He turned from her to Major Dormouse. "Ah, Major, and how many of the enemy have you swatted to death today with your pretty little yellow rag?" He smiled pleasantly at a pimply young man with a camera. "Major, you've brought a professional peeping tom. More stories in the paper, with pictures this time?" The pimply young man shifted his position, fidgeted with the camera. The major was fiery; Mrs. Bellbottom was on her knees peering under a bush, looking for her skirt. Darin blinked. None of them had on any clothing. He turned toward the window. The chimps were drawing up a table, laden with tea things, silver, china, tiny finger sandwiches. The chimps were all wearing flowered shirts and dresses. Hortense had on

54

a ridiculous flop-brimmed sun hat of pale green straw. Darin leaned against the fence to control his laughter.

"Soluble ribonucleic acid," Dr. Johnson was saying when Darin recovered, "sRNA for short. So from the gross beginnings when entire worms were trained and fed to other worms that seemed to benefit from the original training, we have come to these more refined methods. We now extract the sRNA molecule from the trained animals and feed it, the sRNA molecules in solution, to untrained specimens and observe the results."

The young man was snapping pictures as Jacobsen talked. Mrs. Whoosis was making notes, her mouth a lipless line, the sun hat tinging her skin with green. The sun on her patterned red and yellow dress made it appear to jiggle, giving her fleshy hips a constant rippling motion. Darin watched, fascinated. She was about sixty.

". . . my colleague, who proposed this line of experimentation, Dr. Darin," Jacobsen said finally, and Darin bowed slightly. He wondered what Jacobsen had said about him, decided to wait for any questions before he said anything.

"Dr. Darin, is it true that you also extract this substance from people?"

"Every time you scratch yourself, you lose this substance," Darin said. "Every time you lose a drop of blood, you lose it. It is in every cell of your body. Sometimes we take a sample of human blood for study, yes."

"And inject it into those animals?"

"Sometimes we do that," Darin said. He waited for the next, the inevitable question, wondering how he would answer it. Jacobsen had briefed them on what to answer, but he couldn't remember what Jacobsen had said. The question didn't come. Mrs. Whoosis stepped forward, staring at the window.

Darin turned his attention to her; she averted her eyes, quickly fixed her stare again on the chimps in the compound. "Yes, Mrs. uh . . . Madam?" Darin prompted her. She didn't look at him.

"Why? What is the purpose of all this?" she asked. Her voice sounded strangled. The pimpled young man was inching toward the next window.

"Well," Darin said, "our theory is simple. We believe that learning ability can be improved drastically in nearly every species. The learning curve is the normal, expected bell-

55

shaped curve, with a few at one end who have the ability to learn quite rapidly, with the majority in the center who learn at an average rate, and a few at the other end who learn quite slowly. With our experiments we are able to increase the ability of those in the broad middle, as well as those in the deficient end of the curve so that their learning abilities match those of the fastest learners of any given group. . . ."

No one was listening to him. It didn't matter. They would be given the press release he had prepared for them, written in simple language, no polysyllables, no complicated sentences. They were all watching the chimps through the windows. He said, "So we gabbled the gazooka three times wretchedly until the spirit of camping fired the girls." One of the committee members glanced at him. "Whether intravenously or orally, it seems to be equally effective," Darin said, and the perspiring man turned again to the window. "Injections every morning . . . rejections, planned diet, planned parenthood, planned plans planning plans." Jacobsen eyed him suspiciously. Darin stopped talking and lighted a cigarette. The woman with the unquiet hips turned from the window, her face very red. "I've seen enough," she said. "This sun is too hot out here. May we see the inside laboratories now?"

Darin turned them over to Stu Evers inside the building. He walked back slowly to the compound. There was a grin on his lips when he spotted Adam on the far side, swaggering triumphantly, paying no attention to Hortense who was rocking back and forth on her haunches, looking very dazed. Darin saluted Adam, then, whistling, returned to his office. Mrs. Driscoll was due with Sonny at 1 P.M.

Sonny Driscoll was fourteen. He was five feet nine inches, weighed one hundred sixty pounds. His male nurse was six feet two inches and weighed two hundred twenty-seven pounds. Sonny had broken his mother's arm when he was twelve; he had broken his father's arm and leg when he was thirteen. So far the male nurse was intact. Every morning Mrs. Driscoll lovingly washed and dressed her baby, fed him, walked him in the yard, spoke happily to him of plans for the coming months, or sang nursery songs to him. He never seemed to see her. The male nurse, Johnny, was never farther than three feet from his charge when he was on duty.

Mrs. Driscoll refused to think of the day when she would have to turn her child over to an institution. Instead she placed her faith and hope in Darin.

They arrived at two-fifteen, earlier than he had expected them, later than they had promised to be there.

"The kid kept taking his clothes off," Johnny said morosely. The kid was taking them off again in the office. Johnny started toward him, but Darin shook his head. It didn't matter. Darin got his blood sample from one of the muscular arms, shot the injection into the other one. Sonny didn't seem to notice what he was doing. He never seemed to notice. Sonny refused to be tested. They got him to the chair and table, but he sat staring at nothing, ignoring the blocks, the bright balls, the crayons, the candy. Nothing Darin did or said had any discernible effect. Finally the time was up. Mrs. Driscoll and Johnny got him dressed once more and left. Mrs. Driscoll thanked Darin for helping her boy.

Stu and Darin held class from four to five daily. Kelly O'Grady had the monkeys tagged and ready for them when they showed up at the schoolroom. Kelly was very tall, very slender and red-haired. Stu shivered if she accidentally brushed him in passing; Darin hoped one day Stu would pull an Adam on her. She sat primly on her high stool with her notebook on her knee, unaware of the change that came over Stu during school hours, or, if aware, uncaring. Darin wondered if she was really a Barbie doll fully programmed to perform laboratory duties, and nothing else.

He thought of the Finishing School for Barbies where long-legged, high-breasted, stomachless girls went to get shaved clean, get their toenails painted pink, their nipples removed, and all body openings sewn shut, except for their mouths, which curved in perpetual smiles and led nowhere.

The class consisted of six black spider-monkeys who had not been fed yet. They had to do six tasks in order: 1) pull a rope; 2) cross the cage and get a stick that was released by the rope; 3) pull the rope again; 4) get the second stick that would fit into the first; 5) join the sticks together; 6) using the lengthened stick, pull a bunch of bananas close enough to the bars of the cage to reach them and take them inside where they could eat them. At five the monkeys were returned to Kelly, who wheeled them away one by one back to the stockroom. None of them had performed all the tasks, although two had gone through part of them before the time ran out.

Waiting for the last of the monkeys to be taken back to its quarters, Stu asked, "What did you do to that bunch of idiots this morning? By the time I got them, they all acted dazed."

Darin told him about Adam's performance; they were both laughing when Kelly returned. Stu's laugh turned to something that sounded almost like a sob. Darin wanted to tell him about the school Kelly must have attended, thought better of it, and walked away instead.

His drive home was through the darkening forests of interior Florida for sixteen miles on a narrow straight road.

"Of course, I don't mind living here," Lea had said once, nine years ago when the Florida appointment had come through. And she didn't mind. The house was air-conditioned; the family car, Lea's car, was air-conditioned; the back yard had a swimming pool big enough to float the Queen Mary. A frightened, large-eyed Florida girl did the housework, and Lea gained weight and painted sporadically, wrote sporadically—poetry—and entertained faculty wives regularly. Darin suspected that sometimes she entertained faculty husbands also.

"Oh, Professor Dimples, one hour this evening? That will be fifteen dollars, you know." He jotted down the appointment and turned to Lea. "Just two more today and you will have your car payment. How about that!" She twined slinky arms about his neck, pressing tight high breasts hard against him. She had to tilt her head slightly for his kiss. "Then your turn, darling. For free." He tried to kiss her; something stopped his tongue, and he realized that the smile was on the outside only, that the opening didn't really exist at all.

He parked next to an MG, not Lea's, and went inside the house where the martinis were always snapping cold.

"Darling, you remember Greta, don't you? She is going to give me lessons twice a week. Isn't that exciting?"

"But you already graduated." Darin murmured. Greta was not tall and not long-legged. She was a little bit of a thing. He thought probably he did remember her from somewhere or other, vaguely. Her hand was cool in his.

"Greta has moved in; she is going to lecture on modern art for the spring semester. I asked her for private lessons and she said yes."

"Greta Farrel," Darin said, still holding her small hand. They moved away from Lea and wandered through the open windows to the patio where the scent of orange blossoms was heavy in the air.

"Greta thinks it must be heavenly to be married to a

58

psychologist." Lea's voice followed them. "Where are you two?"

"What makes you say a thing like that?" Darin asked.

"Oh, when I think of how you must understand a woman, know her moods and the reasons for them. You must know just what to do and when, and when to do something else . . . Yes, just like that."

His hands on her body were hot, her skin cool. Lea's petulant voice drew closer. He held Greta in his arms and stepped into the pool where they sank to the bottom, still together. She hadn't gone to the Barbie school. His hands learned her body; then his body learned hers. After they made love, Greta drew back from him regretfully.

"I do have to go now. You are a lucky man, Dr. Darin. No doubts about yourself, complete understanding of what makes you tick."

He lay back on the leather couch staring at the ceiling. "It's always that way, Doctor. Fantasies, dreams, illusions. I know it is because this investigation is hanging over us right now, but even when things are going relatively well, I still go off on a tangent like that for no real reason." He stopped talking.

In his chair Darin stirred slightly, his fingers drumming softly on the arm, his gaze on the clock whose hands were stuck. He said, "Before this recent pressure, did you have such intense fantasies?"

"I don't think so," Darin said thoughtfully, trying to remember.

The other didn't give him time. He asked, "And can you break out of them now when you have to, or want to?"

"Oh, sure," Darin said.

Laughing, he got out of his car, patted the MG, and walked into his house. He could hear voices from the living room and he remembered that on Thursdays Lea really did have her painting lesson.

Dr. Lacey left five minutes after Darin arrived. Lacey said vague things about Lea's great promise and untapped talent, and Darin nodded sober agreement. If she had talent, it certainly was untapped so far. He didn't say so.

Lea was wearing a hostess suit, flowing sheer panels of pale blue net over a skin-tight leotard that was midnight blue. Darin wondered if she realized that she had gained weight in the past few years. He thought not.

"Oh, that man is getting impossible," she said when the MG blasted away from their house. "Two years now, and he still doesn't want to put my things on show."

Looking at her, Darin wondered how much more her things could be on show.

"Don't dawdle too long with your martini," she said. "We're due at the Ritters' at seven for clams."

The telephone rang for him while he was showering. It was Stu Evers. Darin stood dripping water while he listened.

"Have you seen the evening paper yet? That broad made the statement that conditions are extreme at the station, that our animals are made to suffer unnecessarily."

Darin groaned softly. Stu went on, "She is bringing her entire women's group out tomorrow to show proof of her claims. She's a bigwig in the SPCA, or something."

Darin began to laugh then. Mrs. Whoosis had her face pressed against one of the windows, other fat women in flowered dresses had their faces against the rest. None of them breathed or moved. Inside the compound Adam laid Hortense, then moved on to Esmeralda, to Hilda . . .

"God damn it, Darin, it isn't funny!" Stu said.

"But it is. It is."

Clams at the Ritters' were delicious. Clams, hammers, buckets of butter, a mountainous salad, beer, and finally coffee liberally laced with brandy. Darin felt cheerful and contented when the evening was over. Ritter was in Med. Eng. Lit. but he didn't talk about it, which was merciful. He was sympathetic about the stink with the SPCA. He thought scientists had no imagination. Darin agreed with him and soon he and Lea were on their way home.

"I am so glad that you didn't decide to stay late," Lea said, passing over the yellow line with a blast oᶜ the horn. "There is a movie on tonight that I am dying to see."

She talked, but he didn't listen, training of twelve years drawing out an occasional grunt at what must have been appropriate times. "Ritter is such a bore," she said. They were nearly home. "As if you had anything to do with that incredible statement in tonight's paper."

"What statement?"

"Didn't you even read the article? For heaven's sake, why not? Everyone will be talking about it . . ." She sighed theatrically. "Someone quoted a reliable source who said that within the foreseeable future, simply by developing the leads you now have, you will be able to produce monkeys that are as smart as normal human beings." She laughed, a brittle meaningless sound.

"I'll read the article when we get home," he said. She didn't ask about the statement, didn't care if it was true or false, if he had made it or not. He read the article while she settled down before the television. Then he went for a swim. The water was warm, the breeze cool on his skin. Mosquitoes found him as soon as he got out of the pool, so he sat behind the screening of the verandah. The bluish light from the living room went off after a time and there was only the dark night. Lea didn't call him when she went to bed. He knew she went very softly, closing the door with care so that the click of the latch wouldn't disturb him if he was dozing on the verandah.

He knew why he didn't break it off. Pity. The most corrosive emotion endogenous to man. She was the product of the doll school that taught that the trip down the aisle was the end, the fulfillment of a maiden's dreams; shocked and horrified to learn that it was another beginning, some of them never recovered. Lea never had. Never would. At sixty she would purse her lips at the sexual display of uncivilized animals, whether human or not, and she would be disgusted and help formulate laws to ban such activities. Long ago he had hoped a child would be the answer, but the school did something to them on the inside too. They didn't conceive, or if conception took place, they didn't carry the fruit, and if they carried it, the birth was of a stillborn thing. The ones that did live were usually the ones to be pitied more than those who fought and were defeated *in utero*.

A bat swooped low over the quiet pool and was gone again against the black of the azaleas. Soon the moon would appear, and the chimps would stir restlessly for a while, then return to deep untroubled slumber. The chimps slept companionably close to one another, without thought of sex. Only the nocturnal creatures, and the human creatures, performed coitus in the dark. He wondered if Adam remembered his human captors. The colony in the compound had been started almost twenty years ago, and since then none of the chimps had seen a human being. When it was necessary to enter the grounds, the chimps were fed narcotics in the evening to insure against their waking. Props were changed then, new obstacles added to the old conquered ones. Now and then a chimp was removed for study, usually ending up in dissection. But not

61

Adam. He was father of the world. Darin grinned in the darkness.

Adam took his bride aside from the other beasts and knew that she was lovely. She was his own true bride, created for him, intelligence to match his own burning intelligence. Together they scaled the smooth walls and glimpsed the great world that lay beyond their garden. Together they found the opening that led to the world that was to be theirs, and they left behind them the lesser beings. And the god searched for them and finding them not, cursed them and sealed the opening so that none of the others could follow. So it was that Adam and his bride became the first man and woman and from them flowed the progeny that was to inhabit the entire world. And one day Adam said, for shame woman, seest thou that thou art naked? And the woman answered, so are you, big boy, so are you. So they covered their nakedness with leaves from the trees, and thereafter they performed their sexual act in the dark of night so that man could not look on his woman, nor she on him. And they were thus cleansed of shame. Forever and ever. Amen. Hallelujah.

Darin shivered. He had drowsed after all, and the night wind had grown chill. He went to bed. Lea drew away from him in her sleep. She felt hot to his touch. He turned to his left side, his back to her, and he slept.

"There is potential x," Darin said to Lea the next morning at breakfast. "We don't know where x is actually. It represents the highest intellectual achievement possible for the monkeys, for example. We test each new batch of monkeys that we get and sort them—x-1, x-2, x-3, suppose, and then we breed for more x-1's. Also we feed the other two groups the sRNA that we extract from the original x-1's. Eventually we get a monkey that is higher than our original x-1, and we reclassify right down the line and start over, using his sRNA to bring the others up to his level. We make constant checks to be sure we aren't allowing inferior strains to mingle with our highest achievers, and we keep control groups that are given the same training, the same food, the same sorting process, but no sRNA. We test them against each other."

Lea was watching his face with some interest as he talked. He thought he had got through, until she said, "Did you realize that your hair is almost solid white at the temples? All at once it is turning white."

Carefully he put his cup back on the saucer. He smiled at her and got up. "See you tonight," he said.

They also had two separate compounds of chimps that had started out identically. Neither had received any training whatever through the years; they had been kept isolated from each other and from man. Adam's group had been fed sRNA daily from the most intelligent chimps they had found. The control group had been fed none. The control-group chimps had yet to master the intricacies of the fountain with its ice-cold water; they used the small stream that flowed through the compound. The control group had yet to learn that fruit on the high, fragile branches could be had, if one used the telescoping sticks to knock them down. The control group huddled without protection, or under the scant cover of palm-trees when it rained and the dome was opened. Adam long ago had led his group in the construction of a rude but functional hut where they gathered when it rained.

Darin saw the women's committee filing past the compound when he parked his car. He went straight to the console in his office, flicked on a switch and manipulated buttons and dials, leading the group through the paths, opening one, closing another to them, until he led them to the newest of the compounds, where he opened the gate and let them inside. Quickly he closed the gate again and watched their frantic efforts to get out. Later he turned the chimps loose on them, and his grin grew broader as he watched the new-men ravage the old women. Some of the offspring were black and hairy, others pink and hairless, some intermediate. They grew rapidly, lined up with arms extended to receive their daily doses, stood before a machine that tested them instantaneously, and were sorted. Some of them went into a disintegration room, others out into the world.

A car horn blasted in his ears. He switched off his ignition and he got out as Stu Evers parked next to his car. "I see the old bats got here," Stu said. He walked toward the lab with Darin. "How's the Driscoll kid coming along?"

"Negative," Darin said. Stu knew they had tried using human sRNA on the boy, and failed consistently. It was too big a step for his body to cope with. "So far he has shown total intolerance to A-127. Throws it off almost instantly."

Stuart was sympathetic and noncommittal. No one else had any faith whatever in Darin's own experiment. A-127 might be too great a step upward, Darin thought. The *Ateles* spider monkey from Brazil was too bright.

He called Kelly from his office and asked about the newly arrived spider monkeys they had tested the day before. Blood had been processed; a sample was available. He looked over his notes and chose one that had shown interest in the tasks without finishing any of them. Kelly promised him the prepared syringe by 1 P.M.

What no one connected with the project could any longer doubt was that those simians, and the men that had been injected with sRNA from the Driscoll boy, had actually had their learning capacities inhibited, some of them apparently permanently.

Darin didn't want to think about Mrs. Driscoll's reaction if ever she learned how they had been using her boy. Rae sat at the corner of his desk and drawled insolently, "I might tell her myself, Dr. Darin. I'll say, Sorry, Ma'am, you'll have to keep your idiot out of here; you're damaging the brains of our monkeys with his polluted blood. Okay, Darin?"

"My God, what are you doing back again?"

"Testing," she said. "That's all, just testing."

Stu called him to observe the latest challenge to Adam's group, to take place in forty minutes. Darin had forgotten that he was to be present. During the night a tree had been felled in each compound, its trunk crossing the small stream, damming it. At eleven the water fountains were to be turned off for the rest of the day. The tree had been felled at the far end of the compound, close to the wall where the stream entered, so that the trickle of water that flowed past the hut was cut off. Already the group not taking sRNA was showing signs of thirst. Adam's group was unaware of the interrupted flow.

Darin met Stu and they walked together to the far side where they would have a good view of the entire compound. The women had left by then. "It was too quiet for them this morning," Stu said. "Adam was making his rounds; he squatted on the felled tree for nearly an hour before he left it and went back to the others."

They could see the spreading pool of water. It was muddy, uninviting looking. At eleven-ten it was generally known within the compound that the water supply had failed. Some of the old chimps tried the fountain; Adam tried it several times. He hit it with a stick and tried it again. Then he sat

64

on his haunches and stared at it. One of the young chimps whimpered pitiably. He wasn't thirsty yet, merely puzzled and perhaps frightened. Adam scowled at him. The chimp cowered behind Hortense, who bared her fangs at Adam. He waved menacingly at her, and she began picking fleas from her offspring. When he whimpered again, she cuffed him. The young chimp looked from her to Adam, stuck his forefinger in his mouth and ambled away. Adam continued to stare at the useless fountain. An hour passed. At last Adam rose and wandered nonchalantly toward the drying stream. Here and there a shrinking pool of muddy water steamed in the sun. The other chimps followed Adam. He followed the stream through the compound toward the wall that was its source. When he came to the pool he squatted again. One of the young chimps circled the pool cautiously, reached down and touched the dirty water, drew back, reached for it again, and then drank. Several of the others drank also. Adam continued to squat. At twelve-forty Adam moved again. Grunting and gesturing to several younger males, he approached the tree-trunk. With much noise and meaningless gestures, they shifted the trunk. They strained, shifted it again. The water was released and poured over the heaving chimps. Two of them dropped the trunk and ran. Adam and the other two held. The two returned.

They were still working when Darin had to leave, to keep his appointment with Mrs. Driscoll and Sonny. They arrived at one-ten. Kelly had left the syringe with the new formula in Darin's small refrigerator. He injected Sonny, took his sample, and started the tests. Sometimes Sonny cooperated to the extent of lifting one of the articles from the table and throwing it. Today he cleaned the table within ten minutes. Darin put a piece of candy in his hand; Sonny threw it from him. Patiently Darin put another piece in the boy's hand. He managed to keep the eighth piece in the clenched hand long enough to guide the hand to Sonny's mouth. When it was gone, Sonny opened his mouth for more. His hands lay idly on the table. He didn't seem to relate the hands to the candy with the pleasant taste. Darin tried to guide a second to his mouth, but Sonny refused to hold a piece a second time.

When the hour was over and Sonny was showing definite signs of fatigue, Mrs. Driscoll clutched Darin's hands in hers. Tears stood in her eyes. "You actually got him to feed himself a little bit," she said brokenly. "God bless you, Dr. Darin.

God bless you!" She kissed his hand and turned away as the tears started to spill down her cheeks.

Kelly was waiting for him when the group left. She collected the new sample of blood to be processed. "Did you hear about the excitement down at the compound? Adam's building a dam of his own."

Darin stared at her for a moment. The breakthrough? He ran back to the compound. The near side this time was where the windows were being used. It seemed that the entire staff was there, watching silently. He saw Stu and edged in by him. The stream twisted and curved through the compound, less than ten inches deep, not over two feet anywhere. At one spot stones lay under it; elsewhere the bottom was of hardpacked sand. Adam and his crew were piling up stones at the one suitable place for their dam, very near their hut. The dam they were building was two feet thick. It was less than five feet from the wall, fifteen feet from where Darin and Stu shared the window. When the dam was completed, Adam looked along the wall. Darin thought the chimp's eyes paused momentarily on his own. Later he heard that nearly every other person watching felt the same momentary pause as those black, intelligent eyes sought out and held other intelligence.

". . . next thunderstorm. Adam and the flood . . ."

". . . eventually seeds instead of food . . ."

". . . his brain. Convolutions as complex as any man's."

Darin walked away from them, snatches of future plans in his ears. There was a memo on his desk. Jacobsen was turning over the SPCA investigatory committee to him. He was to meet with the university representatives, the local SPCA group, and the legal representatives of all concerned on Monday next at 10 A.M. He wrote out his daily report on Sonny Driscoll. Sonny had been on too good behavior for too long. Would this last injection give him just the spark of determination he needed to go on a rampage? Darin had alerted Johnny, the bodyguard, whoops, male nurse, for just such a possibility, but he knew Johnny didn't think there was any danger from the kid. He hoped Sonny wouldn't kill Johnny, then turn on his mother and father. He'd probably rape his mother, if that much goal-directedness ever flowed through him. And the three men who had volunteered for the injections from Sonny's blood? He didn't want to think of them at all, therefore couldn't get them out of his mind as

66

he sat at his desk staring at nothing. Three convicts. That's all, just convicts hoping to get a parole for helping science along. He laughed abruptly. They weren't planning anything now. Not that trio. Not planning for a thing. Sitting, waiting for something to happen, not thinking about what it might be, or when, or how they would be affected. Not thinking. Period.

"But you can always console yourself that your motives were pure, that it was all for Science, can't you, Dr. Darin?" Rae asked mockingly.

He looked at her. "Go to hell," he said.

It was late when he turned off his light. Kelly met him in the corridor that led to the main entrance. "Hard day, Dr. Darin?"

He nodded. Her hand lingered momentarily on his arm. "Good night," she said, turning in to her own office. He stared at the door for a long time before he let himself out and started toward his car. Lea would be furious with him for not calling. Probably she wouldn't speak at all until nearly bedtime, when she would explode into tears and accusations. He could see the time when her tears and accusations would strike home, when Kelly's body would still be a tangible memory, her words lingering in his ears. And he would lie to Lea, not because he would care actually if she knew, but because it would be expected. She wouldn't know how to cope with the truth. It would entangle her to the point where she would have to try an abortive suicide, a screaming-for-attention attempt that would ultimately tie him in tear-soaked knots that would never be loosened. No, he would lie, and she would know he was lying, and they would get by. He started the car, aimed down the long sixteen miles that lay before him. He wondered where Kelly lived. What it would do to Stu when he realized. What it would do to his job if Kelly should get nasty, eventually. He shrugged. Barbie dolls never got nasty. It wasn't built in.

Lea met him at the door, dressed only in a sheer gown, her hair loose and unsprayed. Her body flowed into his, so that he didn't need Kelly at all. And he was best man when Stu and Kelly were married. He called to Rae, "Would that satisfy you?" but she didn't answer. Maybe she was gone for good this time. He parked the car outside his darkened house and leaned his head on the steering wheel for a moment before getting out. If not gone for good, at least for a long time. He hoped she would stay away for a long time.

SWORD GAME

H. H. Hollis

Late in the afternoon of an ugly fall day, a forty-year-old topologist, employed to teach mathematics at a university he despised, bored by his students and frightened that he had done everything of significance in his life that he would ever do, blundered head-down into a group of students handing out flowers and handbills. Before he could retrieve his dropped book bag and move on to continue composing in his head a memorable letter of resignation, his eye had fallen on a grubby teen-age girl and he was hopelessly entrapped.

Thinking to break the spell, he boldly said to her, "Aren't you in my class in elementary topology?"

She licked the raspberry snow cone she was holding and said, without a trace of a smile, "You must be mad. I'm not a student, just a wandering Gypsy fortune teller." She held out the snow cone for him to take a lick. "Do you have a place where we could go, and I would tell your fortune?"

The mathematician knew she was no Gypsy, for your modern, urban Romany never allows himself to be as dirty as she was. He was certain she was putting him on, but his mood of desperate boredom was such that he said, "Cra-a-a-zy, Gypsy! Fall up to my pad, and we'll tell fortunes and other lies till the world melts."

They left hand in hand under the eyes of forty witnesses. Within their own subculture, however, the rebel students conformed to a rigid code; and they would have died rather than give information to the fuzz or even to the Dean of the Faculty; so the professor's absolute breach of propriety in picking up a student went unremarked and unreported.

When he had taken off her clothes, the girl was every bit as dirty as she appeared to be, but this only made him more determined to take advantage of her. Later, he persuaded her to shower by promising to bathe with her; and she looked, when she left, with her rum-colored hair in two long plaits, like a fresh-scrubbed Girl Scout.

The crust turned out to be her equivalent of the makeup squares use; when he came past the common the next day, she was as delectably grimy as ever, and she held a fresh snow cone purple with grape syrup.

The two joined hands and went directly to his apartment. The young woman hardly spoke until late in the evening, after they had showered together. She was toweling her hair and the information came indistinctly. "I went to the Provost's office today," she said, "and told him about us."

The professor was so uncharacteristically content he contemplated the ruin of his academic career with pleasure. "All right, big mouth, how are we going to live?"

"I'm not really a Gypsy," she said, "but I really was in a carnival once, when I ran away before. I know how to dodge swords in a sword basket. Could you be an East Indian sword magician? We could pick up a show somewhere and travel right along with them."

"By God," cried the topologist, "I can do better than that! It's been a long time since I did any engineering work, but I have a little laboratory curiosity that will just fill the bill. Come with me to the animal house in the basement of the Psychology Department, and I'll show you something you won't believe."

"Try me, baby," replied his inamorata. "You'd be surprised at what *I* can believe."

They repaired to the noisome cages in which the experimental animals were kept, and the professor secured a sturdy mouse. Selecting a few strips of clear plastic from a rack, he lit a burner and uncorked a container of plastic adhesive. In a few minutes, the topologist had cobbled up a container which defied the eye to define its exact shape, but which most often seemed to be a lumpy cylinder. In a trice, he thrust the mouse in and clapped the square top down. The mouse could be seen through the plastic, but he seemed to be in a single fixed position, floating in midair with his paws and tail extended just as when he was inserted.

Heating a pointed rod, the professor pierced a hole first in one side of the bulgy cylinder and then in the other. In a moment, when the long pin had cooled, he introduced its sharp point through the hole again, and having located the mouse properly, skewered the rodent through the heart so that the point of the sharpened rod came out the second hole. Swinging the cylinder over the girl's hand with a little shake, the professor deposited a tiny drop of bright arterial mouse blood on her wrist.

As she looked at the crimson drop, tears appeared, sparkling on her eyelids. "Big deal, big man," she said. "Mouse murder. I don't think a wild mouse would walk into that plastic pipe, do you?"

"Heart of my heart," he replied, "it's not a *pipe*. It isn't even a cylinder, and it certainly isn't a mousetrap. This is a tesseract, as you would know if you had ever read a popular work on topology."

"Oh, all right, I know what a tesseract is: an expanded cube, a cube with a cube on each face. That mouse cage doesn't look like six cubes surrounding a cube to me."

"No, otherwise our mouse would be dead all over. This is a tesseract which is a temporal illusion."

"A *temporal* illusion!"

"Yes, my dear," he said, "a temporal illusion. Topology teaches us that mathematical properties can be quite independent of apparent shape. A circle is still a circle, even though it *looks* like a scalloped pie crust—as it may, if it is drawn on a wavy surface. This mouse cage is a cubed cage which is partly displaced along the dimension of time. That's why it appears formless and shifting. Here, feel it."

Sure enough, to the touch it was solid enough: a cube with a cube on each face; but even when held in the hand and sensed by touch, the object still appeared to be a rippling cylinder and the mouse still appeared to be stock still.

"This mouse looks dead. Eccch!" she said.

Deftly the topologist withdrew the tiny sword, pried off the top, and shook Mr. Mouse out in his hand, where the charming little fellow at once sat up on his haunches and waved his forepaws, as if demanding cheese.

"How did you do that?" cried the girl.

"Simple, really," replied the tinker. "The exterior flickers in and out of this moment of time, because of the subtle twist I imparted to the shape when I made it; but the inside is *fixed* in time, because much of the internal mass is stretched all the way around the very large but finite continuum of space and time which is our universe. This little rascal's 'time' has passed so slowly that the powerful regenerative and repair processes of his body have worked as if instantaneously, and

70

the apparently mortal wound I dealt him was no more than a pin prick. Do you think you could get into a large tesseract like this one and let me run a rapier through you . . . knowing it would do you no harm?"

She clapped her hands in pleasure. "Oh yes, lover! That'll be so much more of a mind buster than some old wicker basket that everybody knows I dodge the sword in."

So they hied themselves to a plastic supply house and thence to a dog-and-pony show that was in the neighborhood, and for a long time, everything went like a guided trip with Tim Leary. Audiences were transfixed by the girl's beauty. She was considerably cleaner under the difficult circumstances of carnival trouping than she had been when soap and water were conveniently to be had, and when the topologist drove a sharpened fencing foil through her lovely body, clad as lightly as local ordinance allowed, the crowds gasped. When the box was rotated to show the point of the sword encarnadined, strong men fainted. Later they would press forward and pay a dollar apiece to examine the tiny wound as it closed up and disappeared, usually midway up her delightfully articulated rib cage.

Trouping the carnival together was an idyll. Still, even if forty years is not *old*, neither is it young; and the doctor of mathematics at last realized that he was bored again. The girl's vocabulary never enlarged itself appreciably, and the snow cone remained her favorite confection. The difference in their ages was sufficient for their basic sex attitudes to be irreconcilable. For him, a certain overtone of the forbidden gave carnal love its highest stimulation; but for her, sex was just another natural function, like perspiring or excreting, so that the level of their love-making remained at mere technical proficiency.

After the fashion her generation had adopted, she was faithful. There might be others later, her manner implied by its playfulness; but for now, she did not share her favors out. He was denied even the sour spice of jealousy.

At the end of their last appearance each evening, she was often wearing only transparent pantaloons and a shiny little brief, and when they had walked back to their quarters, she would hold up her arms, and stamping her naked feet softly like a harem dancer, say, "Help me get ready for my bath, lover." If he approached and began to roll down the waistband of her sateen pants, she would drop her arms and begin to undress him too. Later they would bathe each other.

They had almost no other conversation.

At last the idyll became an enslavement to the professor. He found some respite when he learned that a Hindu torture-man, their neighbor in the show, who slept on nails, poured boiling lead in his eyes, and so on, was a Failed M.A. in Mathematics from the University of Rawalpindi. By talking to him, the topologist was able to keep from going quite mad. Still, he was a little off. He loathed the girl and dreamed only of what he would do when she left him; but she would not leave, and continued to raise her arms to him and stamp her feet, as exquisitely irritating as a kitten which continues to claw one's sock after one has done playing with it.

He began to do everything badly, even their turn in the show, which had never much interested him after he put the big tesseract together. Once he missed the hole with his thrust, and the plastic deflected the point of the foil into his toe. This was a real wound, in real time, not spread along the space-time continuum, and was extremely painful for a week. Each time he limped, the pain made him more resolved to be quit of her, until at last his fertile topological mind saw the way.

He had a regular armorer's store of swords with which he made play in their act, and one evening he laid handy, next their bed, a very passable imitation of a Roman short sword. In its day, that design had been a great technological break-through for the weapons makers, and it was beautifully shaped for destructive stabbing.

When they came in that night, he skimmed off her tawdry cape with a flourish, and as she lifted her round arms and stamped one foot, he peeled the bottom of her costume off in one extravagant gesture, and then gave her the pleasure of chasing him and tearing off his garments. As they were toweling each other after their ritual coupling and bathing, he kissed her, tender but preoccupied, as it were, and said, "My dear, would you mind letting me practice that last pass in the act? I just don't seem to be putting that foil home right."

She was so pleased to have him pleasant again that she scampered into the spare tesseract they had in the quarters, a few drops from the bath still glistening on one flank. She turned her face up to him with a grin that almost made him reconsider the irreversible act he had planned. Then he remembered the months of boredom and hardened his heart. Decisively, he tapped the top home. Without a tremor, he put the Roman short sword as nearly into her heart as he could judge its location through the subtle time shifting in the plastic. With that, he snapped off the blade, so that the sword *also* was within the spread, slowed effect of the moving time field, and gave the construction a knowledgeable kick or two which caused it to collapse into itself. Instead of a knobby cylinder, as it had appeared when it was an expanded cube blurred by time, it now appeared to be a single cube about six inches on a side, with an abstract pattern in each face.

The collapsed cube was much heavier than it looked, but not nearly as heavy as the girl, for a substantial part of her mass was distributed along the whole of the cylindrico-spherical space-time continuum. As he gazed at the mirror-like surface of one square face, an eye and eyebrow slowly spread flatly across the plane; but there was neither panic nor recognition as he stared into it. He realized that to the occupant of this peculiar box, his movements were so fast in appearance as to be a mere blur. Whistling, the professor packed the weighty cube into his bag and strolled off the lot, casually remarking to his old Hindu neighbor, "So long, we're jumping this flea circus." By changing into one of his wrinkled natural shoulder suits at the bus station, he simply disappeared as Grax, the Swordsman of Time (his carnival billing), and reincarnated himself as a topologist of considerable talent who had been vaguely on sabbatical for a while.

The frustrations that had so nearly consumed him before his adventure seemed to have been burned and purged away. He settled with pleasure into a new academic routine and became expert in its execution. Once in five years, perhaps, he had a really promising student; but the scarcity no longer bothered him. As he advanced up the ladder of academic tenure and preferment, he was able to place a few brilliant people about himself, and life was as good, he now knew, as it was ever going to be.

The heavy cube was a paperweight on the desk in his apartment. No one else ever recognized the shifting abstract patterns in its silvery sides as the topologized contours of a dead human being. At great intervals, there would drift across

73

one face or another of the prism some recognizable anatomical feature with which the professor was intimately acquainted, and he would feel a vague regret for his act and a light stirring, as of the ashes in a cold grate, of his appetite for the one adventure of his life. He would stuff his pipe, turn the pages of the *Journal of Topology,* and immerse himself once more in the calm, sweet life of the university.

When he was sixty years old and almost bald, there appeared in his classes the student of his dreams, who understood everything he said in his arcane specialty, and replied with fresh and elegant insights into the intuitive sort of math in which they both delighted. Objectively, he knew the boy was neat and trim rather than handsome, yet subjectively (and privately, of course: he was very proper now), he always felt the boy was "good-looking." This feeling puzzled him until one day he had to move a stack of old college annuals, and browsing as one will, he suddenly came upon his own senior picture. His best student was enough like his youthful self to be a double, or at least a younger brother.

Shortly after that, the professor confided the story of his escapade to the boy. He could not have said why he did so, and it certainly was not wise; but the student was beginning to betray the same weird talent the professor had for translating topological abstractions into hardware that did peculiar things; and somehow the tale just told itself. He had become very fond indeed of his disciple. The boy, who affected the total amorality which was the fashion of *his* generation, was nevertheless shocked; but he was also intrigued. He picked up the box and shook it. "Maybe she's alive," he said. "After all, inside it's only been an instant. Let's unlock it."

"Don't be ridiculous," the professor said, taking the cube back and setting it on his desk in a definite manner. "In the first place, she's not alive. While she's in the construction, there's no evidence of the crime. Second, if she were alive, she might go to the police; or worse yet, she might expect me to take up that dreadful, boring liaison with her again. And in the third place, we *can't* unlock it. That was the whole point of breaking the sword. The cube's a closed system now, and no part of the interior is available to this aspect of time and space. Eventually she'll be equally distributed through the entire universe. Absolutely not! I forbid you to think about it. When are you going to give me that paper on topological re-intervertebrates?"

Conversation languished, and the student shortly took his leave. A day or two later, the professor found the boy fiddling the edges of the cube with a device made of mirrors, and they had a genuine quarrel; but gradually they fell back almost into their former sympathetic teacher-student relation.

One day the student appeared in the professor's apartment with a tiny glittering piece of metal in his hand, the shape of which was extraordinarily hard to see. The whole thing seemed to flicker in and out of the mathematician's sight. "What the hell have you got there?" he asked the boy in irritation.

"It's a chrome-plated, self-powered, retractable, inverted, universally jointed, and fully gurgitated Möbius strip," the young man said.

The professor laughed. Every schoolboy knows a Möbius strip is a band, one end of which has been given a half twist before joining it to the other end to make a circlet. The consequence of that little twist (try it) is that the Möbius strip is a geometric figure which has only one side and one edge, though common sense, looking at it, can plainly discern two sides and two edges. However, a pencil drawn down the center of "one side" will meet its own mark and there will then be seen to be a line drawn on "both sides" . . . because there *is* only one side, you see?

But every schoolboy knows that's all a Möbius strip is: just a curiosity. Anything else you do to it changes it from being a Möbius strip. So it can't be improved by chroming it or powering it or anything else. The professor pointed all this out to his student in a rather overbearing manner. He finished by saying, "And I suppose you're going to tell me it has some practical application."

"Yes," said the boy, "it has." And before the professor could stop him, he had reached across the desk, penetrated into the shiny cube with one half of the glittering Möbius strip, and fished out the shattered remnant of a short Roman stabbing sword.

In an instant, the old familiar bulgy cylinder was present on the desk, full-size, and in another, a completely naked young woman had leaped out of it onto the floor. In stupefaction, the professor saw a pink, three-cornered scar, obviously just healing, on her rib cage, and noticed there were still drops of water glistening on her flank.

"Sweetheart!" she cried. "What was that *butcher* knife? I

had to dodge like crazy!" And she engulfed the student in a squid-like embrace. A moment later she saw the professor and recoiled.

"Who is this bald-headed old creep?" she said. "I draw the line at voyeurs, honey." And with a wink and a nod, she and the student dumped the professor into the expanded cube and collapsed it about him.

Even in the endless instant which is the inside of his device, time has begun to seem long to the topologist. He knows the girl and the student are long since dust in the whirling, kaleidoscopic world outside. He is beginning to be transparent, so he knows his substance is slowly plating out along the entire cylindrico-spherical space-time continuum. He has realized that when he is fully distributed, the universe will be at an end; and he has composed a most astounding paper in his head explaining the whole phenomenon. His only regret is that he will never be able to send it to the *Journal of Topology* for publication.

THE LISTENERS

James E. Gunn

> *"Is there anybody there?" said the Traveler,*
> *Knocking on the moonlit door. . . .*

The voices babbled.

MacDonald heard them and knew that there was meaning in them, that they were trying to communicate and that he could understand them and respond to them if he could only concentrate on what they were saying, but he couldn't bring himself to make the effort. He tried again.

"Back behind everything, lurking like a silent shadow behind the closed door, is the question we can never answer except positively: Is there anybody there?"

That was Bob Adams, eternally the devil's advocate, looking querulously at the others around the conference table. His round face was sweating, although the mahogany-paneled room was cool.

Saunders puffed hard on his pipe. "But that's true of all science. The image of the scientist eliminating all negative possibilities is ridiculous. Can't be done. So he goes ahead on faith and statistical probability."

MacDonald watched the smoke rise above Saunders' head in clouds and wisps until it wavered in the draft from the air duct, thinned out, disappeared. He could not see it, but the odor reached his nostrils. It was an aromatic blend easily distinguishable from the flatter smell of cigarettes being smoked by Adams and some of the others.

Wasn't this their task? MacDonald wondered. To detect the thin smoke of life that drifts through the universe, to separate one trace from another, molecule by molecule, and then force them to reverse their entropic paths into their ordered and meaningful original form.

All the king's horses, and all the king's men. . . . Life itself is impossible, he thought, but men exist by reversing entropy.

77

Down the long table cluttered with overflowing ash trays and coffee cups and doodled scratch pads Olsen said, "We always knew it would be a long search. Not years but centuries. The computers must have sufficient data, and that means bits of information approximating the number of molecules in the universe. Let's not chicken out now."

> "If seven maids with seven mops
> Swept it for half a year,
> Do you suppose," the Walrus said,
> "That they could get it clear?"

". . . ridiculous," someone was saying, and then Adams broke in, "It's easy for you to talk about centuries when you've been here only three years. Wait until you've been at it for ten years, like I have. Or Mac here who has been on the Project for twenty years and head of it for fifteen."

"What's the use of arguing about something we can't know anything about?" Sonnenborn said reasonably. "We have to base our position on probabilities. Shklovskii and Sagan estimated that there are more than one thousand million habitable planets in our galaxy alone. Von Hoerner estimated that one in three million have advanced societies in orbit around them; Sagan said one in one hundred thousand. Either way it's good odds that there's somebody there—three hundred or ten thousand in our segment of the universe. Our job is to listen in the right place or in the right way or understand what we hear."

Adams to MacDonald. "What do you say, Mac?"

"I say these basic discussions are good for us," MacDonald said mildly, "and we need to keep reminding ourselves what it is we're doing, or we'll get swallowed in a quicksand of data. I also say that it's time now to get down to the business at hand—what observations do we make tonight and the rest of the week before our next staff meeting?"

Saunders began, "I think we should make a methodical sweep of the entire galactic lens, listening on all wavelengths—"

"We've done that a hundred times," said Sonnenborn.

"Not with my new filter—"

"Tau Ceti still is the most likely," said Olsen. "Let's really give it a hearing—"

MacDonald heard Adams grumbling half to himself, "If

there is anybody, and they are trying to communicate, some amateur is going to pick it up on his ham set, decipher it on his James Bond coderule, and leave us sitting here on one hundred million dollars of equipment with egg all over our faces—"

"And don't forget," MacDonald said, "tomorrow is Saturday night and Maria and I will be expecting you all at our place at eight for the customary beer and bull. Those who have more to say can save it for then."

MacDonald did not feel as jovial as he tried to sound. He did not know whether he could stand another Saturday night session of drink and discussion and dissension about the Project. This was one of his low periods when everything seemed to pile up on top of him, and he could not get out from under, or tell anybody how he felt. No matter how he felt, the Saturday nights were good for the morale of the others.

> *Pues no es posible que esté continuo el arco armado*
> *ni la condición y flaqueza humana se pueda sustenar*
> *sin alguna lícita recreación*

Within the Project, morale was always a problem. Besides, it was good for Maria. She did not get out enough. She needed to see people. And then. . . .

And then maybe Adams was right. Maybe nobody was there. Maybe nobody was sending signals because there was nobody to send signals. Maybe man was all alone in the universe. Alone with God. Or alone with himself, whichever was worse.

Maybe all the money was being wasted, and the effort, and the preparation—all the intelligence and education and ideas being drained away into an endlessly empty cavern.

> *Habe nun, ach! Philosophie,*
> *Juristerei und Medizin,*
> *Under leider auch Theologie*
> *Durchaus studiert, mit heissem Bemühn.*
> *Da steh' ich nun, ich armer Tor!*
> *Und bin so klug als wie zuvor;*
> *Heisse Magister, heisse Doktor gar,*
> *Und ziehe schon an die zehen Jahr*
> *Herauf, herab und quer und krumm*

Meine Schüler an der Nase herum—
Und sehe, dass wir nichts wissen können!

Poor fool. Why me? MacDonald thought. Could not some other lead them better, not by the nose but by his real wisdom? Perhaps all he was good for was the Saturday night parties. Perhaps it was time for a change.

He shook himself. It was the endless waiting that wore him down, the waiting for something that did not happen, and the Congressional hearings were coming up again. What could he say that he had not said before? How could he justify a project that already had gone on for nearly fifty years without results and might go on for centuries more?

"Gentlemen," he said briskly, "to our listening posts."

By the time he had settled himself at his disordered desk, Lily was standing beside him.

"Here's last night's computer analysis," she said, putting down in front of him a thin folder. "Reynolds says there's nothing there, but you always want to see it anyway. Here's the transcription of last year's Congressional hearings." A thick binder went on top of the folder. "The correspondence and the actual appropriation measure are in another file if you want them."

MacDonald shook his head.

"There's a form letter here from NASA establishing the ground rules for this year's budget and a personal letter from Ted Wartinian saying that conditions are really tight and some cuts look inevitable. In fact, he says there's a possibility the Project might be scrubbed."

Lily glanced at him. "Not a chance," MacDonald said confidently.

"There's a few applications for employment. Not as many as we used to get. The letters from school children I answered myself. And there's the usual nut letters from people who've been receiving messages from outer space, and from one who's had a ride in a UFO. That's what he called it—not a saucer or anything. A feature writer wants to interview you and some others for an article on the Project. I think he's with us. And another one who sounds as if he wants to do an exposé."

MacDonald listened patiently. Lily was a wonder. She could handle everything in the office as well as he could. In fact, things might run smoother if he were not around to take up her time.

"They've both sent some questions for you to answer. And Joe wants to talk to you."

"Joe?"

"One of the janitors."

"What does he want?" They couldn't afford to lose a janitor. Good janitors were harder to find than astronomers, harder even than electronicians.

"He says he has to talk to you, but I've heard from some of the lunchroom staff that he's been complaining about getting messages on his—on his—"

"Yes?"

"On his false teeth."

MacDonald sighed. "Pacify him somehow, will you, Lily? If I talk to him we might lose a janitor."

"I'll do my best. And Mrs. MacDonald called. Said it wasn't important and you needn't call back."

"Call her," MacDonald said. "And, Lily—you're coming to the party tomorrow night, aren't you?"

"What would I be doing at a party with all the brains?"

"We want you to come. Maria asked particularly. It isn't all shop talk, you know. And there are never enough women. You might strike it off with one of the young bachelors."

"At my age, Mr. MacDonald? You're just trying to get rid of me."

"Never."

"I'll get Mrs. MacDonald." Lily turned at the door. "I'll think about the party."

MacDonald shuffled through the papers. Down at the bottom was the only one he was interested in—the computer analysis of last night's listening. But he kept it there, on the bottom, as a reward for going through the others. Ted was really worried. *Move over, Ted.* And then the writers. He supposed he would have to work them in somehow. At least it was part of the fallout to locating the Project in Puerto Rico. Nobody just dropped in. And the questions. Two of them caught his attention.

How did you come to be named Project Director? That was the friendly one. *What are your qualifications to be Director?* That was the other. How would he answer them? Could he answer them at all?

Finally he reached the computer analysis, and it was just

like those for the rest of the week, and the week before that, and the months and the years before that. No significant correlations. Noise. There were a few peaks of reception—at the twenty-one-centimeter line, for instance—but these were merely concentrated noise. Radiating clouds of hydrogen, as the Little Ear functioned like an ordinary radio telescope.

At least the Project showed some results. It was feeding star survey data tapes into the international pool. Fallout. Of a process that had no other product except negatives.

Maybe the equipment wasn't sensitive enough. Maybe. They could beef it up some more. At least it might be a successful ploy with the Committee, some progress to present, if only in the hardware. You don't stand still. You spend more money or they cut you back—or off.

Note: Saunders—plans to increase sensitivity.

Maybe the equipment wasn't discriminating enough. But they had used up a generation of ingenuity canceling out background noise, and in its occasional checks the Big Ear indicated that they were doing adequately on terrestrial noise, at least.

Note: Adams—new discrimination gimmick.

Maybe the computer wasn't recognizing a signal when it had one fed into it. Perhaps it wasn't sophisticated enough to perceive certain subtle relationships. . . . And yet sophisticated codes had been broken in seconds. And the Project was asking it to distinguish only where a signal existed, whether the reception was random noise or had some element of the unrandom. At this level it wasn't even being asked to note the influence of consciousness.

Note: ask computer—is it missing something? Ridiculous? Ask Olsen.

Maybe they shouldn't be searching the radio spectrum at all. Maybe radio was a peculiarity of man's civilization. Maybe others had never had it or had passed it by and now had more sophisticated means of communication. Lasers, for instance. Telepathy, or what might pass for it with man. Maybe gamma rays, as Morrison sugested years before Ozma.

Well, maybe. But if it were so, somebody else would have to listen for those. He had neither the equipment nor the background nor the working lifetime left to tackle something new.

And maybe Adams was right.

He buzzed Lily. "Have you reached Mrs. MacDonald?"

"The telephone hasn't answered—"

Unreasoned panic. . . .

"—oh, here she is now. Mr. MacDonald, Mrs. Mac-Donald."

"Hello, darling. I was alarmed when you didn't answer." That had been foolish, he thought, and even more foolish to mention it.

Her voice was sleepy. "I must have been dozing." Even drowsy, it was an exciting voice, gentle, a little husky, that speeded MacDonald's pulse. "What did you want?"

"You called me," MacDonald said.

"Did I? I've forgotten."

"Glad you're resting. You didn't sleep well last night."

"I took some pills."

"How many?"

"Just the two you left out."

"Good girl. I'll see you in a couple of hours. Go back to sleep. Sorry I woke you."

But her voice wasn't sleepy any more. "You won't have to go back tonight, will you? We'll have the evening together?"

"We'll see," he promised.

But he knew he would have to return.

MacDonald paused outside the long, low concrete building which housed the offices and laboratories and computers. It was twilight. The sun had descended below the green hills, but orange and purpling wisps of cirrus trailed down the western sky.

Between MacDonald and the sky was a giant dish held aloft by skeleton metal fingers—held high as if to catch the star dust that drifted down at night from the Milky Way.

> Go and catch a falling star,
>   Get with child a mandrake root,
> Tell me where all past years are,
>   Or who cleft the Devil's foot;
> Teach me to hear mermaids singing,
>   Or to keep off envy's stinging,
>   And find
>   What wind
> Serves to advance an honest mind.

Then the dish began to turn, noiselessly, incredibly, and to tip. And it was not a dish any more but an ear, a listening ear cupped by the surrounding hills to overhear the whispering universe.

Perhaps this was what kept them at their jobs, MacDonald thought. In spite of all disappointments, in spite of all vain efforts, perhaps it was this massive machinery, as sensitive as their fingertips, which kept them struggling with the unfathomable. When they grew weary at their electronic listening posts, when their eyes grew dim with looking at unrevealing dials and studying uneventful graphs, they could step outside their concrete cells and renew their dull spirits in communion with the giant mechanism they commanded, the silent, sensing instrument in which the smallest packets of energy, the smallest waves of matter, were detected in their headlong, eternal flight across the universe. It was the stethoscope with which they took the pulse of the all and noted the birth and death of stars, the probe with which, here on an insignificant planet of an undistinguished star on the edge of its galaxy, they explored the infinite.

Or perhaps it was not just the reality but the imagery, like poetry, which soothed their doubting souls, the bowl held up to catch Donne's falling star, the ear cocked to catch the suspected shout that faded to an indistinguishable murmur by the time it reached them. And one thousand miles above them was the giant, five-mile-in-diameter network, the largest radio telescope ever built, which men had cast into the heavens to catch the stars.

If they had the Big Ear for more than an occasional reference check, MacDonald thought practically, then they might get some results. But he knew the radio astronomers would never relinquish time to the frivolity of listening for signals that never came. It was only because of the Big Ear that the Project had inherited the Little Ear. There had been talk recently about a larger net, twenty miles in diameter. Perhaps when it was done, if it were done, the Project might inherit time on the Big Ear.

If they could endure until then, MacDonald thought, if they could steer their fragile vessel of faith between the Scylla of self-doubt and the Charybdis of Congressional appropriations.

The images were not all favorable. There were others that went boomp in the night. There was the image, for instance, of man listening, listening, listening to the silent stars, listening for an eternity, listening for signals that would never come, because—the ultimate horror—man was alone in the universe, a cosmic accident of self-awareness which needed and would never receive the comfort of companionship. To be alone, to be all alone, would be like being all alone on earth, with no one to talk to, ever—like being alone inside a bone prison, with no way to get out, no way to communicate with anyone outside, no way to know if anyone was outside. . . .

Perhaps that, in the end, was what kept them going—to stave off the terrors of the night. While they listened there was hope; to give up now would be to admit final defeat. Some said they should never have started; then they never would have the problem of surrender. Some of the new religions said that. The Solitarians, for one. There is nobody there; we are the one, the only created intelligence in the universe. Let us glory in our uniqueness. But the older religions encouraged the Project to continue. Why would God have created the myriads of other stars and other planets if He had not intended them for living creatures; why should man only be created in His image? Let us find out, they said. Let us communicate with them. What revelations have they had? What saviors have redeemed them?

These are the words which I spake unto you, while I was yet with you, that all things must be fulfilled, which were written in the law of Moses, and in the prophets, and in the psalms, concerning me. . . . Thus it is written, and thus it behoved Christ to suffer, and to rise from the dead the third day: and that repentance and remission of sins should be preached in his name among all nations, beginning at Jerusalem. And ye are witnesses of these things.

And, behold, I send the promise of my Father upon you: but tarry ye in the city of Jerusalem, until ye be endued with power from on high.

Dusk had turned to night. The sky had turned to black. The stars had been born again. The listening had begun. MacDonald made his way to his car in the parking lot behind the building, coasted until he was behind the hill, and turned on the motor for the long drive home.

85

The hacienda was dark. It had that empty feeling about it that MacDonald knew so well, the feeling it had for him when Maria went to visit friends in Mexico City. But it was not empty now. Maria was here.

He opened the door and flicked on the hall light. "Maria?" He walked down the tiled hall, not too fast, not too slow. "¿Querida?" He turned on the living room light as he passed. He continued down the hall, past the dining room, the guest room, the study, the kitchen. He reached the dark doorway to the bedroom. "Maria Chavez?"

He turned on the bedroom light, low. She was asleep, her face peaceful, her dark hair scattered across the pillow. She lay on her side, her legs drawn up under the covers.

> *Men che dramma*
> *Di sangue m'e rimaso, che no tremi;*
> *Conosco i segni dell' antica fiamma.*

MacDonald looked down at her, comparing her features one by one with those he had fixed in his memory. Even now, with those dark, expressive eyes closed, she was the most beautiful woman he had ever seen. What glories they had known! He renewed his spirit in the warmth of his remembrances, recalling moments with loving details.

C'est de quoy j'ay le plus de peur que la peur.

He sat down upon the edge of the bed and leaned over to kiss her upon the cheek and then upon her upthrust shoulder where the gown had slipped down. She did not waken. He shook her shoulder gently. "Maria!" She turned upon her back, straightening. She sighed, and her eyes came open, staring blankly. "It is Robby," MacDonald said, dropping unconsciously into a faint brogue.

Her eyes came alive and her lips smiled sleepily. "Robby. You're home."

"Yo te amo," he murmured, and kissed her. As he pulled himself away, he said, "I'll start dinner. Wake up and get dressed. I'll see you in half an hour. Or sooner."

"Sooner," she said.

He turned and went to the kitchen. There was romaine lettuce in the refrigerator, and as he rummaged further, some thin slices of veal. He prepared Caesar salad and veal scallopine, doing it all quickly, expertly. He liked to cook. The salad was ready, and the lemon juice, tarragon, white wine, and a minute later, the beef bouillon had been added to the browned veal when Maria appeared.

She stood in the doorway, slim, lithe, lovely, and sniffed the air. "I smell something delicious."

It was a joke. When Maria cooked, she cooked Mexican, something peppery that burned all the way into the stomach and lay there like a banked furnace. When MacDonald cooked, it was something exotic—French, perhaps, or Italian, or Chinese. But whoever cooked, the other had to appreciate it or take over all the cooking for a week.

MacDonald filled their wine glasses. *"A la très-bonne, à la très-belle,"* he said, *"qui fait ma joie et ma santé."*

"To the Project," Maria said. "May there be a signal received tonight."

MacDonald shook his head. One should not mention what one desires too much. "Tonight there is only us."

Afterward there were only the two of them, as there had been now for twenty years. And she was as alive and as urgent, as filled with love and laughter, as when they first had been together.

At last the urgency was replaced by a vast ease and contentment in which for a time the thought of the Project faded into something remote which one day he would return to and finish. "Maria," he said.

"Robby?"

"Yo te amo, corazón."

"Yo te amo, Robby."

Gradually then, as he waited beside her for her breathing to slow, the Project returned. When he thought she was asleep, he got up and began to dress in the dark.

"Robby?" Her voice was awake and frightened.

"¿Querida?"

"You are going again?"

"I didn't want to wake you."

"Do you have to go?"

"It's my job."

"Just this once. Stay with me tonight."

He turned on the light. In the dimness he could see that her face was concerned but not hysterical. *"Rast ich, so rost ich.* Besides, I would feel ashamed."

"I understand. Go, then. Come home soon."

He put out two pills on the little shelf in the bathroom and put the others away again.

The headquarters building was busiest at night when the radio noise of the sun was least and listening to the stars was best. Girls bustled down the halls with coffee pots, and men stood near the water fountain, talking earnestly.

MacDonald went into the control room. Adams was at the control panel; Montaleone was the technician. Adams looked up, pointed to his earphones with a gesture of futility, and shrugged. MacDonald nodded at him, nodded at Montaleone, and glanced at the graph. It looked random to him.

Adams leaned past him to point out a couple of peaks. "These might be something." He had removed the earphones.

"Odds," MacDonald said.

"Suppose you're right. The computer hasn't sounded any alarms."

"After a few years of looking at these things, you get the feel of them. You begin to think like a computer."

"Or you get oppressed by failure."

"There's that."

The room was shiny and efficient, glass and metal and plastic, all smooth and sterile; and it smelled like electricity. MacDonald knew that electricity had no smell, but that was the way he thought of it. Perhaps it was the ozone that smelled or warm insulation or oil. Whatever it was, it wasn't worth the time to find out, and MacDonald didn't really want to know. He would rather think of it as the smell of electricity. Perhaps that was why he was a failure as a scientist. "A scientist is a man who wants to know why," his teachers always had told him.

MacDonald leaned over the control panel and flicked a switch. A thin, hissing noise filled the room. It was something like air escaping from an inner tube—a susurration of surreptitious sibilants from subterranean sessions of seething serpents.

He turned a knob and the sound became what someone—Tennyson?—had called "the murmuring of innumerable bees." Again, and it became Matthew Arnold's

> . . . *melancholy, long withdrawing roar*
> *Retreating, to the breath*
> *Of the night wind, down the vast edges drear*
> *And naked shingles of the world.*

He turned the knob once more, and the sound was a babble of distant voices, some shouting, some screaming, some conversing calmly, some whispering—all of them trying beyond desperation to communicate, and everything just below the level of intelligibility. If he closed his eyes, MacDonald could almost see their faces, pressed against a distant screen, distorted with the awful effort to make themselves heard and understood.

But they all insisted on speaking at once. MacDonald wanted to shout at them. "Silence, everybody! All but you— there, with the purple antenna. One at a time and we'll listen to all of you if it takes a hundred years or a hundred lifetimes."

"Sometimes," Adams said, "I think it was a mistake to put in the speaker system. You begin to anthropomorphize. After a while you begin to hear things. Sometimes you even get messages. I don't listen to the voices any more. I used to wake up in the night with someone whispering to me. I was just on the verge of getting the message that would solve everything, and I would wake up." He flicked off the switch.

"Maybe someday somebody will get the message," MacDonald said. "That's what the audio frequency translation is intended to do. To keep the attention focused. It can mesmerize and it can torment, but these are the conditions out of which spring inspiration."

"Also madness," Adams said. "You've got to be able to continue."

"Yes." MacDonald picked up the earphones Adams had put down and held one of them to his ear.

"Tico-tico, tico-tico," it sang. "They're listening in Puerto Rico. Listening for words that never come. Tico-tico, tico-tico. They're listening in Puerto Rico. Can it be the stars are stricken dumb?"

MacDonald put the earphones down and smiled. "Maybe there's inspiration in that, too."

"At least it takes my mind off the futility."

"Maybe off the job, too? Do you really want to find anyone out there?"

"Why else would I be here? But there are times when I wonder if we would not be better off not knowing."

"We all think that sometimes," MacDonald said.

In his office he attacked the stack of papers and letters again. When he had worked his way to the bottom, he sighed and got up, stretching. He wondered if he would feel better, less frustrated, less uncertain, if he were working on the

Problem instead of just working so somebody else could work on the Problem. But somebody had to do it. Somebody had to keep the Project going, personnel coming in, funds in the bank, bills paid, feathers smoothed.

Maybe it was more important that he do all the dirty little work in the office. Of course it was routine. Of course Lily could do it as well as he. But it was important that he do it, that there be somebody in charge who believed in the Project —or who never let his doubts be known.

Like the Little Ear, he was a symbol—and it is by symbols men live—or refuse to let their despair overwhelm them.

The janitor was waiting for him in the outer office.

"Can I see you, Mr. MacDonald?" the janitor said.

"Of course, Joe," MacDonald said, locking the door of his office carefully behind him. "What is it?"

"It's my teeth, sir." The old man got to his feet and with a deft movement of his tongue and mouth dropped his teeth into his hand.

MacDonald stared at them with a twinge of revulsion. There was nothing wrong with them. They were a carefully constructed pair of false teeth, but they looked too real. MacDonald always had shuddered away from those things which seemed to be what they were not, as if there were some treachery in them.

"They talk to me, Mr. MacDonald," the janitor mumbled, staring at the teeth in his hand with what seemed like suspicion. "In the glass beside my bed at night, they whisper to me. About things far off, like. Messages, like."

MacDonald stared at the janitor. It was a strange word for the old man to use, and hard to say without teeth. Still, the word had been "messages." But why should it be strange? He could have picked it up around the offices or the laboratories. It would be odd, indeed, if he had not picked up something about what was going on. Of course: messages.

"I've heard of that sort of thing happening," MacDonald said. "False teeth accidentally constructed into a kind of crystal set, that pick up radio waves. Particularly near a powerful station. And we have a lot of stray frequencies floating around, what with the antennas and all. Tell you what, Joe. We'll make an appointment with the Project dentist to fix your teeth so that they don't bother you. Any small alteration should do it."

"Thank you, Mr. MacDonald," the old man said. He fitted

90

his teeth back into his mouth. "You're a great man, Mr. MacDonald."

MacDonald drove the ten dark miles to the hacienda with a vague feeling of unease, as if he had done something during the day or left something undone that should have been otherwise.

But the house was dark when he drove up in front, not empty-dark as it had seemed to him a few hours before, but friendly-dark. Maria was asleep, breathing peacefully.

The house was brilliant with lighted windows that cast long fingers into the night, probing the dark hills, and the sound of many voices stirred echoes until the countryside itself seemed alive.

"Come in, Lily," MacDonald said at the door, and was reminded of a winter scene when a Lily had met the gentlemen at the door and helped them off with their overcoats. But that was another Lily and another occasion and another place and somebody else's imagination. "I'm glad you decided to come." He had a can of beer in his hand, and he waved it in the general direction of the major center of noisemaking. "There's beer in the living room and something more potent in the study—190 proof grain alcohol, to be precise. Be careful with that. It will sneak up on you. But—*nunc est bibendum!*"

"Where's Mrs. MacDonald?" Lily asked.

"Back there, somewhere." MacDonald waved again. "The men, and a few brave women, are in the study. The women, and a few brave men, are in the living room. The kitchen is common territory. Take your choice."

"I really shouldn't have come," Lily said. "I offered to spell Mr. Saunders in the control room, but he said I hadn't been checked out. It isn't as if the computer couldn't handle it all alone, and I know enough to call somebody if anything unexpected should happen."

"Shall I tell you something, Lily?" MacDonald said. "The computer could do it alone. And you and the computer could do it better than any of us, including me. But if the men ever feel that they are unnecessary, they would feel more useless than ever. They would give up. And they mustn't do that."

"Oh, Mac!" Lily said.

"They mustn't do that. Because one of them is going to come up with the inspiraton that solves it all. Not me. One of them. We'll send somebody to relieve Charley before the evening is over."

Wer immer strebens sich bemüht,
Den können wir erlösen.

Lily sighed. "Okay, boss."

"And enjoy yourself!"

"Okay, boss, okay."

"Find a man, Lily," MacDonald muttered. And then he, too, turned toward the living room, for Lily had been the last who might come.

He listened for a moment at the doorway, sipping slowly from the warming can.

"—work more on gamma rays—"

"Who's got the money to build a generator? Since nobody's built one yet, we don't even know what it might cost."

"—gamma-ray sources should be a million times more rare than radio sources at twenty-one centimeters—"

"That's what Cocconi said nearly fifty years ago. The same arguments. Always the same arguments."

"If they're right, they're right."

"But the hydrogen-emission line is so uniquely logical. As Morrison said to Cocconi—and Cocconi, if you remember, agreed—it represents a logical, prearranged rendezvous point. 'A unique, objective standard of frequency, which must be known to every observer of the universe,' was the way they put it."

"—but the noise level—"

MacDonald smiled and moved on to the kitchen for a cold can of beer.

"—Bracewell's 'automated messengers'?" a voice asked querulously.

"What about them?"

"Why aren't we looking for them?"

"The point of Bracewell's messengers is that they make themselves known to us!"

"Maybe there's something wrong with ours. After a few million years in orbit—"

"—laser beams make more sense."

"And get lost in all that star shine?"

"As Schwartz and Townes pointed out, all you have to do is select a wavelength of light that is absorbed by stellar atmospheres. Put a narrow laser beam in the center of one of the calcium absorption lines—"

In the study they were talking about quantum noise.

"Quantum noise favors low frequencies."

"But the noise itself sets a lower limit on those frequencies."

"Drake calculated the most favorable frequencies, considering the noise level, lie between 3.2 and 8.1 centimeters."

"Drake! Drake! What did he know? We've had nearly fifty years experience on him. Fifty years of technological advance. Fifty years ago we could send radio messages one thousand light-years and laser signals ten light-years. Today those figures are ten thousand and five hundred at least."

"What if nobody's there?" Adams said gloomily.

Ich bin der Geist der stets verneint.

"Short-pulse it, like Oliver suggested. One hundred million billion watts in a ten billionth of a second would smear across the entire radio spectrum. Here, Mac, fill this, will you?"

And MacDonald wandered away through the clustering guests toward the bar.

"And I told Charley," said a woman to two other women in the corner, "if I had a dime for every dirty diaper I've changed, I sure wouldn't be sitting here in Puerto Rico—"

"—neutrinos," said somebody.

"Nuts," said somebody else, as MacDonald poured grain alcohol carefully into the glass and filled it with orange juice, "the only really logical medium is Q waves."

"I know—the waves we haven't discovered yet but are going to discover about ten years from now. Only here it is nearly fifty years after Morrison suggested it, and we still haven't discovered them."

MacDonald wended his way back across the room.

"It's the night work that gets me," said someone's wife. "The kids up all day, and then he wants me there to greet him when he gets home at dawn. Brother!"

"Or what if everybody's listening?" Adams said gloomily. "Maybe everybody's sitting there, listening, just the way we are, because it's so much cheaper than sending."

"Here you are," MacDonald said.

"But don't you suppose somebody would have thought of that by this time and begun to send?"

"Double-think it all the way through and figure what just occurred to you would have occurred to everybody else, so you might as well listen. Think about it—everybody sitting around, listening. If there is anybody. Either way it makes the skin creep."

"All right, then, we ought to send something."

"What would you send?"

"I'd have to think about it. Prime numbers, maybe."

"Think some more. What if a civilization weren't mathematical?"

"Idiot! How would they build an antenna?"

"Maybe they'd rule-of-thumb it, like a ham. Or maybe they have built-in antennae."

"And maybe you have built-in antennae and don't know it."

MacDonald's can of beer was empty. He wandered back toward the kitchen again.

"—insist on equal time with the Big Ear. Even if nobody's sending we could pick up the normal electronic commerce of a civilization tens of light-years away. The problem would be deciphering, not hearing."

"They're picking it up now, when they're studying the relatively close systems. Ask for a tape and work out your program."

"All right, I will. Just give me a chance to work up a request—"

MacDonald found himself beside Maria. He put his arm around her waist and pulled her close. "All right?" he said.

"All right."

Her face was tired, though, MacDonald thought. He dreaded the notion that she might be growing older, that she was entering middle age. He could face it for himself. He could feel the years piling up inside his bones. He still thought of himself, inside, as twenty, but he knew that he was forty-seven, and mostly he was glad that he had found happiness and love and peace and serenity. He even was willing to pay the price in youthful exuberance and belief in his personal immortality. But not Maria!

Nel mezzo del cammin di nostra vita
Mi ritrovai per una selva oscura,
Che la diritta via era smarrita.

"Sure?"

She nodded.

He leaned close to her ear. "I wish it was just the two of us, as usual."

"I, too."

"I'm going to leave in a little while—"

"Must you?"

"I must relieve Saunders. He's on duty. Give him an opportunity to celebrate a little with the others."

"Can't you send somebody else?"

"Who?" MacDonald gestured with good-humored futility at all the clusters of people held together by bonds of ordered sounds shared consecutively. "It's a good party. No one will miss me."

"I will."

"Of course, *querida*."

"You are their mother, father, priest, all in one," Maria said. "You worry about them too much."

"I must keep them together. What else am I good for?"

"For much more."

MacDonald hugged her with one arm.

"Look at Mac and Maria, will you?" said someone who was having trouble with his consonants. "What god-damned devotion!"

MacDonald smiled and suffered himself to be pounded on the back while he protected Maria in front of him. "I'll see you later," he said.

As he passed the living room someone was saying, "Like Eddie said, we ought to look at the long-chain molecules in carbonaceous chondrites. No telling how far they've traveled —or been sent—or what messages might be coded in the molecules."

As he closed the front door behind him, the noise dropped to a roar and then a mutter. He stopped for a moment at the door of the car and looked up at the sky.

E quindi uscimmo a riveder le stelle.

The noise from the hacienda reminded him of something— the speakers in the control room. All those voices talking, talking, talking, and from here he could not understand a thing.

Somewhere there was an idea if he could only concentrate on it hard enough. But he had drunk one beer too many—or perhaps one too few.

After the long hours of listening to the voices, MacDonald always felt a little crazy, but tonight it was worse than usual.

Perhaps it was all the conversation before, or the beers, or something else—some deeper concern that would not surface.

But then the listeners had to be crazy to begin with—to get committed to a project that might go for centuries without results.

Tico-tico, tico-tico. . . .

Even if they could pick up a message, they still would likely be dead and gone before any exchange could take place even with the nearest likely star. What kind of mad dedication could sustain such perseverance?

They're listening in Puerto Rico. . . .

Religion could. At least once it did, during the era of cathedral building in Europe, the cathedrals that took centuries to build.

"What are you doing, fellow?"

"I'm working for ten francs a day."

"And what are you doing?"

"I'm laying stone."

"And you—what are you doing?"

"I am building a cathedral."

They were building cathedrals, most of them. Most of them had that religious mania about their mission that would sustain them through a lifetime of labors in which no progress could be seen.

Listening for words that never come. . . .

The mere layers of stone and those who worked for pay alone eliminated themselves in time and left only those who kept alive in themselves the concept, the dream.

But they had to be a little mad to begin with.

Can it be the stars are stricken dumb?

Tonight he had heard the voices nearly all night long. They kept trying to tell him something, something urgent, something he should do, but he could not quite make out the words. There was only the babble of distant voices, urgent and unintelligible.

Tico-tico, tico-tic. . . .

He had wanted to shout "Shut up!" to the universe. "One at a time!" "You first!" But of course there was no way to do that. Or had he tried? Had he shouted?

They're listening with ears this big!

Had he dozed at the console with the voices mumbling in his ears, or had he only thought he dozed? Or had he only dreamed he waked. Or dreamed he dreamed?

96

Listening for thoughts just like their own.

There was a madness to it all, but perhaps it was a divine madness, a creative madness. And is not that madness that which sustains man in his terrible self-knowledge, the driving madness which demands reason of a casual universe, the awful aloneness which seeks among the stars for companionship?

Can it be that we are all alone?

The ringing of the telephone half penetrated through the mists of mesmerization. He picked up the handset, half expecting that it would be the universe calling, perhaps with a clipped British accent, "Hello there, Man. Hello. Hello. I say, we seem to have a bad connection, what? Just wanted you to know that we're here. Are you there? Are you listening? Message on the way. May not get there for a couple of centuries. Do be around to answer, will you? That's a good being. Righto. . . ."

Only it wasn't. It was the familiar American voice of Charley Saunders saying, "Mac, there's been an accident. Olsen is on his way to relieve you, but I think you'd better leave now. It's Maria."

Leave it. Leave it all. What does it matter? But leave the controls on automatic; the computer can take care of it all. Maria! Get in the car. Start it. Don't fumble! That's it. Go. Go. Car passing. Must be Olsen. No matter.

What kind of accident? Why didn't I ask? What does it matter what kind of accident? Maria. Nothing could have happened. Nothing serious. Not with all those people around. *Nil desperandum.* And yet—why did Charley call if it was not serious? Must be serious. I must be prepared for something bad, something that will shake the world, that will tear my insides.

I must not break up in front of them. Why not? Why must I appear infallible? Why must I always be cheerful, imperturbable, my faith unshaken? Why me? If there is something bad, if something impossibly bad has happened to Maria, what will matter? Ever? Why didn't I ask Charley what it was? Why? The bad can wait; it will get no worse for being unknown.

What does the universe care for my agony? I am nothing. My feelings are nothing to anyone but me. My only possible meaning to the universe is the Project. Only this slim potential links me with eternity. My love and my agony are me, but the significance of my life or death are the Project.

HIC·SITVS·EST·PHAETHON·CVRRVS·AVRIGA·PATERNI
QVEM·SI·NON·TENVTI·MAGNIS·TAMEN·EXCIDIT·AVSIS

By the time he reached the hacienda, MacDonald was breathing evenly. His emotions were under control. Dawn had grayed the eastern sky. It was a customary hour for Project personnel to be returning home.

Saunders met him at the door. "Dr. Lessenden is here. He's with Maria."

The odor of stale smoke and the memory of babble still lingered in the air, but someone had been busy. The party remains had been cleaned up. No doubt they all had pitched in. They were good people.

"Betty found her in the bathroom off your bedroom. She wouldn't have been there except the others were occupied. I blame myself. I shouldn't have let you relieve me. Maybe if you had been here—But I knew you wanted it that way."

"No one's to blame. She was alone a great deal," Mac-Donald said. "What happened?"

"Didn't I tell you? Her wrists. Slashed with a razor. Both of them. Betty found her in the bathtub. Like pink lemonade, she said."

Percé jusques au fond du coeur
D'une atteinte imprévue aussi bien que mortelle.

A fist tightened inside MacDonald's gut and then slowly relaxed. Yes, it had been that. He had known it, hadn't he? He had known it would happen ever since the sleeping pills, even though he had kept telling himself, as she had told him, that the overdose had been an accident.

Or had he known? He knew only that Saunders' news had been no surprise.

Then they were at the bedroom door, and Maria was lying under a blanket on the bed, scarcely making it mound over her body, and her arms were on top of the blankets, palms up, bandages like white paint across the olive perfection of her arms, now, MacDonald reminded himself, no longer perfection but marred with ugly red lips that spoke of hidden misery and untold sorrow and a life that was a lie. . . .

Dr. Lessenden looked up, sweat trickling down from his hairline. "The bleeding is stopped, but she's lost a good deal of blood. I've got to take her to the hospital for a transfusion. The ambulance should be here any minute." He paused. MacDonald looked at Maria's face. It was paler than he had ever seen it. It looked almost waxen, as if it were already arranged for all time on a satin pillow. "Her chances are fifty-fifty," Lessenden said in answer to his unspoken question.

And then the attendants brushed their way past him with their litter.

"Betty found this on her dressing table," Saunders said. He handed MacDonald a slip of paper folded once.

MacDonald unfolded it: *Je m'en vay chercher un grand Peut-être.*

Everyone was surprised to see MacDonald at the office. They did not say anything, and he did not volunteer the information that he could not bear to sit at home, among the remembrances, and wait for word to come. But they asked him about Maria, and he said, "Dr. Lessenden is hopeful. She's still unconscious. Apparently will be for some time. The doctor said I might as well wait here as at the hospital. I think I made them nervous. They're hopeful. Maria's still unconscious. . . ."

O lente, lente currite, noctis equi!

The stars move still, time runs, the clock will strike. . . .

Finally MacDonald was alone. He pulled out paper and pencil and worked for a long time on the statement, and then he balled it up and threw it into the wastebasket, scribbled a single sentence on another sheet of paper, and called Lily.

"Send this!"

She glanced at it. "No, Mac."

"Send it!"

"But—"

"It's not an impulse. I've thought it over carefully. Send it."

Slowly she left, holding the piece of paper gingerly in her fingertips. MacDonald pushed the papers around on his desk, waiting for the telephone to ring. But without knocking, unannounced, Saunders came through the door first.

"You can't do this, Mac," Saunders said.

MacDonald sighed. "Lily told you. I would fire that girl if she weren't so loyal."

"Of course she told me. This isn't just you. It affects the whole Project."

"That's what I'm thinking about."

"I think I know what you're going through, Mac—" Saunders stopped. "No, of course I don't know what you're going through. It must be hell. But don't desert us. Think of the Project!"

"That's what I'm thinking about. I'm a failure, Charley. Everything I touch—ashes."

"You're the best of us."

"A poor linguist? An indifferent engineer? I have no qualifications for this job, Charley. You need someone with ideas to head the Project, someone dynamic, someone who can lead, someone with—charisma."

A few minutes later he went over it all again with Olsen. When he came to the qualifications part, all Olsen could say was, "You give a good party, Mac."

It was Adams, the skeptic, who affected him most. "Mac, you're what I believe in instead of God."

Sonnenborn said, "You are the Project. If you go, it all falls apart. It's over."

"It seems like it, always, but it never happens to those things that have life in them. The Project was here before I came. It will be here after I leave. It must be longer lived than any of us, because we are for the years and it is for the centuries."

After Sonnenborn, MacDonald told Lily wearily, "No more, Lily."

None of them had had the courage to mention Maria, but MacDonald considered that failure, too. She had tried to communicate with him a month ago when she took the pills, and he had been unable to understand. How could he riddle the stars when he couldn't even understand those closest to him? Now he had to pay.

> *Meine Ruh' ist hin,*
> *Meine Herz ist schwer.*

What would Maria want? He knew what she wanted, but if she lived, he could not let her pay that price. Too long she had been there when he wanted her, waiting like a doll put away on a shelf for him to return and take her down, so that he could have the strength to continue.

And somehow the agony had built up inside her, the dreadful progress of the years, most dread of all to a beautilful woman growing old, alone, too much alone. He had been selfish. He had kept her to himself. He had not wanted children to mar the perfection of their being together.

Perfection for him; less than that for her.

Perhaps it was not too late for them if she lived. And if she died—he would not have the heart to go on with work to which, he knew now, he could contribute nothing.

> *Que acredito su ventura,*
> *Morir querdo y vivir loco.*

And finally the call came. "She's going to be all right, Mac," Lessenden said. And after a moment, "Mac, I said—"

"I heard."

"She wants to see you."

"I'll be there."

"She said to give you a message. 'Tell Robby I've been a little crazy in the head. I'll be better now. That "great perhaps" looks too certain from here. And tell him not to be crazy in the head, too.' "

MacDonald put down the telephone and walked through the doorway and through the outer office, a feeling in his chest as if it were going to burst. "She's going to be all right," he threw over his shoulder at Lily.

"Oh, Mac—"

In the hall, Joe the janitor stopped him. "Mr. Mac-Donald—"

MacDonald stopped. "Been to the dentist yet, Joe?"

"No, sir, not yet, but it's not—"

"Don't go. I'd like to put a tape recorder beside your bed for a while, Joe. Who knows?"

"Thank you, sir. But it's— They say you're leaving, Mr. MacDonald."

"Somebody else will do it."

"You don't understand. Don't go, Mr. MacDonald!"

"Why not, Joe?"

"You're the one who cares."

MacDonald had been about to move on, but that stopped him.

Ful wys is he that can himselven knowe!

He turned and went back to the office. "Have you got that sheet of paper, Lily?"

"Yes, sir."

"Have you sent it?"

"No, sir."

"Bad girl. Give it to me."

He read the sentence on the paper once more: *I have great confidence in the goals and ultimate success of the Project, but for personal reasons I must submit my resignation.*

He studied it for a moment.

Pigmæi gigantum humeris impositi plusquam ipsi gigantes vidant.

And he tore it up.

TRANSLATIONS

1. *Pues no es possible . . .*
   The bow cannot always stand bent, nor can human frailty subsist without some lawful recreation.

   Cervantes, *Don Quixote*

2. *Habe nun, ach! Philosophie, . . .*
   Now I have studied philosophy,
   Medicine and the law,
   And, unfortunately, theology,
   Wearily sweating, yet I stand now,
   Poor fool, no wiser than I was before;
   I am called Master, even Doctor,
   And for these last ten years have drawn
   My students, by the nose, up, down,
   Crosswise and crooked. Now I see
   That we can know nothing finally.

   Goethe, *Faust*, opening lines

3. *Men che dramma . . .*
   Less than a drop
   Of blood remains in me that does not tremble;
   I recognize the signals of the ancient flame.

   Dante, *The Divine Comedy*,
   Purgatorio

4. *C'est de quoy j'ay le plus de peur que la peur.*
   The thing of which I have most fear is fear.

   Montaigne, *Essays*

5. *A la très-bonne, à la très-belle, qui fait ma joie et ma santé.*
   To the best, to the most beautiful, who is my joy and my well-being.

   Baudelaire, *Les Epaves*

6. *Rast ich, so rost ich.*
   When I rest, I rust.

   German proverb

7. *Nunc est bibendum!*
   Now's the time for drinking!

   Horace, *Odes,* Book I

8. *Wer immer strebens sich bemüht, . . .*
   Who strives always to the utmost,
   Him can we save.

   Goethe, *Faust,* Part I

9. *Ich bin der Geist der stets verneint.*
   I am the spirit that always denies.

   Goethe, *Faust,* Part I

10. *Nel mezzo del cammin di nostra vita . . .*
    In the middle of the journey of our life
    I came to myself in a dark wood,
    Where the straight way was lost.

    Dante, *The Divine Comedy,*
    Inferno, opening lines

11. *E quindi uscimmo a riveder le stelle.*
    And thence we issued out, again to see the stars.

    Dante, *The Divine Comedy,*
    Inferno

12. *Nil desperandum.*
    There's no cause for despair.

    Horace, *Odes,* Book I

13. *HIC · SITVS · EST · PHAETHON · CVRRVS · AVRIGA · PATERNI . . .*
    Here Phaeton lies: in Phoebus' car he fared,
    And though he greatly failed, more greatly dared.

    Ovid, *Metamorphoses*

14. *Percé jusques au fond du coeur . . .*
   Pierced to the depth of my heart
   By a blow unforeseen and mortal.

   Corneille, *Le Cid*

15. *Je m'en vay chercher un grand Peut-être.*
   I am going to seek a great Perhaps.

   Rabelais on his deathbed

16. *O lente, lente currite, noctis equi!*
   Oh, slowly, slowly run, horses of the night!

   Marlowe, *Dr. Faustus*

   (Faustus is quoting Ovid. He waits for Mephistopheles to appear to claim his soul at midnight. The next line: "The devil will come and Faustus must be damn'd.")

17. *Mein, Ruh' ist hin, . . .*
   My peace is gone,
   My heart is heavy.

   Goethe, *Faust*, Part I

18. *Que acredito su ventura, . . .*
   For if he like a madman lived,
   At least he like a wise one died.

   Cervantes, *Don Quixote*
   (Don Quixote's epitaph)

19. *Ful wys is he that can himselven knowe!*
   Very wise is he that can know himself!

   Chaucer, *The Canterbury
   Tales*, "The Monk's Tale"

20. *Pigmæi gigantum humeris impositi plusquam ipsi gigantes vidant.*
   A dwarf standing on the shoulder of a giant may see further than the giant himself.

   Didacus Stella, in
   Lucan, *De Bello Civili*

DRAGONRIDER

Anne McCaffrey

Editor's note: What follows is self-contained and self-explanatory. That's obvious; how else could it have won an award? At the same time, it is the concluding half of a larger work, part of which appeared in Nebula Three. *Therefore Karen Anderson has prepared a synopsis of what went before. You may well prefer to skip that and go directly on to the gorgeously colored world of dragons and their riders which Anne McCaffrey has created for you. On the other hand, many travelers prefer to read a guidebook before they leave home.*

On the world called Pern, the human inhabitants have no tradition of Earth or of space travel. There is a legendary vagueness about the menace of the Threads wh:ch fall when the freakish orbit of the Red Star (a captured planet) brings it close to Pern. Though nobles and commoners are in awe of the Dragons and the elite corps who ride them, they are ignorant of the nature of the powers bred into both Dragons and riders.

In the Hold of Ruatha, young Lessa had for half her life used her inborn mental powers to camouflage herself from the men of Fax, the brigand lord who slaughtered her entire family to secure his seizure of their Hold. She also managed, by small subtle interferences, to disrupt all the workings of Ruatha, so that Fax had no profit from his conquest.

Fax did not know of her existence; but when the dragonrider F'lar inspected Fax's Holds in search of a potential Weyrwoman, he knew that someone at Ruatha had the abilities he was looking for—especially when he realized that he had been maneuvered into a duel with Fax. The latter dead, Lessa claimed Ruatha. But in the fury to which she had

 Nebula Award, Best Novella 1968

provoked him, Fax had renounced this unprofitable Hold in favor of his youngest son, born that night. F'lar told Lessa that the infant's claim must stand, but that she had the Power needed in a Weyrwoman. She agreed to go with him to the Weyr.

This had fallen very low in prestige, due in part to the incompetence of the last Weyrwoman, Jora, now dead. The last clutch of the dying queen-dragon Nemorth included one queen-egg; they had been sired by Hath, and consequently his rider R'gul was Weyrleader.

On hatching, the queen-chick chose Lessa after clumsily injuring two other candidates. At the moment their eyes met, their minds joined in joyful rapport. Lessa and the golden dragon Ramoth would now be devoted to each other for the rest of their lives.

R'gul remained Weyrleader while Ramoth grew up, and taught Lessa her duties. Meanwhile few Holds sent tithes and the Lords of the others called the dragonriders parasites, the legendary Threads a lie. After Lessa secretly encouraged raids on the herds of disaffected Holds to make up the shortage of food, there was active revolt. But by the time troops marched on the Weyr, the situation had drastically changed. Ramoth, now two Turns old, was full-grown and larger even than F'lar's bronze Mnementh. She had made her nuptial flight, and Mnementh had claimed her. Their rapport with the dragons brought F'lar and Lessa together with the same passion.

The new Weyrleader F'lar was quick-witted and decisive: he sent parties of dragonriders to make hostages of the womenfolk of the rebel lords. Their Holds were unguarded, for they had forgotten that a dragon can fly *between*, passing almost instantly from one place to another. So the tithes would be paid; the Weyr would prosper again.

> The Finger points
> At an Eye blood-red.
> Alert the Weyrs
> To sear the Thread.

"You STILL doubt, R'gul?" F'lar asked, appearing slightly amused by the older bronze rider's perversity.

R'gul, his handsome features stubbornly set, made no reply

to the Weyrleader's taunt. He ground his teeth together as if he could grind away F'lar's authority over him.

"There have been no Threads in Pern's skies for over four hundred Turns. There are no more!"

"There is always that possibility," F'lar conceded amiably. There was not, however, the slightest trace of tolerance in his amber eyes. Nor the slightest hint of compromise in his manner.

He was more like F'lon, his sire, R'gul decided, than a son had any right to be. Always so sure of himself, always slightly contemptuous of what others did and thought. Arrogant, that's what F'lar was. Impertinent, too, and underhanded in the matter of that young Weyrwoman. Why, R'gul had trained her up to be one of the finest Weyrwomen in many Turns. Before he'd finished her instruction, she'd known all the Teaching Ballads and Sagas letter-perfect. And then the silly child had turned to F'lar. Didn't have sense enough to appreciate the merits of an older, more experienced man. Undoubtedly she felt a first obligation to F'lar for discovering her on Search.

"You do, however," F'lar was saying, "admit that when the sun hits the Finger Rock at the moment of dawn, winter solstice has been reached?"

"Any fool knows that's what the Finger Rock is for," R'gul grunted.

"Then why don't you, you old fool, admit that the Eye Rock was placed on Star Stone to bracket the Red Star when it's about to make a Pass?" burst out K'net.

R'gul flushed, half-starting out of his chair, ready to take the young sprout to task for such insolence.

"K'net!" F'lar's voice cracked authoritatively. "Do you really like flying the Igen patrol so much you want another few weeks at it?"

K'net hurriedly seated himself, flushing at the reprimand and the threat.

"There is, you know, R'gul, incontrovertible evidence to support my conclusions," F'lar went on with deceptive mildness. " 'The Finger points/At an Eye blood-red . . .' "

"Don't quote me verses I taught you as a weyrling," R'gul exclaimed heatedly.

"Then have faith in what you taught," F'lar snapped back, his amber eyes flashing dangerously.

R'gul, stunned by the unexpected forcefulness, sank back into his chair.

"You cannot deny, R'gul," F'lar continued quietly, "that no less than half an hour ago the sun balanced on the Finger's tip at dawn and the Red Star was squarely framed by the Eye Rock."

The other dragonriders, bronze as well as brown, murmured and nodded their agreement to that phenomenon. There was also an undercurrent of resentment for R'gul's continual contest of F'lar's policies as the new Weyrleader. Even old S'lel, once R'gul's avowed supporter, was following the majority.

"There have been no Threads in four hundred Turns. There are no Threads," R'gul muttered.

"Then, my fellow dragonman," F'lar said cheerfully, "all you have taught is falsehood. The dragons are, as the Lords of the Holds wish to believe, parasites on the economy of Pern, anachronisms. And so are we.

"Therefore, far be it from me to hold you here against the dictates of your conscience. You have my permission to leave the Weyr and take up residence where you will."

Someone laughed.

R'gul was too stunned by F'lar's ultimatum to take offense at the ridicule. Leave the Weyr? Was the man mad? Where would he go? The Weyr had been his life. He had been bred up to it for generations. All his male ancestors had been dragonriders. Not all bronze, true, but a decent percentage. His own dam's sire had been a Weyrleader just as he, R'gul, had been until F'lar's Mnementh had flown the new queen.

But dragonmen never left the Weyr. Well, they did if they were negligent enough to lose their dragons, like that Lytol fellow at Ruath Hold. And how could he leave the Weyr *with* a dragon?

What did F'lar want of him? Was it not enough that he was Weyrleader now in R'gul's stead? Wasn't F'lar's pride sufficiently swollen by having bluffed the Lords of Pern into disbanding their army when they were all set to coerce the Weyr and dragonmen? Must F'lar dominate *every* dragonman, body and will, too? He stared a long moment, incredulous.

"I do not believe we are parasites," F'lar said, breaking the silence with a soft, persuasive voice. "Nor anachronistic. There have been long Intervals before. The Red Star does not always pass close enough to drop Threads on Pern. Which is why our ingenious ancestors thought to position the Eye Rock and the Finger Rock as they did . . . to confirm *when* a Pass will be made. And another thing"—his face turned grave—"there have been other times when dragonkind has all but died out . . . and Pern with it because of skeptics like you." F'lar smiled and relaxed indolently in his chair. "I prefer not to be recorded as a skeptic. How shall we record you, R'gul?"

The Council Room was tense. R'gul was aware of someone breathing harshly and realized it was himself. He looked at the adamant face of the young Weyrleader and knew that the threat was not empty. He would either concede to F'lar's authority completely, though concession rankled deeply, or leave the Weyr.

And where could he go, unless to one of the other Weyrs, deserted for hundreds of Turns? And—R'gul's thoughts were savage—wasn't that indication enough of the cessation of Threads? Five empty Weyrs? No, by the Egg of Faranth, he would practice some of F'lar's own brand of deceit and bide his time. When all Pern turned on the arrogant fool, he, R'gul, would be there to salvage something from the ruins.

"A dragonman stays in his Weyr," R'gul said with what dignity he could muster.

"And accepts the policies of the current Weyrleader?" The tone of F'lar's voice made it less of a question and more of an order.

So as not to perjure himself, R'gul gave a curt nod of his head. F'lar continued to stare at him and R'gul wondered if the man could read his thoughts as his dragon might. He managed to return the gaze calmly. His turn would come. He'd wait.

Apparently accepting the capitulation, F'lar stood up and crisply delegated patrol assignments for the day.

"T'bor, you're weather-watch. Keep an eye on those tithing trains as you do. Have you the morning's report?"

"Weather is fair at dawning . . . all across Telgar and Keroon . . . if all too cold," T'bor said with a wry grin. "Tithing trains have good hard roads, though, so they ought to be here soon." His eyes twinkled with anticipation of the feasting that would follow the supplies' arrival—a mood shared by all, to judge by the expressions around the table.

F'lar nodded. "S'lan and D'nol, you are to continue an adroit Search for likely boys. They should be striplings, if possible, but do not pass over anyone suspected of talent.

It's all well and good to present for Impression boys reared up in the Weyr traditions." F'lar gave a one-sided smile. "But there are not enough in the Lower Caverns. We, too, have been behind in begetting. Anyway, dragons reach full growth faster than their riders. We must have more young *men* to Impress when Ramoth hatches. Take the southern holds, Ista, Nerat, Fort, and South Boll where maturity comes earlier. You can use the guise of inspecting Holds for greenery to talk to the boys. And take along firestone and run a few flaming passes on those heights that haven't been scoured in—oh—dragon's years. A flaming beast impresses the young and arouses envy."

F'lar deliberately looked at R'gul to see the ex-Weyrleader's reaction to the order. R'gul had been dead set against going outside the Weyr for more candidates. In the first place, R'gul had argued that there were eighteen youngsters in the Lower Caverns, some quite young, to be sure, but R'gul would not admit that Ramoth would lay more than the dozen Nemorth had always dropped. In the second place, R'gul persisted in wanting to avoid any action that might antagonize the Lords.

R'gul made no overt protest, and F'lar went on.

"K'net, back to the mines. I want the dispositions of each firestone-dump checked and quantities available. R'gul, continue drilling recognition points with the weyrlings. They must be positive about their references. If they're used as messengers and suppliers, they may be sent out quickly and with no time to ask questions.

"F'nor, T'sum"—F'lar turned to his own brown riders—"you're clean-up squad today." He allowed himself a grin at their dismay. "Try Ista Weyr. Clear the Hatching Cavern and enough weyrs for a double wing. And, F'nor, don't leave a single Record behind. They're worth preserving.

"That will be all, dragonmen. Good flying." And with that, F'lar rose and strode from the Council Room up to the queen's weyr.

Ramoth still slept, her hide gleaming with health, its color deepening to a shade of gold closer to bronze, indicating her pregnancy. As he passed her, the tip of her long tail twitched slightly.

All the dragons were restless these days, F'lar reflected. Yet when he asked Mnementh, the bronze dragon could give no reason. He woke, he went back to sleep. That was all. F'lar couldn't ask a leading question for that would defeat his purpose. He had to remain discontented with the vague fact that the restlessness was some kind of instinctive reaction.

Lessa was not in the sleeping room, nor was she still bathing. F'lar snorted. That girl was going to scrub her hide off with this constant bathing. She'd had to live grimy to protect herself in Ruath Hold, but bathing twice a day? He was beginning to wonder if this might be a subtle Lessa-variety insult to him personally. F'lar sighed. That girl. Would she never turn to him of her own accord? Would he ever touch that elusive inner core of Lessa? She had more warmth for his half brother, F'nor, and for K'net, the youngest of the bronze riders than she had for F'lar who shared her bed.

He pulled the curtain back into place, irritated. Where had she gone to today when, for the first time in weeks, he had been able to get all the wings out of the Weyr just so he could teach her to fly *between*?

Ramoth would soon be too egg-heavy for such activity. He had promised the Weyrwoman, and he meant to keep that promise. She had taken to wearing the wher-hide riding gear as a flagrant reminder of his unfulfilled pledge. From certain remarks she had dropped, he knew she would not wait much longer for his aid. That she would try it on her own didn't suit him at all.

He crossed the queen's weyr again and peered down the passage that led to the Records Room. She was often to be found there, poring over the musty skins. And that was one more matter that needed urgent consideration. Those Records were deteriorating past legibility. Curiously enough, earlier ones were still in good condition and readable. Another technique forgotten.

That girl! He brushed his thick forelock of hair back from his brow in a gesture habitual to him when he was annoyed or worried. The passage was dark, which meant she could not be below in the Records Room.

"Mnementh," he called silently to his bronze dragon, sunning on the ledge outside the queen's weyr. "What is that girl doing?"

Lessa, the dragon replied, stressing the Weyrwoman's name with pointed courtesy, *is talking to Manora. She's dressed for riding,* he added after a slight pause.

F'lar thanked the bronze sarcastically and strode down the passage to the entrance. As he turned the last bend, he all but ran Lessa down.

You hadn't asked me where *she was,* Mnementh plaintively answered F'lar's blistering reprimand.

Lessa rocked back on her heels from the force of their encounter. She glared up at him, her lips thin with displeasure, her eyes flashing.

"Why didn't I have the opportunity of seeing the Red Star through the Eye Rock?" she demanded in a hard, angry voice.

F'lar pulled at his hair. Lessa at her most difficult would complete the list of this morning's trials.

"Too many to accommodate on the Peak as it was," he muttered, determined not to let her irritate him today. "And you already believe."

"I'd've liked to see it," she snapped and pushed past him toward the weyr. "If only in my capacity as Weyrwoman and Recorder."

He caught her arm and felt her body tense. He set his teeth, wishing, as he had a hundred times since Ramoth rose in her first mating flight, that Lessa had not been virgin, too. He had not thought to control his dragon-incited emotions, and Lessa's first sexual experience had been violent. It had surprised him to be first, considering that her adolescent years had been spent drudging for lascivious warders and soldier-types. Evidently no one had bothered to penetrate the curtain of rags and the coat of filth she had carefully maintained as a disguise. He had been a considerate and gentle bedmate ever since, but, unless Ramoth and Mnementh were involved, he might as well call it rape.

Yet he knew someday, somehow, he would coax her into responding wholeheartedly to his lovemaking. He had a certain pride in his skill, and he was in a position to persevere.

Now he took a deep breath and released her arm slowly.

"How fortunate you're wearing riding gear. As soon as the wings have cleared out and Ramoth wakes, I shall teach you to fly *between.*"

The gleam of excitement in her eyes was evident even in the dimly lit passageway. He heard her inhale sharply.

"Can't put it off too much longer or Ramoth'll be in no shape to fly at all," he continued amiably.

"You mean it?" Her voice was low and breathless, its usual acid edge missing. "You will teach us today?" He wished he could see her face clearly.

Once or twice he had caught an unguarded expression on her face, loving and tender. He would give much to have

112

that look turned on him. However, he admitted wryly to himself, he ought to be glad that melting regard was directed only at Ramoth and not at another human.

"Yes, my dear Weyrwoman, I mean it. I will teach you to fly *between* today. If only," and he bowed to her with a flourish, "to keep you from trying it yourself."

Her low chuckle informed him his taunt was well-aimed.

"Right now, however," he said, indicating for her to lead the way back to the weyr, "I could do with some food. We were up before the kitchen."

They had entered the well-lighted weyr, so he did not miss the trenchant look she shot him over her shoulder. She would not so easily forgive being left out of the group at the Star Stone this morning, certainly not with the bribe of flying *between*.

How different this inner room was now that Lessa was Weyrwoman, F'lar mused as Lessa called down the service shaft for food. During Jora's incompetent tenure as Weyrwoman, the sleeping quarters had been crowded with junk, unwashed apparel, uncleared dishes. The state of the Weyr and the reduced number of dragons were as much Jora's fault as R'gul's, for she had indirectly encouraged sloth, negligence, and gluttony.

If he, F'lar, had been just a few years older when F'lon, his father, had died . . . Jora had been disgusting, but when dragons rose in mating flight, the condition of your partner counted for nothing.

Lessa took a tray of bread and cheese, and mugs of the stimulating *klah* from the platform. She served him deftly.

"You'd not eaten, either?" he asked.

She shook her head vigorously, the braid into which she had plaited her thick, fine dark hair bobbing across her shoulders. The hairdressing was too severe for her narrow face, but it did not, if that was her intention, disguise her femininity or the curious beauty of her delicate features. Again F'lar wondered that such a slight body contained so much shrewd intelligence and resourceful . . . cunning—yes, that was the word, cunning. F'lar did not make the mistake, as others had, of underestimating her abilities.

"Manora called me to witness the birth of Kylara's child."

F'lar maintained an expression of polite interest. He knew perfectly well that Lessa suspected the child was his, and it could have been, he admitted privately, but he doubted it.

113

Kylara had been one of the ten candidates from the same Search three years ago which had discovered Lessa. Like others who survived Impression, Kylara had found certain aspects of Weyr life exactly suited to her temperament. She had gone from one rider's weyr to another's. She had even seduced F'lar—not at all against his will, to be sure. Now that he was Weyrleader, he found it wiser to ignore her efforts to continue the relationship. T'bor had taken her in hand and had had his hands full until he retired her to the Lower Caverns, well advanced in pregnancy.

Aside from having the amorous tendencies of a green dragon, Kylara was quick and ambitious. She would make a strong Weyrwoman, so F'lar had charged Manora and Lessa with the job of planting the notion in Kylara's mind. In the capacity of Weyrwoman . . . of another Weyr . . . her intense drives would be used to Pern's advantage. She had not learned the severe lessons of restraint and patience that Lessa had, and she didn't have Lessa's devious mind. Fortunately she was in considerable awe of Lessa, and F'lar suspected that Lessa was subtly influencing this attitude. In Kylara's case, F'lar preferred not to object to Lessa's meddling.

"A fine son," Lessa was saying.

F'lar sipped his *klah*. She was not going to get him to admit any responsibility.

After a long pause Lessa added, "She has named him T'kil."

F'lar suppressed a grin at Lessa's failure to get a rise from him.

"Discreet of her."

"Oh?"

"Yes," F'lar replied blandly. "T'lar might be confusing if she took the second half of her name as is customary. 'T'kil,' however, still indicates sire as well as dam."

"While I was waiting for Council to end," Lessa said after clearing her throat, "Manora and I checked the supply caverns. The tithing trains, which the Holds have been so gracious as to send us"—her voice was sharp—"are due within the week. There will shortly be bread fit to eat," she added, wrinkling her nose at the crumbling gray pastry she was attempting to spread with cheese.

"A nice change," F'lar agreed.

She paused.

"The Red Star performed its scheduled antic?"

114

He nodded.

"And R'gul's doubts have been wiped away in the enlightening red glow?"

"Not at all." F'lar grinned back at her, ignoring her sarcasm. "Not at all, but he will not be so vocal in his criticism."

She swallowed quickly so she could speak. "You'd do well to cut out his criticism," she said ruthlessly, gesturing with her knife as if plunging it into a man's heart. "He is never going to accept your authority with good grace."

"We need every bronze rider . . . there are only seven, you know," he reminded her pointedly. "R'gul's a good wingleader. He'll settle down when the Threads fall. He needs proof to lay his doubts aside."

"And the Red Star in the Eye Rock is not proof?" Lessa's expressive eyes were wide.

F'lar was privately of Lessa's opinion—that it might be wiser to remove R'gul's stubborn contentiousness. But he could not sacrifice a wingleader, needing every dragon and rider as badly as he did.

"I don't trust him," she added darkly. She sipped at her hot drink, her gray eyes dark over the rim of her mug. As if, F'lar mused, she didn't trust him, either.

And she didn't, past a certain point. She had made that plain, and, in honesty, he couldn't blame her. She did recognize that every action F'lar took was toward one end . . . the safety and preservation of dragonkind and weyrfolk and consequently the safety and preservation of Pern. To effect that end, he needed her full cooperation. When Weyr business or dragonlore were discussed, she suspended the antipathy he knew she felt for him. In conferences she supported him wholeheartedly and persuasively, but always he suspected the double edge to her comments and saw a speculative, suspicious look in her eyes. He needed not only her tolerance but her empathy.

"Tell me," she said after a long silence, "did the sun touch the Finger Rock before the Red Star was bracketed in the Eye Rock or after?"

"Matter of fact, I'm not sure, as I did not see it myself . . . the concurrence lasts only a few moments . . . but the two are supposed to be simultaneous."

She frowned at him sourly. "Whom did you waste it on?

R'gul?" She was provoked, her angry eyes looked everywhere but at him.

"I am Weyrleader," he informed her curtly. She was unreasonable.

She awarded him one long, hard look before she bent to finish her meal. She ate very little, quickly and neatly. Compared to Jora, she didn't eat enough in the course of an entire day to nourish a sick child. But then, there was no point in ever comparing Lessa to Jora.

He finished his own breakfast, absently piling the mugs together on the empty tray. She rose silently and removed the dishes.

"As soon as the Weyr is free, we'll go," he told her.

"So you said." She nodded toward the sleeping queen, visible through the open arch. "We still must wait upon Ramoth."

"Isn't she rousing? Her tail's been twitching for an hour."

"She always does that about this time of day."

F'lar leaned across the table, his brows drawn together thoughtfully as he watched the golden-forked tip of the queen's tail jerk spasmodically from side to side.

"Mnementh, too. And always at dawn and early morning. As if somehow they associate that time of day with trouble . . ."

"Or the Red Star's rising?" Lessa interjected.

Some subtle difference in her tone caused F'lar to glance quickly at her. It wasn't anger now over having missed the morning's phenomenon. Her eyes were fixed on nothing; her face, smooth at first, was soon wrinkled with a vaguely anxious frown as tiny lines formed between her arching, well-defined brows.

"Dawn . . . that's when all warnings come," she murmured.

"What kind of warnings?" he asked with quiet encouragement.

"There was that morning . . . a few days before . . . before you and Fax descended on Ruath Hold. Something woke me . . . a feeling, like a very heavy pressure . . . the sensation of some terrible danger threatening." She was silent. "The Red Star was just rising." The fingers of her left hand opened and closed. She gave a convulsive shudder. Her eyes refocused on him.

"You and Fax did come out of the northeast from Crom,"

she said sharply, ignoring the fact, F'lar noticed, that the Red Star also rises north of true east.

"Indeed we did," he grinned at her, remembering that morning vividly. "Although," he added, gesturing around the great cavern to emphasize, "I prefer to believe I served you well that day . . . you remember it with displeasure?"

The look she gave him was coldly inscrutable.

"Danger comes in many guises."

"I agree," he replied amiably, determined not to rise to her bait. "Had any other rude awakenings?" he inquired conversationally.

The absolute stillness in the room brought his attention back to her. Her face had drained of all color.

"The day Fax invaded Ruath Hold." Her voice was a barely articulated whisper. Her eyes were wide and staring. Her hands clenched the edge of the table. She said nothing for such a long interval that F'lar became concerned. This was an unexpectedly violent reaction to a casual question.

"Tell me," he suggested softly.

She spoke in unemotional, impersonal tones, as if she were reciting a Traditional Ballad or something that had happened to an entirely different person.

"I was a child. Just eleven. I woke at dawn . . ." Her voice trailed off. Her eyes remained focused on nothing, staring at a scene that had happened long ago.

F'lar was stirred by an irresistible desire to comfort her. It struck him forcibly, even as he was stirred by this unusual compassion, that he had never thought that Lessa, of all people, would be troubled by so old a terror.

Mnementh sharply informed his rider that Lessa was obviously bothered a good deal. Enough so that her mental anguish was rousing Ramoth from sleep. In less accusing tones Mnementh informed F'lar that R'gul had finally taken off with his weyrling pupils. His dragon, Hath, however, was in a fine state of disorientation due to R'gul's state of mind. Must F'lar unsettle everyone in the Weyr . . .

"Oh, be quiet," F'lar retorted under his breath.

"Why?" Lessa demanded in her normal voice.

"I didn't mean you, my dear Weyrwoman," he assured her, smiling pleasantly, as if the entranced interlude had never occurred. "Mnementh is full of advice these days."

"Like rider, like dragon," she replied tartly.

Ramoth yawned mightily. Lessa was instantly on her feet,

running to her dragon's side, her slight figure dwarfed by the six-foot dragon head.

A tender, adoring expression flooded her face as she gazed into Ramoth's gleaming opalescent eyes. F'lar clenched his teeth, envious, by the Egg, of a rider's affection for her dragon.

In his mind he heard Mnementh's dragon equivalent of laughter.

"She's hungry," Lessa informed F'lar, an echo of her love for Ramoth lingering in the soft line of her mouth, in the kindness of her gray eyes.

"She's always hungry," he observed and followed them out of the weyr.

Mnementh hovered courteously just beyond the ledge until Lessa and Ramoth had taken off. They glided down the Weyr Bowl, over the misty bathing lake, toward the feeding ground at the opposite end of the long oval that comprised the floor of Benden Weyr. The striated, precipitous walls were pierced with the black mouths of single weyr entrances, deserted at this time of day by the few dragons who might otherwise doze on their ledges in the wintry sun.

As F'lar vaulted to Mnementh's smooth bronze neck, he hoped that Ramoth's clutch would be spectacular, erasing the ignominy of the paltry dozen Nemorth had laid in each of her last few clutches.

He had no serious doubts of the improvement after Ramoth's remarkable mating flight with his Mnementh. The bronze dragon smugly echoed his rider's certainty, and both looked on the queen possessively as she curved her wings to land. She was twice Nemorth's size, for one thing; her wings were half-a-wing again longer than Mnementh's, who was the biggest of the seven male bronzes. F'lar looked to Ramoth to repopulate the five empty Weyrs, even as he looked to himself and Lessa to rejuvenate the pride and faith of dragon-riders and of Pern itself. He only hoped time enough remained to him to do what was necessary. The Red Star had been bracketed by the Eye Rock. The Threads would soon be falling. Somewhere, in one of the other Weyrs' Records, must be the information he needed to ascertain *when*, exactly, Threads would fall.

Mnementh landed. F'lar jumped down from the curving neck to stand beside Lessa. The three watched as Ramoth, a buck grasped in each of her forefeet, rose to a feeding ledge.

"Will her appetite never taper off?" Lessa asked with affectionate dismay.

As a dragonet, Ramoth had been eating to grow. Her full stature attained, she was, of course, now eating for her young, and she applied herself conscientiously.

F'lar chuckled and squatted, hunter fashion. He picked up shale-flakes, skating them across the flat dry ground, counting the dust puffs boyishly.

"The time will come when she won't eat everything in sight," he assured Lessa. "But she's young . . ."

". . . and needs her strength," Lessa interrupted, her voice a fair imitation of R'gul's pedantic tones.

F'lar looked up at her, squinting against the wintry sun that slanted down at them.

"She's a finely grown beast, especially compared to Nemorth." He gave a contemptuous snort. "In fact, there *is* no comparison. However, look here," he ordered peremptorily.

He tapped the smoothed sand in front of him, and she saw that his apparently idle gestures had been to a purpose. With a sliver of stone, he drew a design in quick strokes.

"In order to fly a dragon *between,* he has to know where to go. And so do you." He grinned at the astonished and infuriated look of comprehension on her face. "Ah, but there are certain consequences to an ill-considered jump. Badly visualized reference points often result in staying *between.*" His voice dropped ominously. Her face cleared of its resentment. "So there are certain reference or recognition points arbitrarily taught all weyrlings. "That,"—he pointed first to his facsimile and then to the actual Star Stone with its Finger and Eye Rock companions, on Benden Peak—"is the first recognition point a weyrling learns. When I take you aloft, you will reach an altitude just above the Star Stone, near enough for you to be able to see the hole in the Eye Rock clearly. Fix that picture sharply in your mind's eye, relay it to Ramoth. That will always get you home."

"Understood. But how do I learn recognition points of places I've never seen?"

He grinned up at her. "You're drilled in them. First by your instructor," and he pointed the sliver at his chest, "and then by going there, having directed your dragon to get the visualization from her instructor," and he indicated Mnementh. The bronze dragon lowered his wedge-shaped head

119

until one eye was focused on his rider and his mate's rider. He made a pleased noise deep in his chest.

Lessa laughed up at the gleaming eye and, with unexpected affection, patted the soft nose.

F'lar cleared his throat in surprise. He had been aware that Mnementh showed an unusual affection for the Weyrwoman, bue he had had no idea Lessa was fond of the bronze. Perversely, he was irritated.

"However," he said, and his voice sounded unnatural to himself, "we take the young riders constantly to and from the main reference points all across Pern, to all the Holds so that they have eyewitness impressions on which to rely. As a rider becomes adept in picking out landmarks, he gets additional references from other riders. Therefore, to go *between,* there is actually only one requirement: a clear picture of where you want to go. *And* a dragon!" He grinned at her. "Also, you should always plan to arrive above your reference point in clear air."

Lessa frowned.

"It is better to arrive in open air"—F'lar waved a hand above his head—"rather than underground," and he slapped his open hand onto the dirt. A puff of dust rose warningly.

"But the wings took off within the Bowl itself the day the Lords of the Hold arrived," Lessa reminded him.

F'lar chuckled at her uptake. "True, but only the most seasoned riders. Once we came across a dragon and a rider entombed together in solid rock. They . . . were . . . very young." His eyes were bleak.

"I take the point," she assured him gravely. "That's her fifth," she added, pointing toward Ramoth, who was carrying her latest kill up to the bloody ledge.

"She'll work them off today, I assure you," F'lar remarked. He rose, brushing off his knees with sharp slaps of his riding gloves. "Test her temper."

Lessa did so with a silent, *Had enough?* She grimaced at Ramoth's indignant rejection of the thought.

The queen went swooping down for a huge fowl, rising in a flurry of gray, brown and white feathers.

"She's not as hungry as she's making you think, the deceitful creature," F'lar chuckled and saw that Lessa had reached the same conclusion. Her eyes were snapping with vexation.

"When you've finished the bird, Ramoth, do let us learn

how to fly *between*," Lessa said aloud for F'lar's benefit, "before our good Weyrleader changes his mind."

Ramoth looked up from her gorging, turned her head toward the two riders at the edge of the feeding ground. Her eyes gleamed. She bent her head again to her kill, but Lessa could sense the dragon would obey.

It was cold aloft. Lessa was glad of the fur lining in her riding gear, and the warmth of the great golden neck which she bestrode. She decided not to think of the absolute cold of *between* which she had experienced only once. She glanced below on her right where bronze Mnementh hovered, and she caught his amused thought.

F'lar tells me to tell Ramoth to tell you to fix the alignment of the Star Stone firmly in your mind as a homing. Then, Mnementh went on amiably, *we shall fly down to the lake. You will return from* between *to this exact point. Do you understand?*

Lessa found herself grinning foolishly with anticipation and nodded vigorously. How much time was saved because she could speak directly to the dragons! Ramoth made a disgruntled noise deep in her throat. Lessa patted her reassuringly.

"Have you got the picture in your mind, dear one?" she asked, and Ramoth again rumbled, less annoyed, because she was catching Lessa's excitement.

Mnementh stroked the cold air with his wings, greenish-brown in the sunlight, and curved down gracefully toward the lake on the plateau below Benden Weyr. His flight line took him very low over the rim of the Weyr. From Lessa's angle, it looked like a collision course. Ramoth followed closely in his wake. Lessa caught her breath at the sight of the jagged boulders just below Ramoth's wing tips.

It was exhilarating, Lessa crowed to herself, doubly stimulated by the elation that flowed back to her from Ramoth.

Mnementh halted above the farthest shore of the lake, and there, too, Ramoth came to hover.

Mnementh flashed the thought to Lessa that she was to place the picture of where she wished to go firmly in her mind and direct Ramoth to get there.

Lessa complied. The next instant the awesome, bone-penetrating cold of black *between* enveloped them. Be ore either she or Ramoth were aware of more than that biting touch of cold and impregnable darkness, they were above the Star Stone.

Lessa let out a cry of pure triumph.

It is extremely simple. Ramoth seemed disappointed.

Mnementh reappeared beside and slightly below them.

You are to return by the same route to the Lake, he ordered, and before the thought had finished, Ramoth took off.

Mnementh was beside them above the lake, fuming with his own and F'lar's anger. *You did not visualize before transferring. Don't think a first successful trip makes you perfect. You have no conception of the dangers inherent in* between. *Never fail to picture your arrival point again.*

Lessa glanced down at F'lar. Even two wingspans apart, she could see the vivid anger on his face, almost feel the fury flashing from his eyes. And laced through the wrath, a terrible sinking fearfulness for her safety that was a more effective reprimand than his wrath. Lessa's safety, she wondered bitterly, or Ramoth's?

You are to follow us, Mnementh was saying in a calmer tone, *rehearsing in your mind the two reference points you have already learned. We shall jump to and from them this morning, gradually learning other points around Benden.*

They did. Flying as far away as Benden Hold itself, nestled against the foothills above Benden Valley, the Weyr Peak a far point against the noonday sky, Lessa did not neglect to visualize a clearly detailed impression each time.

This was as marvelously exciting as she had hoped it would be, Lessa confided to Ramoth. Ramoth replied: yes, it was certainly preferable to the time-consuming methods others had to use, but she didn't think it was exciting at all to jump *between* from Benden Weyr to Benden Hold and back to Benden Weyr again. It was dull.

They had met with Mnementh above the Star Stone again. The bronze dragon sent Lessa the message that this was a very satisfying initial session. They would practice some distant jumping tomorrow.

Tomorrow, thought Lessa glumly, some emergency will occur or our hard-working Weyrleader will decide today's session constitutes keeping his promise and that will be that.

There was one jump she could make *between,* from anywhere on Pern, and not miss her mark.

She visualized Ruatha for Ramoth as seen from the heights

122

above the Hold . . . to satisfy that requirement. To be scrupulously clear, Lessa projected the pattern of the firepits. Before Fax invaded and she had had to manipulate its decline, Ruatha had been such a lovely, prosperous valley. She told Ramoth to jump *between*.

The cold was intense and seemed to last for many heartbeats. Just as Lessa began to fear that she had somehow lost them *between*, they exploded into the air above the Hold. Elation filled her. That for F'lar and his excessive caution! With Ramoth she could jump anywhere! For there was the distinctive pattern of Ruatha's fire-guttered heights. It was just before dawn, the Breast Pass between Crom and Ruatha, black cones against the lightening gray sky. Fleetingly she noticed the absence of the Red Star that now blazed in the dawn sky. And fleetingly she noticed a difference in the air. Chill, yes, but not wintry . . . the air held that moist coolness of early spring.

Startled, she glanced downward, wondering if she could have, for all her assurance, erred in some fashion. But no, this was Ruath Hold. The Tower, the inner Court, the aspect of the broad avenue leading down to the crafthold were just as they should be. Wisps of smoke from distant chimneys indicated people were making ready for the day.

Ramoth caught the tenor of her insecurity and began to press for an explanation.

This is Ruatha, Lessa replied stoutly. *It can be no other. Circle the heights. See, there are the firepit lines I gave you. . . .*

Lessa gasped, the coldness in her stomach freezing her muscles.

Below her in the slowly lifting predawn gloom, she saw the figures of many men toiling over the breast of the cliff from the hills beyond Ruatha, men moving with quiet stealth like criminals.

She ordered Ramoth to keep as still as possible in the air so as not to direct their attention upward. The dragon was curious but obedient.

Who would be attacking Ruatha? It seemed incredible. Lytol was, after all, a former dragonman and had savagely repelled one attack already. Could there possibly be a thought of aggression among the Holds now that F'lar was Weyrleader? And what Hold Lord would be foolish enough to mount a territorial war in the winter?

No, not winter. The air was definitely springlike.

The men crept on, over the firepits to the edge of the heights. Suddenly Lessa realized they were lowering rope ladders over the face of the cliff, down toward the open shutters of the Inner Hold.

Wildly she clutched at Ramoth's neck, certain of what she saw.

This was the invader Fax, now dead nearly three Turns—Fax and his men as they began their attack on Ruatha nearly thirteen Turns ago.

Yes, there was the Tower guard, his face a white blot turned toward the Cliff itself, watching. He had been paid his bribe to stand silent this morning.

But the watch-wher, trained to give alarm for any intrusion—why was it not trumpeting its warning? Why was it silent?

Because, Ramoth informed her rider with calm logic, *it senses your presence as well as mine, so how could the Hold be in danger?*

No, No! Lessa moaned. *What can I do now? How can I wake them? Where is the girl I was? I was asleep, and then I woke. I remember. I dashed from my room. I was so scared. I went down the steps and nearly fell. I knew I had to get to the watch-wher's kennel. . . . I knew. . . .*

Lessa clutched at Ramoth's neck for support as past acts and mysteries became devastatingly clear.

She herself had warned herself, just as it was her presence on the queen dragon that had kept the watch-wher from giving alarm. For as she watched, stunned and speechless, she saw the small, gray-robed figure that could only be herself as a youngster, burst from the Hold Hall door, race uncertainly down the cold stone steps into the Court, and disappear into the watch-wher's stinking den. Faintly she heard it crying in piteous confusion.

Just as Lessa-the-girl reached that doubtful sanctuary, Fax's invaders swooped into the open window embrasures and began the slaughter of her sleeping family.

"Back—back to the Star Stone!" Lessa cried. In her wide and staring eyes she held the image of the guiding rocks like a rudder for her sanity as well as Ramoth's direction.

The intense cold acted as a restorative. And then they were above the quiet, peaceful wintry Weyr as if they had never paradoxically visited Ruatha.

F'lar and Mnementh were nowhere to be seen.

Ramoth, however, was unshaken by the experience. She had only gone where she had been told to go and had not quite understood that going where she had been told to go had shocked Lessa. She suggested to her rider that Mnementh had probably followed them to Ruatha so if Lessa would give her the *proper* references, she'd take her there. Ramoth's sensible attitude was comforting.

Lessa carefully drew for Ramoth not the child's memory of a long-vanished, idyllic Ruatha but her more recent recollection of the Hold, gray, sullen, at dawning, with a Red Star pulsing on the horizon.

And there they were again, hovering over the valley, the Hold below them on the right. The grasses grew untended on the heights, clogging firepit and brickwork; the scene showed all the deterioration she had encouraged in her effort to thwart Fax of any profit from conquering Ruath Hold.

But, as she watched, vaguely disturbed, she saw a figure emerge from the kitchen, saw the watch-wher creep from its lair and follow the raggedly dressed figure as far across the Court as the chain permitted. She saw the figure ascend the Tower, gaze first eastward, then northeastward. This was still not Ruatha of today and now! Lessa's mind reeled, disoriented. This time she had come back to visit herself of three Turns ago, to see the filthy drudge plotting revenge on Fax.

She felt the absolute cold of *between* as Ramoth snatched them back, emerging once more above the Star Stone. Lessa was shuddering, her eyes frantically taking in the reassuring sight of the Weyr Bowl, hoping she had not somehow shifted backward in time yet again. Mnementh suddenly erupted into the air a few lengths below and beyond Ramoth. Lessa greeted him with a cry of intense relief.

Back to your weyr! There was no disguising the white fury in Mnementh's tone. Lessa was too unnerved to respond in any way other than instant compliance. Ramoth glided swiftly to their ledge, quickly clearing the perch for Mnementh to land.

The rage on F'lar's face as he leaped from Mnementh and advanced on Lessa brought her wits back abruptly. She made no move to evade him as he grabbed her shoulders and shook her violently.

"How dare you risk yourself and Ramoth? Why must you defy me at every opportunity? Do you realize what would happen to all Pern if we lost Ramoth? Where did you go?" He was spitting with anger, punctuating each question that tumbled from his lips by giving her a head-wrenching shake.

"Ruatha," she managed to say, trying to keep herself erect. She reached out to catch at his arms, but he shook her again.

"Ruatha? We were there. You weren't. Where did you go?"

"Ruatha!" Lessa cried louder, clutching at him distractedly because he kept jerking her off balance. She couldn't organize her thoughts with him jolting her around.

She was at Ruatha, Mnementh said firmly.

We were there twice, Ramoth added.

As the dragons' calmer words penetrated F'lar's fury, he stopped shaking Lessa. She hung limply in his grasp, her hands weakly plucking at his arms, her eyes closed, her face gray. He picked her up and strode rapidly into the queen's weyr, the dragons following. He placed her upon the couch, wrapping her tightly in the fur cover. He called down the service shaft for the duty cook to send up hot *klah.*

"All right, what happened?" he demanded.

She didn't look at him, but he got a glimpse of her haunted eyes. She blinked constantly as if she longed to erase what she had just seen.

Finally she got herself somewhat under control and said in a low, tired voice. "I did go to Ruatha. Only . . . I went *back* to Ruatha."

"Back to Ruatha?" F'lar repeated the words stupidly; the significance momentarily eluded him.

It certainly does, Mnementh agreed and flashed to F'lar's mind the two scenes he had picked out of Ramoth's memory.

Staggered by the import of the visualization, F'lar found himself slowly sinking to the edge of the bed.

"You went *between* times?"

She nodded slowly. The terror was beginning to leave her eyes.

"Between times," F'lar murmured. "I wonder . . ."

His mind raced through the possibilities. It might well tip the scales of survival in the Weyr's favor. He couldn't think exactly how to use this extraordinary ability, but there *must* be an advantage in it for dragonfolk.

The service shaft rumbled. He took the pitcher from the platform and poured two mugs.

Lessa's hands were shaking so much that she couldn't get hers to her lips. He steadied it for her, wondering if going *between* times would regularly cause this kind of shock. If so, it wouldn't be any advantage at all. If she'd had enough of a scare this day, she might not be so contemptuous of his orders the next time; which would be to his benefit.

Outside in the weyr, Mnementh snorted his opinion on that. F'lar ignored him.

Lessa was trembling violently now. He put an arm around her, pressing the fur against her slender body. He held the mug to her lips, forcing her to drink. He could feel the tremors ease off. She took long, slow, deep breaths between swallows, equally determined to get herself under control. The moment he felt her stiffen under his arm, he released her. He wondered if Lessa had ever had someone to turn to. Certainly not after Fax invaded her family Hold. She had been only eleven, a child. Had hate and revenge been the only emotions the growing girl had practiced?

She lowered the mug, cradling it in her hands carefully as if it had assumed some undefinable importance to her.

"Now. Tell me," he ordered evenly.

She took a long deep breath and began to speak, her hands tightening around the mug. Her inner turmoil had not lessened; it was merely under control now.

"Ramoth and I were bored with the weyrling exercises," she admitted candidly.

Grimly F'lar recognized that, while the adventure might have taught her to be more circumspect, it had not scared her into obedience. He doubted that anything would.

"I gave her the picture of Ruatha so we could go *between* there." She did not look at him, but her profile was outlined against the dark fur of the rug. "The Ruatha I knew so well —I accidentally sent myself backward in time to the day Fax invaded."

Her shock was now comprehensible to him.

"And . . ." he prompted her, his voice carefully neutral.

"And I saw myself—" Her voice broke off. With an effort she continued. "I had visualized for Ramoth the designs of the firepits and the angle of the Hold if one looked down from the pits into the Inner Court. That was where we emerged. It was just dawn"—she lifted her chin with a nervous jerk—"and there was no Red Star in the sky." She gave him a quick, defensive look as if she expected him to contest this detail. "And I saw men creeping over the firepits, lowering rope ladders to the top windows of the Hold. I saw

127

the Tower guard watching. Just watching." She clenched her teeth at such treachery, and her eyes gleamed malevolently. "And I saw myself run from the Hall into the watch-wher's lair. And do you know why"—her voice lowered to a bitter whisper—"the watch-wher did not alarm the Hold?"

"Why?"

"Because there was a dragon in the sky, and *I*, Lessa of Ruatha, was on her." She flung the mug from her as if she wished she could reject the knowledge, too. "Because *I* was there, the watch-wher did not alarm the Hold, thinking the intrusion legitimate, with one of the Blood on a dragon in the sky. So I"—her body grew rigid, her hands clasped so tightly that the knuckles were white—"*I* was the cause of my family's massacre. Not Fax! If I had not acted the captious fool today, I would not have been there with Ramoth and the watch-wher would—"

Her voice had risen to an hysterical pitch of recrimination. He slapped her sharply across the cheeks, grabbing her, robe and all, to shake her.

The stunned look in her eyes and the tragedy in her face alarmed him. His indignation over her willfulness disappeared. Her unruly independence of mind and spirit attracted him as much as her curious dark beauty. Infuriating as her fractious ways might be, they were too vital a part of her integrity to be exorcised. Her indomitable will had taken a grievous shock today, and her self-confidence had better be restored quickly.

"On the contrary, Lessa," he said sternly, "Fax would still have murdered your family. He had planned it very carefully, even to scheduling his attack on the morning when the Tower guard was one who could be bribed. Remember, too, it was dawn and the watch-wher, being a nocturnal beast, blind by daylight, is relieved of responsibility at dawn and knows it. Your presence, damnable as it may appear to you, was not the deciding factor by any means. It did, and I draw your attention to this very important fact, cause you to save yourself, by warning Lessa-the-child. Don't you see that?"

"I could have called out," she murmured, but the frantic look had left her eyes and there was a faint hint of normal color in her lips.

"If you wish to flail around in guilt, go right ahead," he said with deliberate callousness.

Ramoth interjected a thought that, since the two of them had been there that previous time as Fax's men had prepared to invade, it had already happened, so how could it be changed? The act was inevitable both that day and today. For how else could Lessa have lived to come to the Weyr and impress Ramoth at the hatching?

Mnementh relayed Ramoth's message scrupulously, even to imitating Ramoth's egocentric nuances. F'lar looked sharply at Lessa to see the effect of Ramoth's astringent observation.

"Just like Ramoth to have the final word," she said with a hint of her former droll humor.

F'lar felt the muscles along his neck and shoulders begin to relax. She'd be all right, he decided, but it might be wiser to make her talk it all out now, to put the whole experience into proper perspective.

"You said you were there twice?" He leaned back on the couch, watching her closely. "When was the second time?"

"Can't you guess?" she asked sarcastically.

"No," he lied.

"When else but the dawn I was awakened, feeling the Red Star was a menace to me? . . . Three days before you and Fax came out of the northeast."

"It would seem," he remarked dryly, "that you were your own premonition both times."

She nodded.

"Have you had any more of these presentiments . . . or should I say reinforced warnings?"

She shuddered but answered him with more of her old spirit.

"No, but if I should, *you* go. I don't want to."

F'lar grinned maliciously.

"I would, however," she added, "like to know why and how it could happen."

"I've never run across a mention of it anywhere," he told her candidly. "Of course, if you have done it—and you undeniably have," he assured her hastily at her indignant protest, "it obviously can be done. You say you thought of Ruatha, but you thought of it as it was on that particular day. Certainly a day to be remembered. You thought of spring, before dawn, no Red Star—yes, I remember your mentioning that—so one would have to remember references peculiar to a significant day to return to *between* times to the past."

She nodded slowly, thoughtfully.

"You used the same method the second time, to get to the Ruatha of three Turns ago. Again, of course, it was spring."

He rubbed his palms together, then brought his hands down on his knees with an emphatic slap and rose to his feet.

"I'll be back," he said and strode from the room, ignoring her half-articulated cry of warning.

Ramoth was curling up in the weyr as he passed her. He noticed that her color remained good in spite of the drain on her energies by the morning's exercises. She glanced at him, her many-faceted eye already covered by the inner, protective lid.

Mnementh awaited his rider on the ledge, and the moment F'lar leaped to his neck, took off. He circled upward, hovering above the Star Stone.

You wish to try Lessa's trick, Mnementh said, unperturbed by the prospective experiment.

F'lar stroked the great curved neck affectionately. *You understand how it worked for Ramoth and Lessa?*

As well as anyone can, Mnementh replied with the approximation of a shrug. *When did you have in mind?*

Before that moment F'lar had had no idea. Now, unerringly, his thoughts drew him backward to the summer day R'gul's bronze Hath had flown to mate the grotesque Nemorth, and R'gul had become Weyrleader in place of his dead father, F'lon.

Only the cold of *between* gave them any indication that they had transferred; they were still hovering above the Star Stone. F'lar wondered if they had missed some essential part of the transfer. Then he realized that the sun was in another quarter of the sky and the air was warm and sweet with summer. The Weyr below was empty; there were no dragons sunning themselves on the ledges, no women busy at tasks in the Bowl. Noises impinged on his senses: raucous laughter, yells, shrieks, and a soft crooning noise that dominated the bedlam.

Then, from the direction of the weyrling barracks in the Lower Caverns, two figures emerged—a stripling and a young bronze dragon. The boy's arm lay limply along the beast's neck. The impression that reached the hovering observers was one of utter dejection. The two halted by the lake, the boy peering into the unruffled blue waters, then glancing upward toward the queen's weyr.

130

F'lar knew the boy for himself, and compassion for that younger self filled him. If only he could reassure that boy, so torn by grief, so filled with resentment, that he would one day become Weyrleader. . . .

Abruptly, startled by his own thoughts, he ordered Mnementh to transfer back. The utter cold of *between* was like a slap in his face, replaced almost instantly as they broke out of *between* into the cold of normal winter.

Slowly, Mnementh flew back down to the queen's weyr, as sobered as F'lar by what they had seen.

Rise high in glory,	Count three months and more,
Bronze and gold.	And five heated weeks,
Dive entwined,	A day of glory and
Enhance the Hold.	In a month, who seeks?

A strand of silver
In the sky . . .
With heat, all quickens
And all times fly.

"I don't know why you insisted that F'nor unearth these ridiculous things from Ista Weyr," Lessa exclaimed in a tone of exasperation. "They consist of nothing but trivial notes on how many measures of grain were used to bake daily bread."

F'lar glanced up at her from the Records he was studying. He sighed, leaned back in his chair in a bone-popping stretch.

"And I used to think," Lessa said with a rueful expression on her vivid, narrow face, "that those venerable Records would hold the total sum of all dragonlore and human wisdom. Or so I was led to believe," she added pointedly.

F'lar chuckled. "They do, but you have to disinter it."

Lessa wrinkled her nose. "Phew. They smell as if we had . . . and the only decent thing to do would be to rebury them."

"Which is another item I'm hoping to find . . . the old preservative technique that kept the skins from hardening and smelling."

"It's stupid, anyhow, to use skins for recording. There ought to be something better. We have become, dear Weyrleader, entirely too hidebound."

While F'lar roared with appreciation of her pun, she

regarded him impatiently. Suddenly she jumped up, fired by another of her mercurial moods.

"Well, you won't find it. You won't find the facts you're looking for. Because I know what you're really after, and it isn't recorded!"

"Explain yourself."

"It's time we stopped hiding a rather brutal truth from ourselves."

"Which is?"

"Our mutual feeling that the Red Star is a menace and that the Threads *will* come! *We* decided that out of pure conceit and then went back *between* times to particularly crucial points in our lives and strengthened that notion, in our earlier selves. And for you, it was when you decided you were destined"—her voice made the word mocking—"to become Weyrleader one day.

"Could it be," she went on scornfully, "that our ultraconservative R'gul has the right of it? That there have been no Threads for four hundred Turns because there are no more? And that the reason we have so few dragons is because the dragons sense they are no longer essential to Pern? That we *are* anachronisms as well as parasites?"

F'lar did not know how long he sat looking up at her bitter face or how long it took him to find answers to her probing questions.

"Anything is possible, Weyrwoman," he heard his voice replying calmly. "Including the unlikely fact that an eleven-year-old child, scared stiff, could plot revenge on her family's murderer and—against all odds—succeed."

She took an involuntary step forward, struck by his unexpected rebuttal. She listened intently.

"I prefer to believe," he went on inexorably, "that there is more to life than raising dragons and playing spring games. That is not enough for me. And I have made others look further, beyond self-interest and comfort. I have given them a purpose, a discipline. Everyone, dragonfolk and Holder alike, profits.

"I am not looking in these Records for reassurance. I'm looking for solid facts.

"I can prove, Weyrwoman, that there have been Threads. I can prove that there have been Intervals during which the Weyrs have declined. I can prove that if you sight the Red Star directly bracketed by the Eye Rock at the moment of winter solstice, the Red Star will pass close enough to Pern to throw off Threads. Since I can prove these facts, I believe Pern is in danger. *I* believe . . . not the youngster of fifteen Turns ago. F'lar, the bronze rider, the Weyrleader, believes it!"

He saw her eyes reflecting shadowy doubts, but he sensed his arguments were beginning to reassure her.

"You felt constrained to believe in me once before," he went on in a milder voice, "when I suggested that you could be Weyrwoman. You believed me and . . ." He made a gesture around the weyr as substantiation.

She gave him a weak, humorless smile.

"That was because I had never planned what to do with my life once I did have Fax lying dead at my feet. Of course, being Ramoth's Weyrmate is wonderful, but"—she frowned slightly—"it isn't enough any more, either. That's why I wanted so to learn to fly and . . ."

". . . . that's how this argument started in the first place," F'lar finished for her with a sardonic smile.

He leaned across the table urgently.

"Believe with me, Lessa, until you have cause not to. I respect your doubts. There's nothing wrong in doubting. It sometimes leads to greater faith. But believe with me until spring. If the Threads have not fallen by then . . ." He shrugged fatalistically.

She looked at him for a long moment and then inclined her head slowly in agreement.

He tried to suppress the relief he felt at her decision. Lessa, as Fax had discovered, was a ruthless adversary and a canny advocate. Besides these, she was Weyrwoman: essential to his plans.

"Now, let's get back to the contemplation of trivia. They do tell me, you know, time, place, and duration of Thread incursions," he grinned up at her reassuringly. "And those facts I must have to make up my timetable."

"Timetable? But you said you didn't know the time."

"Not the day to the second when the Threads may spin down. For one thing, while the weather holds so unusually cold for this time of year, the Threads simply turn brittle and blow away like dust. They're harmless. However, when the air is warm, they are viable and . . . deadly." He made fists of both hands, placing one above and to one side of the other. "The Red Star is my right hand, my left is Pern. The

Red Star turns very fast and in the opposite direction to us. It also wobbles erratically."

"How do you know that?"

"Diagram on the walls of the Fort Weyr Hatching Ground. That was the very first Weyr, you know."

Lessa smiled sourly. "I know."

"So, when the Star makes a pass, the Threads spin off, down toward us, in attacks that last six hours and occur approximately fourteen hours apart."

"Attacks last six hours?"

He nodded gravely.

"When the Red Star is closest to us. Right now it is just beginning its Pass."

She frowned.

He rummaged among the skin sheets on the table, and an object dropped to the stone floor with a metallic clatter.

Curious, Lessa bent to pick it up, turning the thin sheet over in her hands.

"What's this?" She ran an exploratory finger lightly across the irregular design on one side.

"I don't know. F'nor brought it back from Fort Weyr. It was nailed to one of the chests in which the Records had been stored. He brought it along, thinking it might be important. Said there was a plate like it just under the Red Star diagram on the wall of the Hatching Ground."

"This first part is plain enough: 'Mother's father's father, who departed for all time *between*, said this was the key to the mystery, and it came to him while doodling: he said that he said: ARRHENIUS? EUREKA! MYCORRHIZA. . . .' Of course, that part doesn't make any sense at all," Lessa snorted. "It isn't even Pernese—just babbling, those last three words."

"I've studied it, Lessa," F'lar replied, glancing at it again and tipping it toward him to reaffirm his conclusions. "The only way to depart for all time *between* is to die, right? People just don't fly away on their own, obviously. So it is a death vision, dutifully recorded by a grandchild, who couldn't spell very well either. 'Doodling' as the present tense of dying!" He smiled indulgently. "And as for the rest of it, after the nonsense—like most death visions, it 'explains' what everyone has always known. Read on."

" 'Flamethrowing fire lizards to wipe out the spores. Q.E.D.'?"

"No help there, either. Obviously just a primitive rejoicing that he is a dragonman, who didn't even know the right word for Threads." F'lar's shrug was expressive.

Lessa wet one fingertip to see if the patterns were inked on. The metal was shiny enough for a good mirror if she could get rid of the designs. However, the patterns remained smooth and precise.

"Primitive or no, they had a more permanent way of recording their visions that is superior to even the well-preserved skins," she murmured.

"Well-preserved babblings," F'lar said, turning back to the skins he was checking for understandable data.

"A badly scored ballad?" Lessa wondered and then dismissed the whole thing. "The design isn't even pretty."

F'lar pulled forward a chart that showed overlapping horizontal bands imposed on the projection of Pern's continental mass.

"Here," he said, "this represents waves of attack, and this one"—he pulled forward the second map with vertical bandings—"shows time zones. So you can see that with a fourteen-hour break only certain parts of Pern are affected in each attack. One reason for spacing of the Weyrs."

"Six full Weyrs," she murmured, "close to three thousand dragons."

"I'm aware of the statistics," he replied in a voice devoid of expression. "It meant no one Weyr was overburdened during the height of the attacks, not that three thousand beasts must be available. However, with these timetables, we can manage until Ramoth's first clutches have matured."

She turned a cynical look on him. "You've a lot of faith in one queen's capacity."

He waved that remark aside impatiently. "I've more faith, no matter what your opinion is, in the startling repetitions of events in these Records."

"Ha!"

"I don't mean how many measures for daily bread, Lessa," he retorted, his voice rising. "I mean such things as the time such and such a wing was sent out on patrol, how long the patrol lasted, how many riders were hurt. The brooding capacities of queens, during the fifty years a Pass lasts and the Intervals between such Passes. Yes, it tells that. By all I've studied here," and he pounded emphatically on the nearest stack of dusty, smelly skins, "Nemorth should have been mating twice a Turn for the last ten. Had she even kept to her paltry twelve a clutch, we'd have two hundred and forty more beasts. . . . Don't interrupt. But we had Jora as Weyrleader, and we had fallen into planet-wide disfavor during a four hundred Turn Interval. Well, Ramoth will brood over no measly dozen, and she'll lay a queen egg, mark my words. She will rise often to mate and lay generously. By the time the Red Star is passing closest to us and the attacks become frequent, we'll be ready."

She stared at him, her eyes wide with incredulity. "Out of Ramoth?"

"Out of Ramoth and out of the queens she'll lay. Remember, there are Records of Faranth laying sixty eggs at a time, including several queen eggs."

Lessa could only shake her head slowly in wonder.

" 'A strand of silver/In the sky. . . . With heat, all quickens/And all times fly,' " F'lar quoted to her.

"She's got weeks more to go before laying, and then the eggs must hatch . . ."

"Been on the Hatching Ground recently? Wear your boots. You'll be burned through sandals."

She dismissed that with a guttural noise. He sat back, outwardly amused by her disbelief.

"And then you have to make Impression and wait till the riders—" she went on.

"Why do you think I've insisted on older boys? The dragons are mature long before their riders."

"Then the system is faulty."

He narrowed his eyes slightly, shaking the stylus at her.

"Dragon tradition started out as a guide . . . but there comes a time when man becomes too traditional, too—what was it you said?—too hidebound? Yes, it's traditional to use the weyrbred, because it's been convenient. And because this sensitivity to dragons strengthens where both sire and dam are weyrbred. That doesn't mean weyrbred is best. You, for example . . ."

"There's Weyrblood in the Ruathan line," she said proudly.

"Granted. Take young Naton; he's craftbred from Nabol, yet F'nor tells me he can make Canth understand him."

"Oh, that's not hard to do," she interjected.

"What do you mean?" F'lar jumped on her statement.

They were both interrupted by a high-pitched, penetrating

whine. F'lar listened intently for a moment and then shrugged, grinning.

"Some green's getting herself chased again."

"And that's another item these so-called all-knowing Records of yours never mention. Why is it that only the gold dragon can reproduce?"

F'lar did not suppress a lascivious chuckle.

"Well, for one thing, firestone inhibits reproduction. If they never chewed stone, a green could lay, but at best they produce small beasts, and we need big ones. And, for another thing"—his chuckle rolled out as he went on deliberately, grinning mischievously—"if the greens could reproduce, considering their amorousness and the numbers we have of them, we'd be up to our ears in dragons in next to no time."

The first whine was joined by another, and then a low hum throbbed as if carried by the stones of the Weyr itself.

F'lar, his face changing rapidly from surprise to triumphant astonishment, dashed up the passage.

"What's the matter?" Lessa demanded, picking up her skirts to run after him. "What does that mean?"

The hum, resonating everywhere, was deafening in the echo-chamber of the queen's weyr. Lessa registered the fact that Ramoth was gone. She heard F'lar's boots pounding down the passage to the ledge, a sharp *ta-ta-tat* over the kettledrum booming hum. The whine was so high-pitched now that it was inaudible, but still nerve-racking. Disturbed, frightened, Lessa followed F'lar out.

By the time she reached the ledge, the Bowl was a-whir with dragons on the wing, making for the high entrance to the Hatching Ground. Weyrfolk, riders, women, children, all screaming with excitement, were pouring across the Bowl to the lower entrance to the Ground.

She caught sight of F'lar, charging across to the entrance, and she shrieked at him to wait. He couldn't have heard her across the bedlam.

Fuming because she had the long stairs to descend, then must double back as the stairs faced the feeding grounds at the opposite end of the Bowl from the Hatching Ground, Lessa realized that she, the Weyrwoman, would be the last one there.

Why had Ramoth decided to be secretive about laying? Wasn't she close enough to her own weyrmate to want her with her?

A dragon knows what to do, Ramoth calmly informed her.
You could have told me, Lessa wailed, feeling much abused.

Why, at the time F'lar had been going on largely about huge clutches and three thousand beasts, that infuriating dragon-child had been doing it!

It didn't improve Lessa's temper to have to recall another remark of F'lar's—on the state of the Hatching Grounds. The moment she stepped into the mountain-high cavern, she felt the heat through the soles of her sandals. Everyone was crowded in a loose circle around the far end of the cavern. And everyone was swaying from foot to foot. As Lessa was short to begin with, this only decreased the likelihood of her ever seeing what Ramoth had done.

"Let me through!" she demanded imperiously, pounding on the wide backs of two tall riders.

An aisle was reluctantly opened for her, and she went through, looking neither to her right or left at the excited weyrfolk. She was furious, confused, hurt, and knew she looked ridiculous because the hot sand made her walk with a curious mincing quickstep.

She halted, stunned and wide-eyed at the mass of eggs, and forgot such trivial things as hot feet.

Ramoth was curled around the clutch, looking enormously pleased with herself. She, too, kept shifting, closing and opening a protective wing over her eggs, so that it was difficult to count them.

No one will steal them, silly, so stop fluttering, Lessa advised as she tried to make a tally.

Obediently Ramoth folded her wings. To relieve her maternal anxiety, however, she snaked her head out across the circle of mottled, glowing eggs, looking all around the cavern, flicking her forked tongue in and out.

An immense sigh, like a gust of wind, swept through the cavern. For there, now that Ramoth's wings were furled, gleamed an egg of glowing gold among the mottled ones. A queen egg!

"A queen egg!" The cry went up simultaneously from half a hundred throats. The Hatching Ground rang with cheers, yells, screams, and howls of exultation.

Someone seized Lessa and swung her around in an excess of feeling. A kiss landed in the vicinity of her mouth. No sooner did she recover her footing than she was hugged by someone else—she thought it was Manora, and then pounded and buffeted around in congratulation until she was reeling in a kind of dance between avoiding the celebrants and easing the growing discomfort of her feet.

She broke from the milling revelers and ran across the Ground to Ramoth. Lessa came to a sudden stop before the eggs. They seemed to be pulsing. The shells looked flaccid. She could have sworn they were hard the day she Impressed Ramoth. She wanted to touch one, just to make sure, but dared not.

You may, Ramoth assured her condescendingly. She touched Lessa's shoulder gently with her tongue.

The egg was soft to touch and Lessa drew her hand back quickly, afraid of doing injury.

The heat will harden it, Ramoth said.

"Ramoth, I'm so proud of you," Lessa sighed, looking adoringly up at the great eyes that shone in rainbows of pride. "You are the most marvelous queen ever. I do believe you will redragon all the Weyrs. I do believe you will."

Ramoth inclined her head regally, then began to sway it from side to side over the eggs, protectingly. She began to hiss suddenly, raising from her crouch, beating the air with her wings, before settling back into the sands to lay yet another egg.

The weyrfolk, uncomfortable on the hot sands, were beginning to leave the Hatching Ground now that they had paid tribute to the arrival of the golden egg. A queen took several days to complete her clutch so there was no point to waiting. Seven eggs already lay beside the important golden one, and if there were seven already, this augured well for the eventual total. Wagers were being made and taken even as Ramoth produced her ninth mottled egg.

"Just as I predicted, a queen egg, by the mother of us all," F'lar's voice said in Lessa's ear. "And I'll wager there'll be ten bronzes at least."

She looked up at him, completely in harmony with the Weyrleader at this moment. She was conscious now of Mnementh, crouching proudly on a ledge, gazing fondly at his mate. Impulsively Lessa laid her hand on F'lar's arm.

"F'lar, I do believe you."

"Only now?" F'lar teased her, but his smile was wide and his eyes proud.

Weyrman, watch; Weyrman, learn
Something new in every Turn.
Oldest may be coldest, too.
Sense the right; find the true!

IF F'LAR'S orders over the next months caused no end of discussion and muttering among the weyrfolk, they seemed to Lessa to be only the logical outcomes of their discussion after Ramoth had finished laying her gratifying total of forty-one eggs.

F'lar discarded tradition right and left, treading on more than R'gul's conservative toes.

Out of perverse distaste for outworn doctrines against which she herself had chafed during R'gul's leadership, and out of respect for F'lar's intelligence, Lessa backed him completely. She might not have respected her earlier promise to him that she would believe him until spring if she had not seen his predictions come true, one after another. These were based, however, not on the premonitions she no longer trusted after her experience *between* times, but on recorded facts.

As soon as the eggshells hardened and Ramoth had rolled her special queen egg to one side of the mottled clutch for attentive brooding, F'lar brought the prospective riders into the Hatching Ground. Traditionally the candidates saw the eggs for the first time on the day of Impression. To this precedent F'lar added others: very few of the sixty-odd were weyrbred, and most of them were in their late teens. The candidates were to get used to the eggs, touch them, caress them, be comfortable with the notion that out of these eggs young dragons would hatch, eager and waiting to be Impressed. F'lar felt that such a practice might cut down on casualties during Impression when the boys were simply too scared to move out of the way of the awkward dragonets.

F'lar also had Lessa persuade Ramoth to let Kylara near her precious golden egg. Kylara readily enough weaned her son and spent hours, with Lessa acting as her tutor, beside the golden egg. Despite Kylara's loose attachment to T'bor, she showed an open preference for F'lar's company. Therefore, Lessa took great pains to foster F'lar's plan for Kylara since it meant her removal, with the new-hatched queen, to Fort Weyr.

F'lar's use of the Hold-born as riders served an additional purpose. Shortly before the actual Hatching and Impression,

Lytol, the Warder appointed at Ruath Hold, sent another message.

"The man positively delights in sending bad news," Lessa remarked as F'lar passed the message skin to her.

"He's gloomy," F'nor agreed. He had brought the message. "I feel sorry for that youngster cooped up with such a pessimist."

Lessa frowned at the brown rider. She still found distasteful any mention of Gemma's son, now Lord of her ancestral Hold. Yet . . . as she had inadvertently caused his mother's death and she could not be Weyrwoman and Lady Holder at the same time, it was fitting that Gemma's Jaxom be Lord at Ruatha.

"I, however," F'lar said, "am grateful for his warnings. I suspected Meron would cause trouble again."

"He has shifty eyes, like Fax's," Lessa remarked.

"Shifty-eyed or not, he's dangerous," F'lar answered. "And I cannot have him spreading rumors that we are deliberately choosing men of the Blood to weaken Family Lines."

"There are more craftsmen's sons than Holders' boys, in any case," F'nor snorted.

"I don't like him questioning that the Threads have not appeared," Lessa said gloomily.

F'lar shrugged. "They'll appear in due time. Be thankful the weather has continued cold. When the weather warms up and still no Threads appear, then I will worry." He grinned at Lessa in an intimate reminder of her promise.

F'nor cleared his throat hastily and looked away.

"However," the Weyrleader went on briskly, "I can do something about the other accusation."

So, when it was apparent that the eggs were about to hatch, he broke another long-standing tradition and sent riders to fetch the fathers of the young candidates from craft and Hold.

The great Hatching Cavern gave the appearance of being almost full as Holder and Weyrfolk watched from the tiers above the heated Ground. This time, Lessa observed, there was no aura of fear. The youthful candidates were tense, yes, but not frightened out of their wits by the rocking, shattering eggs. When the ill-coordinated dragonets awkwardly stumbled —it seemed to Lessa that they deliberately looked around at the eager faces as though pre-Impressed—the youths either stepped to one side or eagerly advanced as a crooning dragonet made his choice. The Impressions were made quickly and with no accidents. All too soon, Lessa thought, the triumphant procession of stumbling dragons and proud new riders moved erratically out of the Hatching Ground to the barracks.

The young queen burst from her shell and moved unerringly for Kylara, standing confidently on the hot sands. The watching beasts hummed their approval.

"It was over too soon," Lessa said in a disappointed voice that evening to F'lar.

He laughed indulgently, allowing himself a rare evening of relaxation now that another step had gone as planned. The Holder folk had been ridden home, stunned, dazed, and themselves impressed by the Weyr and the Weyrleader.

"That's because you were watching this time," he remarked, brushing a lock of her hair back. It obscured his view of her profile. He chuckled again. "You'll notice Naton . . ."

"N'ton," she corrected him.

"All right, N'ton—Impressed a bronze."

"Just as you predicted," she said with some asperity.

"And Kylara is Weyrwoman for Pridith."

Lessa did not comment on that, and she did her best to ignore his laughter.

"I wonder which bronze will fly her," he murmured softly.

"It had better be T'bor's Orth," Lessa said, bridling.

He answered her the only way a wise man could.

Crack dust, blackdust,
Turn in freezing air.
Waste dust, spacedust,
From Red Star bare.

LESSA WOKE abruptly, her head aching, her eyes blurred, her mouth dry. She had the immediate memory of a terrible nightmare that, just as quickly, escaped recall. She brushed her hair out of her face and was surprised to find that she had been sweating heavily.

"F'lar?" she called in an uncertain voice. He had evidently risen early. "F'lar," she called again, louder.

He's coming, Mnementh informed her. Lessa sensed that the dragon was just landing on the ledge. She touched Ramoth and found that the queen, too, had been bothered by formless, frightening dreams. The dragon roused briefly and then fell back into deeper sleep.

Disturbed by her vague fears, Lessa rose and dressed, forgoing a bath for the first time since she had arrived at the Weyr.

She called down the shaft for breakfast, then plaited her hair with deft fingers as she waited.

The tray appeared on the shaft platform just as F'lar entered. He kept looking back over his shoulder at Ramoth.

"What's gotten into her?"

"Echoing my nightmare. I woke in a cold sweat."

"You were sleeping quietly enough when I left to assign patrols. You know, at the rate those dragonets are growing, they're already capable of limited flight. All they do is eat and sleep, and that's . . ."

". . . what makes a dragon grow," Lessa finished for him and sipped thoughtfully at her steaming hot *klah*. "You are going to be extra-careful about their drill procedures, aren't you?"

"You mean to prevent an inadvertent flight *between* times? I certainly am," he assured her. "I don't want bored dragon-riders irresponsibly popping in and out." He gave her a long, stern look.

"Well, it wasn't my fault no one taught me to fly early enough," she replied in the sweet tone she used when she was being especially malicious. "If I'd been drilled from the day of Impression to the day of my first flight, I'd never have discovered that trick."

"True enough," he said solemnly.

"You know, F'lar, if I discovered it, someone else must have, and someone else may. If they haven't already."

F'lar drank, making a face as the *klah* scalded his tongue. "I don't know how to find out discreetly. We would be foolish to think we were the first. It is, after all, an inherent ability in dragons, or you would never have been able to do it."

She frowned, took a quick breath, and then let it go, shrugging.

"Go on," he encouraged her.

"Well, isn't it possible that our conviction about the imminence of the Threads could stem from one of us coming back when the Threads are actually falling? I mean . . ."

"My dear girl, we have both analyzed every stray thought

143

and action—even your dream this morning upset you, although it was no doubt due to all the wine you drank last night—until we wouldn't know an honest presentiment if it walked up and slapped us in the face."

"I can't dismiss the thought that this *between* times ability is of crucial value," she said emphatically.

"That, my dear Weyrwoman, *is* an honest presentiment."

"But why?"

"Not why," he corrected her cryptically. *"When."* An idea stirred vaguely in the back of his mind. He tried to nudge it out where he could mull it over. Mnementh announced that F'nor was entering the weyr.

"What's the matter with you?" F'lar demanded of his half brother, for F'nor was choking and sputtering, his face red with the paroxysm.

"Dust . . ." he coughed, slapping at his sleeves and chest with his riding gloves. "Plenty of dust, but no Threads," he said, describing a wide arc with one arm as he fluttered his fingers suggestively. He brushed his tight wher-hide pants, scowling as a fine black dust drifted off.

F'lar felt every muscle in his body tense as he watched the dust float to the floor.

"Where did you get so dusty?" he demanded.

F'nor regarded him with mild surprise. "Weather patrol in Tillek. Entire north has been plagued with dust storms lately. But what I came in for . . ." He broke off, alarmed by F'lar's taut immobility. "What's the matter with dust?" he asked in a baffled voice.

F'lar pivoted on his heel and raced for the stairs to the Record Room. Lessa was right behind him, F'nor belatedly trailing after.

"Tillek, you said?" F'lar barked at his wingsecond. He was clearing the table of stacks for the four charts he then laid out. "How long have these storms been going on? Why didn't you report them?"

"Report dust storms? You wanted to know about warm air masses."

"How long have these storms been going on?" F'lar's voice crackled.

"Close to a week."

"How close?"

"Six days ago the first storm was noticed in upper Tillek.

144

They have been reported in Bitra, Upper Telgar, Crom, and the High Reaches," F'nor reported tersely.

He glanced hopefully at Lessa but saw she, too, was staring at the four unusual charts. He tried to see why the horizontal and vertical strips had been superimposed on Pern's land mass, but the reason was beyond him.

F'lar was making hurried notations, pushing first one map and then another away from him.

"Too involved to think straight, to see clearly, to understand," the Weyrleader snarled to himself, throwing down the stylus angrily.

"You did say only warm air masses," F'nor heard himself saying humbly, aware that he had somehow failed his Weyrleader.

F'lar shook his head impatiently.

"Not your fault, F'nor. Mine. I should have asked. I knew it was good luck that the weather held so cold." He put both hands on F'nor's shoulders, looking directly into his eyes. "The Threads have been falling," he announced gravely. "Falling into the cold air, freezing into bits to drift on the wind"—F'lar imitated F'nor's finger-fluttering—"as specks of black dust."

" 'Crack dust, blackdust,' " Lessa quoted. "In 'The Ballad of Moreta's Ride,' the chorus is all about black dust."

"I don't need to be reminded of Moreta right now," F'lar growled, bending to the maps. "She could talk to any dragon in the Weyrs."

"But I can do that!" Lessa protested.

Slowly, as if he didn't quite credit his ears, F'lar turned back to Lessa. "What did you just say?"

"I said I can talk to any dragon in the Weyr."

Still staring at her, blinking in utter astonishment, F'lar sank down to the table top.

"How long," he managed to say, "have you had *this* particular skill?"

Something in his tone, in his manner, caused Lessa to flush and stammer like an erring weyrling.

"I . . . I always could. Beginning with the watch-wher at Ruatha." She gestured indecisively in Ruatha's westerly direction. "And I talked to Mnementh at Ruatha. And . . . when I got here, I could . . ." Her voice faltered at the accusing look in F'lar's cold, hard eyes. Accusing and, worse, contemptuous.

"I thought you had agreed to help me, to believe in me."

"I'm truly sorry, F'lar. It never occurred to me it was of any use to anyone, but . . ."

F'lar exploded onto both feet, his eyes blazing with aggravation.

"The one thing I could not figure out was how to direct the wings and keep in contact with the Weyr during an attack, how I was going to get reinforcements and firestone in time. And you . . . you have been sitting there, spitefully hiding the . . ."

"I am NOT spiteful," she screamed at him. "I said I was sorry. I am. But you've a nasty, smug habit of keeping your own council. How was I to know you didn't have the same trick? You're F'lar, the Weyrleader, you can do *anything*. Only you're just as bad as R'gul because you never *tell* me half the things I ought to know . . ."

F'lar reached out and shook her until her angry voice was stopped.

"Enough. We can't waste time arguing like children." Then his eyes widened, his jaw dropped. "Waste time? That's it."

"Go *between* times?" Lessa gasped.

"*Between* times!"

F'nor was totally confused. "What are you two talking about?"

"The Threads started falling at dawn in Nerat," F'lar said, his eyes bright, his manner decisive.

F'nor could feel his guts congealing with apprehension. At dawn in Nerat? Why, the rainforests would be demolished. He could feel a surge of adrenalin charging through his body at the thought of danger.

"So we're going *back* there, *between* times, and be there when the Threads started falling, two hours ago. F'nor, the dragons can go not only where we direct them but *when*."

"Where? When?" F'nor repeated, bewildered. "That could be dangerous."

"Yes, but today it will save Nerat. Now, Lessa," and F'lar gave her another shake, compounded of pride and affection, "order out all the dragons, young, old, any that can fly. Tell them to load themselves down with firestone sacks. I don't know if you can talk across time . . ."

"My dream this morning . . ."

"Perhaps. But right now rouse the Weyr." He pivoted to F'nor. "If Threads are falling . . . were falling . . . at Nerat

146

at dawn, they'll be falling on Keroon and Ista right now, because they are in that time pattern. Take two wings to Keroon. Arouse the plains. Get them to start the firepits blazing. Take some weyrlings with you and send them on to Igen and Ista. Those Holds are not in as immediate danger as Keroon. I'll reinforce you as soon as I can. And . . . keep Canth in touch with Lessa."

F'lar clapped his brother on the shoulder and sent him off. The brown rider was too used to taking orders to argue.

"Mnementh says R'gul is duty officer and R'gul wants to know . . ." Lessa began.

"C'mon, girl," F'lar said, his eyes brilliant with excitement. He grabbed up his maps and propelled her up the stairs.

They arrived in the weyr just as R'gul entered with T'sum. R'gul was muttering about this unusual summons.

"Hath told me to report," he complained. "Fine thing when your own dragon . . ."

"R'gul, T'sum, mount your wings. Arm them with all the firestone they can carry, and assemble above Star Stone. I'll join you in a few minutes. We go to Nerat at dawn."

"Nerat? I'm watch officer, not patrol . . ."

"This is no patrol," F'lar cut him off.

"But, sir," T'sum interrupted, his eyes wide. "Nerat's dawn was two hours ago, the same as ours."

"And that is *when* we are going to, brown rider. The dragons, we have discovered, can go *between* places temporally as well as geographically. At dawn Threads fell at Nerat. We're going back, *between* time, to sear them from the sky."

F'lar paid no attention to R'gul's stammered demand for explanation. T'sum, however, grabbed up firestone sacks and raced back to the ledge and his waiting Munth.

"Go on, you old fool," Lessa told R'gul irascibly. "The Threads are here. You were wrong. Now be a dragonman! Or go *between* and stay there!"

Ramoth, awakened by the alarms, poked at R'gul with her man-sized head, and the ex-Weyrleader came out of his momentary shock. Without a word he followed T'sum down the passageway.

F'lar had thrown on his heavy wher-hide tunic and shoved on his riding boots.

"Lessa, be sure to send messages to all the Holds. Now, this attack will stop about four hours from now. So the

147

farthest west it can reach will be Ista. But I want every Hold and craft warned."

She nodded, her eyes intent on his face lest she miss a word.

"Fortunately, the Star is just beginning its Pass, so we won't have to worry about another attack for a few days. I'll figure out the next one when I get back.

"Now, get Manora to organize her women. We'll need pails of ointment. The dragons are going to be laced, and that hurts. Most important, if something goes wrong, you'll have to wait till a bronze is at least a year old to fly Ramoth . . ."

"No one's flying Ramoth but Mnementh," she cried, her eyes sparkling fiercely.

F'lar crushed her against him, his mouth bruising hers as if all her sweetness and strength must come with him. He released her so abruptly that she staggered back against Ramoth's lowered head. She clung for a moment to her dragon, as much for support as for reassurance.

That is, if Mnementh can catch me, Ramoth amended smugly.

> Wheel and turn
> Or bleed and burn.
> Fly *between,*
> Blue and green.
> Soar, dive down,
> Bronze and brown
> Dragonmen must fly
> When Threads are in the sky.

As F'LAR raced down the passageway to the ledge, fire-sacks bumping against his thighs, he was suddenly grateful for the tedious sweeping patrols over every Hold and hollow of Pern. He could see Nerat clearly in his mind's eye. He could see the many-petaled vineflowers which were the distinguishing feature of the rainforests at this time of year. Their ivory blossoms would be glowing in the first beams of sunlight like dragon eyes among the tall, wide-leaved plants.

Mnementh, his eyes flashing with excitement, hovered skittishly over the ledge. F'lar vaulted to the bronze neck.

The Weyr was seething with wings of all colors, noisy with shouts and countercommands. The atmosphere was electric, but F'lar could sense no panic in that ordered confusion.

Dragon and human bodies oozed out of openings around the Bowl walls. Women scurried across the floor from one Lower Cavern to another. The children playing by the lake were sent to gather wood for a fire. The weyrlings, supervised by old C'gan, were forming outside their barracks. F'lar looked up to the Peak and approved the tight formation of the wings assembled there in close flying order. Another wing formed up as he watched. He recognized brown Canth, F'nor on his neck, just as the entire wing vanished.

He ordered Mnementh aloft. The wind was cold and carried a hint of moisture. A late snow? This was the time for it, if ever.

R'gul's wing and T'bor's fanned out on his left, T'sum and D'nol on his right. He noted each dragon was well-laden with sacks. Then he gave Mnementh the visualization of the early spring rainforest in Nerat, just before dawn, the vineflowers gleaming, the sea breaking against the rocks of the High Shoal. . . .

He felt the searing cold of *between*. And he felt a stab of doubt. Was he injudicious, sending them all possibly to their deaths *between* times in this effort to outtime the Threads at Nerat?

Then they were all there, in the crepuscular light that promises day. The lush, fruity smells of the rainforest drifted up to them. Warm, too, and that was frightening. He looked up and slightly to the north. Pulsing with menace, the Red Star shone down.

The men had realized what had happened, their voices raised in astonishment. Mnementh told F'lar that the dragons were mildly surprised at their riders' fuss.

"Listen to me, dragonriders," F'lar called, his voice harsh and distorted in an effort to be heard by all. He waited till the men had moved as close as possible. He told Mnementh to pass the information on to each dragon. Then he explained what they had done and why. No one spoke, but there were many nervous looks exchanged across bright wings.

Crisply he ordered the dragonriders to fan out in a staggered formation, keeping a distance of five wings' spread up or down.

The sun came up.

Slanting across the sea, like an ever-thickening mist, Threads were falling, silent, beautiful, treacherous. Silvery gray were those space-transversing spores, spinning from hard

149

frozen ovals into coarse filaments as they penetrated the warm atmospheric envelope of Pern. Less than mindless, they had been ejected from their barren planet toward Pern, a hideous rain that sought organic matter to nourish it into growth. One Thread, sinking into fertile soil, would burrow deep, propagating thousands in the warm earth, rendering it into a black-dusted wasteland. The southern continent of Pern had already been sucked dry. The true parasites of Pern were Threads.

A stifled roar from the throats of eighty men and dragons broke the dawn air above Nerat's green heights—as if the Threads might hear this challenge, F'lar mused.

As one, dragons swiveled their wedge-shaped heads to their riders for firestone. Great jaws macerated the hunks. The fragments were swallowed and more firestone was demanded. Inside the beasts, acids churned and the poisonous phosphines were readied. When the dragons belched forth the gas, it would ignite in the air into ravening flame to sear the Threads from the sky. And burn them from the soil.

Dragon instinct took over the moment the Threads began to fall above Nerat's shores.

As much admiration as F'lar had always held for his bronze companion, it achieved newer heights in the next hours. Beating the air in great strokes, Mnementh soared with flaming breath to meet the down-rushing menace. The fumes, swept back by the wind, choked F'lar until he thought to crouch low on the lee side of the bronze neck. The dragon squealed as a Thread flicked the tip of one wing. Instantly F'lar and he ducked into *between*, cold, calm, black. The frozen Thread cracked off. In the flicker of an eye, they were back to face the reality of Threads.

Around him F'lar saw dragons winking in and out of *between*, flaming as they returned, diving, soaring. As the attack continued and they drifted across Nerat, F'lar began to recognize the pattern in the dragons' instinctive evasion-attack movements. And in the Threads. For, contrary to what he had gathered from his study of the Records, the Threads fell in patches. Not as rain will, in steady unbroken sheets, but like flurries of snow, here, above, there, whipped to one side suddenly. Never fluidly, despite the continuity their name implied.

You could see a patch above you. Flaming, your dragon would rise. You'd have the intense joy of seeing the clump shrivel from bottom to top. Sometimes, a patch would fall between riders. One dragon would signal he would follow and, spouting flame, would dive and sear.

Gradually the dragonriders worked their way over the rain-forests, so densely, so invitingly green. F'lar refused to dwell on what just one live Thread burrow would do to that lush land. He would send back a low-flying patrol to quarter every foot. One Thread, just one Thread, could put out the ivory eyes of every luminous vineflower.

A dragon screamed somewhere to his left. Before he could identify the beast, it had ducked *between*. F'lar heard other cries of pain, from men as well as dragons. He shut his ears and concentrated, as dragons did, on the here-and-now. Would Mnementh remember those piercing cries later? F'lar wished he could forget them now.

He, F'lar, the bronze rider, felt suddenly superfluous. It was the dragons who were fighting this engagement. You encouraged your beast, comforted him when the Threads burned, but you depended on his instinct and speed.

Hot fire dripped across F'lar's cheeks, burrowing like acid into his shoulder . . . a cry of surprised agony burst from F'lar's lips. Mnementh took them to merciful *between*. The dragonmen battled with frantic hands at the Threads, felt them crumble in the intense cold of *between* and break off. Revolted, he slapped at injuries still afire. Back in Nerat's humid air, the sting seemed to ease. Mnementh crooned comfortingly and then dove at a patch, breathing fire.

Shocked at self-consideration, F'lar hurriedly examined his mount's shoulder for telltale score marks.

I duck very quickly, Mnementh told him and veered away from a dangerously close clump of Threads. A brown dragon followed them down and burned them to ash.

It might have been moments, it might have been a hundred hours later when F'lar looked down in surprise at the sunlit sea. Threads now dropped harmlessly into the salty waters. Nerat was to the east of him on his right, the rocky tip curling westward.

F'lar felt weariness in every muscle. In the excitement of frenzied battle, he had forgotten the bloody scores on cheek and shoulder. Now, as he and Mnementh glided slowly, the injuries ached and stung.

He flew Mnementh high and when they had achieved sufficient altitude, they hovered. He could see no Threads falling landward. Below him, the dragons ranged, high and low, searching for any sign of a burrow, alert for any suddenly toppling trees or disturbed vegetation.

"Back to the Weyr," he ordered Mnementh with a heavy sigh. He heard the bronze relay the command even as he himself was taken *between*. He was so tired he did not even visualize where—much less, when—relying on Mnementh's instinct to bring him safely home through time and space.

> Honor those the dragons heed,
> In thought and favor, word and deed.
> Worlds are lost or worlds are saved
> From those dangers dragon-braved.

CRANING HER neck toward the Star Stone at Benden Peak, Lessa watched from the ledge until she saw the four wings disappear from view.

Sighing deeply to quiet her inner fears, Lessa raced down the stairs to the floor of Benden Weyr. She noticed that someone was building a fire by the lake and that Manora was already ordering her women around, her voice clear but calm.

Old C'gan had the weyrlings lined up. She caught the envious eyes of the newest dragonriders at the barracks windows. They'd have time enough to fly a flaming dragon. From what F'lar had intimated, they'd have Turns.

She shuddered as she stepped up to the weyrlings but managed to smile at them. She gave them their orders and sent them off to warn the Holds, checking quickly with each dragon to be sure the rider had given clear references. The Holds would shortly be stirred up to a froth.

Canth told her that there were Threads at Keroon, falling on the Keroon side of Nerat Bay. He told her that F'nor did not think two wings were enough to protect the meadowlands.

Lessa stopped in her tracks, trying to think how many wings were already out.

K'net's wing is still here, Ramoth informed her. *On the Peak.*

Lessa glanced up and saw bronze Piyanth spread his wings in answer. She told him to get *between* to Keroon, close to Nerat Bay. Obediently the entire wing rose and then disappeared.

She turned with a sigh to say something to Manora when

a rush of wind and a vile stench almost overpowered her. The air above the Weyr was full of dragons. She was about to demand of Piyanth why he hadn't gone to Keroon when she realized there were far more beasts a-wing than K'net's twenty.

But you just left, she cried as she recognized the unmistakable bulk of bronze Mnementh.

That was two hours ago for us, Mnementh said with such weariness in his tone that Lessa closed her eyes in sympathy.

Some dragons were gliding in fast. From their awkwardness it was evident that they were hurt.

As one, the women grabbed salve pots and clean rags and beckoned the injured down. The numbing ointment was smeared on score marks where wings resembled black and red lace.

No matter how badly injured he might be, every rider tended his beast first.

Lessa kept one eye on Mnementh, sure that F'lar would not keep the huge bronze hovering like that if he'd been hurt. She was helping T'sum with Munth's cruelly pierced right wing when she realized that sky above the Star Stone was empty.

She forced herself to finish with Munth before she went to find the bronze and his rider. When she did locate them, she also saw Kylara smearing salve on F'lar's cheek and shoulder. She was advancing purposefully across the sands toward the pair when Canth's urgent plea reached her. She saw Mnementh's head swing upward as he, too, caught the brown's thought.

"F'lar, Canth says they need help," Lessa cried. She didn't notice then that Kylara slipped away into the busy crowd.

F'lar wasn't badly hurt. She reassured herself about that. Kylara had treated the wicked burns that seemed to be shallow. Someone had found him another fur to replace the tatters of the Thread-bared one. He frowned—and winced because the frown creased his burned cheek. He gulped hurriedly at his *klah.*

Mnementh, what's the tally of able-bodied? Oh, never mind, just get 'em aloft with a full load of firestone.

"You're all right?" Lessa asked, a detaining hand on his arm. He couldn't just go off like this, could he?

He smiled tiredly down at her, pressed his empty mug into her hands, giving them a quick squeeze. Then he vaulted to

153

Mnementh's neck. Someone handed him a heavy load of sacks.

Blue, green, brown, and bronze dragons lifted from the Weyr Bowl in quick order. A trifle more than sixty dragons hovered briefly above the Weyr where eighty had lingered so few minutes before.

So few dragons. So few riders. How long could they take such toll?

Canth said F'nor needed more firestone.

She looked about anxiously. None of the weyrlings were back yet from their messenger rounds. A dragon was crooning plaintively, and she wheeled, but it was only young Pridith, stumbling across the Weyr to the feeding grounds, butting playfully at Kylara as they walked. The only other dragons were injured or—her eye fell on C'gan, emerging from the weyrling barracks.

"C'gan, can you and Tagath get more firestone to F'nor at Keroon?"

"Of course," the old blue rider assured her, his chest lifting with pride, his eyes flashing. She hadn't thought to send him anywhere, yet he had lived his life in training for this emergency. He shouldn't be deprived of a chance at it.

She smiled her approval at his eagerness as they piled heavy sacks on Tagath's neck. The old blue dragon snorted and danced as if he were young and strong again. She gave them the references Canth had visualized to her.

She watched as the two blinked out above the Star Stone. *It isn't fair. They have all the fun,* said Ramoth peevishly. Lessa saw her sunning herself on the Weyr ledge, preening her enormous wings.

"You chew firestone and you're reduced to a silly green," Lessa told her Wyermate sharply. She was inwardly amused by the queen's disgruntled complaint.

Lessa passed among the injured then. B'fol's dainty green beauty moaned and tossed her head, unable to bend one wing that had been threaded to bare cartilage. She'd be out for weeks, but she had the worst injury among the dragons. Lessa looked quickly away from the misery in B'fol's worried eyes.

As she did the rounds, she realized that more men were injured than beasts. Two in R'gul's wing had sustained serious head damages. One man might lose an eye completely. Manora had dosed him unconscious with numb-weed. Another man's arm had been burned clear to the bone. Minor though most of the wounds were, the tally dismayed Lessa. How many more would be disabled at Keroon?

Out of one hundred and seventy-two dragons, fifteen already were out of action, some only for a day or two, however.

A thought struck Lessa. If N'ton had actually ridden Canth, maybe he could ride out on the next dragonade on an injured man's beast, since there were more injured riders than dragons. F'lar broke traditions as he chose. Here was another one to set aside—if the dragon was agreeable.

Presuming N'ton was not the only new rider able to transfer to another beast, what good would such flexibility do in the long run? F'lar had definitely said the incursions would not be so frequent at first, when the Red Star was just beginning its fifty-Turn long circling pass of Pern. How frequent was frequent? He would know, but he wasn't here.

Well, he *had* been right this morning about the appearance of Threads at Nerat, so his exhaustive study of those old Records had proved worthwhile.

No, that wasn't quite accurate. He had forgotten to have the men alert for signs of black dust as well as warming weather. As he had put the matter right by going *between* times, she would graciously allow him that minor error. But he did have an infuriating habit of guessing correctly. Lessa corrected herself again. He didn't guess. He studied. He planned. He thought and then he used common good sense. Like figuring out where and when Threads would strike according to entries in those smelly Records. Lessa began to feel better about their future.

Now, if he would just make the riders learn to trust their dragons' sure instinct in battle, they would keep casualties down, too.

A shriek pierced air and ear as a blue dragon emerged above the Star Stone.

"*Ramoth!*" Lessa screamed in an instinctive reaction, hardly knowing why. The queen was a-wing before the echo of her command had died. For the careering blue was obviously in grave trouble. He was trying to brake his forward speed, yet one wing would not function. His rider had slipped forward over the great shoulder, precariously clinging to his dragon's neck with one hand.

Lessa, her hands clapped over her mouth, watched fearfully. There wasn't a sound in the Bowl but the flapping of Ramoth's immense wings. The queen rose swiftly to position herself against the desperate blue, lending him wing support on the crippled side.

The watchers gasped as the rider slipped, lost his hold, and fell—landing on Ramoth's wide shoulders.

The blue dropped like a stone. Ramoth came to a gentle stop near him, crouching low to allow the weyrfolk to remove her passenger.

It was C'gan.

Lessa felt her stomach heave as she saw the ruin the Threads had made of the old harper's face. She dropped beside him, pillowing his head in her lap. The weyrfolk gathered in a respectful, silent circle.

Manora, her face, as always, serene, had tears in her eyes. She knelt and placed her hand on the old rider's heart. Concern flicked in her eyes as she looked up at Lessa. Slowly she shook her head. Then, setting her lips in a thin line, she began to apply the numbing salve.

"Too toothless old to flame and too slow to get *between*," C'gan mumbled, rolling his head from side to side. "Too old. But 'Dragonmen must fly/When Threads are in the sky. . . .'" His voice trailed off into a sigh. His eyes closed.

Lessa and Manora looked at each other in anguish. A terrible, ear-shattering note cut the silence. Tagath sprang aloft in a tremendous leap. C'gan's eyes rolled slowly open, sightless. Lessa, breath suspended, watched the blue dragon, trying to deny the inevitable as Tagath disappeared in mid-air.

A low moan sprang up around the Weyr, like the torn, lonely cry of a keening wind. The dragons uttered tribute.

"Is he . . . gone?" Lessa asked, although she knew.

Manora nodded slowly, tears streaming down her cheeks as she reached over to close C'gan's dead eyes.

Lessa rose slowly to her feet, motioning to some of the women to remove the old rider's body. Absently she rubbed her bloody hands dry on her skirts, trying to concentrate on what might be needed next.

Yet her mind turned back to what had just happened. A dragonrider had died. His dragon, too. The Threads had claimed one pair already. How many more would die this cruel Turn? How long could the Weyr survive? Even after

Ramoth's forty matured, and the ones she soon would conceive, and her queen-daughters, too?

Lessa walked apart to quiet her uncertainties and ease her grief. She saw Ramoth wheel and glide aloft, to land on the Peak. One day soon would Lessa see those golden wings laced red and black from Thread marks? Would Ramoth . . . disappear?

No, Ramoth would not. Not while Lessa lived.

F'lar told her long ago that she must learn to look beyond the narrow confines of Hold Ruatha and mere revenge. He was, as usual, right. As Weyrwoman under his tutelage, she had further learned that living *was* more than raising dragons and Spring Games. Living was struggling to do something impossible—to succeed, or die, knowing you had tried!

Lessa realized that she had, at last, fully accepted her role: as Weyrwoman and as mate, to help F'lar shape men and events for many Turns to come—to secure Pern against the Threads.

Lessa threw back her shoulders and lifted her chin high. Old C'gan had had the right of it.

> Dragonmen *must* fly
> When Threads are in the sky!
>
> Worlds are lost or worlds are saved
> By those dangers dragon-braved.

As F'LAR had predicted, the attack ended by high noon, and weary dragons and riders were welcomed by Ramoth's high-pitched trumpeting from the Peak.

Once Lessa assured herself that F'lar had taken no additional injury, that F'nor's were superficial and that Manora was keeping Kylara busy in the kitchens, she applied herself to organizing the care of the injured and the comfort of the worried.

As dusk fell, an uneasy peace settled on the Weyr—the quiet of minds and bodies too tired or too hurtful to talk. Lessa's own words mocked her as she made out the list of wounded men and beasts. Twenty-eight men or dragons were out of the air for the next Thread battle. C'gan was the only fatality, but there had been four more seriously injured dragons at Keroon and seven badly scored men, out of action entirely for months to come.

Lessa crossed the Bowl to her Weyr, reluctant but resigned to giving F'lar this unsettling news.

She expected to find him in the sleeping room, but it was vacant. Ramoth was asleep already as Lessa passed her on the way to the Council Room—also empty. Puzzled and a little alarmed, Lessa half-ran down the steps to the Records Room, to find F'lar, haggard of face, poring over musty skins.

"What are you doing here?" she demanded angrily. "You ought to be asleep."

"So should you," he drawled, amused.

"I was helping Manora settle the wounded . . ."

"Each to his own craft." But he did lean back from the table, rubbing his neck and rotating the uninjured shoulder to ease stiffened muscles.

"I couldn't sleep," he admitted, "so I thought I'd see what answers I might turn up in the Records."

"More answers? To what?" Lessa cried, exasperated with him. As if the Records ever answered anything. Obviously the tremendous responsibilities of Pern's defense against the Threads were beginning to tell on the Weyrleader. After all, there had been the stress of the first battle, not to mention the drain of the traveling *between* time itself to get to Nerat to forestall the Threads.

F'lar grinned and beckoned Lessa to sit beside him on the wall bench.

"I need the answer to the very pressing question of how one understrength Weyr can do the fighting of six."

Lessa fought the panic that rose, a cold flood, from her guts.

"Oh, your time schedules will take care of that," she replied gallantly. "You'll be able to conserve the dragon-power until the new forty can join the ranks."

F'lar raised a mocking eyebrow.

"Let us be honest between ourselves, Lessa."

"But there have been Long Intervals before," she argued, "and since Pern survived them, Pern can again."

"Before there were always six Weyrs. And twenty so Turns before the Red Star was due to begin its Pass, the queens would start to produce enormous clutches. All the queens, not just one faithful golden Ramoth. Oh, how I curse Jora!" He slammed to his feet and started pacing, irritably brushing the lock of black hair that fell across his eyes.

Lessa was torn with the desire to comfort him and the

sinking, choking fear in her belly that made it difficult to think at all.

"You were not so doubtful . . ."

He whirled back to her. "Not until I had actually had an encounter with the Threads and reckoned up the numbers of injuries. That sets the odds against us. Even supposing we can mount other riders to uninjured dragons, we will be hard put to keep a continuously effective force in the air and still maintain a ground guard." He caught her puzzled frown. "There's Nerat to be gone over on foot tomorrow. I'd be a fool indeed if I thought we'd caught and seared every Thread in mid-air."

"Get the Holders to do that. They can't just immure themselves safely in their Inner Holds and let us do all. If they hadn't been so miserly and stupid . . ."

He cut off her complaint with an abrupt gesture. "They'll do their part all right," he assured her. "I'm sending for a full Council tomorrow, all Hold Lords and all Craftmasters. But there's more to it than just marking where Threads fall. How do you destroy a burrow that's gone deep under the surface? A dragon's breath is fine for the air and surface work but no good three feet down."

"Oh, I hadn't thought of that aspect. But the firepits . . ."

". . . are only on the heights and around human habitations, not on the meadowlands of Keroon or on Nerat's so green rainforests."

This consideration was daunting indeed. She gave a rueful little laugh.

"Shortsighted of me to suppose our dragons are all poor Pern needs to dispatch the Threads. Yet . . ." She shrugged expressively.

"There are other methods," F'lar said, "or there were. There must have been. I have run across frequent mention that the Holds were organizing ground groups and that they were armed with fire. What kind is never mentioned because it was so well-known." He threw up his hands in disgust and sagged back down on the bench. "Not even five hundred dragons could have seared all the Threads that fell today. Yet *they* managed to keep Pern Thread-free."

"Pern, yes, but wasn't the Southern Continent lost? Or did they just have their hands too full with Pern itself?"

"No one's bothered with the Southern Continent in a hundred thousand Turns," F'lar snorted.

"It's on the maps," Lessa reminded him.

He scowled disgustedly at the Records, piled in uncommunicative stacks on the long table.

"The answer must be there. Somewhere."

There was an edge of desperation in his voice, the hint that he held himself to blame for not having discovered those elusive facts.

"Half those things couldn't be read by the man who wrote them," Lessa said tartly. "Besides that, it's been your *own* ideas that have helped us most so far. You compiled the time maps, and look how valuable they have been already."

"I'm getting too hidebound again, huh?" he asked, a half smile tugging at one corner of his mouth.

"Undoubtedly," she assured him with more confidence than she felt. "We both know the Records are guilty of the most ridiculous omissions."

"Well said, Lessa. So let us forget these misguiding and antiquated precepts and think up our own guides. First, we need more dragons. Second, we need them now. Third, we need something as effective as a flaming dragon to destroy Threads which have burrowed."

"Fourth, we need sleep, or we won't be able to think of anything," she added with a touch of her usual asperity.

F'lar laughed outright, hugging her.

"You've got your mind on one thing, haven't you?" he teased, his hands caressing her eagerly.

She pushed ineffectually at him, trying to escape. For a wounded, tired man, he was remarkably amorous. One with that Kylara. Imagine that woman's presumption, dressing his wounds.

"My responsibility as Weyrwoman includes care of you, the Weyrleader."

"But you spend hours with blue dragonriders and leave me to Kylara's tender ministrations."

"You didn't look as if you objected."

F'lar threw back his head and roared. "Should I open Fort Weyr and send Kylara on?" he taunted her.

"I'd as soon Kylara were Turns as well as miles away from here," Lessa snapped, thoroughly irritated.

F'lar's jaw dropped, his eyes widened. He leaped to his feet with an astonished cry.

"You've said it!"

"Said what?"

"Turns away! That's it. We'll send Kylara back, *between* times, with her queen and the new dragonets." F'lar excitedly paced the room while Lessa tried to follow his reasoning. "No, I'd better send at least one of the older bronzes. F'nor, too . . . I'd rather have F'nor in charge. . . . Discreetly, of course—"

"Send Kylara back . . . where to? When to?" Lessa interrupted him.

"Good point." F'lar dragged out the ubiquitous charts. "Very good point. Where can we send them around here without causing anomalies by being present at one of the other Weyrs? The High Reaches are remote. No, we've found remains of fires there, you know, still warm, and no inkling as to who built them or why. And if we had already sent them back, they'd've been ready for today, and they weren't. So they can't have been in two places already. . . ." He shook his head, dazed by the paradoxes.

Lessa's eyes were drawn to the blank outline of the neglected Southern Continent.

"Send them there," she suggested sweetly, pointing.

"There's nothing there."

"Then bring in what they need. There must be water, for Threads can't devour that. We fly in whatever else is needed, fodder for the herdbeasts, grain. . . ."

F'lar drew his brows together in concentration, his eyes sparkling with thought, the depression and defeat of a few moments ago forgotten.

"Threads wouldn't be there ten Turns ago. And haven't been there for close to four hundred. Ten Turns would give Pridith time to mature and have several clutches. Maybe more queens."

Then he frowned and shook his head dubiously. "No, there's no Weyr there. No Hatching Ground, no . . ."

"How do we know that?" Lessa caught him up sharply, too delighted with many aspects of this project to give it up easily. "The Records don't mention the Southern Continent, true, but they omit a great deal. How do we know it isn't green again in the four hundred Turns since the Threads last spun? We do know that Threads can't last long unless there is something organic on which to feed and that once they've devoured all, they dry up and blow away."

F'lar looked at her admiringly. "Now, why hasn't someone wondered about that before?"

161

"Too hidebound." Lessa wagged her finger at him. "Besides, there's been no need to bother with it."

"Necessity—or is it jealousy?—hatches many a tough shell." There was a smile of pure malice on his face, and Lessa whirled away as he reached for her.

"The good of the Weyr," she retorted.

"Furthermore, I'll send you along with F'nor tomorrow to look. Only fair, since it is your idea."

Lessa stood still. "You're not going?"

"I feel confident I can leave this project in your very capable, interested hands." He laughed and caught her against his uninjured side, smiling down at her, his eyes glowing. "I must play ruthless Weyrleader and keep the Hold Lords from slamming shut their Inner Doors. And I'm hoping"—he raised his head, frowning slightly—"one of the Craftmasters may know the solution to the third problem—getting rid of Thread burrows."

"But . . ."

"The trip will give Ramoth something to stop her fuming." He pressed the girl's slender body more closely to him, his full attention at last on her odd, delicate face. "Lessa, you are my fourth problem." He bent to kiss her.

At the sound of hurried steps in the passageway, F'lar scowled irritably, releasing her.

"At this hour?" he muttered, ready to reprove the intruder scathingly. "Who goes there?"

"F'lar?" It was F'nor's voice, anxious, hoarse.

The look on F'lar's face told Lessa that not even his half brother would be spared a reprimand, and it pleased her irrationally. But the moment F'nor burst into the room, both Weyrleader and Weyrwoman were stunned silent. There was something subtly wrong with the brown rider. And as the man blurted out his incoherent message, the difference suddenly registered in Lessa's mind. He was tanned! He wore no bandages and hadn't the slightest trace of the Thread-mark along his cheek that she had tended this evening!

"F'lar, it's not working out! You can't be alive in two times at once!" F'nor was exclaiming distractedly. He staggered against the wall, grabbing the sheer rock to hold himself upright. There were deep circles under his eyes, visible despite the tan. "I don't know how much longer we can last like this. We're all affected. Some days not as badly as others."

"I don't understand."

"Your dragons are all right," F'nor assured the Weyrleader with a bitter laugh. "It doesn't bother them. They keep all their wits about them. But their riders . . . all the weyr-folk . . . we're shadows, half alive, like dragonless men, part of us gone forever. Except Kylara." His face contorted with intense dislike. "All she wants to do is go back and watch herself. The woman's egomania will destroy us all, I'm afraid."

His eyes suddenly lost focus, and he swayed wildly. His eyes widened, and his mouth fell open. "I can't stay. I'm here already. Too close. Makes it twice as bad. But I had to warn you. I promise, F'lar, we'll stay as long as we can, but it won't be much longer . . . so it won't be long enough, but we tried. We tried!"

Before F'lar could move, the brown rider whirled and ran, half-crouched, from the room.

"But he hasn't gone yet!" Lessa gasped. "He hasn't even gone yet!"

F'lar stared after his half brother, his brows contracting with the keen anxiety he felt.

"What can have happened?" Lessa demanded of the Weyrleader. "We haven't even told F'nor. We ourselves just finished considering the idea." Her hand flew to her own cheek. "And the Thread-mark—I dressed it myself tonight—it's gone. Gone. So he's been gone a long while." She sank down to the bench.

"However, he has come back. So he did go," F'lar remarked slowly in a reflective tone of voice. "Yet we now know the venture is not entirely successful even before it begins. And knowing this, we have sent him back ten Turns for whatever good it is doing." F'lar paused thoughtfully. "Consequently we have no alternative but to continue with the experiment."

"But what could be going wrong?"

"I think I know and there is no remedy." He sat down beside her, his eyes intent on hers. "Lessa, you were very upset when you got back from going *between* to Ruatha that first time. But I think now it was more than just the shock of seeing Fax's men invading your own Hold or in thinking your return might have been responsible for that disaster. I think it has to do with being in two times at once." He hesitated again, trying to understand this immense new concept even as he voiced it.

Lessa regarded him with such awe that he found himself laughing with embarrassment.

"It's unnerving under any conditions," he went on, "to think of returning and seeing a younger self."

"That must be what he meant about Kylara," Lessa gasped, "about her wanting to go back and watch herself . . . as a child. Oh, that wretched girl!" Lessa was filled with anger for Kylara's self-absorption. "Wretched, selfish creature. She'll ruin everything."

"Not yet," F'lar reminded her. "Look, although F'nor warned us that the situation in his time is getting desperate, he didn't tell us how much he was able to accomplish. But you noticed that his scar had healed to invisibility—consequently some Turns must have elapsed. Even if Pridith lays one good-sized clutch, even if just the forty of Ramoth's are mature enough to fight in three days' time, we have accomplished something. Therefore, Weyrwoman," and he noticed how she straightened up at the sound of her title, "we must disregard F'nor's return. When you fly to the Southern Continent tomorrow, make no allusion to it. Do you understand?"

Lessa nodded gravely and then gave a little sigh. "I don't know if I'm happy or disappointed to realize, even before we get there tomorrow, that the Southern Continent obviously will support a Weyr," she said with dismay. "It was kind of exciting to wonder."

"Either way," F'lar told her with a sardonic smile, "we have found only part of the answers to problems one and two."

"Well, you'd better answer number four right now!" Lessa suggested. "Decisively!"

> Weaver, Miner, Harper, Smith,
> Tanner, Farmer, Herdsman, Lord,
> Gather, wingsped, listen well
> To the Weyrman's urgent word.

THEY BOTH managed to guard against any reference to his premature return when they spoke to F'nor the next morning. F'lar asked brown Canth to send his rider to the queen's weyr as soon as he awoke and was pleased to see F'nor almost immediately. If the brown rider noticed the curiously intent stare Lessa gave his bandaged face, he gave no sign of it. As a matter of fact, the moment F'lar outlined the bold venture of scouting the Southern Continent with the possibility of starting a Weyr ten Turns back in time, F'nor forgot all about his wounds.

"I'll go willingly only if you send T'bor along with Kylara. I'm not waiting till N'ton and his bronze are big enough to take her on. T'bor and she are as—" F'nor broke off with a grimace in Lessa's direction. "Well, they're as near a pair as can be. I don't object to being . . . importuned, but there are limits to what a man is willing to do out of loyalty to dragon-kind."

F'lar barely managed to restrain the amusement he felt over F'nor's reluctance. Kylara tried her wiles on every rider, and, because F'nor had not been amenable, she was determined to succeed with him.

"I hope two bronzes are enough. Pridith may have a mind of her own, come matingtime."

"You can't turn a brown into a bronze!" F'nor exclaimed with such dismay that F'lar could no longer restrain himself.

"Oh, stop it!" And that touched off Lessa's laughter. "You're as bad a pair," F'nor snapped, getting to his feet. "If we're going south, Weyrwoman, we'd better get started. Particularly if we're going to give this laughing maniac a chance to compose himself before the solemn Lords descend. I'll get provisions from Manora. Well, Lessa? *Are* you coming with me?"

Muffling her laughter, Lessa grabbed up her furred flying cloak and followed him. At least the adventure was starting off well.

Carrying the pitcher of *klah* and his cup, F'lar adjourned to the Council Room, debating whether to tell the Lords and Craftmasters of this southern venture or not. The dragons' ability to fly *between* times as well as places was not yet well-known. The Lords might not realize it had been used the previous day to forestall the Threads. If F'lar could be sure that project was going to be successful—well, it would add an optimistic note to the meeting.

Let the charts, with the waves and times of the Thread attacks clearly visible, reassure the Lords.

The visitors were not long in assembling. Nor were they all successful in hiding their apprehension and the shock they had received now that Threads had again spun down from the Red Star to menace all life on Pern. This was going to be a difficult session, F'lar decided grimly. He had a fleeting wish, which he quickly suppressed, that he had gone with F'nor and Lessa to the Southern Continent. Instead, he bent with apparent industry to the charts before him.

Soon there were but two more to come, Meron of Nabol (whom he would have liked not to include, for the man was a troublemaker) and Lytol of Ruatha. F'lar had sent for Lytol last because he did not wish Lessa to encounter the man. She was still overly—and, to his mind, foolishly—sensitive at having had to resign her claim to Ruatha Hold for the Lady Gemma's posthumous son. Lytol, as Warder of Ruatha, had a place in this conference. The man was also an ex-dragonman, and his return to the Weyr was painful enough without Lessa's compounding it with her resentment. Lytol was, with the exception of young Larad of Telgar, the Weyr's most valuable ally.

S'lel came in with Meron a step behind him. The Holder was furious at this summons; it showed in his walk, in his eyes, in his haughty bearing. But he was also as inquisitive as he was devious. He nodded only to Larad among the Lords and took the seat left vacant for him by Larad's side. Meron's manner made it obvious that that place was too close to F'lar by half a room.

The Weyrleader acknowledged S'lel's salute and indicated the bronze rider should be seated. F'lar had given thought to the seating arrangements in the Council Room, carefully interspersing brown and bronze dragonriders with Holders and Craftsmen. There was now barely room to move in the generously proportioned cavern, but there was also no room in which to draw daggers if tempers got hot.

A hush fell on the gathering, and F'lar looked up to see that the stocky, glowering ex-dragonman from Ruatha had stopped on the threshold of the Council. He slowly brought his hand up in a respectful salute to the Weyrleader. As F'lar returned the salute, he noticed that the tic in Lytol's left cheek jumped almost continuously.

Lytol's eyes, dark with pain and inner unquiet, ranged the room. He nodded to the members of his former wing, to Larad and Zurg, head of his own weavers' craft. Stiff-legged, he walked to the remaining seat, murmuring a greeting to T'sum on his left.

F'lar rose.

"I appreciate your coming, good Lords and Craftmasters. The Threads spin once again. The first attack has been met and seared from the sky. Lord Vincet," and the worried Holder of Nerat looked up in alarm, "we have dispatched a patrol to the rainforest to do a low-flight sweep to make certain there are no burrows."

Vincet swallowed nervously, his face paling at the thought of what Threads could do to his fertile, lush holdings.

"We shall need your best junglemen to help—"

"Help? But you said . . . the Threads were seared in the sky?"

"There is no point in taking the slightest chance," F'lar replied, implying that the patrol was only a precaution instead of the necessity he knew it would be.

Vincet gulped, glancing anxiously around the room for sympathy, and found none. Everyone would soon be in his position.

"There is a patrol due at Keroon and at Igen." F'lar looked first at Lord Corman, then at Lord Banger, who gravely nodded. "Let me say by way of reassurance that there will be no further attacks for three days and four hours." F'lar tapped the appropriate chart. "The Threads will begin approximately here on Telgar, drift westward through the southernmost portion of Crom, which is mountainous, and on, through Ruatha and the southern end of Nabol."

"How can you be so certain of that?"

F'lar recognized the contemptuous voice of Meron of Nabol.

"The Threads do not fall like a child's jackstraws, Lord Meron," F'lar replied. "They fall in a definitely predictable pattern; the attacks last exactly six hours. The intervals between attacks will gradually shorten over the next few Turns as the Red Star draws closer. Then, for about forty full Turns, as the Red Star swings past and around us, the attacks occur every fourteen hours, marching across our world in a time-able fashion."

"So *you* say," Meron sneered, and there was a low mumble of support.

"So the Teaching Ballads say," Larad put in firmly.

Meron glanced at Telgar's Lord and went on, "I recall another of your predictions about how the Threads were supposed to begin falling right after Solstice."

"Which they did," F'lar interrupted him. "As black dust in the Northern Holds. For the reprieve we've had, we can

167

thank our lucky stars that we have had an unusually hard and long Cold Turn."

"Dust?" demanded Nessel of Crom. "That dust was Threads?" The man was one of Fax's blood connections and under Meron's influence: an older man who had learned lessons from his conquering relative's bloody ways and had not the wit to improve or alter the original. "My Hold is still blowing with them. They're dangerous?"

F'lar shook his head emphatically. "How long has the black dust been blowing in your Hold? Weeks? Done any harm yet?"

Nessel frowned.

"I'm interested in your charts, Weyrleader," Larad of Telgar said smoothly. "Will they give us an accurate idea of how often we may expect Threads to fall in our own Holds?"

"Yes. You may also anticipate that the dragonmen will arrive shortly before the invasion is due," F'lar went on. "However, additional measures of your own are necessary, and it is for this that I called the Council."

"Wait a minute," Corman of Keroon growled. "I want a copy of those fancy charts of yours for my own. I want to know what those bands and wavy lines really mean. I want . . ."

"Naturally you'll have a timetable of your own. I mean to impose on Masterharper Robinton"—F'lar nodded respectfully toward that Craftmaster—"to oversee the copying and make sure everyone understands the timing involved."

Robinton, a tall, gaunt man with a lined, saturnine face, bowed deeply. A slight smile curved his wide lips at the now hopeful glances favored him by the Hold Lords. His craft, like that of the dragonmen, had been much mocked, and this new respect amused him. He was a man with a keen eye for the ridiculous, and an active imagination. The circumstances in which doubting Pern found itself were too ironic not to appeal to his innate sense of justice. He now contented himself with a deep bow and a mild phrase.

"Truly all shall pay heed to the master." His voice was deep, his words enunciated with no provincial slurring.

F'lar, about to speak, looked sharply at Robinton as he caught the double barb of that single line. Larad, too, looked around at the Masterharper, clearing his throat hastily.

"We shall have our charts," Larad said, forestalling Meron, who had opened his mouth to speak. "We shall have the dragonmen when the Threads spin. What are these additional measures? And why are they necessary?"

All eyes were on F'lar again.

"We have one Weyr where six once flew."

"But word is that Ramoth has hatched over forty more," someone in the back of the room declared. "And why did you Search out still more of our young men?"

"Forty-one as yet unmatured dragons," F'lar said. Privately, he hoped that this southern venture would still work out. There was real fear in that man's voice. "They grow well and quickly. Just at present, while the Threads do not strike with great frequency as the Red Star begins its Pass, our Weyr is sufficient . . . if we have your cooperation on the ground. Tradition is that"—he nodded tactfully toward Robinton, the dispenser of Traditional usage—"you Holders are responsible for only your dwellings, which, of course, are adequately protected by firepits and raw stone. However, it is spring and our heights have been allowed to grow wild with vegetation. Arable land is blossoming with crops. This presents vast acreage vulnerable to the Threads which one Weyr, at this time, is not able to patrol without severely draining the vitality of our dragons and riders."

At this candid admission, a frightened and angry mutter spread rapidly throughout the room.

"Ramoth rises to mate again soon," F'lar continued in a matter-of-fact way. "Of course, in other times, the queens started producing heavy clutches many Turns before the critical solstice as well as more queens. Unfortunately, Jora was ill and old, and Nemorth intractable. The matter—" He was interrupted.

"Your dragonmen with your high and mighty airs will bring destruction on us all!"

"You have yourselves to blame," Robinton's voice stabbed across the ensuing shouts. "Admit it, one and all. You've paid less honor to the Weyr than you would your watch-wher's kennel—and that not much! But now the thieves are on the heights, and you are screaming because the poor reptile is nigh to death from neglect. Beat him, will you? When you exiled him to his kennel because he tried to warn you? Tried to get you to prepare against the invaders? It's on *your* conscience, not the Weyrleader's or the dragonriders', who have honestly done their duty these hundreds of Turns in keeping dragonkind alive . . . against your protests. How many of you"—his tone was scathing—"have been generous in thought and favor toward dragonkind? Even since I became master of my craft, how often have my harpers told me of being beaten for singing the old songs as is their duty? You earn only the right, good Lords and Craftsmen, to squirm inside your stony Holds and writhe as your crops die a-borning."

He rose.

" 'No Threads will fall. It's a harper's winter tale,' " he whined, in faultless imitation of Nessel. " 'These dragonmen leech us of heir and harvest,' " and his voice took on the constricted, insinuating tenor that could only be Meron's. "And now the truth is as bitter as a brave man's fears and as difficult as mockweed to swallow. For all the honor you've done them, the dragonmen should leave you to be spun on the Threads' distaff."

"Bitra, Lemos, and I," spoke up Raid, the wiry Lord of Benden, his blunt chin lifted belligerently, "have always done our duty to the Weyr."

Robinton swung around to him, his eyes flashing as he gave that speaker a long, slow look.

"Aye, and you have. Of all the Great Holds, you three have been loyal. But you others," and his voice rose indignantly, "as spokesman for my craft, I know, to the last full stop in your score, your opinion of dragonkind. I heard the first whisper of your attempt to ride out against the Weyr." He laughed harshly and pointed a long finger at Vincet. "Where would you be today, good Lord Vincet, if the Weyr had *not* sent you packing back, hoping your ladies would be returned you? All of you," and his accusing finger marked each of the Lords of the abortive effort, "actually rode against the Weyr because . . . 'there . . . were . . . no . . . more . . . Threads!' "

He planted his fists on either hip and glared at the assembly. F'lar wanted to cheer. It was easy to see why the man was Masterharper, and he thanked circumstance that such a man was the Weyr's partisan.

"And now, at this critical moment, you have the incredible presumption to protest against any measure the Weyr suggests?" Robinton's supple voice oozed derision and amazement. "Attend what the Weyrleader says and spare him your petty carpings!" He snapped those words out as a father might enjoin an erring child. "You were," and he switched

170

to the mildest of polite conversational tones as he addressed F'lar, "I believe, asking our cooperation, good F'lar? In what capacities?"

F'lar hastily cleared his throat.

"I shall require that the Holds police their own fields and woods, during the attacks if possible, definitely once the Threads have passed. All burrows which might land must be found, marked, and destroyed. The sooner they are located, the easier it is to be rid of them."

"There's no time to dig firepits through all the lands . . . we'll lose half our growing space," Nessel exclaimed.

"There were other ways, used in olden times, which I believe our Mastersmith might know." F'lar gestured politely toward Fandarel, the archetype of his profession if ever such existed.

The Smith Craftmaster was by several inches the tallest man in the Council Room, his massive shoulders and heavily muscled arms pressed against his nearest neighbors, although he had made an effort not to crowd against anyone. He rose, a giant tree-stump of a man, hooking thumbs like beast-horns in the thick belt that spanned his waistless midsection. His voice, by no means sweet after Turns of bellowing above roaring hearths and hammers, was, by comparison to Robinton's superb delivery, a diluted, unsupported light baritone.

"There were machines, that much is true," he allowed in deliberate, thoughtful tones. "My father, it was he, told me of them as a curiosity of the Craft. There may be sketches in the Hall. There may not. Such things do not keep on skins for long." He cast an oblique look under beetled brows at the Tanner Craftmaster.

"It is our own hides we must worry about preserving," F'lar remarked to forestall any intercraft disputes.

Fandarel grumbled in his throat in such a way that F'lar was not certain whether the sound was the man's laughter or a guttural agreement.

"I shall consider the matter. So shall all my fellow craftsmen," Fandarel assured the Weyrleader. "To sear Threads from the ground without damaging the soil may not be so easy. There are, it is true, fluids which burn and sear. We use an acid to etch design on daggers and ornamental metals. We of the Craft call it agenothree. There is also the black heavy-water that lies on the surface of pools in Igen and Boll. It burns hot and long. And if, as you say, the Cold Turn made the Threads break into dust, perhaps ice from the coldest northlands might freeze and break grounded Threads. However, the problem is to bring such to the Threads where they fall since they will not oblige us by falling where we want them. . . ." He screwed up his face in a grimace.

F'lar stared at him, surprised. Did the man realize how humorous he was? No, he was speaking with sincere concern. Now the Mastersmith scratched his head, his tough fingers making audible grating sounds along his coarse hair and heat-toughened scalp.

"A nice problem. A nice problem," he mused, undaunted. "I shall give it every attention." He sat down, the heavy bench creaking under his weight.

The Masterfarmer raised his hand tentatively.

"When I became Craftmaster, I recall coming across a reference to the sandworms of Igen. They were once cultivated as a protective—"

"Never heard Igen produced anything useful except heat and sand," quipped someone.

"We need every suggestion," F'lar said sharply, trying to identify that heckler. "Please find that reference, Craftmaster. Lord Banger of Igen, find me some of those sandworms!"

Banger, equally surprised that his arid Hold had a hidden asset, nodded vigorously.

"Until we have more efficient ways of killing Threads, all Holders must be organized on the ground during attacks, to spot and mark burrows, to set firestone to burn in them. I do not wish any man to be scored, but we know how quickly Threads burrow deep, and no burrow can be left to multiply. You stand to lose more," and he gestured emphatically at the Holder Lords, "than any others. Guard not just yourselves, for a burrow on one man's border may grow across to his neighbor's. Mobilize every man, woman, and child, farm and crafthold. Do it now."

The Council Room was fraught with tension and stunned reflection until Zurg, the Masterweaver, rose to speak.

"My craft, too, has something to offer . . . which is only fair since we deal with thread every day of our lives . . . in regard to the ancient methods." Zurg's voice was light and dry, and his eyes, in their creases of spare, lined flesh, were busy, darting from one face in his audience to another. "In Ruath Hold I once saw upon the wall . . . where the tapestry now resides, who knows?" He slyly glanced at Meron of

Nabol and then at Bargen of the High Reaches who had succeeded to Fax's title there. "The work was as old as dragonkind and showed, among other things, a man on foot, carrying upon his back a curious contraption. He held within his hand a rounded, sword-long object from which tongues of flame . . . magnificently woven in the orange-red dyes now lost to us . . . spouted toward the ground. Above, of course, were dragons in close formation, bronzes predominating . . . again we've lost that true dragon-bronze shade. Consequently I remember the work as much for what we now lack as for its subject matter."

"A flamethrower?" the Smith rumbled. "A flamethrower," he repeated with a falling inflection. "A flamethrower," he murmured thoughtfully, his heavy brows drawn into a titanic scowl. "A thrower of what sort of flame? It requires thought." He lowered his head and didn't speak, so engrossed in the required thought that he lost interest in the rest of the discussion.

"Yes, good Zurg, there have been many tricks of every trade lost in recent Turns," F'lar commented sardonically. "If we wish to continue living, such knowledge must be revived . . . fast. I would particularly like to recover the tapestry of which Master Zurg speaks."

F'lar looked significantly at those Lords who had quarreled over Fax's seven Holds after his death.

"It may save all of you much loss. I suggest that it appear at Ruatha. Or at Zurg's or at Fandarel's crafthall. Whichever is most convenient."

There was some shuffling of feet, but no one admitted ownership.

"It might then be returned to Fax's son, who is now Ruatha's Lord," F'lar added, wryly amused at such magnanimous justice.

Lytol snorted softly and glowered around the room. F'lar supposed Lytol to be amused and experienced a fleeting regret for the orphaned Jaxom, reared by such a cheerless if honest guardian.

"If I may, Lord Weyrleader," Robinton broke in, "we might all benefit, as your maps prove to us, from research in our own Records." He smiled suddenly, an unexpectedly embarrassed smile. "I own I find myself in some disgrace for we Harpers have let slip unpopular ballads and skimped on some of the longer Teaching Ballads and Sagas . . . for lack of listeners and, occasionally, in the interest of preserving our skins."

F'lar stifled a laugh with a cough. Robinton was a genius.

"I must see that Ruathan tapestry," Fandarel suddenly boomed out.

"I'm sure it will be in your hands very soon," F'lar assured him with more confidence than he dared feel. "My Lords, there is much to be done. Now that you understand what we all face, I leave it in your hands as leaders in your separate Holds and crafts how best to organize your own people. Craftsmen, turn your best minds to our special problems: review all Records that might turn up something to our purpose. Lords Telgar, Crom, Ruatha, and Nabol, I shall be with you in three days. Nerat, Keroon, and Igen, I am at your disposal to help destroy any burrow on your lands. While we have the Masterminer here, tell him your needs. How stands your craft?"

"Happy to be so busy at our trade, Weyrleader," piped up the Masterminer.

Just then F'lar caught sight of F'nor, hovering about in the shadows of the hallway, trying to catch his eye. The brown rider wore an exultant grin, and it was obvious he was bursting with news.

F'lar wondered how they could have returned so swiftly from the Southern Continent, and then he realized that F'nor—again—was tanned. He gave a jerk of his head, indicating that F'nor take himself off to the sleeping quarters and wait.

"Lords and Craftmasters, a dragonet will be at the disposal of each of you for messages and transportation. Now, good morning."

He strode out of the Council Room, up the passageway into the queen's weyr, and parted the still swinging curtains into the sleeping room just as F'nor was pouring himself a cup of wine.

"Success!" F'nor cried as the Weyrleader entered. "Though how you knew to send just thirty-two candidates I'll never understand. I thought you were insulting our noble Pridith. But thirty-two eggs she laid in four days. It was all I could do to keep from riding out when the first appeared."

F'lar responded with hearty congratulations, relieved that there would be at least that much benefit from this apparently

174

ill-fated venture. Now all he had to figure out was how much longer F'nor had stayed south until his frantic visit the night before. For there were no worry lines or strain in F'nor's grinning, well-tanned face.

"No queen egg?" asked F'lar hopefully. With thirty-two in the one experiment, perhaps they could send a second queen back and try again.

F'nor's face lengthened. "No, and I was sure there would be. But there are fourteen bronzes. Pridith out-matched Ramoth there," he added proudly.

"Indeed she did. How goes the Weyr otherwise?"

F'nor frowned, shaking his head against an inner bewilderment. "Kylara's . . . well, she's a problem. Stirs up trouble constantly. T'bor leads a sad time with her, and he's so touchy everyone keeps a distance from him." F'nor brightened a little. "Young N'ton is shaping up into a fine wingleader, and his bronze may outfly T'bor's Orth when Pridith flies to mate the next time. Not that I'd wish Kylara on N'ton . . . or anyone."

"No trouble then with supplies?"

F'nor laughed outright. "If you hadn't made it so plain we must not communicate with you here, we could supply you with fruits and fresh greens that are superior to anything in the north. We eat the way dragonmen should! F'lar, we must consider a supply Weyr down there. Then we shall never have to worry about tithing trains and . . ."

"In good time. Get back now. You know you must keep these visits short."

F'nor grimaced. "Oh, it's not so bad. I'm not here in this time, anyway."

"True," F'lar agreed, "but don't mistake the time and come while you're still here."

"Hmmm? Oh, yes, that's right. I forget time is creeping for us and speeding for you. Well, I shan't be back again till Pridith lays the second clutch."

With a cheerful good-bye, F'nor strode out of the weyr. F'lar watched him thoughtfully as he slowly retraced his steps to the Council Room. Thirty-two new dragons, fourteen of them bronzes, was no small gain and seemed worth the hazard. Or would the hazard wax greater?

Someone cleared his throat deliberately. F'lar looked up to see Robinton standing in the archway that led to the Council Room.

"Before I can copy and instruct others about those maps, Weyrleader, I must myself understand them completely. I took the liberty of remaining behind."

"You make a good champion, Masterharper."

"You have a noble cause, Weyrleader," and then Robinton's eyes glinted maliciously. "I've been begging the Egg for an opportunity to speak out to so noble an audience."

"A cup of wine first?"

"Benden grapes are the envy of Pern."

"If one has the palate for such a delicate bouquet."

"It is carefully cultivated by the knowledgeable."

F'lar wondered when the man would stop playing with words. He had more on his mind than studying the time-charts.

"I have in mind a ballad which, for lack of explanation, I had set aside when I became the Master of my crafthall," he said judiciously after an appreciative savoring of his wine. "It is an uneasy song, both the tune and the words. One develops, as a harper must, a certain sensitivity for what will be received and what will be rejected . . . forcefully," and he winced in retrospect. "I found that this ballad unsettled singer as well as audience and retired it from use. Now, like that tapestry, it bears rediscovery."

After his death C'gan's instrument had been hung on the Council Room wall till a new Weyrsinger could be chosen. The guitar was very old, its wood thin. Old C'gan had kept it well-tuned and covered. The Masterharper handled it now with reverence, lightly stroking the strings to hear the tone, raising his eyebrows at the fine voice of the instrument.

He plucked a chord, a dissonance. F'lar wondered if the instrument was out of tune or if the harper had, by some chance, struck the wrong string. But Robinton repeated the odd discord, then modulating into a weird minor that was somehow more disturbing than the first notes.

"I told you it was an uneasy song. And I wonder if you know the answers to the questions it asks. For I've turned the puzzle over in my mind many times of late."

Then abruptly he shifted from the spoken to the sung tone.

> Gone away, gone ahead,
> Echoes roll unansweréd.
> Empty, open, dusty, dead,
> Why have all the Weyrfolk fled?

Where have dragons gone together?
Leaving Weyrs to wind and weather?
Setting herdbeasts free of tether?
Gone, our safeguards, gone, but whither?

Have they flown to some new Weyr
Where cruel Threads some others fear?
Are they worlds away from here?
Why, oh, why, the empty Weyr?

The last plaintive chord reverberated.

"Of course, you realize that the song was first recorded in the craft annals some four hundred Turns ago," Robinton said lightly, cradling the guitar in both arms. "The Red Star had just passed beyond attack-proximity. The people had ample reason to be stunned and worried over the sudden loss of the populations of five Weyrs. Oh, I imagine at the time they had any one of a number of explanations, but none . . . not one explanation . . . is recorded." Robinton paused significantly.

"I have found none recorded, either," F'lar replied. "As a matter of fact, I had all the Records brought here from the other Weyrs . . . in order to compile accurate attack timetables. And those other Weyr Records simply end—" F'lar made a chopping gesture with one hand. "In Benden's Records there is no mention of sickness, death, fire, disaster —not one word of explanation for the sudden lapse of the usual intercourse between the Weyrs. Benden's Records continue blithely, but only for Benden. There is one entry that pertains to the mass disappearance . . . the initiation of a Pernwide patrol routing, not just Benden's immediate responsibility. And that is all."

"Strange," Robinton mused. "Once the danger from the Red Star was past, the dragons and riders may have gone *between* to ease the drain on the Holds. But I simply cannot believe that. Our craft Records do mention that harvests were bad and that there had been several natural catastrophes . . . other than the Threads. Men may be gallant and your breed the most gallant of all, but mass suicide? I simply do not accept that explanation . . . not for dragonmen."

"My thanks," F'lar said with mild irony.

"Don't mention it," Robinton replied with a gracious nod.

F'lar chuckled appreciatively. "I see we have been too weyrbound as well as too hidebound."

Robinton drained his cup and looked at it mournfully until F'lar refilled it.

"Well, your isolation served some purpose, you know, and you handled that uprising of the Lords magnificently. I nearly choked to death laughing," Robinton remarked, grinning broadly. "Stealing their women in the flash of a dragon's breath!" He chuckled again, then suddenly sobered, looking F'lar straight in the eye. "Accustomed as I am to hearing what a man does *not* say aloud, I suspect there is much you glossed over in that Council meeting. You may be sure of my discretion . . . and . . . you may be sure of my wholehearted support and that of my not ineffectual craft. To be blunt, how may my harpers aid you?" and be strummed a vigorous marching air. "Stir men's pulses with ballads of past glories and success?" The tune, under his flashing fingers, changed abruptly to a stern but determined rhythm. "Strengthen their mental and physical sinews for hardship?"

"If all your harpers could stir men as you yourself do, I should have no worries that five hundred or so additional dragons would not immediately end."

"Oh, then despite your brave words and marked charts, the situation is"—a dissonant twang on the guitar accented his final words—"more desperate than you carefully did not say."

"It may be."

"The flamethrowers old Zurg remembered and Fandarel must reconstruct—will they tip the scales?"

F'lar regarded this clever man thoughtfully and made a quick decision.

"Even Igen's sandworms will help, but as the world turns and the Red Star nears, the interval between daily attacks shortens and we have only seventy-two new dragons to add to those we had yesterday. One is now dead and several will not fly for several weeks."

"Seventy-two?" Robinton caught him up sharply. "Ramoth hatched but forty, and they are still too young to eat firestone."

F'lar outlined F'nor and Lessa's expedition, taking place at that moment. He went on to F'nor's reappearance and warning, as well as the fact that the experiment had been success-

178

ful in part with the hatching of thirty-two new dragons from Pridith's first clutch. Robinton caught him up.

"How can F'nor already have returned when you haven't heard from Lessa and him that there is a breeding place on the Southern Continent?"

"Dragons can go *between* times as well as places. They go as easily to a *when* as to a *where*."

Robinton's eyes widened as he digested this astonishing news.

"That is how we forestalled the attack on Nerat yesterday morning. We jumped back two hours *between* time to meet the Threads as they fell."

"You can actually jump backward? How far back?"

"I don't know. Lessa, when I was teaching her to fly Ramoth, inadvertently returned to Ruath Hold, to the dawn thirteen Turns ago when Fax's men invaded from the heights. When she returned to the present, I attempted a *between* times jump of some ten Turns. To the dragons it is a simple matter to go *between* times or spaces, but there appears to be a terrific drain on the rider. Yesterday, by the time we returned from Nerat and had to go on to Keroon, I felt as though I had been pounded flat and left to dry for a summer on Igen Plain." F'lar shook his head. "We have obviously succeeded in sending Kylara, Pridith, and the others ten Turns *between*, because F'nor has already reported to me that he has been there several Turns. The drain on humans, however, is becoming more and more marked. But even seventy-two more mature dragons will be a help."

"Send a rider ahead in time to see if it is sufficient," Robinton suggested helpfully. "Save you a few days' worrying."

"I don't know how to get to a *when* that has not yet happened. You must give your dragon reference points, you know. How can you refer him to times that have not yet occurred?"

"You've got an imagination. Project it."

"And perhaps lose a dragon when I have none to spare? No, I must continue . . . because obviously I have, judging by F'nor's returns . . . as I decided to start. Which reminds me, I must give orders to start packing. Then I shall go over the time-charts with you."

It wasn't until after the noon meal, which Robinton took

with the Weyrleader, that the Masterharper was confident that he understood the charts and left to begin their copying.

> Across a waste of lonely tossing sea,
> Where no dragonwings had lately spread,
> Flew a gold and sturdy brown in spring,
> Searching if a land be dead.

As RAMOTH and Canth bore Lessa and F'nor up to the Star Stone, they saw the first of the Hold Lords and Craftmasters arriving for the Council.

In order to get back to the Southern Continent of ten Turns ago, Lessa and F'nor had decided it was easiest to transfer first *between* times to the Weyr of ten Turns back which F'nor remembered. Then they would go *between* places to a seapoint just off the coast of the neglected Southern Continent which was as close to it as the Records gave any references.

F'nor put Canth in mind of a particular day he remembered ten Turns back, and Ramoth picked up the references from the brown's mind. The awesome cold of *between* times took Lessa's breath away, and it was with intense relief that she caught a glimpse of the normal weyr activity before the dragons took them *between* places to hover over the turgid sea.

Beyond them, smudged purple on this overcast and gloomy day, lurked the Southern Continent. Lessa felt a new anxiety replace the uncertainty of the temporal displacement. Ramoth beat forward with great sweeps of her wings, making for the distant coast. Canth gallantly tried to maintain a matching speed.

He's only a brown, Lessa scolded her golden queen.

If he is flying with me, Ramoth replied coolly, *he must stretch his wings a little.*

Lessa grinned, thinking very privately that Ramoth was still piqued that she had not been able to fight with her weyrmates. All the males would have a hard time with her for a while.

They saw the flock of wherries first and realized that there would have to be some vegetation on the Continent. Wherries needed greens to live, although they could subsist on little else besides occasional grubs if necessary.

Lessa had Canth relay questions to his rider. *If the South-*

ern Continent was rendered barren by the Threads, how did
new growth start? Where did the wherries come from?

Ever notice the seed pods split open and the flakes car-
ried away by the winds? Ever notice that wherries fly south
after the autumn solstice?

Yes, but . . .

Yes, but!

But the land was Thread-bared!

In less than four hundred Turns even the scorched hill-
tops of our Continent begin to sprout in the springtime,
F'nor *replied by way of* Canth, *so it is easy to assume the*
Southern Continent could revive, too.

Even at the pace Ramoth set, it took time to reach the
jagged shoreline with its forbidding cliffs, stark stone in the
sullen light. Lessa groaned inwardly but urged Ramoth
higher to see over the masking highlands. All seemed gray
and desolate from that altitude.

Suddenly the sun broke through the cloud cover and the
gray dissolved into dense greens and browns, living colors,
the live greens of lush tropical growth, the browns of vigorous trees and vines. Lessa's cry of triumph was echoed by
F'nor's hurrah and the brass voices of the dragons. Wherries, startled by the unusual sound, rose in squeaking alarm
from their perches.

Beyond the headland, the land sloped away to jungle and
grassy plateau, similar to mid-Boll. Though they searched all
morning, they found no hospitable cliffs wherein to found
a new Weyr. Was that a contributing factor in the southern
venture's failure, Lessa wondered.

Discouraged, they landed on a high plateau by a small
lake. The weather was warm but not oppressive, and while
F'nor and Lessa ate their noonday meal, the two dragons
wallowed in the water, refreshing themselves.

Lessa felt uneasy and had little appetite for the meat
and bread. She noticed that F'nor was restless, too, shooting
surreptitious glances around the lake and the jungle verge.

"What under the sun are we expecting? Wherries don't
change, and wild whers would come nowhere near a dragon.
We're ten Turns before the Red Star, so there can't be
any Threads."

F'nor shrugged, grimacing sheepishly as he tossed his un-
finished bread back into the food pouch.

"Place feels so empty, I guess," he tendered, glancing

around. He spotted ripe fruit hanging from a moonflower vine. "Now that looks familiar and good enough to eat, without tasting like dust in the mouth."

He climbed nimbly and snagged the orange-red fruit.

"Smells right, feels ripe, looks ripe," he announced and deftly sliced the fruit open. Grinning, he landed Lessa the first slice, carving another for himself. He lifted it challengingly. "Let us eat and die together!"

She couldn't help but laugh and saluted him back. They bit into the succulent flesh simultaneously. Sweet juices dribbled from the corners of her mouth, and Lessa hurriedly licked her lips to capture the least drop of the delicious liquid.

"Die happy—I will," F'nor cried, cutting more fruit.

Both were subtly reassured by the experiment and were able to discuss their discomposure.

"I think," F'nor suggested, "it is the lack of cliff and cavern and the still, still quality of the place, the knowing that there are no other men or beasts about but us."

Lessa nodded her head in agreement. "Ramoth, Canth, would having no Weyr upset you?"

We didn't always live in caves, Ramoth replied, somewhat haughtily as she rolled over in the lake. Sizable waves rushed up the shore almost to where Lessa and F'nor were seated on a fallen tree trunk. *The sun here is warm and pleasant, the water cooling. I would enjoy it here, but I am not to come.*

"She is out of sorts," Lessa whispered to F'nor. "Let Pridith have it, dear one," she called soothingly to the golden queen. "You've the Weyr and all!"

Ramoth ducked under the water, blowing up a froth in disgruntled reply.

Canth admitted that he had no reservations at all about living Weyrless. The dry earth would be warmer than stone to sleep on, once a suitably comfortable hollow had been achieved. No, he couldn't object to the lack of the cave as long as there was enough to eat.

"We'll have to bring herdbeasts in," F'nor mused. "Enough to start a good-sized herd. Of course, the wherries here are huge. Come to think of it, I believe this plateau has no exits. We wouldn't need to pasture it off. I'd better check. Otherwise, this pleateau with the lake and enough clear space for Holds seems ideal. Walk out and pick breakfast from the tree."

"It might be wise to choose those who were not Hold-reared," Lessa added. "They would not feel so uneasy away from protecting heights and stone-security." She gave a short laugh. "I'm more a creature of habit than I suspected. All these open spaces, untenanted and quiet, seem . . . indecent." She gave a delicate shudder, scanning the broad and open plain beyond the lake.

"Fruitful and lovely," F'nor amended, leaping up to secure more of the orange-red succulents. "This tastes uncommonly good to me. Can't remember anything this sweet and juicy from Nerat, and yet it's the same variety."

"Undeniably superior to what the Weyr gets. I suspect Nerat serves home first, Weyr last."

They both stuffed themselves greedily.

Further investigation proved that the plateau was isolated, and ample to pasture a huge herd of foodbeasts for the dragons. It ended in a sheer drop of several dragonlengths into denser jungle on one side, the sea-side escarpment on the other. The timber stands would provide raw material from which dwellings could be made for the Weyrfolk. Ramoth and Canth stoutly agreed dragonkind would be comfortable enough under the heavy foliage of the dense jungle. As this part of the continent was similar, weatherwise, to Upper Nerat, there would be neither intense heat nor cold to give distress.

However, if Lessa was glad enough to leave, F'nor seemed reluctant to start back.

"We can go *between* time and place on the way back," Lessa insisted finally, "and be in the Weyr by late afternoon. The Lords will surely be gone by then."

F'nor concurred, and Lessa steeled herself for the trip *between*. She wondered why the *when between* bothered her more than the *where*, for it had no effect on the dragons at all. Ramoth, sensing Lessa's depression, crooned encouragingly. The long, long black suspension of the utter cold of *between* where and when ended suddenly in sunlight above the Weyr.

Somewhat startled, Lessa saw bundles and sacks spread out before the Lower Caverns as dragonriders supervised the loading of their beasts.

"What has been happening?" F'nor exclaimed.

"Oh, F'lar's been anticipating success," she assured him glibly.

183

Mnementh, who was watching the bustle from the ledge of the queen's weyr, sent a greeting to the travelers and the information that F'lar wished them to join him in the weyr as soon as they returned.

They found F'lar, as usual, bent over some of the oldest and least legible Record skins that he had had brought to the Council Room.

"And?" he asked, grinning a broad welcome at them.

"Green, lush, and livable," Lessa declared, watching him intently. He knew something else, too. Well, she hoped he'd watch his words. F'nor was no fool, and this foreknowledge was dangerous.

"That is what I had so hoped to hear you say," F'lar went on smoothly. "Come, tell me in detail what you observed and discovered. It'll be good to fill in the blank spaces on the chart."

Lessa let F'nor give most of the account, to which F'lar listened with sincere attention, making notes.

"On the chance that it would be practical, I started packing supplies and alerting the riders to go with you," he told F'nor when the account was finished. "Remember, we've only three days in this time in which to start you back ten Turns ago. *We* have no moments to spare. And we must have many more mature dragons ready to fight at Telgar in three days time. So, though ten Turns will have passed for you, three days only will elapse here. Lessa, your thought that the farm-bred might do better is well-taken. We're lucky that our recent Search for rider candidates for the dragons Pridith will have come mainly from the crafts and farms. No problem there. And most of the thirty-two are in their early teens."

"Thirty-two?" F'nor exclaimed. "We should have fifty. The dragonets must have some choice, even if we get the candidates used to the dragonets before they're hatched."

F'lar shrugged negligently. "Send back for more. *You'll* have time, remember," and F'lar chuckled as though he had started to add something and decided against it.

F'nor had no time to debate with the Weyrleader, for F'lar immediately launched on other rapid instructions.

F'nor was to take his own wingriders to help train the weyrlings. They would also take the forty young dragons of Ramoth's first clutch: Kylara with her queen Pridith, T'bor and his bronze Piyanth. N'ton's young bronze might

184

also be ready to fly and mate by the time Pridith was, so that gave the young queen two bronzes at least.

"Suppose we'd found the continent barren?" F'nor asked, still puzzled by F'lar's assurance. "What then?"

"Oh, we'd've sent them back to, say, the High Reaches," F'lar replied far too glibly, but quickly went on. "I should send on other bronzes, but I'll need everyone else here to ride burrow-search on Keroon and Nerat. They've already unearthed several at Nerat. Vincet, I'm told, is close to heart attack from fright."

Lessa made a short comment on that Hold Lord.

"What of the meeting this morning?" F'nor asked, remembering.

"Never mind that now. You've got to start shifting *between* by evening, F'nor."

Lessa gave the Weyrleader a long hard look and decided she would have to find out what had happened in detail very soon.

"Sketch me some references, will you, Lessa?" F'lar asked.

There was a definite plea in his eyes as he drew clean hide and a stylus to her. He wanted no questions from her now that would alarm F'nor. She sighed and picked up the drawing tool.

She sketched quickly, with one or two details added by F'nor until she had rendered a reasonable map of the plateau they had chosen. Then, abruptly, she had trouble focusing her eyes. She felt light-headed.

"Lessa?" F'lar bent to her.

"Everything's . . . moving . . . circling . . ." and she collapsed backward into his arms.

As F'lar raised her slight body into his arms, he exchanged an alarmed look with his half brother.

"I'll call for Manora," F'nor suggested.

"How do you feel?" the Weyrleader called after his brother.

"Tired but no more than that," F'nor assured him as he shouted down the service shaft to the kitchens for Manora to come and for hot *klah*. He needed that, and no doubt of it.

F'lar laid the Weyrwoman on the sleeping couch, covering her gently.

"I don't like this," he muttered, rapidly recalling what F'nor had said of Kylara's decline, which F'nor could not know was yet to come in his future. Why should it start so swiftly with Lessa?

"Time-jumping makes one feel slightly—" F'nor paused, groping for the exact wording. "Not entirely . . . whole. You fought *between* times at Nerat yesterday. . . ."

"I fought," F'lar reminded him, "but neither you nor Lessa battled anything today. There may be some inner . . . mental . . . stress simply to going *between* times. Look, F'nor, I'd rather only you came back once you reach the southern Weyr. I'll make it an order and get Ramoth to inhibit the dragons. That way no rider can take it into his head to come back even if he wants to. There is some factor that may be more serious than we can guess. Let's take no unnecessary risks."

"Agreed."

"One other detail, F'nor. Be very careful which times you pick to come back to see me. I wouldn't jump *between* too close to any time you were actually here. I can't imagine what would happen if you walked into your own self in the passageway, and I can't lose you."

With a rare demonstration of affection, F'lar gripped his half brother's shoulder tightly.

"Remember, F'nor. I was here all morning and you did not arrive back from the first trip till mid-afternoon. And remember, too, *we* have only three days. You have ten Turns."

F'nor left, passing Manora in the hall.

The woman could find nothing obviously the matter with Lessa, and they finally decided it might be simple fatigue; yesterday's strain when Lessa had to relay messages between dragons and fighters followed by the disjointing *between* times trip today.

When F'lar went to wish the southern ventures a good trip, Lessa was in a normal sleep, her face pale, but her breathing easy.

F'lar had Mnementh relay to Ramoth the prohibition he wished the queen to instill in all dragonkind assigned to the venture. Ramoth obliged, but added in an aside to bronze Mnementh, which he passed on to F'lar, that everyone else had adventures while she, the Weyr queen, was forced to stay behind.

No sooner had the laden dragons, one by one, winked out of the sky above the Star Stone than the young weyrling assigned to Nerat Hold as messenger came gliding down, his face white with fear.

"Weyrleader, many more burrows have been found, and they cannot be burned out with fire alone. Lord Vincet wants you."

F'lar could well imagine that Vincet did.

"Get yourself some dinner, boy, before you start back. I'll go shortly."

As he passed through to the sleeping quarters, he heard Ramoth rumbling in her throat. She had settled herself down to rest.

Lessa still slept, one hand curled under her cheek, her dark hair trailing over the edge of the bed. She looked fragile, childlike, and very precious to him. F'lar smiled to himself. So she was jealous of Kylara's attentions yesterday. He was pleased and flattered. Never would Lessa learn from him that Kylara, for all her bold beauty and sensuous nature, did not have one tenth the attraction for him that the unpredictable, dark, and delicate Lessa held. Even her stubborn intractableness, her keen and malicious humor, added zest to their relationship. With a tenderness he could never show her awake, F'lar bent and kissed her lips. She stirred and smiled, sighing lightly in her sleep.

Reluctantly returning to what must be done, F'lar left her so. As he paused by the queen, Ramoth raised her great, wedge-shaped head; her many-faceted eyes gleamed with bright luminiscence as she regarded the Weyrleader.

"Mnementh, please ask Ramoth to get in touch with the dragonet at Fandarel's crafthall. I'd like the Mastersmith to come with me to Nerat. I want to see what his agenothree does to Threads."

Ramoth nodded her head as the dragon relayed the message to her.

She has done so, and the green dragon comes as soon as he can. Mnementh reported to his rider. *It is easier to do, this talking about, when Lessa is awake,* he grumbled.

F'lar agreed heartily. It had been quite an advantage yesterday in the battle and would be more and more of an asset.

Maybe it would be better if she tried to speak, across time, to F'nor . . . but no, F'nor had come back.

F'lar strode into the Council Room, still hopeful that somewhere within the illegible portions of the old Records was the one clue he so desperately needed. There must be a way out of this impasse. If not the southern venture, then something else. Something!

Fandarel showed himself a man of iron will as well as sinew; he looked calmly at the exposed tangle of perceptibly growing Threads that writhed and intertwined obscenely.

"Hundreds and thousands in this one burrow," Lord Vincet of Nerat was exclaiming in a frantic tone of voice. He waved his hands distractedly around the plantation of young trees in which the burrow had been discovered. "These stalks are already withering even as you hesitate. Do something! How many more young trees will die in this one field alone? How many more burrows escaped dragon's breath yesterday? Where is a dragon to sear them? Why are you just standing there?"

F'lar and Fandarel paid no attention to the man's raving, both fascinated as well as revolted by their first sight of the burrowing stage of their ancient foe. Despite Vincet's panicky accusations, it was the only burrow on this particular slope. F'lar did not like to contemplate how many more might have slipped through the dragons' efforts and had reached Nerat's warm and fertile soil. If they had only had time enough to set out watchmen to track the fall of stray clumps. They could, at least, remedy that error in Telgar, Crom, and Ruatha in three days. But it was not enough. Not enough.

Fandarel motioned forward the two craftsmen who had accompanied him. They were burdened with an odd contraption: a large cylinder of metal to which was attached a wand with a wide nozzle. At the other end of the cylinder was another short pipe-length and then a short cylinder with an inner plunger. One craftsman worked the plunger vigorously, while the second, barely keeping his hands steady, pointed the nozzle end toward the Thread burrow. At a nod from this pumper, the man released a small knob on the nozzle, extending it carefully away from him and over the burrow. A thin spray danced from the nozzle and drifted down into the burrow. No sooner had the spray motes contacted the Thread tangles than steam hissed out of the burrow. Before long, all that remained of the pallid writhing tendrils was a smoking mass of blackened strands. Long after Fandarel had waved the craftsmen back, he stared at the grave. Finally he grunted and found himself a long stick with which he poked and prodded the remains. Not one Thread wriggled.

"Humph," he grunted with evident satisfaction. "However, we can scarcely go around digging up every burrow. I need another."

With Lord Vincet a hand-wringing moaner in their wake, they were escorted by the junglemen to another undisturbed burrow on the sea-side of the rainforest. The Threads had entered the earth by the side of a huge tree that was already drooping.

With his prodding stick Fandarel made a tiny hole at the top of the burrow and then waved his craftsmen forward. The pumper made vigorous motions at his end, while the nozzle-holder adjusted his pipe before inserting it in the hole. Fandarel gave the sign to start and counted slowly before he waved a cutoff. Smoke oozed out of the tiny hole.

After a suitable lapse of time, Fandarel ordered the junglemen to dig, reminding them to be careful not to come in contact with the agenothree liquid. When the burrow was uncovered, the acid had done its work, leaving nothing but a thoroughly charred mass of tangles.

Fandarel grimaced but this time scratched his head in dissatisfaction.

"Takes too much time, either way. Best to get them still at the surface," the Mastersmith grumbled.

"Best to get them in the air," Lord Vincet chattered. "And what will that stuff do to my young orchards? What will it do?"

Fandarel swung around, apparently noticing the distressed Holder for the first time.

"Little man, agenothree in diluted form is what you use to fertilize your plants in the spring. True, this field has been burned out for a few years, but it is *not* Thread-full. It *would* be better if we could get the spray up high in the air. Then it would float down and dissipate harmlessly—fertilizing very evenly, too." He paused, scratched his head gratingly. "Young dragons could carry a team aloft. . . . Hmmm. A possibility, but the apparatus is bulky yet." He turned his back on the surprised Hold Lord then and asked F'lar if the tapestry had been returned. "I cannot yet discover how to make a tube throw flame. I got this mechanism from what we make for the orchard farmers."

"I'm still waiting for word on the tapestry," F'lar replied, "but this spray of yours is effective. The Thread burrow is dead."

"The sandworms are effective too, but not really efficient," Fandarel grunted in dissatisfaction. He beckoned abruptly to his assistants and stalked off into the increasing twilight to the dragons.

Robinton awaited their return at the Weyr, his outward calm barely masking his inner excitement. He inquired politely, however, of Fandarel's efforts. The Mastersmith grunted and shrugged.

"I have all my craft at work."

"The Mastersmith is entirely too modest," F'lar put in. "He has already put together an ingenious device that sprays agenothree into Thread burrows and sears them into a black pulp."

"Not efficient. *I* like the idea of flamethrowers," the smith said, his eyes gleaming in his expressionless face. "A thrower of flame," he repeated, his eyes unfocusing. He shook his heavy head with a bone-popping crack. "I go," and with a curt nod to the harper and the Weyrleader, he left.

"I like that man's dedication to an idea," Robinton observed. Despite his amusement with the man's eccentric behavior, there was a strong undercurrent of respect for the smith. "I must set my apprentices a task for an appropriate Saga on the Mastersmith. I understand," he said, turning to F'lar, "that the southern venture has been inaugurated."

F'lar nodded unhappily.

"Your doubts increase?"

"This *between* times travel takes its own toll," he admitted, glancing anxiously toward the sleeping room.

"The Weyrwoman is ill?"

"Sleeping, but today's journey affected her. We need another, less dangerous answer!" and F'lar slammed one fist into the other palm.

"I came with no real answer," Robinton said then, briskly, "but with what I believe to be another part of the puzzle. I have found an entry. Four hundred Turns ago the then Masterharper was called to Fort Weyr not long after the Red Star retreated away from Pern in the evening sky."

"An entry? What is it?"

"Mind you, the Thread attacks had just lifted and the Masterharper was called one late evening to Fort Weyr. An unusual summons. However," and Robinton emphasized the distinction by pointing a long, callous-tipped finger at F'lar, "no further mention is ever made of that visit. There ought to have been, for all such summonses have a purpose. All such meetings are recorded, yet no explanation of this one is given. The record is taken up several weeks later by the Masterharper as though he had not left his crafthall at all. Some ten months afterward, the Question Song was added to compulsory Teaching Ballads."

"You believe the two are connected with the abandonment of the five Weyrs?"

"I do, but I could not say why. I only feel that the events, the visit, the disappearances, the Question Song, are connected."

F'lar poured them both cups of wine.

"I have checked back, too, seeking some indications." He shrugged. "All must have been normal right up to the point they disappeared. There are Records of tithing trains received, supplies stored, the list of injured dragons and men returning to active patrols. And then the Records cease at full Cold, leaving only Benden Weyr occupied."

"And why that one Weyr of the six to choose from?" Robinton demanded. "Island Ista would be a better choice if only one Weyr was to be left. Benden so far north is not a likely place to pass four hundred Turns."

"Benden is high and isolated. A disease that struck the others and was prevented from reaching Benden?"

"And no explanation of it? They can't all—dragons, riders, weyrfolk—have dropped dead on the same instant and left no carcasses rotting in the sun."

"Then let us ask ourselves, why was the harper called? Was he told to construct a Teaching Ballad covering this disappearance?"

"Well," Robinton snorted, "it certainly wasn't meant to reassure us, not with that tune—if one cares to call it a tune at all, and I don't—nor does it answer any questions! It poses them."

"For us to answer?" suggested F'lar softly.

"Aye." Robinton's eyes shone. "For us to answer, indeed, for it is a difficult song to forget. Which means it was meant to be remembered. Those questions are important, F'lar!"

"Which questions are important?" demanded Lessa, who had entered quietly.

Both men were on their feet. F'lar, with unusual attentiveness, held a chair for Lessa and poured her wine.

"I'm not going to break apart," she said tartly, almost annoyed at the excess of courtesy. Then she smiled up at F'lar to take the sting out of her words. "I slept and I feel much better. What were you two getting so intense about?"

F'lar quickly outlined what he and the Masterharper had been discussing. When he mentioned the Question Song, Lessa shuddered.

"That's one I can't forget, either. Which, I've always been told," and she grimaced, remembering the hateful lessons with R'gul, "means it's important. But why? It only asked questions." Then she blinked, her eyes went wide with amazement.

" 'Gone away, gone . . . ahead!' " she cried, on her feet. "That's it! All five Weyrs went . . . ahead. But to when?"

F'lar turned to her, speechless.

"They came ahead to our time! Five Weyrs full of dragons," she repeated in an awed voice.

"No, that's impossible," F'lar contradicted.

"Why?" Robinton demanded excitedly. "Doesn't that solve the problem we're facing? The need for fighting dragons? Doesn't it explain why they left so suddenly with no explanation except that Question Song?"

F'lar brushed back the heavy lock of hair that overhung his eyes.

"It would explain their actions in leaving," he admitted, "because they couldn't leave any clues saying where they went, or it would cancel the whole thing. Just as I couldn't tell F'nor I knew the southern venture would have problems. But how do they get here—if here is *when* they came? They aren't here now. How would they have known they were needed—or *when* they were needed? And this is the real problem—how can you conceivably give a dragon references to a *when* that has not yet occurred?"

"Someone here must go back to give them the proper references," Lessa replied in a very quiet voice.

"You're mad, Lessa," F'lar shouted at her, alarm written on his face. "You know what happened to you today. How can you consider going back to a *when* you can't remotely imagine? To a *when* four hundred Turns ago? Going back ten Turns left you fainting and half-ill."

"Wouldn't it be worth it?" she asked him, her eyes grave. "Isn't Pern worth it?"

192

F'lar grabbed her by the shoulders, shaking her, his eyes wild with fear.

"Not even Pern is worth losing you, or Ramoth. Lessa, Lessa, don't you dare disobey me in this." His voice dropped to an intense, icy whisper, shaking with anger.

"Ah, there may be a way of effecting that solution, momentarily beyond us, Weyrwoman," Robinton put in adroitly. "Who knows what tomorrow holds? It certainly is not something one does without considering every angle."

Lessa did not shrug off F'lar's viselike grip on her shoulders as she gazed at Robinton.

"Wine?" the Masterharper suggested, pouring a mug for her. His diversionary action broke the tableau of Lessa and F'lar.

"Ramoth is not afraid to try," Lessa said, her mouth set in a determined line.

F'lar glared at the golden dragon who was regarding the humans, her neck curled around almost to the shoulder joint of her great wing.

"Ramoth is young," F'lar snapped and then caught Mnementh's wry thought even as Lessa did.

She threw her head back, her peal of laughter echoing in the vaulting chamber.

"I'm badly in need of a good joke myself," Robinton remarked pointedly.

"Mnementh told F'lar that he was neither young nor afraid to try, either. It was just a long step," Lessa explained, wiping tears from her eyes.

F'lar glanced dourly at the passageway, at the end of which Mnementh lounged on his customary ledge.

A laden dragon comes, the bronze warned those in the Weyr. *It is Lytol behind young B'rant on brown Fanth.*

"Now he brings his own bad news?" Lessa asked sourly.

"It is hard enough for Lytol to ride another's dragon or come here at all, Lessa of Ruatha. Do not increase his torment one jot with your childishness," F'lar said sternly.

Lessa dropped her eyes, furious with F'lar for speaking so to her in front of Robinton.

Lytol stumped into the queen's weyr, carrying one end of a large rolled rug. Young B'rant, struggling to uphold the other end, was sweating with the effort. Lytol bowed respectfully toward Ramoth and gestured the young brown rider to help him unroll their burden. As the immense tapestry uncoiled, F'lar could understand why Masterweaver Zurg had remembered it. The colors, ancient though they undoubtedly were, remained vibrant and undimmed. The subject matter was even more interesting.

"Mnementh, send for Fandarel. Here's the model he needs for his flamethrower," F'lar said.

"That tapestry is Ruatha's," Lessa cried indignantly. "I remember it from my childhood. It hung in the Great Hall and was the most cherished of my Blood Line's possessions. Where has it been?" Her eyes were flashing.

"Lady, it is being returned to where it belongs," Lytol said stolidly, avoiding her gaze. "A masterweaver's work, this," he went on, touching the heavy fabric with reverent fingers. "Such colors, such patterning. It took a man's life to set up the loom, a craft's whole effort to complete, or I am no judge of true craftsmanship."

F'lar walked along the edge of the immense arras, wishing it could be hung to afford the proper perspective of the heroic scene. A flying formation of three wings of dragons dominated the upper portion of half the hanging. They were breathing flame as they dove upon gray, falling clumps of Threads in the brilliant sky. A sky just that perfect autumnal blue, F'lar decided, that cannot occur in warmer weather. Upon the lower slopes of the hills, foliage was depicted as turning yellow from chilly nights. The slatey rocks suggested Ruathan country. Was that why the tapestry had hung in Ruatha Hall? Below, men had left the protecting Hold, cut into the cliff itself. The men were burdened with the curious cylinders of which Zurg had spoken. The tubes in their hands belched brilliant tongues of flame in long streams, aimed at the writhing Threads that attempted to burrow in the ground.

Lessa gave a startled exclamation, walking right onto the tapestry, staring down at the woven outline of the Hold, its massive door ajar, the details of its bronze ornamentation painstakingly rendered in fine yarns.

"I believe that's the design on the Ruatha Hold door," F'lar remarked.

"It is . . . and it isn't," Lessa replied in a puzzled voice.

Lytol glowered at her and then at the woven door. "True. It isn't and yet it is, and I went through that door a scant hour ago." He scowled down at the door before his toes.

194

"Well, here are the designs Fandarel wants to study," F'lar said with relief, as he peered at the flamethrowers.

Whether or not the smith could produce a working model from this woven one in time to help them three days hence F'lar couldn't guess. But if Fandarel could not, no man could.

The Mastersmith was, for him, jubilant over the presence of the tapestry. He lay upon the rug, his nose tickled by the nap as he studied the details. He grumbled, moaned, and muttered as he sat cross-legged to sketch and peer.

"Has been done. Can be done. Must be done," he was heard to rumble.

Lessa called for *klah*, bread, and meat when she learned from young B'rant that neither he nor Lytol had eaten yet. She served all the men, her manner gay and teasing. F'lar was relieved for Lytol's sake. Lessa even pressed food and *klah* on Fandarel, a tiny figure beside the mammoth man, insisting that he come away from the tapestry and eat and drink before he could return to his mumbling and drawing.

Fandarel finally decided that he had enough sketches and disappeared, to be flown back to his crafthold.

"No point in asking him when he'll be back. He's too deep in thought to hear," F'lar remarked, amused.

"If you don't mind, I shall excuse myself as well," Lessa said, smiling graciously to the four remaining around the table. "Good Warder Lytol, young B'rant should soon be excused, too. He's half asleep."

"I most certainly am not, Weyrlady," B'rant assured her hastily, widening his eyes with simulated alertness.

Lessa merely laughed as she retreated into the sleeping chamber. F'lar stared thoughtfully after her.

"I mistrust the Weyrwoman when she uses that particularly docile tone of voice," he said slowly.

"Well, we must all depart," Robinton suggested, rising.

"Ramoth is young but not that foolish," F'lar murmured after the others had left.

Ramoth slept, oblivious of his scrutiny. He reached for the consolation Mnementh could give him, without response. The big bronze was dozing on his ledge.

> Black, blacker, blackest,
> And cold beyond frozen things.
> Where is *between* when there is naught
> To Life but fragile dragon wings?

"I JUST want to see that tapestry back on the wall at Ruatha," Lessa insisted to F'lar the next day. "I want it where it belongs."

They had gone to check on the injured and had had one argument already over F'lar's having sent N'ton along with the southern venture. Lessa had wanted him to try riding another's dragon. F'lar had preferred for him to learn to lead a wing of his own in the south, given the Turns to mature in. He had reminded Lessa, in the hope that it might prove inhibiting to any ideas she had about going four hundred Turns back, about F'nor's return trips, and he had borne down hard on the difficulties she had already experienced.

She had become very thoughtful, although she had said nothing.

Therefore, when Fandarel sent word that he would like to show F'lar a new mechanism, the Weyrleader felt reasonably safe in allowing Lessa the triumph of returning the purloined tapestry to Ruatha. She went to have the arras rolled and strapped to Ramoth's back.

He watched Ramoth rise with great sweeps of her wide wings, up to the Star Stone before going *between* to Ruatha. R'gul appeared on the ledge just then, reporting that a huge train of firestone was entering the Tunnel. Consequently, busy with such details, it was midmorning before he could get to see Fandarel's crude and not yet effective flame-thrower . . . the fire did not "throw" from the nozzle of the tube with any force at all. It was late afternoon before he reached the Weyr again.

R'gul announced sourly that F'nor had been looking for him—twice, in fact.

"Twice?"

"Twice, as I said. He would not leave a message with me for you." R'gul was clearly insulted by F'nor's refusal.

By the evening meal, when there was still no sign of Lessa, F'lar sent to Ruatha to learn that she had indeed brought the tapestry. She had badgered and bothered the entire Hold until the thing was properly hung. For upward of several hours she had sat and looked at it, pacing its length occasionally.

She and Ramoth had then taken to the sky above the Great Tower and disappeared. Lytol had assumed, as had everyone at Ruatha, that she had returned to Benden Weyr.

"Mnementh," F'lar bellowed when the messenger had finished. "Mnementh, where are they?"

Mnementh's answer was a long time in coming.

I cannot hear them, he said finally, his mental voice soft and as full of worry as a dragon's could be.

F'lar gripped the table with both hands, staring at the queen's empty weyr. He knew, in the anguished privacy of his mind, where Lessa had tried to go.

> Cold as death, death-bearing,
> Stay and die, unguided.
> Brave and braving, linger.
> This way was twice decided.

BELOW THEM was Ruatha's Great Tower. Lessa coaxed Ramoth slightly to the left, ignoring the dragon's acid comments, knowing that she was excited, too.

That's right, dear, this is exactly the angle at which the tapestry illustrates the Hold door. Only when that tapestry was designed, no one had carved the lintels or capped the door. And there was no Tower, no inner Court, no gate. She stroked the surprisingly soft skin of the curving neck, laughing to hide her own tense nervousness and apprehension at what she was about to attempt.

She told herself there were good reasons prompting her action in this matter. The ballad's opening phrase, "Gone away, gone ahead," was clearly a reference to *between* times. And the tapestry gave the required reference points for the jump *between* whens. Oh, how she thanked the Masterweaver who had woven that doorway. She must remember to tell him how well he had wrought. She hoped she'd be able to. Enough of that. Of course, she'd be able to. For hadn't the Weyrs disappeared? Knowing they had gone ahead, knowing how to go back to bring them ahead, it was she, obviously, who must go back and lead them. It was very simple, and only she and Ramoth could do it. Because they already had.

She laughed again, nervously, and took several deep, shuddering breaths.

"All right, my golden love," she murmured. "You have the reference. You know when I want to go. Take me *between*, Ramoth, *between* four hundred Turns."

The cold was intense, even more penetrating than she had

197

imagined. Yet it was not a physical cold. It was the awareness of the absence of *everything*. No light. No sound. No touch. As they hovered, longer, and longer, in this nothingness, Lessa recognized full-blown panic of a kind that threatened to overwhelm her reason. She knew she sat on Ramoth's neck, yet she could not feel the great beast under her thighs, under her hands. She tried to cry out inadvertently and opened her mouth to . . . nothing . . . no sound in her own ears. She could not even feel the hands that she knew she had raised to her own cheeks.

I am here, she heard Ramoth say in her mind. *We are together,* and this reassurance was all that kept her from losing her grasp on sanity in that terrifying aeon of unpassing, timeless nothingness.

Someone had sense enough to call for Robinton. The Masterharper found F'lar sitting at the table, his face deathly pale, his eyes staring at the empty weyr. The craftmaster's entrance, his calm voice, reached F'lar in his shocked numbness. He sent others out with a peremptory wave.

"She's gone. She tried to go back four hundred Turns," F'lar said in a tight, hard voice.

The Masterharper sank into the chair opposite the Weyrleader.

"She took the tapestry back to Ruatha," F'lar continued in that same choked voice. "I'd told her about F'nor's returns. I told her how dangerous this was. She didn't argue very much, and I know going *between* times had frightened her, if anything could frighten Lessa." He banged the table with an impotent fist. "I should have suspected her. When she thinks she's right, she doesn't stop to analyze, to consider. She just does it!"

"But she's not a foolish woman," Robinton reminded him slowly. "Not even she would jump *between* times without a reference point. Would she?"

" 'Gone away, gone ahead'—that's the only clue we have!"

"Now wait a moment," Robinton cautioned him, then snapped his fingers. "Last night, when she walked upon the tapestry, she was uncommonly interested in the Hall door. Remember, she discussed it with Lytol."

F'lar was on his feet and halfway down the passageway.

"Come on, man, we've got to get to Ruatha."

Lytol lit every glow in the Hold for F'lar and Robinton to examine the tapestry clearly.

"She spent the afternoon just looking at it," the Warder said, shaking his head. "You're sure she has tried this incredible jump?"

"She must have. Mnementh can't hear either her or Ramoth anywhere. Yet he says he can get an echo from Canth many Turns away and in the Southern Continent." F'lar stalked past the tapestry. "What is it about the door, Lytol? Think, man!"

"It is much as it is now, save that there are no carved lintels, there is no outer Court or Tower . . ."

"That's it. Oh, by the first Egg, it is so simple. Zurg said this tapestry is old. Lessa must have decided it was four hundred Turns, and she has used it as the reference point to go back *between* times."

"Why, then, she's there and safe," Robinton cried, sinking with relief in a chair.

"Oh, no, harper. It is not as easy as that," F'lar murmured, and Robinton caught his stricken look and the despair echoed in Lytol's face.

"What's the matter?"

"There is nothing *between*," F'lar said in a dead voice. "To go *between* places takes only as much time as for a man to cough three times. *Between* four hundred Turns. . . ." His voice trailed off.

Who wills,
Can.
Who tries,
Does.
Who loves,
Lives.

THERE WERE voices that first were roars in her aching ears and then hushed beyond the threshold of sound. She gasped as the whirling, nauseating sensation apparently spun her, and the bed which she felt beneath her, around and around. She clung to the sides of the bed as pain jabbed through her head, from somewhere directly in the middle of her skull. She screamed, as much in protest at the pain as from the terrifying, rolling, whirling, dropping lack of a solid ground.

Yet some frightening necessity kept her trying to gabble out

199

the message she had come to give. Sometimes she felt Ramoth trying to reach her in that vast swooping darkness that enveloped her. She would try to cling to Ramoth's mind, hoping the golden queen could lead her out of this torturing nowhere. Exhausted, she would sink down, down, only to be torn from oblivion by the desperate need to communicate.

She was finally aware of a soft, smooth hand upon her arm, of a liquid, warm and savory, in her mouth. She rolled it around her tongue, and it trickled down her sore throat. A fit of coughing left her gasping and weak. Then she experimentally opened her eyes, and the images before her did not lurch and spin.

"Who . . . are . . . you?" she managed to croak.

"Oh, my dear Lessa . . ."

"Is that who I am?" she asked, confused.

"So your Ramoth tells us," she was assured. "I am Mardra of Fort Weyr."

"Oh, F'lar will be so angry with me," Lessa moaned as her memory came rushing back. "He will shake me and shake me. He always shakes me when I disobey him. But I was right. I was right. Mardra? . . . Oh, that . . . awful . . . nothingness," and she felt herself drifting off into sleep, unable to resist that overwhelming urge. Comfortably, her bed no longer rocked beneath her.

The room, dimly lit by wallglows, was both like her own at Benden Weyr and subtly different. Lessa lay still, trying to isolate that difference. Ah, the weyr-walls were very smooth here. The room was larger, too, the ceiling higher and curving. The furnishings, now that her eyes were used to the dim light and she could distinguish details, were more finely crafted. She stirred restlessly.

"Ah, you're awake again, mystery lady," a man said. Light beyond the parted curtain flooded in from the outer weyr. Lessa sensed rather than saw the presence of others in the room beyond.

A woman passed under the man's arm, moving swiftly to the bedside.

"I remember you. You're Mardra," Lessa said with surprise.

"Indeed I am, and here is T'ton, Weyrleader at Fort."

T'ton was tossing more glows into the wallbasket, peering over his shoulder at Lessa to see if the light bothered her.

"Ramoth!" Lessa exclaimed, sitting upright, aware for the

first time that it was not Ramoth's mind she touched in the outer weyr.

"Oh, that one," Mardra laughed with amused dismay. "She'll eat us out of the Weyr, and even my Loranth has had to call the other queens to restrain her."

"She perches on the Star Stones as if she owned them and keens constantly," T'ton added, less charitably. He cocked an ear. "Ha. She's stopped."

"You can come, can't you?" Lessa blurted out.

"Come? Come where, my dear?" Mardra asked, confused. "You've been going on and on about our 'coming,' and Threads approaching, and the Red Star bracketed in the Eye Rock, and . . . my dear, don't you realize the Red Star has been past Pern these two months?"

"No, no, they've started. That's why I came back *between* times . . ."

"Back? *Between* times?" T'ton exclaimed, striding over to the bed, eyeing Lessa intently.

"Could I have some *klah?* I know I'm not making much sense, and I'm not really awake yet. But I'm not mad or still sick, and this is rather complicated."

"Yes, it is," T'ton remarked with deceptive mildness. But he did call down the service shaft for *klah.* And he did drag a chair over to her bedside, settling himself to listen to her.

"Of course you're not mad," Mardra soothed her, glaring at her weyrmate. "Or she wouldn't ride a queen."

T'ton had to agree to that. Lessa waited for the *klah* to come; when it did, she sipped gratefully at its stimulating warmth.

Then she took a deep breath and began, telling them of the Long Interval between the dangerous passes of the Red Star: how the sole Weyr had fallen into disfavor and contempt, how Jora had deteriorated and lost control over her queen, Nemorth, so that, as the Red Star neared, there was no sudden increase in the size of clutches. How she had Impressed Ramoth to become Benden's Weyrwoman. How F'lar had outwitted the dissenting Hold Lords the day after Ramoth's first mating flight and taken firm command of Weyr and Pern, preparing for the Threads he knew were coming. She told her by now rapt audience of her own first attempts to fly Ramoth and how she had inadvertently gone back *between* time to the day Fax had invaded Ruath Hold.

"Invade . . . my family's Hold?" Mardra cried, aghast.

201

"Ruatha has given the Weyrs many famous Weyrwomen," Lessa said with a sly smile at which T'ton burst out laughing.

"She's Ruathan, no question," he assured Mardra.

She told them of the situation in which dragonmen now found themselves, with an insufficient force to meet the Thread attacks. Of the Question Song and the great tapestry.

"A tapestry?" Mardra cried, her hand going to her cheek in alarm. "Describe it to me!"

And when Lessa did, she saw—at last—belief in both their faces.

"My father has just commissioned a tapestry with such a scene. He told me of it the other day because the last battle with the Threads was held over Ruatha." Incredulous, Mardra turned to T'ton, who no longed looked amused. "She must have done what she has said she'd done. How could she possibly know about the tapestry?"

"You might also ask your queen dragon, and mine," Lessa suggested.

"My dear, we do not doubt you now," Mardra said sincerely, "but it is a most incredible feat."

"I don't think," Lessa said, "that I would ever try it again, knowing what I do know."

"Yes, this shock makes a forward jump *between* times quite a problem if your F'lar must have an effective fighting force," T'ton remarked.

"You will come? You will?"

"There is a distinct possibility we will," T'ton said gravely, and his face broke into a lopsided grin. "You said we left the Weyrs . . . abandoned them, in fact, and left no explanation. We went somewhere . . . somewhen, that is, for we are still here now. . . ."

They were all silent, for the same alternative occurred to them simultaneously. The Weyrs had been vacant, but Lessa had no way of proving that the five Weyrs reappeared in her time.

"There must be a way. There must be a way," Lessa cried distractedly. "And there's no time to waste. No time at all!"

T'ton gave a bark of laughter. "There's plenty of time at this end of history, my dear."

They made her rest then, more concerned than she was that she had been ill some weeks, deliriously screaming that she was falling and could not see, could not hear, could not

202

touch. Ramoth, too, they told her, had suffered from the appalling nothingness of a protracted stay *between*, emerging above ancient Ruatha a pale yellow wraith of her former robust self.

The Lord of Ruatha Hold, Mardra's father, had been surprised out of his wits by the appearance of a staggering rider and a pallid queen on his stone verge. Naturally and luckily he had sent to his daughter at Fort Weyr for help. Lessa and Ramoth had been transported to the Weyr, and the Ruathan Lord kept silence on the matter.

When Lessa was strong enough, T'ton called a Council of Weyrleaders. Curiously, there was no opposition to going . . . provided they could solve the problem of time-shock and find reference points along the way. It did not take Lessa long to comprehend why the dragonriders were so eager to attempt the journey. Most of them had been born during the present Thread incursions. They had now had close to four months of unexciting routine patrols and were bored with monotony. Training Games were pallid substitutes for the real battles they had all fought. The Holds, which once could not do dragonmen favors enough, were beginning to be indifferent. The Weyrleaders could see these incidents increasing as Thread-generated fears receded. It was a morale decay as insidious as a wasting disease in Weyr and Hold. The alternative which Lessa's appeal offered was better than a slow decline in their own time.

Of Benden, only the Weyrleader himself was privy to these meetings. Because Benden was the only Weyr in Lessa's time, it must remain ignorant, and intact, until her time. Nor could any mention be made of Lessa's presence, for that, too, was unknown in her Turn.

She insisted that they call in the Masterharper because her Records said he had been called. But when he asked her to tell him the Question Song, she smiled and demurred.

"You'll write it, or your successor will, when the Weyrs are found to be abandoned," she told him. "But it must be your doing, not my repeating."

"A difficult assignment to know one must write a song that four hundred Turns later gives a valuable clue."

"Only be sure," she cautioned him, "that it is a Teaching tune. It must *not* be forgotten, for it poses questions that I have to answer."

203

As he started to chuckle, she realized she had already given him a pointer.

The discussions—how to go so far safely with no sustained sense deprivations—grew heated. There were more constructive notions, however impractical, on how to find reference points along the way. The five Weyrs had not been ahead in time, and Lessa, in her one gigantic backward leap, had not stopped for intermediate time marks.

"You did say that a *between* times jump of ten years caused no hardship?" T'ton asked of Lessa as all the Weyrleaders and the Masterharper met to discuss this impasse.

"None. It takes . . . oh, twice as long as a *between* places jump."

"It is the four hundred Turn leap that left you imbalanced. Hmmm. Maybe twenty or twenty-five Turn segments would be safe enough."

That suggestion found merit until Ista's cautious leader, D'ram, spoke up.

"I don't mean to be a Hold-hider, but there is one possibility we haven't mentioned. How do we know we made the jump *between* to Lessa's time? Going *between* is a chancy business. Men go missing often. And Lessa barely made it here alive."

"A good point, D'ram," T'ton concurred briskly, "but I feel there is more to prove that we do—did—will—go forward. The clues, for one thing—they were aimed at Lessa. The very emergency that left five Weyrs empty sent her back to appeal for our help—"

"Agreed, agreed," D'ram interrupted earnestly, "but what I mean is can you be sure we reached Lessa's time? It hadn't happened yet. Do we know it can?"

T'ton was not the only one who searched his mind for an answer to that. All of a sudden he slammed both hands, palms down, on the table.

"By the Egg, it's die slow, doing nothing, or die quick, trying. I've had a surfeit of the quiet life we dragonmen must lead after the Red Star passes till we go *between* in old age. I confess I'm almost sorry to see the Red Star dwindle farther from us in the evening sky. I say, grab the risk with both hands and shake it till it's gone. We're dragonmen, aren't we, bred to fight the Threads? Let's go hunting . . . four hundred Turns ahead!"

Lessa's drawn face relaxed. She had recognized the validity

of D'ram's alternate possibility, and it had touched off bitter fear in her heart. To risk herself was her own responsibility, but to risk these hundreds of men and dragons, the Weyrfolk who would accompany their men . . . ?

T'ton's ringing words for once and all dispensed with that consideration.

"And I believe," the Masterharper's exultant voice cut through the answering shouts of agreement, "I have your reference points." A smile of surprised wonder illuminated his face. "Twenty Turns or twenty hundred, you have a guide! And T'ton said it. As the Red Star dwindles in the evening sky . . ."

Later, as they plotted the orbit of the Red Star, they found how easy that solution actually was and chuckled that their ancient foe should be their guide.

Atop Fort Weyr, as on all the Weyrs, were great stones. They were so placed that at certain times of the year they marked the approach and retreat of the Red Star, as it orbited in its erratic two hundred Turn-long course around their sun. By consulting the Records which, among other morsels of information, included the Red Star's wanderings, it was not hard to plan jumps *between* of twenty-five Turns for each Weyr. It had been decided that the complement of each separate Weyr would jump *between* above its own base, for there would unquestionably be accidents if close to eighteen hundred laden beasts tried it at one point.

Each moment now was one too long away from her own time for Lessa. She had been a month away from F'lar and missed him more than she had thought possible. Also, she was worried that Ramoth would mate away from Mnementh. There were, to be sure, bronze dragons and bronze riders eager to do that service, but Lessa had no interest in them.

T'ton and Mardra occupied her with the many details in organizing the exodus, so that no clues, past the tapestry and the Question Song that would be composed at a later date, remained in the Weyrs.

It was with a relief close to tears that Lessa urged Ramoth upward in the night sky to take her place near T'ton and Mardra above the Fort Weyr Star Stone. At five other Weyrs great wings were ranged in formation, ready to depart their own times.

As each Weyrleader's dragon reported to Lessa that all were ready, reference points determined by the Red Star's

205

travels in mind, it was this traveler from the future who gave the command to jump *between.*

> The blackest night must end in dawn,
> The sun dispel the dreamer's fear:
> When shall my soul's black, hopeless pain
> Find solace in its darkening Weyr?

THEY HAD made eleven jumps *between,* the Weyrleaders' bronzes speaking to Lessa as they rested briefly between each jump. Of the eighteen hundred-odd travelers, only four failed to come ahead, and they had been older beasts. All five sections agreed to pause for a quick meal and hot *klah* before the final jump, which would be but twelve Turns.

"It is easier," T'ton commented as Mardra served the *klah,* "to go twenty-five Turns than twelve." He glanced up at the Red Dawn Star, their winking and faithful guide. "It does not alter its position as much. I count on you, Lessa, to give us additional references."

"I want to get us back to Ruatha before F'lar discovers I have gone." She shivered as she looked up at the Red Star and sipped hastily at the hot *klah.* "I've seen the Star just like that, once . . . no, twice . . . before at Ruatha." She stared at T'ton, her throat constricting as she remembered that morning: the time she had decided that the Red Star was a menace to her, three days after which Fax and F'lar had appeared at Ruatha Hold. Fax had died on F'lar's dagger, and she had gone to Benden Weyr. She felt suddenly dizzy, weak, strangely unsettled. She had not felt this way as they paused between other jumps.

"Are you all right, Lessa?" Mardra asked with concern. "You're so white. You're shaking." She put her arm around Lessa, glancing, concerned, at her Weyrmate.

"Twelve Turns ago I was at Ruatha," Lessa murmured, grasping Mardra's hand for support. "I was at Ruatha twice. Let's go on quickly. I'm too many in this morning. I must get back. I must get back to F'lar. He'll be so angry."

The note of hysteria in her voice alarmed both Mardra and T'ton. Hastily the latter gave orders for the fires to be extinguished, for the Weyrfolk to mount and prepare for the final jump ahead.

Her mind in chaos, Lessa transmitted the references to the

206

other Weyrleaders' dragons: Ruatha in the evening light, the Great Tower, the inner Court, the land at springtime. . . .

> A fleck of red in a cold night sky,
> A drop of blood to guide them by,
> Turn away, Turn away, Turn, be gone,
> A Red Star beckons the travelers on.

BETWEEN THEM, Lytol and Robinton forced F'lar to eat, deliberately plying him with wine. At the back of his mind F'lar knew he would have to keep going, but the effort was immense, the spirit gone from him. It was no comfort that they still had Pridith and Kylara to continue dragonkind, yet he delayed sending someone back for F'nor, unable to face the reality of that admission: that in sending for Pridith and Kylara, he had acknowledged the fact that Lessa and Ramoth would not return.

Lessa, Lessa, his mind cried endlessly, damning her one moment for her reckless, thoughtless daring, loving her the next for attempting such an incredible feat.

"I said, F'lar, you need sleep now more than wine." Robinton's voice penetrated his preoccupation.

F'lar looked at him, frowning in perplexity. He realized that he was trying to lift the wine jug that Robinton was holding firmly down.

"What did you say?"

"Come. I'll bear you company to Benden. Indeed, nothing could persuade me to leave your side. You have aged years, man, in the course of hours."

"And isn't it understandable?" F'lar shouted, rising to his feet, the impotent anger boiling out of him at the nearest target in the form of Robinton.

Robinton's eyes were full of compassion as he reached for F'lar's arm, gripping it tightly.

"Man, not even this Masterharper has words enough to express the sympathy and honor he has for you. But you must sleep; you have tomorrow to endure, and the tomorrow after that you have to fight. The dragonmen must have a leader. . . ." His voice trailed off. "Tomorrow you must send for F'nor . . . and Pridith."

F'lar pivoted on his heel and strode toward the fateful door of Ruatha's great hall.

Oh, Tongue, give sound to joy and sing
Of hope and promise on dragonwing.

BEFORE THEM loomed Ruatha's Great Tower, the high walls of the Outer Court clearly visible in the fading light.

The claxon rang violent summons into the air, barely heard over the earsplitting thunder as hundreds of dragons appeared, ranging in full fighting array, wing upon wing, up and down the valley.

A shaft of light stained the flagstones of the Court as the Hold door opened.

Lessa ordered Ramoth down, close to the Tower, and dismounted, running eagerly forward to greet the men who piled out of the door. She made out the stocky figure of Lytol, a handbasket of glows held high above his head. She was so relieved to see him that she forgot her previous antagonism to the Warder.

"You misjudged the last jump by two days, Lessa," he cried as soon as he was near enough for her to hear him over the noise of settling dragons.

"Misjudged? How could I?" she breathed.

T'ton and Mardra came up beside her.

"No need to worry," Lytol reassured her, gripping her hands tightly in his, his eyes dancing. He was actually smiling at her. "You overshot the day. Go back *between,* return to Ruatha of two days ago. That's all." His grin widened at her confusion. "It is all right," he repeated, patting her hands. "Take this same hour, the Great Court, everything, but visualize F'lar, Robinton, and myself here on the flagstones. Place Mnementh on the Great Tower and a blue dragon on the verge. Now go."

Mnementh? Ramoth queried Lessa, eager to see her Weyrmate. She ducked her great head, and her huge eyes gleamed with scintillating fire.

"I don't understand," Lessa wailed. Mardra slipped a comforting arm around her shoulders.

"But I do, I do—trust me," Lytol pleaded, patting her shoulder awkwardly and glancing at T'ton for support. "It is as F'nor has said. You cannot be several places in time without experiencing great distress, and when you stopped twelve Turns back, it threw Lessa all to pieces."

"You know that?" T'ton cried.

"Of course. Just go back two days. You see, I *know* you

have. I shall, of course, be surprised then, but now, tonight, I know you reappeared two days earlier. Oh, go. Don't argue. F'lar was half out of his mind with worry for you."

"He'll shake me," Lessa cried, like a little girl.

"Lessa!" T'ton took her by the hand and led her back to Ramoth, who crouched so her rider could mount.

T'ton took complete charge and had his Fidranth pass the order to return to the references Lytol had given, adding by way of Ramoth, a description of the humans and Mnementh.

The cold of *between* restored Lessa to herself, although her error had badly jarred her confidence. But then there was Ruatha again. The dragons happily arranged themselves in tremendous display. And there, silhouetted against the light from the Hall, stood Lytol, Robinton's tall figure, and . . . F'lar.

Mnementh's voice gave a brassy welcome, and Ramoth could not land Lessa quickly enough to go and twine necks with her mate.

Lessa stood where Ramoth had left her, unable to move. She was aware that Mardra and T'ton were beside her. She was conscious only of F'lar, racing across the Court toward her. Yet she could not move.

He grabbed her in his arms, holding her so tightly to him that she could not doubt the joy of his welcome.

"Lessa, Lessa," his voice raggedly chanted in her ear. He pressed her face against his, crushing her to breathlessness, all his careful detachment abandoned. He kissed her, hugged her, held her, and then kissed her with rough urgency again. Then he suddenly set her on her feet and gripped her shoulders. "Lessa, if you ever . . ." he said, punctuating each word with a flexing of his fingers, then stopped, aware of a grinning circle of strangers surrounding them.

"I told you he'd shake me," Lessa was saying, dashing tears from her face. "But, F'lar, I brought them all . . . all but Benden Weyr. And that is why the five Weyrs were abandoned. I brought them."

F'lar looked around him, looked beyond the leaders to the masses of dragons settling in the valley, on the heights, everywhere he turned. There were dragons, blue, green, bronze, brown, and a whole wingful of golden queen dragons alone.

"You brought the Weyrs?" he echoed, stunned.

"Yes, this is Mardra and T'ton of Fort Weyr, D'ram and . . ."

He stopped her with a little shake, pulling her to his side so he could see and greet the newcomers.

"I am more grateful than you can know," he said and could not go on with all the many words he wanted to add.

T'ton stepped forward, holding out his hand, which F'lar seized and held firmly.

"We bring eighteen hundred dragons, seventeen queens, and all that is necessary to implement our Weyrs."

"And they brought flamethrowers, too," Lessa put in excitedly.

"But—to come . . . to attempt it . . ." F'lar murmured in admiring wonder.

T'ton and D'ram and the others laughed.

"Your Lessa showed the way . . ."

". . . with the Red Star to guide us . . ." she said.

"We are dragonmen," T'ton continued solemnly, "as you are yourself, F'lar of Benden. We were told there are Threads here to fight, and that's work for dragonmen to do . . . in any time!"

> Drummer, beat, and piper, blow,
> Harper, strike, and soldier, go.
> Free the flame and sear the grasses
> Till the dawning Red Star passes.

EVEN AS the five Weyrs had been settling around Ruatha Valley, F'nor had been compelled to bring forward in time his southern Weyrfolk. They had all reached the end of endurance in double-time life, gratefully creeping back to quarters they had vacated two days and ten Turns ago.

R'gul, totally unaware of Lessa's backward plunge, greeted F'lar and his Weyrwoman, on their return to the Weyr, with the news of F'nor's appearance with seventy-two new dragons and the further word that he doubted any of the riders would be fit to fight.

"I've never seen such exhausted men in my life," R'gul rattled on, "can't imagine what could have gotten into them, with sun and plenty of food and all, and no responsibilities."

F'lar and Lessa exchanged glances.

"Well, the southern Weyr ought to be maintained, R'gul. Think it over."

"I'm a fighting dragonman, not a womanizer," the old

210

dragonrider grunted. "It'd take more than a trip *between* times to reduce me like those others."

"Oh, they'll be themselves again in next to no time," Lessa said and, to R'gul's intense disapproval, she giggled.

"They'll have to be if we're to keep the skies Thread-free," R'gul snapped testily.

"No problem about that now," F'lar assured him easily.

"No problem? With only a hundred and forty-four dragons?"

"Two hundred and sixteen," Lessa corrected him firmly.

Ignoring her, R'gul asked, "Has that Mastersmith found a flamethrower that'll work?"

"Indeed he has," F'lar assured R'gul, grinning broadly.

The five Weyrs had also brought forward their equipment. Fandarel all but snatched examples from their backs and, undoubtedly, every hearth and smithy through the continent would be ready to duplicate the design by morning. T'ton had told F'lar that, in his time, each Hold had ample flamethrowers for every man on the ground. In the course of the Long Interval, however, the throwers must have been either smelted down or lost as incomprehensible devices. D'ram, particularly, was very much interested in Fandarel's agenothree sprayer, considering it better than thrown-flame, since it would also act as a fertilizer.

"Well," R'gul admitted gloomily, "a flamethrower or two will be some help day after tomorrow."

"We have found something else that will help a lot more," Lessa remarked and then hastily excused herself, dashing into the sleeping quarters.

The sounds that drifted past the curtain were either laughter or sobs, and R'gul frowned on both. That girl was just too young to be Weyrwoman at such a time. No stability.

"Has she realized how critical our situation is? Even with F'nor's additions? That is, if they can fly?" R'gul demanded testily. "You oughtn't to let her leave the Weyr at all."

F'lar ignored that and began pouring himself a cup of wine.

"You once pointed out to me that the five empty Weyrs of Pern supported your theory that there would be no more Threads."

R'gul cleared his throat, thinking that apologies—even if they might be due from the Weyrleader—were scarcely effective against the Threads.

"Now there was merit in that theory," F'lar went on, filling a cup for R'gul. "Not, however, as you interpreted it. The five Weyrs were empty because they . . . they came here."

R'gul, his cup halfway to his lips, stared at F'lar. This man also was too young to bear his responsibilities. But . . . he seemed actually to believe what he was saying.

"Believe it or not, R'gul—and in a bare day's time you will—the five Weyrs are empty no longer. They're here, in the Weyrs, in this time. And they shall join us, eighteen hundred strong, the day after tomorrow at Telgar, with flame-throwers and with plenty of battle experience."

R'gul regarded the poor man stolidly for a long moment. Carefully he put his cup down and, turning on his heel, left the weyr. He refused to be an object of ridicule. He'd better plan to take over the leadership tomorrow if they were to fight Threads the day after.

The next morning, when he saw the clutch of great bronze dragons bearing the Weyrleaders and their wingleaders to the conference, R'gul got quietly drunk.

Lessa exchanged good mornings with her friends and then, smiling sweetly, left the weyr, saying she must feed Ramoth. F'lar stared after her thoughtfully, then went to greet Robinton and Fandarel, who had been asked to attend the meeting, too. Neither Craftmaster said much, but neither missed a word spoken. Fandarel's great head kept swiveling from speaker to speaker, his deep-set eyes blinking occasionally. Robinton sat with a bemused smile on his face, utterly delighted by ancestral visitors.

F'lar was quickly talked out of resigning his titular position as Weyrleader of Benden on the grounds that he was too inexperienced.

"You did well enough at Nerat and Keroon. Well indeed," T'ton said.

"You call twenty-eight men or dragons out of action good leadership?"

"For a first battle, with every dragonman green as a hatchling? No, man, you were on time at Nerat, however you got there," and T'ton grinned maliciously at F'lar, "which is what a dragonman must do. No, that was well flown, I say. Well flown." The other four Weyrleaders muttered complete agreement with that compliment. "Your Weyr is under-

212

strength, though, so we'll lend you enough odd-wing riders till you've gotten the Weyr up to full strength again. Oh, the queens love these times!" And his grin broadened to indicate that bronze riders did, too.

F'lar returned that smile, thinking that Ramoth was about ready for another mating flight, and this time, Lessa . . . oh, that girl was being too deceptively docile. He'd better watch her closely.

"Now," T'ton was saying, "we left with Fandarel's craft-hold all the flamethrowers we brought up so that the ground-men will be armed tomorrow."

"Aye, and my thanks," Fandarel grunted. "We'll turn out new ones in record time and return yours soon."

"Don't forget to adapt that agenothree for air spraying, too," D'ram put in.

"It is agreed," and T'ton glanced quickly around at the other riders, "that all the Weyrs will meet, full strength, three hours after dawn above Telgar, to follow the Threads' attack across to Crom. By the way, F'lar, those charts of yours that Robinton showed me are superb. We never had them."

"How did you know when the attacks would come?"

T'ton shrugged. "They were coming so regularly even when I was a weyrling, you kind of knew when one was due. But this way is much, much better."

"More efficient," Fandarel added approvingly.

"After tomorrow, when all the Weyrs show up at Telgar, we can request supplies we need to stock the empty Weyrs," T'ton grinned. "Like old times, squeezing extra tithes from the Holders." He rubbed his hands in anticipation. "Like old times."

"There's the southern Weyr," F'nor suggested. "We've been gone from there six Turns in this time, and the herdbeasts were left. They'll have multiplied, and there'll be all that fruit and grain."

"It would please me to see that southern venture continued," F'lar remarked, nodding encouragingly at F'nor.

"Yes, and continue Kylara down there, please, too," F'nor added urgently, his eyes sparkling with irritation.

They discussed sending for some immediate supplies to help out the newly occupied Weyrs, and then adjourned the meeting.

"It is a trifle unsettling," T'ton said as he shared wine with

213

Robinton, "to find that the Weyr you left the day before in good order has become a dusty hulk." He chuckled. "The women of the Lower Caverns were a bit upset."

"We cleaned up those kitchens," F'nor replied indignantly. A good night's rest in a fresh time had removed much of his fatigue.

T'ton cleared his throat. "According to Mardra, no man can *clean* anything."

"Do you think you'll be up to riding tomorrow, F'nor?" F'lar asked solicitously. He was keenly aware of the stress showing in his half brother's face, despite his improvement overnight. Yet those strenuous Turns had been necessary, nor had they become futile even in hindsight with the arrival of eighteen hundred dragons from past time. When F'lar had ordered F'nor ten Turns backward to breed the desperately needed replacements, they had not yet brought to mind the Question Song or known of the tapestry.

"I wouldn't miss that fight if I were dragonless," F'nor declared stoutly.

"Which reminds me," F'lar remarked, "we'll need Lessa at Telgar tomorrow. She can speak to any dragon, you know," he explained, almost apologetically, to T'ton and D'ram.

"Oh, we know," T'ton assured him. "And Mardra doesn't mind." Seeing F'lar's blank expression, he added, "As senior Weyrwoman, Mardra, of course, leads the queens' wing."

F'lar's face grew blanker. "Queens' wing?"

"Certainly," and T'ton and D'ram exchanged questioning glances at F'lar's surprise. "You don't keep your queens from fighting, do you?"

"Our *queens*? T'ton, we at Benden have had only *one* queen dragon—at a time—for so many generations that there are those who denounce the legends of queens in battle as black heresy!"

T'ton looked rueful. "I had not truly realized till this instant how small your numbers were." But his enthusiasms overtook him. "Just the same, queens are very useful with flamethrowers. They get clumps other riders might miss. They fly in low, under the main wings. That's one reason D'ram's so interested in the agenothree spray. Doesn't singe the hair off the Holders' heads, so to speak, and is far better over tilled fields."

"Do you mean to say that you allow your queens to fly—

214

against Threads?" F'lar ignored the fact that F'nor was grinning, and T'ton, too.

"Allow?" D'ram bellowed. "You can't stop them. Don't you know your Ballads?"

" 'Moreta's Ride'?"

"Exactly."

F'nor laughed aloud at the expression on F'lar's face as he irritably pulled the hanging forelock from his eyes. Then, sheepishly, he began to grin.

"Thanks. That gives me an idea."

He saw his fellow Weyrleaders to their dragons, waved cheerfully to Robinton and Fandarel, more lighthearted than he would have thought he'd be the morning before the second battle. Then he asked Mnementh where Lessa might be.

Bathing, the bronze dragon replied.

F'lar glanced at the empty queen's weyr.

Oh, Ramoth is on the Peak, as usual. Mnementh sounded aggrieved.

F'lar heard the sound of splashing in the bathing room suddenly cease, so he called down for hot *klah.* He was going to enjoy this.

"Oh, did the meeting go well?" Lessa asked sweetly as she emerged from the bathing room, drying-cloth wrapped tightly around her slender figure.

"Extremely. You realize, of course, Lessa, that you'll be needed at Telgar?"

She looked at him intently for a moment before she smiled again.

"I *am* the only Weyrwoman who can speak to any dragon," she replied archly.

"True," F'lar admitted blithely. "And no longer the only queen's rider in Benden. . . ."

"I hate you!" Lessa snapped, unable to evade F'lar as he pinned her cloth-swathed body to his.

"Even when I tell you that Fandarel has a flamethrower for you so you can join the queens' wing?"

She stopped squirming in his arms and stared at him, disconcerted that he had outguessed her.

"And that Kylara will be installed as Weyrwoman in the south . . . in this time? As Weyrleader, I need my peace and quiet between battles. . . ."

The cloth fell from her body to the floor as she responded to his kiss as ardently as if dragon-roused.

> From the Weyr and from the Bowl,
> Bronze and brown and blue and green,
> Rise the dragonmen of Pern,
> Aloft, on wing; seen, then unseen.

RANGED ABOVE the Peak of Benden Weyr, a scant three hours after dawn, two hundred and sixteen dragons held their formations as F'lar on bronze Mnementh inspected their ranks.

Below in the Bowl were gathered all the Weyrfolk and some of those injured in the first battle. All the Weyrfolk, that is, except Lessa and Ramoth. They had gone on to Fort Weyr where the queens' wing was assembling. F'lar could not quite suppress a twinge of concern that she and Ramoth would be fighting, too. A holdover, he knew, from the days when Pern had only one queen. If Lessa could jump four hundred Turns *between* and lead five Weyrs back, she could take care of herself and her dragon against Threads.

He checked to be sure that every man was well loaded with firestone sacks, that each dragon was in good color, especially those in from the southern Weyr. Of course, the dragons were fit, but the faces of the men still showed evidences of the temporal strains they had endured. He was procrastinating, and the Threads would be dropping in the skies of Telgar.

He gave the order to go *between*. They reappeared above, and to the south of Telgar Hold itself, and were not the first arrivals. To the west, to the north, and yes, to the east now, wings arrived until the horizon was patterned with the great V's of several thousand dragon wings. Faintly he heard the claxon bell on Telgar Hold Tower as the unexpected dragon strength was acclaimed from the ground.

"Where is she?" F'lar demanded of Mnementh. "We'll need her presently to relay orders . . ."

She's coming, Mnementh interrupted him.

Right above Telgar Hold another wing appeared. Even at this distance, F'lar could see the difference: the golden dragons shone in the bright morning sunlight.

A hum of approval drifted down the dragon ranks, and despite his fleeting worry, F'lar grinned with proud indulgence at the glittering sight.

Just then the eastern wings soared straight upward in the sky as the dragons became instinctively aware of the presence of their ancient foe.

216

Mnementh raised his head, echoing back the brass thunder of the war cry. He turned his head, even as hundreds of other beasts turned to receive firestone from their riders. Hundreds of great jaws masticated the stone, swallowed it, their digestive acids transforming dry stone into flame-producing gases, igniting on contact with oxygen.

Threads! F'lar could see them clearly now against the spring sky. His pulses began to quicken, not with apprehension, but with a savage joy. His heart pounded unevenly. Mnementh demanded more stone and began to speed up the strokes of his wings in the air, gathering himself to leap upward when commanded.

The leading Weyr already belched gouts of orange-red flame into the pale blue sky. Dragons winked in and out, flamed and dove.

The great golden queens sped at cliff-skimming height to cover what might have been missed.

Then F'lar gave the command to gain altitude to meet the Threads halfway in their abortive descent. As Mnementh surged upward, F'lar shook his fist defiantly at the winking Red Eye of the Star.

"One day," he shouted, "we will not sit tamely here, awaiting your fall. We will fall on you, where you spin, and sear you on your own ground."

By the Egg, he told himself, if we can travel four hundred Turns backward and across seas and lands in the blink of an eye, what is travel from one world to another but a different kind of step?

F'lar grinned to himself. He'd better not mention that audacious notion in Lessa's presence.

Clumps ahead, Mnementh warned him.

As the bronze dragon charged, flaming, F'lar tightened his knees on the massive neck. Mother of us all, he was glad that now, of all times conceivable, he, F'lar, rider of bronze Mnementh, was a dragonman of Pern!

IN MEMORIAM

Among many science fiction people, be they professionals, amateur but valuable scholars of the field, or simply readers, there exists an intimacy unique in literature. Over the years it has kept a small glow of humanness alive for us in this darkening world. But friendship and love have their price, which death finally exacts. The year 1968—actually, counting from late 1967—was as disastrous for our little circle as for the whole planet.

Space does not allow that we here memorialize any but those who worked with text for pay. You, the general public, never knew the rest. It was your loss. The women who have departed—Helen Bretnor, Anna-Louise Germeshausen, Barbara Pollard—were more than wives, more even than beautiful and gracious ladies, they were outstanding achievers in their special lines of endeavor. Likewise, George Salter was important in fantasy art. The other men were not just fans (though several of them had much to do with making fandom what it is), they counted for a great deal in their daily lives: Ron Ellik, Lewis Grant, Jr., Andy Harris, Dale Hart, Lee Jacobs, Harry Sanders.

We will always miss them.

Meanwhile, in honor and as a contribution to literary history, a number of writers have kindly donated obituaries of their colleagues.

Anthony Boucher

Anthony Boucher died last April. He has been gone over a year now, and as James Reach wrote in *Ellery Queen's Mystery Magazine*, "How shall we manage without him?" The answer is that we haven't managed too well.

Tony Boucher was the Renaissance ideal of the universal man. He was an editor, a writer, a reviewer, a writer for radio and television, a musicologist, an opera critic. In addition to all these, he was a lover of sports, a shrewd and deadly poker player, a devout Catholic who knew his church's doctrine better than some priests, and a man who took a friendly interest in the activities and professions of his fellow man.

There was seldom a day that passed that I didn't phone to Tony about some problem—of the detective story, who wrote what and when, of the science fiction world, of a myriad things. In answer to the query of Mr. Reach, I, for one, have found a goodly portion of my life empty with Tony's passing. There is no one to pose questions to, to discuss politics, football, or cookery, no one to argue with about a score of subjects.

We who knew him are doing a memorial anthology of crime and science fiction. It sums up what people felt about Anthony Boucher, I think, when I state that we have been swamped with submissions by writers who wish to use this opportunity to do him homage. He was a pre-eminent critic but a just and gentle one. What man can say more of him?   J. FRANCIS MCCOMAS

Rosel George Brown

When Damon Knight *(Orbit 3)* admitted ". . . I was [wrong] . . . when I told Rosel George Brown she couldn't sell a novel about a female private eye . . ." he paid deserved tribute to the outstanding craftsmanship-under-handicap of this "handsome Southern gentlewoman," as Horace Gold once described her. For Rosel, who died of lymphatic-system malignancy in November 1967, and whose eminently successful achievements in science fiction coincided with a decade of illness, produced increasingly notable and major works during the terminal phase of her affliction. Moreover, despite her infirmity, she remained, at forty-one, "handsome"—petite, attractive, delightful; "gentle"—as the wife of Dr. William Burlie Brown, Tulane University history professor, and mother of two children; and "Southern"—but only geographically and in the sense of suggesting picturesque regional charm, for hers was a broad, cosmopolitan outlook. Even as she pursued the distinctive and unique in futuristic fiction, she lived in a large, old home in New Orleans' quiet university section, where sprawling plantations once drowsed.

But Rosel, indeed, neither drowsed nor bent under affliction. Her novel "about a female private eye" (*Sibyl Sue Blue,* Doubleday, 1966) came as somewhat of a landmark in science fiction and underscored the authoress' ranging skill at cloaking unconventional protagonists with vividly drawn credibility—in this case a cigar-smoking, gin-guzzling matron who likes her investigative chores well spiced with sensual interludes. Had Rosel lived, Sibyl Sue Blue would have become a familiar serial adventuress in this genre. Fortunately, Sibyl will wade daintily-swashbucklingly through *The Waters of Centaurus,* still to be published by Doubleday; unfortunately, the third of this series was never finished. Then there was Rosel's noteworthy Nebula Award nominee, *Earthblood* (Doubleday, 1966; Science Fiction Book Club selection, January 1967), written in collaboration with Keith Laumer and again expanding standards of characterization and exotic situation. Heralding Rosel's promise of signal accomplishment as a crisp stylist were her short stories, rich in emotion and satirical content—"Visiting Professor," "Car Pool," "Fruiting Body," and many others. In not a few of these she drew heavily upon academic knowledge deriving from her University of Minnesota master's degree in Greek. "Rosel George Brown," wrote James Blish in *The Issue at Hand* (Advent, 1966), "is the only one of F&SF's recent gaggle of housewives who knows how to write." An overstatement, of course. But Rosel, a charter member of the Science Fiction Writers of America, stood among the very best of them.

DANIEL F. GALOUYE

Groff Conklin

In 1946 there appeared *The Best of Science Fiction,* the first of the science fiction anthologies to attract general notice and the first, as it happened, to contain a story by myself. The editor was Groff Conklin, and over the next twenty years he remained the master anthologizer. He was not to remain alone on the heights; others joined him; but he was there first.

In those twenty years, I saw him all too rarely, but letters flowed back and forth freely. He loved science fiction with a childlike delight that infused itself into all who would listen to him. He was acerbic in his criticism but always fair, and when he didn't like one of my stories (as sometimes happened) his words cut deep but left no sting behind. He was a lovable fellow, good-natured and kind, but he smoked too many cigarettes and they killed him at last.

ISAAC ASIMOV

Bernard I. Kahn

Bernard Kahn's first story arrived at my office by mail, landed in the "slush pile"—stories from people we've never heard of, or who have not merited special attention—and promptly earned a place in the magazine—*Astounding* then, *Analog* now. I'd bought a second Bernard Kahn story before I met the man; he lived in San Francisco, I in the New York area. Then I found out that the stories had a large autobiographical component. Dr. Bernard I. Kahn had Been There in the governmental medical business. A Navy doctor during the early part of World War II, he learned about sinuses and infected ears during a winter in the Aleutian Islands. The latter part of the war he spent as chief of psychiatric research for the Navy at Mare Island Navy Base. After the war he joined in setting up the Kaiser Foundation Hospital's unique Family Health Plan, which treated the whole family as whole individuals, both minds and bodies.

He knew the problems of the medical-psychiatric public service. He was, also, one of the few psychiatrists I fully respected as a man, as a person, and as a psychiatrist. There is a tendency among psychiatrists to consider that Being A Psychiatrist means that they are a few notches above such fumbling things as mere human beings. Bernard Kahn knew he was a human being practicing psychiatry.

The trouble with that approach is that it means they take on the woes of many men—and that's very hard on a human heart. It's not a safe or a smart thing to do.

My friend Barney Kahn died of heart failure during 1968.

JOHN W. CAMPBELL

Anna Kavan

Anna Kavan's name may be little known among science fiction readers; yet to those readers who also take their pleasure in wider fields of literature, her short stories—in which a frequent streak of fantasy is blended with a sense of apprehension, with abrupt changs of mood, and with a keen though veiled sense of humor—have great appeal. At her best, she recalls Kafka. Back in the fifties, she was doing effortlessly the sort of story that, ten years later, would appear rather stylishly modern in an sf magazine.

Born at about the turn of the century, Anna Kavan was a cosmopolitan; of British parents, she first saw the light of day in France, spent much of her childhood in Europe and the United States, and lived in Burma after her first marriage. She pursued her writing career despite frequent illness. Her first novel, *Asylum Piece*, was published in England in 1940—not a good year for publication!—and in the States by Doubleday in 1946. Her last novel, *Ice,* a powerfully conceived and mysterious piece of higher science fiction, was published in 1967. I nominated it the Best SF Novel of 1967 in my *Oxford Mail* column. Now, I am happy to say, Doubleday has accepted *Ice* for future publication. This good news, unfortunately, failed to reach Anna by about a week; she died in her beautiful little home in Kensington on 5 December 1968.

BRIAN W. ALDISS

Gerald Kersh

When he wrote good, few men could touch him at what he did best. When he wrote bad, at his worst he was merely dull. A writer could go to meet his maker with few regrets if he knew that to be true. It was true of Kersh, and he certainly knew it. Despite the short shrift he got from most American publishers and critics, who chose to ignore the almost legendary awe in which he was held by Continental authorities, he continued working, producing, and besides the stature acquired from simply brilliant novels like *Fowler's End, Night and the Ci y,* and *The Implacable Hunter,* he assured himself a place in the hall of fame of fantasy writers with short stories like "Whatever happened to Corporal Cuckoo?" "The Queen of Pig Island," and "Men Without Bones."

I never met him, but it fell to me to edit the last book of his work ever published, just last year. He died soon after, on Novmber 7, 1968. The throat cancer that killed him had first led to the removal of his larynx. The few letters we exchanged testify to his unbroken courage and steady grip on reality.

The last sentence he wrote to me was, "I hope we may meet when you are in my part of the world, or I am in yours." Looks like it'll have to be in his part of the world, now. But that's cool. I suspect I'd come upon Kersh, with his voice restored, playing some five-card stud with Cyril Kornbluth, Henry Kuttner, and Chuck Beaumont—and ignoring boring mothers like Shakespeare and Thomas Wolfe, over there in the corner, brooding because they hadn't written the way Kersh had. Mary Shelley would be serving the refreshments.

But until that time, there's a quote from a Kersh story that I have over my typewriter; it keeps my head straight. It says:

". . . there are men whom one hates until a certain moment when one sees, through a chink in their armour, the writhing of something nailed down and in torment."

Have you ever noticed: though the good ones go, they never really leave.

HARLAN ELLISON

Edison Marshall

Edison Tesla Marshall, noted author of historical novels, including *Benjamin Blake, Yankee Pasha,* and *The Viking,* as well as a number of lesser-known fantasy novels, died October 29, 1968, at the age of seventy-three.

He was born in Renssalaer, Indiana, where his father edited and published a small newspaper. The family later moved to Oregon, where Edison attended the state university from 1913 to 1915. His first published story was "The Sacred Fire" in *Argosy* for May 1915. For the next twenty to twenty-five years he turned out countless serials and short stories for both pulp and slick magazines before turning to the writing of his colorful and popular historical novels.

Edison Marshall's list of published fantasy is short but generally of a high quality: "Who Killed Charles Avison?" *Argosy,* May 1916, *Famous Fantastic Mysteries,* December 1939; *Ogden's Strange Story,* Kinsey, 1934, *Famous Fantastic Mysteries,* December 1949 (first published in 1928 as *Og, the Dawn Man,* a four-part serial in *Popular Magazine*); his most famous fantasy novel, *Dian of the Lost Land,* Kinsey, 1935, *Famous Fantastic Mysteries,* April 1949; *The Stolen God,* Kinsey, 1936; and *The Jewel of Mahalea,* Kinsey, 1938.   ALVA ROGERS

Frank Owen

In a letter from Frank Owen dated June 6, 1967, Brooklyn, New York, he offered me the following statistics: "I wrote for *Weird Tales* occasionally for over thirty years. . . . Among other things, I have edited eighteen anthologies. . . . I was Hung Long Tom, who wrote the short poems. . . . My own favorite [of my] novel(s) was 'The Scarlet Hill' about China 1200 years ago."

Since his "Shadows" appeared, *Weird Tales,* April 1924, there have been around fifty more Frank Owen fantasies there, and in *Oriental Stories, Dance, Magic Carpet.* A couple novels. A few poems. Seven or eight books, in all. Not a prodigious produce. Yet even his titles evoke. "The Old Man Who Swept the Sky," "Pale Pink Porcelain," "The Tinkle of the Camel's Bell," the classic "The Wind That Tramps the World." Frank Owen's stories weave a fine sorcery for the initiate, for those in tune. It is like holding a tropical sea shell up to your ear, hearing (not what science says) a far-off music of exotic half-remembered dreams. Nobody else quite matched Frank Owen's special delicate whimsey, those splashes of Oriental color, that sly patriarchal philosophy hidden within those sweet small songs.   EMIL PETAJA

Stuart Palmer

Perhaps Stuart Palmer's best-known creation is Hildegarde Withers, the schoolma'am sleuth with the impossible hats and unerring nose for crime. His mystery stories carried the tang of his enthusiasm for science fiction and fantasy; his detective-journalist Howie Rook dreamed of becoming the successor of Charles Fort. In our own field, his tales include "A Bride for the Devil," which was the cover story for V I N 1 of *The Magazine of Fantasy and Science Fiction,* and the charming "Three-Dimensional Valentine" in the same publication.

Stu was a big, hearty man, and if his life was one of uncertainty, he could enjoy its variety: now a reporter covering the Barbara Graham case, now in charge of a correspondence course in writing, now a top-paid private investigator, now editing nudist magazines. To each of his occupations he brought an innate professionalism and a full measure of hard work. Among friends he was warm, generous, irreverent but never discourteous. When he and his wife last stayed with Poul and me, and shortly afterward we with them, he concealed the seriousness of his illness with his usual good cheer for a festive holiday. His fellow writers miss Stu as a colleague and as a friend.   KAREN ANDERSON

Mervyn Peake

Mervyn Peake was a generous man in an ungenerous world. He died on November 17, 1968, having suffered for more than ten years from encephalitis akin to Parkinson's disease. Best known in England for his drawings and paintings, he was considered by many to be the century's greatest illustrator, but he also had a reputation as a poet and won the Heinemann Award and an Award from the Royal Society of Literature. His four novels— the three Titus Groan books and *Mr. Pye*—had a small, devoted audience for years, and it was a bitter irony that he died just as a very much larger public began to appreciate his talents. He was much more than a writer of charming fantasy; his technical range was great and his subject matter was rich and varied, controlled superbly; his characters were as vital as those of Dickens, whom Peake resembled in style and humor.

Born in China in 1911, Mervyn came back to England while

young, studied art, and eventually taught it. It was while teaching that he met and married Maeve Gilmore (a fine artist in her own right). They had three children, Sebastian, Fabian, and Claire. His early reputation was made chiefly as a child portraitist—he could draw children without a trace of sentimentality—and he also designed the sets for the first British production of *The Insect Play*. He illustrated fine editions of *The Rime of the Ancient Mariner, Treasure Island, Alice in Wonderland, Grimm's Household Tales,* and *The Hunting of the Snark*. His play *The Wit to Woo* has been staged in London, Oxford, and Cambridge, and two other plays, *Mr Loftus* and *The Cave* (about an H-bomb shelter), have yet to be produced. His collected poetry includes *Shapes and Sounds* (1944), *The Glassblowers* (1950), *The Rhyme of the Flying Bomb* (1962), and *A Reverie of Bone* (limited to 320 copies, 1967).

He was a man of enormous goodness and vitality, deeply loved by all his friends and as inspiring to know as he was to read. The illness, which grew steadily worse from around 1958, robbed him of his vitality and his ability to create, but his great character remained even when he could no longer frame a sentence. Kind, generous, without any apparent neuroses or hatreds, Peake was badly treated by publishers and galleries. His last book *(Titus Alone)* was savagely and stupidly copy edited by the original publisher when Peake was unable to defend his work (this edition has, unfortunately, been reprinted in the United States, but the original book will probably appear in Britain in 1970), and his books have been erroneously labeled "Gothics": an insult to a subtle, sophisticated, and skillful writer whose work has been a seminal influence on many younger modern writers in this country.

MICHAEL MOORCOCK

Arthur Sellings

Arthur Sellings, pseudonym of Arthur Gordon Ley, a native Londoner, 1921–68, died suddenly September 24. From the wish fulfillment to be a writer at the age of seventeen, he moved steadily through the London book world to start an antiquarian book business in 1946, which mushroomed in the succeeding twenty years into a large successful organization. Poet, wit, raconteur, he acquired a knowledge of typography, book design, and lettering. His sf short stories commenced in 1953, over forty appearing in most of the leading sf magazines prior to his death. His greatest asset, however, apart from intense friendliness, was his driving force on behalf of European sf; in recent years he spent considerable time in France and Spain and devoted great effort to establishing Spanish sf in magazine form.

Two collections of his stories have been published: *Time Transfer* and *The Long Eureka;* five novels, *The Silent Speakers* (*Telepath* in the United States), *The Uncensored Man, The Quy Effect, The Power of X,* and *Intermind* (under the name of "Ray Luther"). A sixth novel, *Junk Day,* completed just before he died, is due for publication in 1969.   TED CARNELL

Harl Vincent

Harl Vincent was a pioneer whose literary career started in the Gernsback "scientifiction" era and continued through forty years into the "sci-fi" era of popular acceptance. At the end of his life he was a member of the Los Angeles Fantasy Society and the Count Dracula Society and enjoyed attending meetings of both and local conventions.

Born Harold Vincent Schoepflin, he was first published in *Amazing Stories* in June 1928: "The Golden Girl of Munan." His book-length novels "Venus Liberated" and its sequel "Faster Than Light" were featured in *Amazing Stories Quarterly*. His two-part novella of Mars, "Red Twilight," appeared in *Argosy* in the thirties; "Rex" was in the paperback anthology *The Coming of the Robots* (Collier Books, 1966), and "Prowler of the Wastelands" same year in the Holt, Rinehart & Winston hardcover anthology *Strange Signposts;* while his original paperback *Doomsday Planet* has had two printings to date from Tower Publications. In all he had seventy-seven science fiction stories in fifteen different publications, two of them being posthumous appearances in *Spaceway* and *Famous Science Fiction.* As he was actively creating to the time of his demise, the total could still rise.

He died of emphysema and pneumonia complications, leaving widow, son, and daughter.   FORREST J. ACKERMAN

A. A. Wyn

A. A. Wyn, truly a self-made man, was at the time of his death the last major publisher who owned his own business outright and who personally ran it in all its aspects. He began a literary career in the early 1920s after the usual variety of odd jobs which, for him, included cowboy and merchant seaman. He tasted success as a pulp writer and became an editor for Dell Magazines in the late twenties. In 1932 he struck out on his own by acquiring and running the Ace magazine chain, one of the pulp magazine giants of the prewar days. In 1952, he started Ace Books and masterminded it into one of the better-established lines in the highly competitive paperback field.

Aaron Wyn, like many writers, was basically a shy man; most of his education had come from his own reading, and he was confident only of his own judgment. His venture into science fiction was one of his few gambles on another person's views, my own, and it paid off by the rise of Ace Books (always marked by Wyn's tight and cautious control) to the point where it is the largest publisher of sf paperbacks and one of the six or seven leading paperback firms. He was a man to be respected, of high intelligence, undoubted literary ability within strict limits, but always a tough, opinionated businessman for whom few ever acquired a warm affection.　　　　　DONALD WOLLHEIM

. . . Something there is more immortal even than the stars, (Many the burials, many the days and nights, passing away,) Something that shall endure longer even than lustrous Jupiter, Longer than any sun or any revolving satellite, Or the radiant sisters the Pleiades.　　　　　WALT WHITMAN

NEBULA AWARDS 1965

Best Novel: *Dune,* by Frank Herbert.
Best Novella (tie): "The Saliva Tree," by Brian Aldiss; "He who Shapes," by Roger Zelazny.
Best Novelette: "The Doors of His Face, the Lamps of His Mouth," by Roger Zelazny.
Best Short Story: " 'Repent, Harlequin!' said the Ticktockman," by Harlan Ellison.

NEBULA AWARDS 1966

Best Novel (tie): *Flowers for Algernon,* by Daniel Keyes; *Babel-17,* by Samuel R. Delany.
Best Novella: "The Last Castle," by Jack Vance.
Best Novelette: "Call Him Lord," by Gordon R. Dickson.
Best Short Story: "The Secret Place," by Richard McKenna.

NEBULA AWARDS 1967

Best Novel: *The Einstein Intersection,* by Samuel R. Delany.
Best Novella: "Behold the Man," by Michael Moorcock.
Best Novelette: "Gonna Roll the Bones," by Fritz Leiber.
Best Short Story: "Aye, and Gomorrah," by Samuel R. Delany.

NEBULA AWARDS 1968

Best Novel: *Rite of Passage,* by Alexei Panshin.
Best Novella: "Dragonrider," by Anne McCaffrey.
Best Novelette: "Mother to the World," by Richard Wilson.
Best Short Story: "The Planners," by Kate Wilhelm.